MAGGIE IN·THE MIDDLE

Debbie Viggiano

For all the Golden Oldies with love, especially:
Father Bryant
Mother Bryant
Mama Viggiano

Chapter One

Twelve months ago – Sunday 7th May

I beamed at the eleven people sitting around my extended dining table as they sang a slightly offkey rendition of *Happy Birthday*. My smile widened as the twelfth family member joined us, carefully holding a large cake with flickering candles. Ella set down before me a large sponge-and-cream creation just as the tuneless squawks reached a crescendo.

'Happy   birthday   dear   Magg*ieeee*'   –   everyone momentarily held the note – 'happy birthday to you!'

'Thank you,' I smiled, a little embarrassed at the spotlight of attention.

Leaning forward, I took a deep breath. I now knew how the Big Bad Wolf had felt when he'd told the three little pigs that he was going to blow their house down. I'd certainly have to huff and puff to blow this little lot out. Had Ella *really* put sixty candles on the cake?

'Careful,' she warned. Suddenly she was grabbing my hair and scooping it into a twist at the nape of my neck. 'You might still have flaming-red hair, but we don't want it going up in flames,' she laughed nervously.

I took a deep breath and extinguished all the candles in

one puff. Ha! Beat that, Mr Wolf.

'Make a wish,' Greg whooped.

My blue eyes, now brimming, met my husband's dark ones. They were full of kindness and love. He could see I was in trouble but championing me on.

Come on, Mags. Don't bawl like a baby. Stiff upper lip, girl. You can cry on my shoulder later. When we're in bed. Snuggle up to me. And I'll make love to you. Because even though you're now sixty years old, you've still got it. Still make my heart sing.

Oh, how I adored this man. We'd been through some tricky stuff in the last couple of years. Aging parents had demanded more and more of our time. Then our girls had busted up with their partners – childhood sweethearts no less. At the time, Ruby and Ella had needed lots of emotional support.

Then some financial issues had unexpectedly come along. Greg's parents had got into difficulty when their pension no longer covered the basics. We'd leapt to assist. Then our eldest had found himself out of work. Tim had panicked. Wife Steph had a job but didn't earn enough to cover everything. We'd leapt to assist again. Then, shockingly, my in-laws had died within weeks of each other. Pneumonia. I'd had no idea that funerals were so expensive.

Our 'rainy-day' savings had taken a battering, so we'd forfeited our annual holiday. That hadn't bothered us. Did going away really matter, in the grand scheme of things? No, of course not. Greg and I considered ourselves blessed to be entering our autumn years with our health and to still

2

have one set of parents in this world. Mum and Dad were now creaking through their nineties.

Meanwhile, Ella and Ruby – who had previously sworn off men forever – were in love again and partnered up with Archie and Josh. Good. Greg and I wanted our kids to be happy. To know a love that stood the test of time. Like ours.

Like any couple, we'd had our ups and downs. But we'd always gravitated back into each other's arms. Always kissed each other goodnight. Never gone to bed on an argument.

Thankfully, Tim and Steph, now married for two years, appeared to be following in our footsteps. Again, they'd had the odd spat – as we all do, at the risk of repeating myself – but nothing serious. No cheating. No gambling. No addictions. Their arguments were more a gentle bickering about who got to watch *I'm a Celebrity* when a must-see football match was occurring on another channel. Nothing significant. Nothing major.

'Have you wished?' prompted Ella, keen to whisk the cake away and cut it up.

'Not yet. Hang on.'

I shut my eyes. Wondered what to wish for. My thoughts scrabbled about.

I wish… I wish… I wish for everyone around this table to always be happy.

'All done,' I smiled at Ella. 'You oversee the cake while I put the kettle on.' I pushed back my chair and stood up, addressing everyone. 'Who wants tea, and who wants coffee?'

There was the usual clamour of orders. Dad wanted coffee. Mum didn't, although that might change. Due to severe dementia, her decisions about anything were both erratic and inconsistent. Ruby wanted black decaf. Josh told me to make that two. Ella yodelled from across the kitchen that she'd like a proper coffee, not instant, and to use the cafetiere. My sister Freya asked if there was any green tea lurking at the back of the cupboard. This on account of PG Tips being full of poisonous chemicals.

'Teabags are bleached,' she now declared. I knew from her tone that she was getting in her stride. 'And when did you last change the filter on that water jug?'

'Last week,' I lied.

It was probably overdue for a change. One always knew on account of the water suddenly tasting like the local swimming pool. I turned to Freya's husband.

'What would you like, Vernon?'

My brother-in-law opened his mouth to speak but my sister immediately answered for him.

'He'll have a green tea too. No sugar.'

Greg shot me a look, then gave a discreet eyeroll. Neither Freya nor Vernon had seen, but Ruby had. She gave a snort of laughter, then quickly turned it into a cough. My husband didn't care much for my sister. I knew because he'd once said so. But only to me. He was far too polite to ever go head-to-head with anyone. And Freya had pushed Greg's buttons on numerous occasions.

That said, Freya pushed everyone's buttons. Mine

4

included. She seemed to delight in it. There wasn't a single person around the table that she hadn't upset at some point or another. She had a sharp tongue and sharper opinions.

I was the one who kept quiet. The one who acted as peacemaker if a debate became too heated. The one who put the fire out when a conversation became an argument. I played the role of mediator. Piggy in the middle. Or – as Greg had recently said now that my parents were behaving this way too – Maggie in the middle.

On more than one occasion Freya had washed her hands of me. Sometimes for months at a time. This was usually because I wouldn't agree to her way of thinking. She'd been incensed when I'd squared up to one of her ex-husbands. Robin had slapped Tim for cheeking him. Tim had been seven at the time. I can't now recall why Freya and Robin had been with me and Tim, but they had. And, yes, Tim had been a bit cheeky. But not maliciously so. He'd impishly asked Freya's third husband what it was like to be bald. Robin had touched his combover, turned purple, and shouted at Tim to mind his manners. He'd then delivered a hearty slap to Tim's cheek.

I'd reacted instantly. Grabbed the prat by the shoulders. Thrust my face into his. Mummy Lion. And I'd roared. Said that if he ever laid a finger on my son again, I'd flatten him.

Freya had been apoplectic. Called me a fishwife. Told me it was no wonder Tim was so rude when his own mother was such a terrible example.

Perhaps I should tell you about another significant row –

5

to give you a second flavour of this sibling relationship.

Freya had been put out when I'd refused to photograph her last wedding – photography being my business. I'd been the official photographer at all three of her previous marriages. My gift to her. But I'd drawn the line at the fourth wedding. By this point, Mum had been diagnosed with dementia. She had good days, and bad. My father was also struggling with frailty, periodic confusion and age-related health issues but refused care assistance. "Over my dead body," he'd asserted.

Someone had needed to help the Golden Oldies get ready for the big day, especially as Freya had wanted Dad to walk her down the aisle in full morning suit. That someone had been me. However, I hadn't been able to oversee the parents' needs *and* Freya's wedding photography. It simply hadn't been possible.

I'd done my best to explain to my sister. To compromise with her. I'd said that Greg would oversee Dad and then drop him off to Freya's house, ready to depart in the Roller. Meanwhile, I'd do Mum's makeup, get her dressed, and then drive straight to the venue. However, Freya had wanted me to go to her house before the wedding. Take photographs of her getting into her wedding dress, etcetera, etcetera.

My energy levels, while good, aren't what they used to be. I hadn't been up for rushing around, juggling my confused mother with wedding photography, or a wheelchair with a tripod and lighting equipment. I'd politely suggested Freya appoint another photographer.

My sister had been furious. Told me I was selfish. Unsupportive. Unkind. She'd sent me long ranting texts. Her last one had been so poisonous, somehow so shaming, I'd nearly caved in. Nearly told myself that I *could* get up at five in the morning. *Could* bathe Mum and wash her hair – or not, depending on whether Mum thought I was a stranger trying to drown her. But then I'd hazarded that our mother *might* have a good day. That she *might* let me do her hair and makeup. *Might* allow me to dress her in a new posh frock and not the food-stained old trousers she couldn't bear to be parted from. That hopefully there wouldn't be any dementia tantrums. Or swearing. And then, after several frustrating and exhausting hours, I might even snatch five minutes to do my *own* makeup. Bung a fascinator on my head. Belt off to the church. Camera around my neck. Equipment in the boot, with Mum's wheelchair and walking frame. Get there just in time to photograph Freya on Dad's arm. Ready to walk down the aisle *again.*

When my sister had married her previous three husbands, she'd had two weddings – a registry office and then a church blessing. She'd done the same when she'd married Vernon. By my reckoning she'd walked down the aisle eight times. Anyway, I digress.

I'd stuck to my guns. Told Freya no. That, due to Mum's dementia, it wasn't possible. Freya hadn't spoken to me for six months. At her wedding to Vernon, she'd blanked me.

Our last spat had been over the Covid pandemic. Freya had declared it a hoax.

'It's more bollocks than Boris Johnson's overworked testicles,' she'd ranted.

On this occasion I'd come perilously close to agreeing with her. After all, Boris had cancelled Christmas and then been caught partying. I'd been flabbergasted. No social distancing. No masks. If the country's leader seemed so unconcerned, why the hell was everyone in lockdown?

For decades, Freya had always been something of a conspiracy theorist. From declaring toothpaste *poison* on account of its fluoride content, to Covid vaccinations being a population cull. She was a scaremonger.

My sister had never had children. Her reason? So as not to further burden Mother Earth. Like most childless women, Freya was an authority on how parents should raise their children.

Freya had been vocal over my children wearing disposable nappies. What was wrong with cloth alternatives? And why were the kids bottle fed? What was wrong with breast milk? She'd looked appalled when, after yet another sleepless night, I'd reached for a jar of Mr Heinz instead of pureeing homemade food.

My sister was almost messianic in pointing out where I was going wrong. Whether it be on how to raise my kids or how to leap life's hurdles.

'I don't know why you listen to your sister,' Greg had roared from his sickbed – after having the vaccine that I'd refused (yes, on account of Freya's influence). 'There's a pandemic. People are dying and you don't want to be one of them!' At that point I'd had Covid but hadn't died. This had caused Freya to crow with triumph about the benefits of Vitamin C and D. 'Apart from anything else' – Greg had added – 'your sister isn't even nice to you. Look at all the arguments she's created. The months where she's not spoken to you. I get fed up with it. One of these days she'll overstep the mark and I'll say something I regret.'

He hadn't. Yet. And I doubted he ever would. As I've said, Greg was courteous and polite to people – and that included Freya. But the kids hadn't always followed their father's example.

There had been one memorable Christmas. I'd irritated the kids by doing my sister's bidding. I'd bought organic vegetables instead of supermarket frozen produce. I'd also purchased a cornfed, free-range turkey that had likely listened to panpipes at the time of slaughter. However, I'd cheated over the gravy. Used granules. Freya had loudly deplored this. Tim – now an adult and emboldened by Christmas champers – had told his aunt to get off her soapbox and shut up. Cue Freya going into victim mode.

Her face had crumpled and there had been hysterics of the unfunny kind. My father had then waded in. Told Tim off. Tim had said he was fed up with Aunty Freya putting people down. My mother – confused and panicky – had thought Freya wanted her euthanised.

'More champagne over here, Greg,' I'd trilled gaily, desperate to divert attention. 'Another top up, Freya? And Ruby, don't hog the nibbles. Pass them round!'

But Freya wasn't to be distracted. Between catchy breaths and gulps, she'd pushed back her chair. She wasn't staying. She'd called Vernon to heel and flounced off. Who'd have thought Bisto would cause such a rumpus?

Anyway, I digress. This is my family. And on this occasion, my sixtieth birthday, I'd trodden on eggshells to ensure no feathers were ruffled. And by that, I mean Freya's feathers. I'd sat her next to me so I could instantly diffuse a tricky conversation. No, I didn't want her winding up Tim – a doctor – about paracetamol being the devil's invention. Or telling the girls that their gorgeous new lipsticks contained metal and would cause early dementia. You get the gist.

All that was now left to do was hand out the sliced-up birthday cake with the coffees and teas.

I went to the fridge and discreetly decanted the milk into a glass jug. I didn't want Freya seeing the carton – yes, plastic – and discovering the milk wasn't organic.

Chapter Two

Twelve months later – Tuesday 7th May

'Happy birthday, Mum.'

Ella stooped, pecked me on the cheek, then flopped down on the squashy sofa opposite me.

Thanks to the still relatively early hour, I'd managed to bag a window seat at the local Costa. The only other current occupants were a handful of mums. They'd pulled some tables together to enable a group gossip. Having safely overseen their offspring to the school gates they were discussing someone called Mr Hadley. According to the platinum blonde with dark roots, Mr Hadley was sex on legs, and she wanted a one-to-one with him on Parents' Evening. Cue much cackling, nudging and winking.

'How does it feel to be sixty-one?' asked Ella with an impish grin.

Sixty-one. *Sixty-sodding-one.* How the hell could I be sixty-one when my heart was only twenty-one? But mirrors don't lie. There were blue bags under my eyes that hadn't been there last year. I was also aware that, when I swung my legs out of bed in the morning, there was a moment of stiffness. That the body took a moment to recalibrate. Bones would crack, as if remembering where they belonged

11

before realigning themselves.

'It feels fine,' I shrugged.

'Good,' she nodded. 'And I'm looking forward to spending the day with you. Some girly time at Bluewater. Lots of shopping. Then dinner at Browns with the others.'

My heart rose at the thought of later seeing Tim, Ruby and their partners. Showing off what I'd bought with Ella. Ruby agreeing that of *course* I could still get away with a short skirt, so long as I teamed it with dark tights and fashionable lace-up boots.

I leant across the table and squeezed my youngest's hand.

'Thanks for taking the day off work, darling. I hope your boss isn't missing you.'

'Too bad if he is.' Ella pulled a face. 'I didn't take all my holiday last year. Nor was I allowed to carry it over. I'm not losing out *this* year,' she said fiercely. 'Anyway, it's your birthday and I want to spend it with you.'

I could see Ella discreetly scanning my face. Looking for signs of tension. My youngest was the one that worried about anything and everything – and that included me.

The last few months had been awful, but I didn't want the parent-child roles reversing. Not yet. It was too soon. Maybe in another thirty years. When I was ninety-one. Although hopefully I would've popped my clogs before such role reversal.

I didn't want the kids experiencing what I was enduring with my own parents. Where, almost daily, I reached screaming point with two stubborn oldies who refused any outside assistance.

'Why do I need help' – my father had recently roared – 'when I have you and Freya.'

'Freya?' I'd snorted. 'Dad, you know full well that Freya doesn't help. She leaves it all to me.'

'She's a busy lady,' my father had countered. 'She works.'

'And I don't?'

'You know what I mean,' he'd harrumphed.

Yes, I'd known what he'd meant. Freya worked in an office in London, whereas I was self-employed. My sister had made it clear that her job as a PA was utterly exhausting. Totally stressful. Under no circumstances was she to be disturbed at work – although she would make an exception if one of the parents was gasping their last.

'Ultimately, Freya's job is more important than yours,' Dad had said.

'I'm not sure my brides would agree,' I'd muttered.

'What?' he'd barked.

'Nothing,' I'd quickly answered. I hadn't wanted an argument.

My father believed that being a photographer was no different to being a window cleaner. That my job was flexible. I could pick it up and put it down as and when. Certainly, he had no compunction about expecting me to drop everything at a moment's notice. To beetle up the motorway and do whatever bidding was required. From acting as chaperone when visiting the doctor. Taxi driver to the dentist… the chiropodist… or the dementia clinic for Mum. Then there were the trips to the supermarket – Dad abhorred online shopping. And let's not leave out housework, washing, and ironing. Sod Maggie's life. Or that's how it seemed anyway.

I tried hard not to feel resentful, but the human part of me couldn't help it. I wanted my life back. Obviously, I didn't wish my parents dead. Of course not. No, what I wanted was for someone else to deal with the daily grind. A live-in carer. After all, it wasn't as if Dad didn't have the financial wherewithal to pay for it.

'Mum to Earth,' Ella prompted.

'Sorry, darling,' I apologised. 'My thoughts were elsewhere.'

'Let me guess. You were thinking about Granny and Grandad, right? Feeling guilty that you've given yourself the day off and won't be calling in on them.'

'Honing your psychic skills?' I grinned.

She gave a half-shrug.

'I don't need to be psychic, Mum. We all know what you do for them. Did you even remind Grandad it was your birthday?'

'No, of course not.' I shook my head. 'My father would feel awful about forgetting. And anyway, as bad as it sounds, the best birthday present he can give me is letting me have an entire day to myself. However, if I'd told him that he'd have been offended. He thinks he and Granny are no trouble at all.'

'Do you think Grandad has dementia too?' said Ella tentatively.

'The thought has crossed my mind. In the last few

months, he's not been so sharp.'

Recently my father had wanted to revise his Will. He'd made an appointment with a local firm of solicitors. I knew because I'd seen it written on his calendar. On this occasion he'd declined using me as taxi, saying it was a private affair and he didn't want me there.

Later, I'd asked how the meeting had gone. Dad hadn't known what I was talking about. His face had then cleared. 'Oh, wait. I remember now.' He'd looked momentarily distressed. 'Maggie, can you ring Gardener and Stewart. Apologise on my behalf. I'll defer the matter for now.'

I sighed and gave Ella a frank look.

'I'm not sure if he's showing signs of dementia or if it's just old age. You know, being a little fuzzy. After all, he is ninety-two. And we can all have moments of forgetfulness.'

'Did you speak to Social Services? You said you wanted to express your concerns. See if they could back you up about having some home help.'

My eyes darted around the coffee shop. A fear response. My parents knew nothing of this. You see, in my head I had a plan. To seek reinforcement. For the officials to get involved. To sternly tell my father that this situation couldn't prevail. That it was, at times, comparable to supervised neglect, particularly where my mother was concerned.

It was one thing to drop everything to do their bidding, but it was quite another to have two Golden Oldies left alone at night.

Last month, my mother had been found wandering by a

15

late-night dog walker. The gentleman was local. He'd recognised Mum and guided her home. I'd known nothing of this until recently. Visiting my parents, I'd parked on their drive and the same man had been passing by with his dog. He'd stopped me. Enquired after the confused old lady within. I'd listened, horrified, as the man had told me about Mum, barefoot, dressed only in a nightdress, roaming the street and unable to convey where she lived.

When I'd confronted Dad, he'd switched to his now familiar default mode. Humour. He'd laughed it off.

'Ah ha ha ha,' he'd chortled. 'How your mother and I split our sides. Your mum simply fancied a bit of fresh air. Unfortunately, she had one of her moments.'

For *one of her moments* read *completely lost the plot*.

'My scatty Deirdre,' Dad had said fondly.

He'd given Mum a misty-eyed look. She'd batted her eyelashes coquettishly.

'I've always been a bit scatty,' she'd giggled, as if we were talking about burning the toast, not disappearing into the night. 'What's the problem?' she'd asked, her eyes wide and uncomprehending.

I'd regarded them both with incredulity. This man. My father. Someone who'd once been so sensible. Or had he? Rather, it had been my mother who'd been the capable one. The practical one. The one who'd waited on my father hand, foot, and finger. All he'd ever had to decide was whether to read his newspaper in the conservatory or the lounge.

Naturally I'd told Freya about Mum's latest dementia

episode.

'You'll have to move in with them,' she'd declared.

I'd held the handset away from my ear. Boggled at it. No way. I'd go loopy within a month. I'd put the receiver back to my ear.

'Absolutely not,' I'd said firmly.

'It's not as if you can't,' she'd pointed out. 'After all, Greg–'

'Leave Greg out of it,' I'd snarled.

I wasn't discussing Greg. Nor was I moving in with the parents. And that was that.

Ella touched my arm, once again scattering my thoughts.

'Mum,' she said, her voice low. 'I'm worried about you.'

'You don't need to worry about me,' I protested, a smile instantly on my face. 'Anyway, look at the two of us sitting here like a pair of ninnies. It's my birthday, for heaven's sake. I need cake!'

Ella relaxed slightly. Leant back. But her eyes were still locked on mine.

'My treat,' she murmured. 'Cappuccino and a slice of carrot cake?'

'Yes, please,' I beamed.

She pushed back her chair.

'Coming right up.'

Chapter Three

The remainder of the day with my youngest was spent shopping at Bluewater. It was both fun and exhausting. And, yes, I did buy a miniskirt.

Now I was seated in Browns Restaurant. The rest of the family had joined me and Ella for an evening celebratory dinner. Ruby wanted to see the skirt I'd bought. Just as I'd suspected, she suggested it should be teamed with tights and chunky boots.

'Ta da!' I trilled, thrusting another carrier bag at her. 'Take a look.'

She peered within and dutifully oohed and aahed.

'Show me what you've been buying,' Tim interrupted. He was sitting at the far end of the table. 'Just because I'm a bloke, doesn't mean I'm not interested – unless you and Ella paid a visit to Victoria's Secret. I draw the line at wanting to see my mother's new frilly knickers.'

'Ha!' I said, rolling my eyes.

I passed the carrier along the table. Archie took it and handed it to Josh who gave it to Steph who dumped it on Tim's lap. He looked inside.

'Very trendy,' my son announced. 'If I didn't know better, Mum, I'd say you were reinventing yourself.'

'Maybe Mum *should* reinvent herself,' said Ruby thoughtfully. 'Out with the old Maggie King, and all that.'

'Less of the old,' I chided. I retrieved the bags. Shoved them under my chair. Picking up my wine, I took an appreciative glug. 'I was toying with the idea of having some of those injectable thingies,' I said idly.

Ruby's eyes widened.

'You mean dermal filler?'

'That's it,' I said.

She looked aghast.

'But... why?'

'Why not?' I countered. 'After all, you girls regularly have it done and you're only in your twenties.'

'We have our *lips* done,' Ella corrected. 'I'm not sure it would look right on you, Mum. Not with...' She trailed off.

'You need to do the other bits first,' said Ruby kindly.

'Brazilian bum lift?' I said sarcastically. The wine was hitting its spot and making me feel somewhat rebellious.

'Oh, please,' Tim interrupted. 'I heard that. It was bad enough not thinking about the frilly knickers, never mind the butt lift. Archie' – he turned to Ella's boyfriend – 'do you have an embarrassing mother?'

Archie laughed good-naturedly.

'If you want to reinvent yourself, Maggie, don't mind me. However, I think you look fabulous just the way you are.'

'Stop sucking up to my mother,' said Ella. She gave Archie a shove in the ribs, although it was done in good humour. 'Seriously though' – she turned back to me – 'if you're up for it, there's a clinic on the upper floor. We could pay a visit after dinner. Have an impromptu consultation.'

'Oh, why not,' I shrugged.

The birthday meal got underway. We ate chargrilled steaks and garden veg, chatted, and laughed. For the next ninety minutes I forgot about the pressures of life. Responsibilities. Challenges. Sadness.

The kids had clubbed together for my birthday present. They'd bought a beautiful chain with heart-shaped locket. Inside was a picture of Tim, Ruby and Ella taken with a selfie stick and grinning away.

I swallowed down the lump of emotion suddenly wedged in my throat. Said thank you. Embraced them one by one. Each hug said what words didn't. *Thanks for everything. Thanks for being here. Thanks for your love and support.*

Eventually, the others peeled away. They headed home, leaving me and Ella standing outside the beauty clinic.

'Come on then, Mother,' said Ella as she led me into the clinic's brightly lit interior. 'Ruby is right. It's time to reinvent yourself.'

'I was joking,' I said nervously.

Unusually – or maybe not, due to the recent hike in inflation – the consultant was available. She talked me into an on-the-spot treatment. I left with slight bruising but was secretly impressed.

The blue undereye bags had disappeared and I had

plumper cheeks. The difference was subtle, but fresh. As if someone had taken my crumpled face and given it an iron.

'You look great,' Ella beamed, as we headed off to the car park. 'Really fab. I wonder if Aunty Freya will notice.'

My stomach instantly contracted with anxiety.

'Please don't tell her,' I implored. 'I don't want a lecture about whatever was in those syringes. It will either be bad for the environment or bad for me.'

'Don't worry,' Ella assured. 'Your secret is safe. Anyway, so what? Aunty Freya has injections in her face.'

'Yes, but they're different. Organic. Liquid vitamins and whatnot.'

'Mum, you do *you*, okay?' Ella looked cross for a moment. 'Stuff Aunty Freya, and stuff her opinions.'

'You're right,' I said.

Later – much later – I showed Greg my birthday purchases. I also opened the locket. Let him see the precious photograph within. He made no comment, so I decided not to tell him about the visit to the beauty clinic.

Feeling slightly deflated, I went to the bathroom to clean my teeth and get ready for bed.

.

Chapter Four

I awoke the following morning minutes before the alarm went off.

Six fifty-five. Always six fifty-five. It didn't matter whether I set the clock for seven or later, my body was a law unto itself. I lay there for a moment, gently coming to.

The house was quiet. I put out a hand. Touched the area beside me. The space was empty. The cold sheet let me know that Greg hadn't been in bed for a while. Again. I sighed and threw back the duvet. Padded off to the bathroom.

Fifteen minutes later, I went downstairs and headed for the kitchen. Greg was already there. I gave him a friendly smile.

'Morning,' I chirped. I didn't wait for an answer. Instead, I busied myself. Filled the kettle. Slotted bread in the toaster. I made a large pot of tea and gestured to Greg.

'Help yourself when you're ready. I won't pour for you. After all, you have a habit of letting my cuppas go cold.'

It was said lightly. After all, there was no need for any bad feeling. Neither of us liked undercurrents. I got on with buttering my toast. Spreading marmalade. Gave Greg another pleasant smile as I picked up my plate and cup.

'I'll be in the study. I've been making some notes about the Golden Oldies. I have something else to add. I'm convinced Dad isn't feeding Mum properly. There's more flesh on a scarecrow. Dad doesn't look much better. Most men of his age have a paunch. Instead, his belly button is cosying up with his spine. It's ridiculous. Do you know, only the other day I insisted on putting his shopping away and, when I went to the fridge, I was horrified. There were eggs dating back to last Christmas, and all the fresh veg I'd previously bought hadn't been touched. Most of it had gone off. The cabbage stank.' I heaved a sigh. 'The two of them seem to exist on tinned salmon and sweetcorn. All the dinners I made them are still in the freezer. Why can't my father use the microwave? It's not rocket science. That said, I have a feeling he's forgotten how to use it. But he'd never confess to that truth. Anyway, later on, I'm going to phone Social Services. See if I can get someone to pay a visit and talk some sense into Dad.'

I rattled to a stop. Glanced at Greg. He met my eyes.

'Well,' I said, suddenly awkward. 'I'll… er… you know.' I nodded my head in the direction of the study. 'If you, um, want me, I'll be in there.'

God how I hated this. This wall of silence. It wasn't fair. It just wasn't. I didn't deserve this. I really didn't.

Come on, Maggie, said my inner voice. *Buck up. Don't waste your breath. You know it isn't going to get you anywhere. Drink your tea. Eat your toast. Catch up with your emails. You have a wedding this Saturday and the*

23

bride hasn't paid the balance. A polite reminder is required. By the time you've emptied your Inbox, the phone lines will be open to Social Services. And then you can pour your heart out. Hopefully that person will be sympathetic or, at the very least, offer some solutions.

By nine o'clock, I was on my second cup of tea and had the handset clamped to my head. After going through a merry-go-round of an automated phone system, I ended up speaking to a lady called Irene. She was part of the Old People's Team. As I opened my mouth to relay the concerns about my ancient parents, to my shame, I burst into tears.

'Sorry,' I said, trying to get a grip on the waterworks. 'It's such a relief to talk to someone.'

At the other end of the line, Irene gave a wry chuckle.

'If I had a pound for every person who's said that to me, I'd be able to give up work. So, Maggie. Give me some background on your parents.'

'I think my mother is dying,' I said, stemming a fresh flow of tears. 'I don't mean to sound dramatic, but my father doesn't feed her properly. He doesn't feed *himself* properly. They've lost so much weight. Sometimes I cook extra food in my house, then run two hot meals over to them. However, unless I do that, I'm not sure they're eating. But I can't keep doing it, night after night. Not when I've already spent half the day with them. I have my own life.' I foraged up my sleeve for a tissue. Blew my nose. 'Sorry,' I said. 'You have no idea how ashamed I feel admitting all this.'

'Please don't feel guilty,' said Irene. 'You're entitled to a life of your own. Is there any other family member who can help?'

I told Irene that the kids pitched in where they could. Visited their grandparents. Gave me respite. But they were young. Had their own lives. My parents weren't *their* responsibility.

'And there's my sister Freya,' I added. 'But she works.'

'I see.' I could hear a keyboard being tapped. Irene was making notes. 'I take it you're retired?'

I blinked.

'No. I work too.'

'Part time, then?'

'Well, not really, although I suppose it might seem that way. I'm a wedding photographer. The work is seasonal. I do other stuff. You know, parties. Teens that want to glam up. Family portraits. I'm never not busy. There's always something to do, even if it's just admin and promo work.'

'I see,' said Irene thoughtfully. The keyboard continued to rattle away in the background. 'I'm second-guessing that, because you can juggle your work schedule, the care has mainly fallen to you.'

'Yes,' I nodded. At last. Someone who understood. I wasn't sure Freya would appreciate Irene putting it so succinctly.

Irene continued making notes. How my father sometimes took himself off. Left my mother alone. How Mum wandered. Got lost. Didn't recognise where she lived. That, left to her own devices, she was dangerous.

How Dad had once returned home to a plastic kettle melting over the gas hob, smoke alarm screeching.

Irene gave me a list of numbers which included a 'sitting service'. This provided three free hours a week allowing Dad to go out leaving his wife in safe hands. Irene also gave me the number of an Alzheimer's support group. She suggested Dad could take Mum for a coffee, and at the same time chat to other carers. Make new friends. I noted everything down. However, I knew Dad would refuse to follow up on any of this information.

A care assessment was also arranged. Irene warned me to be patient. There was a waiting list, and every name upon it was urgent. I told her that I understood.

The relief was huge. I'd now taken a positive step in asking for help. However, I wasn't looking forward to telling my father what I'd done. He might be ninety-two and frail, but when he lost his temper there was nothing doddery about his voice.

Chapter Five

'I've done it,' I said to Greg.

We were in the lounge. I was scoffing a mid-morning sandwich, suddenly ravenous. Talking to the Old People's Team had been liberating.

I brought Greg up to date. Told him what Irene had advised. He listened to me patiently. Also, silently. The air positively vibrated with all my words tumbling out. But still he didn't respond. At length, I burbled myself to a standstill.

I couldn't go on like this. It was getting me down. For a moment I didn't say anything. I licked my finger. Dabbed up some crumbs. Then took a deep breath.

'Look,' I said, choosing my words carefully. 'I know things have changed. Between us.' I licked my lips nervously. 'And I accept that. But I'm finding it hard, Greg.' I spread my hands wide. My eyes momentarily brimmed. I blinked rapidly. Willed the tears back into their ducts. 'Anyway,' I said, chin jutting slightly. Defiance. 'I want a dog. I know you're not into animals. You've said they're a tie. A liability.' My chin jutted further. I'd be looking like Bruce Forsyth shortly. 'But I don't care. I'm prepared to take full responsibility. Pay any vet's bills. Clean up any muddy paw prints. I'll make sure your precious lawn isn't wrecked. Pick up the whoopsies.' I looked my husband in the eye and, at the same time, squared my shoulders. 'Anyway, my mind's made up. I don't want a row about it, okay?'

After mentioning the *row* word, I found my heart beating rather fast. I didn't like verbally asserting myself. It was uncomfortable.

Scooping up my empty plate and cup, I hurried out to the kitchen. The plate and cup clattered down on the worktop. I realised I was shaking.

Well done for speaking up, girl, said my inner voice. *One down, one to go.*

Yes, there was still my father to deal with. I wouldn't telephone him with the news about a care assessment. These things were better done face to face. Even if it meant another round of stony silence.

As I rinsed the mug and washed the plate, I determined to get the visit over and done with. Picking up my car keys, I went out to the hallway. I grabbed my jacket and handbag from where they'd been hanging over the banister.

'I'm off,' I called to Greg. 'See you later.'

I didn't bother waiting for a reply and let myself out.

I reversed off the driveway and set off to Mum and Dad's. As I drove through the village of Little Waterlow, I allowed the pretty scenery to distract me. So many trees were in blossom. It reminded me of pink and white candy floss. A whole riot of new foliage was going on. Spring had sprung and summer was just around the corner. My heart lifted at the thought.

Greg and I had lived in this village all our married life. Little Waterlow was a small hamlet perched high on the North Downs of Kent. This was a place where everyone knew everybody – and that included everybody's business. It was for this reason that I hadn't cultivated any deep friendships here. Yes, I knew everyone. But not everyone knew me. I was a private person. I didn't want people knowing what was going on within my four walls.

Only a handful of people knew the details about what had happened between me and Greg. Lyn, from school days, who now lived on the other side of the Dartford Bridge. Also, Nell, Vicky, and Bette. They'd been on the same ward as me when I'd gone into hospital to give birth to Tim. Despite everyone now being scattered around the London Boroughs, these friendships had held. Greg had once jokingly referred to us all as the *Witches of Feastwick*. This on account of how we all ate cake and cackled with laughter whenever we got together.

But there was none of that camaraderie with the folks of Little Waterlow. You wouldn't find me gossiping with the village's oldest resident. Mabel Plaistow held the crown for being top busybody. Nor would you catch me gassing away at the local village store – always a hotbed of regurgitated gossip.

Don't get me wrong. I wasn't rude to people. Just… a little aloof as I went about my business. I didn't stop – when driving past fields full of sheep and cows – to talk to the farmer who'd pulled over on his tractor. I didn't tell Cathy, the landlady at our local pub, all about my new kitchen while sharing a meal with Greg. Nor did I make idle chatter with the postmistress who'd worked for thirty years on the old-fashioned high street, with its quaint shops and bow windows.

I braked and negotiated a truck coming towards me. Squeezed into a hedgerow to let it pass, then moved off again.

Eventually, I picked up the M20 and accelerated into the outside lane. As the car ate up the miles, my heart began to bang about. Adrenalin. God, and I hadn't even arrived at Mum and Dad's yet. I needed to distract myself. Think of something good.

I'd already decided – after having that firm chat with the Golden Oldies – to detour home via the local animal rescue centre. I wanted to make a new friend. Of the four-legged variety. To have a companion. Someone to walk with me. Exercise with me. Yes, that would be wonderful. Perhaps I could start jogging again. Through Trosley Woods.

The last time I'd gone there, I'd been alone. Greg had stayed at home. I'd suddenly found the woods creepy, especially with its early morning fog. A thick mist had shrouded the trees, turning them into monsters with outstretched arms. However, with a dog by my side, I'd no longer feel twitchy.

As I overtook a lorry, I smiled to myself. My heart had now stopped banging about, and my brain was positively buzzing. A pooch. How exciting. Someone to chat to. A dog could *talk* in so many ways. A wag of the tail. A panting grin – and a smattering of halitosis. Eyes that lit up the moment you opened the biscuit tin.   Sharing a shortbread – oh, too much sugar.   Make that a Bonio.   For the dog, not me.   A slobbery kiss.   The dog, again.   Oh, and a hug.   Even if its body was more hirsute than Greg's.

And dammit, I *soooo* wanted a hug.

Chapter Six

'Hello, darling,' said Dad.

My father stood in the open doorway. The light from the inner hallway haloed his body. He seemed stiffer. More stooped. Why was it that some old folks seemed to collapse in upon themselves, while others strode about as if they owned the planet? I remembered how I'd once admired a photograph of the Queen riding her pony. It had been taken at the time of her ninetieth birthday. Yet my father couldn't mount a stepladder to change a lightbulb, never mind a horse.

Because he hasn't moved, said my inner voice. *He worked at a desk for years. Now he sits in front of a television.*

I made a mental note to move more. To keep moving with the years. Thank goodness I'd defied Greg about getting a dog. There was no excuse not to move when you had a four-legged friend. I'd be out in wind, rain, and shine.

Dad stepped forward to kiss my cheek, wincing as he did so.

'I was going to ring you later,' he said. 'I need a few things from Asda.'

'In which case' – I pecked him back – 'give me your

shopping list. I might as well go now.'

'Oh, I don't need much. A loaf of bread. Some more milk. Maybe one of those iced walnut cakes. Your mother is very partial.'

'I can get those things from the corner shop. Tell you what, you put the kettle on. I'll be two minutes.'

Dad's local shop was run by the Patels and was open all hours, including Christmas Day. The owner, Sanjit, was a kindly man who always asked after my father. He'd been amazing during lockdown, always leaving a bag of groceries outside my parents' front door. Letting my father settle-up later.

Sanjit greeted me with a grin.

'Hello, Maggie, love. How are you?'

'Not so bad, thanks, Sanjit.' I returned his smile, then quickly located the bread, milk, and cake. There was no one else in the shop as I went to pay.

'If you don't mind me saying' – Sanjit's brow furrowed as he scanned the items – 'you're looking a little tired.' He popped everything into a small paper carrier. 'I expect you've been worrying about your father, eh? Especially after that nasty fall.'

'What fall?' I frowned.

Sanjit looked at me curiously.

'Didn't your dad tell you?'

I felt the familiar knot of anxiety start up in my gut. It was as if my intestines were being squeezed by an invisible hand.

'He hasn't told me anything. What fall?' I repeated.

Sanjit looked wary. As if he'd said too much.

'Perhaps he didn't want you fretting,' he said carefully. 'But I was very concerned. Trevor stumbled up the pavement kerb. Just outside this shop. He tripped and went down with a bang. Hurt both wrists and his ribs. An off-duty paramedic happened to be passing, which was a stroke of luck. The guy gave your dad the onceover, before helping him home.'

My mouth pursed. It seemed to be doing a lot of that lately.

'Thank you for telling me,' I said quietly.

I couldn't believe my father hadn't told me. Well, actually, I could.

'There's something else, Maggie.' Sanjit regarded me anxiously. Unsure whether to impart further information.

I took a deep breath.

'Spit it out,' I sighed.

'I don't think your father should be driving.'

'I agree. However, he won't listen to me. Dad tells me to stop interfering. He can get very… you know… angry. And when he's angry, he says rotten things.'

'I sympathise. Truly. But, well, he was wearing shorts the last time I saw him, and I couldn't help but notice his right leg. And the foot. Both are very swollen. I don't think his foot can properly feel the pedals in his car. Recently, I witnessed him having a confrontation with another motorist. It got ugly.'

'What?' I gasped.

'It happened outside the shop. At the junction. Trevor

34

was in his car. He had trouble braking. He nearly ploughed into a vehicle that was travelling in the opposite direction.'

I briefly closed my eyes, imagining the scene.

'The other driver' – Sanjit continued – 'was furious. He got out of his car. Strode over to your dad's vehicle. Then banged on the window. There was a big commotion. Enough to have me running outside. Trevor had buzzed down the side window. He was yelling at the other driver. A young man. Shouting that he was a lunatic. I thought the man might punch your father. Instead, he leant into Trevor's car. Snatched the keys from the ignition. Yelled that old people shouldn't be allowed to drive. At this point, I intervened. Tried to calm down both men. The young guy gave me Trevor's keys. He was furious. He said he'd made a note of your father's licence plate and would be reporting him to the DVLA.'

'Oh God,' I breathed. If Dad was banned from driving, he'd be apoplectic. And yet I knew it was the best thing that could happen. My father should *not* be driving.

'Anyway,' Sanjit sighed. 'I'm sorry to be the bearer of bad news, Maggie. You have enough on your plate. I heard about Greg–'

'Thanks,' I interrupted. 'We're okay. *I'm* okay. It's all fine.' Sanjit gave me a look that suggested otherwise. 'I'm getting a dog,' I said brightly, abruptly changing the subject. 'Greg has never been a fan of dogs but, you know' – I gave a little shrug – 'I thought it might be therapeutic. Help the situation.'

'Yes,' he nodded, but I'd caught the look in his eyes.

He knew my mother had lost the plot. That my father *might* be losing the plot. Was the daughter, perhaps, going gaga too?

'Right,' I said, suddenly brisk. 'I'd better get back to the parents.'

'Give them my regards.'

'I will. Thank you. And give Sushma my love.'

I left with my head bowed, paper bag tucked under one arm.

Breathe, Maggie. Breathe. Don't return to your parents' house and explode with frustration and anger. It won't resolve anything.

'That was quick, darling,' said Dad, as he opened the door. I had my own key to the house. However, I didn't like to assume to let myself in, unless he was indisposed. 'I envy you having a pair of pins that work properly.'

'Indeed,' I said, with a tight smile. 'Shall we have our coffee in the kitchen?'

'Yes. I did what you said. Put the kettle on. It won't take a second to re-boil.'

He shuffled off and I followed slowly behind.

'Where's Mum?' I asked. I placed the cake on the table, put the loaf in the breadbin, and left the milk alongside the kettle.

'Upstairs,' said Dad, as he pottered about.

'What's she doing?'

'Oh, you know,' he said vaguely.

No. I didn't. I hadn't a Scooby what my mother did in her bedroom. But whatever it was, it could keep her occupied for hours. Literally.

'Is she getting dressed?' I hazarded. Any time before lunch would be a miracle.

'Having a wash I expect.'

Dad abandoned making the drinks. Instead, he pulled out a chair and sat down heavily. I took over. Found a jar of instant.

'Don't you help her?' I asked, spooning coffee granules into cups.

'Why would I do that?'

'Because I recently caught her putting soap on her toothbrush. She wondered why it wouldn't foam.' I added the hot water and milk. Stirred the drinks overvigorously. An outlet for further frustration. 'Don't you see, Dad? The poor woman no longer recognises certain things.'

'Nonsense,' he protested. 'Anyway, interrupting her is more than my life's worth. She's a fiery little thing, your mum. The last time I checked on her, she told me to fuck off. I only wanted to see if she was up for watching Coronation Street.'

Of late, Mum's language had become rather fruity. The dementia had taken an aggressive turn. In the beginning, it had been mildly amusing to see this tiny lady balling up her fists and threatening to *punch your lights out*. But now it was alarming. I'd spoken about it with my mother's surgery. Tried to personally speak to her GP. But they'd refused to address my concerns on account of me not producing a Power of Attorney.

'Oh, but there *is* a document,' I'd breathed. 'I'll find it.

Show it to you.'

'Is it registered?'

I'd blinked.

'Um, what do you mean?'

'You need to see a solicitor. Get the POA registered. Then and only then can a doctor speak to you about your mother.'

'Right,' I'd said, making a note in my diary. Why was life so full of red tape?

I took the drinks to the table. Gave my father one of my looks. One that said I was not going to be fobbed off.

'Dad,' I said, sitting down opposite him. 'Don't you think it's time to get some help?'

His eyes bulged, and he instantly looked outraged.

'Absolutely not. We manage perfectly well.'

I didn't immediately answer.

That's it, Maggie. Count to ten before speaking. Stay calm.

'I know Mum isn't easy to manage,' I said, picking my words carefully. 'You're doing a good job, Dad.' I took a sip of coffee. 'A *very* good job.'

His chest swelled. Flattery could achieve much.

'I know,' he agreed. 'There aren't many folks in their nineties living on their own.'

'Sanjit told me about your fall,' I said abruptly.

'It was a stumble,' he quickly countered.

'He also told me about your altercation with another motorist.'

Dad rolled his eyes.

'I always knew Sanjit was a bloody gossip. That's what comes from owning a corner shop. Nattering with all the people that come in. Finding out their business. Then telling others.'

'I'm not *others*, Dad. I'm your daughter. Sanjit was right to tell me. What if you'd busted a rib? Broken your wrist? Had to go to hospital?'

'Well I didn't,' said Dad belligerently. 'So, change the topic, Maggie. You're starting to sound like a stuck record. And I have enough of that listening to your mother all day, repeating herself over and over. It's very wearing.'

'I can imagine,' I said quietly. Frankly, I couldn't begin to understand how he coped with it all day, every day, every week, month, and year. 'The thing is, Dad' – I licked my lips – 'what if you *had* broken something?'

'I'd have been plastered up and sent home good as new.' His jaw was set. Eyes unblinking. *Don't challenge me*, they said.

'Not necessarily,' I persisted.

'Maggie,' Dad growled.

He was warning me. *Don't push it.* But I couldn't back off. Not now. This situation, bad enough for the last twelve months, was rapidly becoming dire. I tried a different tack.

'I don't know what the big deal is,' I said carelessly. 'You once said you'd get help when you'd turned ninety, and that birthday has long been and gone. I mean, obviously you're doing brilliantly,' I added, once again resorting to shameless flattery. 'Everyone says you're amazing. Still driving.' Best not to mention that it might not be for much longer. 'Still independent. Fantastic.' My father relaxed slightly, possibly thinking he was off the hook. 'But it's Mum I'm worried about,' I pressed on. 'Not you.' That's it, throw in some reverse psychology. Let him think he was marvelous as he roared around town. Narrowly avoiding collisions. Missing that young mother pushing her pram – *oh God, Maggie, don't torture yourself.* Yes, let him think it was only my mother who needed care. Brilliant idea!

'But the thing *is*' – I continued – 'if you suddenly weren't here, who would look after Mum?'

His eyes slowly as he comprehended that possibility. That he might die before his wife.

Nobody liked to mention the *death* word. Certainly not Dad. It was a taboo. He, Trevor King, was going to live to one hundred years old. And he, Trevor King, would single-handedly take care of the demented Deirdre King. And when he'd outlived his wife – and *only* then – would he ask Creator to be returned to the stars. Or wherever one's essence went. Dad cleared his throat.

'I understand what you're saying.' Hurrah! 'If anything happens to me, then your mother will live with you.'

Pardon?

'Dad' – I shook my head helplessly – 'I can't cope with Mum.'

'Poppycock!' His hand waved away my words.

'Apart from the fact that I still work' – why did nobody in my family take my job seriously? – 'I don't want to look after her.'

Dad's eyes flashed.

40

'What sort of a daughter says such a thing?'

'An honest one,' I asserted. 'And because I'm honest, I might as well tell you something else. This morning, I spoke to Social Services.'

'About what?' said Dad in astonishment.

'About my grave concerns over Mum. Have you noticed how much weight she's lost? She's fading away before your eyes.'

'Who's fading away?' said my mother, making me jump.

She was hovering in the doorway. She looked like an apparition. Hair standing on end. Face so pale it matched the nightdress she was still wearing. She'd teamed the nightie with some socks and sandals.

'Deirdre, darling,' said Dad, patting the chair beside him. 'Come and sit down. Maggie will make you a nice coffee.'

'Yes,' I said, pasting on a smile. 'Would you like something to eat as well? After all, the time's getting on. It's almost lunch–'

The words died on my lips. What was that terrible smell?

'Maggie?' said Dad. His horrified expression matched mine. And then we both looked at my mother. Her hands. They were covered in excrement.

'Er, Mum' – I hastily propelled her towards the sink – 'I think you need to wash your hands.'

I shoved her hands under running water. Squirted her palms with washing-up liquid. She needed a nailbrush too. Did this house even possess one?

'What are you doing?' she screeched. 'Get off me.'

She snatched her hands away, then gave me a shove. For a woman who weighed less than a hundred pounds, she was surprisingly strong.

'Stop it,' I said, grabbing her wrists. It was like dealing with a child. 'Look at your hands.'

'What's wrong with them?' she demanded.

'They're covered in poo. You need to clean them. Now.'

'How dare you?' she hissed, rheumy eyes narrowing with fury. 'How DARE you say such lies. How FUCKING *DARE* YOU.'

Oh God. Not the swearing and aggression. Please.

My mother then caught me by surprise. She slapped me. Hard. Across the face. The sound was not dissimilar to a swimmer bellyflopping into a pool.

'I don't know who you are' – my mother's cheeks were pink with fury – 'but I want you OUT OF MY FUCKING HOUSE.'

My cheek stung. The smell of shit and soapy water shot up my nostrils. For a moment I was too shocked to react. I glanced at my father. He was slumped in his seat. Head bowed. I couldn't see his face, but his body language said it all. He was used to this behaviour. This outburst was one of many. I wondered *how* many. I didn't know. Certainly, enough to desensitise my father. His response was zero. Just another day of dementia. Another variation of its behaviour. Another version of the brain firing incoherently.

I took a step away from my mother. Picked up my handbag. Burrowed within for the wet wipes I always

42

carried. Cleaned my face and hands.

'I'll see myself out, Dad.'

He didn't look up.

'Where are you going, dear?' said my mother.

Her cheeks were still pink from the outburst, but already the memory of what she'd done had disappeared.

'I have things to do,' I said, forcing myself to smile at her.

'Oh, that's a shame,' she said. She sat down on the chair I'd recently vacated, shitty hands all over the kitchen table. 'Oooh, cake.' Her eyes lit up as she reached for the box. 'Shall we all have a slice?'

Chapter Seven

It was only when I was in the car that I allowed myself to cry.

But the tears weren't those of a victim. Instead, they were a result of the emotion my mother had invoked. In that moment, I'd hated her. Despised her for what she'd become. And yet the rational part of me knew it wasn't her that had been screaming at me. It was the dementia. My poor mother. My poor, *poor* mother.

I drove off but, after two minutes, had to pull over. The tears were blinding me. I parked illegally in a bus stop layby and trumpeted into a fistful of tissues. I then fired off a text to Freya.

I've just been assaulted by Mum. I can't deal with her anymore. I've spoken to Social Services.

Her reply came back almost immediately.

Do what you have to do. However, please remember I'm at work. I don't need this distraction.

My lip curled. In a fit of temper, I lobbed the phone into the car's passenger footwell.

'Fuck you, Freya,' I screeched at the mobile. 'FUCK YOU!'

Oh God. I was turning into my mother. Sixty-one

years old and I was losing my marbles.

No, you're not, said my inner voice. *You're feeling stressed. That's all. Take some deep breaths. That's it. Now drive to the animal sanctuary. Go and do something for you. Something nice.*

Yes. Something nice. Something for me. Indeed.

Feeling calmer, I turned the engine over, signalled, spotted a gap in the stream of oncoming traffic, and seamlessly joined it.

The local animal sanctuary had achieved overnight fame when one of Little Waterlow's residents, Sadie Harding, had rescued a dog from the centre.

It transpired that William Beagle had been dognapped. The legal owner, Jack Farrell, was a local resident. It had only been a matter of time before his path had crossed with Sadie's – and a certain beagle's. The events that had followed had made the national papers.

As I now drove through the gates of the sanctuary, I perked up. My future companion was here!

I locked the car and looked about. The carpark wasn't vast. At the far end, a couple of other motors were parked up. A fair-haired man was unloading a transit van. He was transferring animal food and pet products on to a large trolley. I caught a glimpse of dog and cat baskets being piled on. He saw me looking and paused.

'If you're looking to rehome, Reception is over there.' He pointed to a door. 'My wife should be around. Her name's Rachel.'

'Okay,' I said, putting up a hand. 'Thank you.'

As I pushed through the door, I immediately spotted Rachel. She was talking to a tall man who had his back to me. She paused to quickly address me.

'Won't be a mo.'

The man swung round to see who Rachel was talking to. As he caught my eye, my heart inexplicably did a few skippy beats. Wow. Good looking or what? He had dark hair, and lots of it. The slight greying at his temples set off a pair of eyes the colour of the Mediterranean Sea.

Why are you checking out men? enquired my inner voice.

I'm not, I silently retorted.

He's too young for you.

Do you think?

The man turned back to Rachel, but not before my brain had taken a snapshot of his face and filed it to memory.

As I waited for the pair of them to finish talking, I turned away. Mentally retrieved the snapshot. Studied it. Yes, he was younger than me. Late forties? Maybe early fifties. His physique told me he worked out. Unlike me, he had yet to reach his autumn years. However, I had a feeling he'd be the type to always stay in shape. I instantly thought of my own figure with its thickening midriff. At least my hair – naturally red – had yet to require help from the hairdresser. These days one had to be grateful for small mercies.

The man was then directed to go through another door. Presumably it led to the area where dogs were up for adoption.

Rachel then turned to me.

'Looking to rehome?' she enquired.

Her face was kind, but I sensed a brisk, no-nonsense person.

Er, yes,' I said timidly. 'If that's okay.'

'It's okay if you meet our criteria,' she replied. 'Don't look so anxious. I don't bite. Nor do any of our dogs,' she added. 'We don't rehome any dogs that are aggressive. They've been thoroughly vetted – and that's before they even get to this area.' She nodded at the door that the good-looking man had gone through. 'So, what sort of pooch are you looking for?'

'Um, well, I haven't given it much thought,' I said vaguely. My comment earnt a raised eyebrow from Rachel. 'I mean' – I stumbled on – 'I don't know what sort of dog to pick. I'm looking for… a friend, I suppose. Not that I'm Billy-No-Mates,' I added, laughing nervously. 'What I mean is I don't know whether to get a big dog or… a small dog,' I finished lamely.

Careful, Maggie. You'll be saying 'fat dog' or 'thin dog' next.

'Do you have children?' asked Rachel.

'Yes, but they're all grown up and independent.'

'Grandchildren?'

'No, not yet. But Tim and Steph – that's my eldest and his wife – they're talking about starting a family.'

'In which case, be sure to carefully read all the information about each dog. Some are better suited than others to be around kids. You'll find a potted history about each dog directly outside each kennel.'

'Okay, thanks for that,' I nodded.

There was more to this than I'd realised.

'Do you have any other pets?' Rachel asked. 'A cat, for example?'

'No. Not even a goldfish.'

'Good to know. Some of our residents aren't great with moggies, although I've never considered how they might behave upon seeing an aquarium full of fish,' she laughed. 'Just be aware of all factors. You don't want to feel stressed over a neighbour's cat possibly being chased up a tree.'

'Quite,' I agreed. 'But, er, I don't think any of my immediate neighbours have cats.'

'Good. Is there anyone else at home, or is it just you?' Rached asked.

'I have an empty nest,' I said, deliberately not mentioning Greg. I didn't want any awkward questions about my husband. He was neither a pet fan nor by my side. Action speaks louder than words, etcetera.

'If you go through that door' – Rached pointed ahead – 'you'll be able to view our residents. Like I said, read their info. Keep the obvious in mind.

'The obvious?' I repeated blankly.

'Yes,' she nodded. 'The size of a dog in relation to the size of your home and outdoor area. After all, it's no good rehoming Denny, our Great Dane, if you live in a maisonette with a patio garden.'

'Oh, I see,' I said. 'Right, I'll do that. Thanks.'

'Good.' Rachel gave me a brisk nod. 'Well, I hope one

of our boys or girls capture your heart.'

'Me too,' I said, suddenly excited.

'Also, be aware that if you do find a companion, either me or Luke – that's my husband – will assess both you and your home.' I gave Rachel a horrified look. I didn't want any anxiety over Greg. 'I'm sure you have nothing to worry about,' she said kindly. She suddenly smiled, and her stern features softened. 'It's just a precaution,' she assured. 'After all, our boys and girls don't want to find themselves back here.'

'I see,' I said, relaxing slightly. 'In which case, I'll just…' I trailed off and gestured at the door to the kennel area.

'Yes, yes' – she made a shooing motion with her hands – 'off you go. I'll be in Reception if you need me.'

Refraining from giving a sudden skip of joy, I pushed open the door.

Chapter Eight

Whatever I'd been anticipating on the other side of that door, it wasn't what I got.

In my head I had a hazy idea of my future furry friend. Small. A dog that bounced up to the cage door.

Hello! Is it me you're looking for? as a Lionel Ritchie soundtrack played in my head.

What I hadn't been expecting was the noise. The cacophony of barking.

Pick me!

No, me!

Hey, over here! Look! See my tail? It wags faster than a metronome.

Hellooo! Here's my paw. High-five me!

Oh God, this was awful. How was I going to choose one dog from so many?

Ahead I could see the man who'd been talking to Rachel minutes earlier. He was crouching down. One hand through the bars of a door as he caressed a shaggy head.

I looked away. Concentrated on the immediate kennels closest to me. A grinning chihuahua. A Jack Russell with a curling lip. A cheeky looking mongrel straight out of *Lady and the Tramp*. A Springer Spaniel practically doing cartwheels to get my attention. A dull-eyed German Shepherd curled up in her basket. I paused. Stared at her. She looked like she'd given up hope.

I walked on. Past Denny the Great Dane. Then a cute Yorkshire Terrier. Several Staffies. A Border Collie.

There were about forty kennels in all. Each housed a dog that wanted to know what was going on. Who was walking through. All, apart from that German Shepherd.

I was now approaching the good-looking man. He was still down on his haunches, making a fuss of a brown-and-white mongrel. The dog's ecstatic body language conveyed that it had found Nirvana. The man rocked back on his heels. Glanced up. To my surprise, he spoke to me.

'Have you found your fur-ever friend?' he enquired pleasantly.

I paused. Stood uncertainly.

'I'm not sure,' I said honestly. 'There's a miserable looking Alsatian back there, but I'm terrified of the breed.' I gave a helpless shrug. 'Pathetic, eh.'

'Not at all,' he said. 'When I was a kid, I used to be scared of Rotties. That is, until my mate got himself a pup. He called her Mabel, and she was so cute. I watched her grow up. Indeed, I ended up regularly walking with my friend and Mabel. It was then that I lost my fear of the breed. My friend had her for fourteen years. We cried together when Mabel crossed the Rainbow Bridge.'

The man stopped making a fuss of the mongrel and stood up. His knees briefly cracked, and he laughed.

'It doesn't matter how many times a week I go to the

gym' – he pulled a face – 'it doesn't stop my bones from making that sound.'

'I know the feeling,' I said, grinning.

'Come on.' He jerked his head. 'Let's look at that German Shepherd. I'll bet she's not scary at all.' He turned to speak to the mongrel. 'I'll be back in a bit, fella,' he assured. 'You're coming home with me.'

The dog gave a woof of delight.

'That was a quick decision,' I said, as we walked over to the German Shepherd's kennel. 'I won't be able to make up my mind so quickly. If anything, I want to take *all* of them home. Obviously, that's not possible. What made you choose the mongrel?'

'Because' – the man touched his heart – 'I felt it here. And I suspect you might have felt it there too when you walked past the German Shepherd's kennel.'

'Well, it was more… feeling sorry for the dog,' I said carefully.

'Here she is,' he said. We paused to read the information about the dog within. 'Hi, I'm Bess,' the man read. 'I'm eight years old and here through no fault of my own. You see, my owner died–'

'Oh!' I exclaimed. My eyes brimmed. I blinked away the tears that momentarily threatened to ambush me.

The man made no comment about my reaction, but I noticed his raised eyebrow. He carried on reading.

'Consequently, I've been feeling very depressed. Currently, I don't want to interact with visitors. People assume I'm being stand-offish and aloof. The truth is that

I'm feeling miserable and sorry for myself.'

'That's why she's so despondent,' I breathed. Nothing like stating the obvious.

'Also' – the man continued to read from the poster – 'because I'm an older dog, I'm worried about finding a new home. However, there are lots of advantages to having a Golden Oldie.' Upon hearing those last two words, something stirred in my heart. 'First off, I'm house-trained. Second, I'm obedient. Third, I'm a little stiff in my hips so only need short walks or a garden to play in.' I thought about the garden at home. It was perfect for a dog of this size. 'In return, I will be your loyal companion and never leave your side.'

Hmm. I wondered what Greg would make of a dog like this one. I had a sudden vision of a huge beast slumped on our bed. Of me waking up with a whiskery muzzle pressed into my face. But then again, if Bess had arthritic hips, maybe she wouldn't be able to climb the stairs?

The man had finished reading and was now studying Bess.

'C'mon, girl,' he coaxed. He stuck one hand through the bars. 'Come and say hello.'

Bess remained in her basket. She was coiled up so tightly her nose was touching her bottom. Only her eyes moved. They were watchful as the man continued to click his fingers.

'Bess,' the stranger crooned. 'Bessie baby. Let me make a fuss of you.' She ignored him. 'Boy, she really depressed,' he said, extracting his hand. He turned to me.

'I'm Dylan, by the way.' He offered me the same hand that he'd shown Bess. I shook it.

'Maggie,' I said.

Dylan's palm was large and warm. His touch unleashed an unexpected stream of feelings within me. Contact. Tenderness. Companionship. Also, a terrible, terrible yearning. When had Greg last held my hand? When had my husband last touched me? And the answer was… well, not for a while.

But something else had also registered. Something that I didn't want to acknowledge. But the tingles shooting up my fingers… into my wrist… up my arm… straight into my armpit… they told another story. Attraction. Chemistry. Well, likely not on this man's part. Of course not. He was a good-looking guy, and years younger than me. But what this electric sensation told me was that there was something very wrong with my own marriage. And sooner or later, it was going to have to be addressed.

Chapter Nine

Dylan and I continued to stand there, alongside Bess's kennel.

For a moment we were both silent, simply observing the depressed caged dog. Bess gazed back. My heart went out to her. I understood her depression to a degree. But, unlike Bess, I could distract myself. See my kids. Go shopping. Work. Visit my parents. Ring friends. Attempt clinging to my marriage. In other words, there was plenty to occupy me. But for Bess? Nothing. Four walls. Bars. A walk around the exercise space while her kennel was being cleaned. For her, this place was a prison.

As I continued to watch her, I told myself that it was impossible to even consider rehoming her. Look at the length of that muzzle! It contained hundreds of sharp teeth. Okay, maybe not hundreds. An exaggeration. But certainly, some enormous incisors, the length of which would make Dracula envious.

And then something happened. Bess uncoiled herself. She stood up. Stretched stiffly, then stepped out of her basket. She was still staring at me. Her gaze didn't waver. Suddenly, the breath caught in my throat.

'She's going to check you out,' Dylan whispered.

'Oh,' I murmured.

'Put your hand through the bars,' he instructed, sotto voce.

'I really can't,' I protested.

'Okay, I will,' he said.

He stuck his hand through the bars. Bess began to approach the cage door but ignored Dylan's hand. Her eyes remained locked on mine. She paused at the edge of her cell, then gave one wag of the tail. Was I imagining it, or did those eyes hold a glimmer of hope?

I was rooted to the spot. I felt so sorry for her but was too frightened to lean in and touch her. The light in her eyes dimmed. She turned away and headed back to her basket.

'Bess,' I croaked. I found myself hunkering down, as Dylan had earlier. The dog turned but didn't come back over. She looked at me, but her eyes were dull again.

Don't raise my hopes, she seemed to say.

Cautiously, heart pounding, I tentatively stuck one hand through the bars. Made a fist. If she was going to bite me, better to chomp on that than snap off a finger. I offered my balled-up hand to her. She regarded it, as if considering.

'I can't begin to describe how scared I am,' I muttered to Dylan.

'You don't need to anxious,' he assured. 'She likes you. I can tell.'

To my delight – and horror – Bess came over. She ignored my hand and instead sat down.

I'm not going to touch you, those eyes seemed to say. *Instead, I'm going to wait for YOU to touch me.*

Whenever you're ready,' said Dylan quietly.

It was now or never. I took a deep breath and reached out. My fingers touched her head. The fur was baby soft. I traced one finger up a huge ear. It felt like velvet. Bess didn't move. I then held her cheek. Cupped my palm against the side of her face. Then stroked her. Slowly. Carefully. I was all too aware of the proximity of her muzzle, just millimetres from my fingers. Without warning, she opened her mouth. For a split second, I was privy to a long pink tongue. Terror rose up in my throat and I let out a strangled squeak just as Bess licked the inside of my wrist. Once. Then twice.

'She's kissing you,' whispered Dylan.

'Really?' I breathed. The terror was receding, although I could feel my heart thudding away under my ribs. However, I no longer felt quite so anxious. In fact, as Bess licked my wrist for a third time, I was aware of a fuzzy sensation in my heart. Love.

'This is fantastic,' said a delighted Dylan. 'Listen, I'm going to find Rachel and ask if I can take Charlie Boy' – he pointed to the far end of the kennel area – 'for a walk. Why don't you ask if you can bring Bess along? We can walk together. And don't worry' – Dylan grinned mischievously – 'if for any reason Bess goes berserk, I will rescue you.'

'Okay,' I said nervously.

Taking Bess for a walk was a good idea. I could get to know her a little. And vice versa. Maybe I was being fanciful, but Bess's eyes seemed to convey that she thought this was a good idea too.

Chapter Ten

'Take your time walking Bess and Charlie,' said Rachel to Dylan and me. 'Rehoming a dog is a huge decision. Choosing *which* dog is even more difficult.'

Bess was now wearing a Halti, a sort of doggy bridle. Charlie was straining on a leash. His body language was clear: *get me out of here.* Unlike the hyper Charlie, Bess was very calm.

Rachel then guided us through the exercise area, and over to a steel gate. She paused to punch in a code. The gate swung open. Suddenly we were in the carpark.

'Be good,' said Rachel to Bess and Charlie. She gave both dogs a pat on the head. 'Hopefully Bess will be a calming influence on young Charlie,' she smiled, and held up two crossed fingers.

'I reckon this lad needs some intensive training,' said Dylan, as Charlie once again tugged on the lead.

'Enjoy yourselves,' said Rachel. 'Don't rush back.'

'Thanks,' I said gratefully.

The gate clanged shut behind us. Bess and I followed Dylan and Charlie across the carpark. We crossed the road, heading for fields and footpaths. Walking along side by side, Dylan and I fell into step. We were now taking long strides with the dogs trotting briskly at our heels.

'How did Charlie end up at the sanctuary?' I asked.

'A bit of an unhappy story,' said Dylan. 'A couple bought him for their two-year-old daughter. A cute puppy gift.'

'Oh dear,' I murmured, already knowing how this tale was going to pan out.

'Indeed,' Dylan agreed. 'Mum found no time to walk Charlie. Or train him, for that matter. Dad wasn't interested. Then Mum discovered she was expecting a second baby, which meant even less time for Charlie. So, he ended up at the sanctuary through no fault of his own. And now, of course, Charlie is the doggy equivalent of a juvenile delinquent,' Dylan chuckled.

'Doesn't that put you off?'

We were currently walking along a bridle path. I was grateful that the May weather had stayed dry because my sandals weren't appropriate for mud and puddles.

'Not at all.' Dylan shook his head. 'Charlie and I will be going to training classes. In a few weeks he will be a happy – but disciplined – pooch. Won't you, boy?'

Without pausing, Dylan leant down and rubbed Charlie behind one ear. The mongrel continued trotting along, his tail wagging jauntily.

'How do you feel about being out with Bess?' he asked.

'Happy,' I acknowledged. 'It feels… nice.'

'You look right together,' said Dylan approvingly.

'Dare I say it, but it *feels* right,' I confessed.

We were now approaching a point in the footpath where it divided. To the right was Trosley Country Park.

To the left, Vigo Village.

'Okay with you if we go this way?' asked Dylan, indicating the country park.

'Sure.'

We walked on for another ten minutes or so, then Dylan pointed out a large woodland area.

'On the other side of those trees is the Bluebell Café. Let's grab a coffee and see how our charges behave around food, children, and other dogs.'

'Okay,' I agreed.

'I reckon Bess will be well-mannered, and that Charlie might be a bit of a nutter. Ah well. In for a penny,' Dylan laughed.

We walked into a clearing which had been made into an outside eating area. I quickly bagged one of several trestle tables. Dylan went off to get the drinks while I minded the dogs. I marvelled at how natural it felt.

Sitting down on a wooden bench, I glanced around. To the casual onlooker, I appeared to be just another dog walker about to enjoy a cuppa after a stroll through the woods.

Most of the other tables were occupied by ramblers and dog walkers alike. Nearby, a couple with two young children were enjoying a drink. At their heels sat a well-behaved Golden Retriever. The woman was talking to a beagle that kept trying to jump on the table.

'No, William,' I heard her say. 'You're *not* having my toasted teacake, so please stop dribbling everywhere.'

Thanks to Little Waterlow's grapevine, I knew of the couple. The Farrell family had made headlines when their own secrets and drama had played out in a most public way. I looked away, not wishing to be caught staring.

At that moment Dylan returned with a tray.

'Coffee for us. I thought a bit of cake might be nice too.'

'Oooh, a man after my own heart,' I said carelessly, then immediately blushed. 'I mean–'

'I get it,' said Dylan rescuing me. He smiled kindly. 'It's nice to have someone to be naughty with.' Then it was his turn to redden. 'Oh dear! That didn't come out quite the way–'

'I get it,' I laughed, repeating back his words.

He nodded, and his eyes showed both relief and merriment. Their bright blue colour was accentuated by sun-kissed skin. At his temples, lines fanned out. This told me he was a man who liked to laugh. Like Greg.

My mind slithered away. Right now, I didn't want to think about my husband. I instantly felt disloyal.

'I also bought' – Dylan waggled two baked bread bones – 'doggy biscuits for Bess and Charlie. 'Let's see how they both behave around food.'

Bess was already sitting politely at my feet, but Charlie seemed to be impersonating the nearby William Beagle. His front paws were stretched up on the bench-seat. It was clear from his foxy expression that he was plotting the fastest route to the food.

'Oh no you don't,' said Dylan. He swiftly intercepted Charlie. 'Wait!' he commanded. Amazingly, Charlie paused – one paw suspended in mid-air. 'Sit!' said Dylan. Suddenly

Charlie's bottom was parked on the grassy floor. 'Good heavens.' Dylan looked at me in astonishment. 'I'll make an obedient hound of him yet.' He broke the biscuit in half. 'One bit for you,' he said to Charlie. The mongrel greedily snatched the treat. 'And the other half for you,' he said to Bess.

I watched in delight as Bess gently took the offering from Dylan.

'Good girl,' I said, giving her a pat.

Omigod. I was really doing this. I was enjoying a moment in time with this huge, ferocious looking dog. Although… was she truly ferocious? Of course not.

I broke the second biscuit in half and timidly offered it to Bess. Once again, she gently took the treat. My heart swelled.

I instantly recognised the feeling. It was one of falling in love. And it was beautiful. It had been too long since love had been in my life. Way too long.

Chapter Eleven

Twelve months ago

'Hey, sexy lady,' said Greg, as I flounced past him. He grabbed my wrist. Pulled me towards him. 'What's up?'

I paused. Allowed him to wrap his arms around me.

'Nothing,' I mumbled. 'Everything.'

Greg sighed and hugged me tightly.

'Is it that sister of yours again? Come on. Let me make you a cup of tea and you can tell me all about it.' He led me into the kitchen. Pulled out a chair at the table. 'Sit down.' Checking the kettle's water level, he pressed the switch. 'What's Freya done now?'

'The usual,' I glowered.

Greg opened a cupboard. Searched for mugs. Most of the cupboard's contents were currently in the dishwasher. The hum of the machine and slosh of water indicated it was cleaning everything within. This included pots and pans from the roast dinner I'd cooked earlier. Greg had volunteered to be taxi driver. He'd driven over to my parents' place and picked them up, leaving me free to get on with the cooking.

The kids hadn't joined us for dinner on this occasion. Much as my parents loved their grandchildren, they couldn't cope with their boisterousness. Tim's voice, always the loudest, played havoc with Dad's hearing aids.

After a leisurely meal, I'd cleared up, and Greg had run the Golden Oldies back.

Now home again, Greg had been all set to watch some late-night telly while I indulged in a bubble bath. Except, just as I'd been about to hop in the tub, my phone had dinged. Due to the late hour – and always mindful of a potential emergency – I'd dithered. One foot had momentarily hovered over the bubbly water. Then I'd stepped back. Opened the message. It had been from Freya.

Evening! I completely forgot to tell you. Visited the parents yesterday. Mum has blocked the downstairs loo – toilet paper, I hasten to add, nothing nasty. She's obsessed with the stuff. Anyway, can you call a plumber on Monday morning? Oh, and go over there to let him in and make sure he does the job properly. I didn't deal with it myself as didn't want to pay a plumber's weekend rate. And obviously I can't sort it out myself tomorrow because I'll be at work. So over to you. Ta! xx

I gnashed my teeth together as I now reread the text to Greg.

He set the teas on the table and sat down beside me.

'Why couldn't she have told me earlier?' I complained.

Greg rubbed his hands wearily over his eyes.

'Never mind Freya,' he said dismissively. 'Why didn't your father mention it when I was there? I could have had a go at sorting the loo out myself.'

'Dad is getting so forgetful,' I tutted.

'Mind you, if it's as bad as last time around' – my mother often blocked the loos thanks to her tissue fascination

– 'then it will require a specialist company. They'll use a pump and a reinforced hose to clear the pipe. There's only so much I can do with my plunger.' He waggled his eyebrows suggestively.

'Not funny,' I said grumpily. 'To hell with the weekend callout charge. If Freya had bothered to communicate, it would have been fixed by now.' I took a sip of my tea. 'And Dad is starting to seriously worry me.'

'As we've both established, your father is having his own memory issues, darling.' We were both glum for a moment. 'Anyway, it would have been difficult for your dad to tell me without your mother overhearing. She's always glued to his side. And you know what she's like. If Deirdre had heard Trevor telling tales, she'd have gone berserk. It's a no-win situation.'

'I know.' I sighed again. 'But I do wish Freya wouldn't always assume that I'm available. I was meant to see my accountant tomorrow morning. I'd also set the afternoon aside to do a recce on a hotel. One of my clients is getting married there. Ah well.' I blew out my cheeks. 'I'll have to juggle my diary. At least the parents have two loos in their house, otherwise it would be a problem.'

'Until your mother blocks that one too,' Greg chuckled. He gave my hand a squeeze. 'Have I told you lately that I love you?'

'No,' I said despondently.

My husband leant in. Put an arm around my shoulders.

'I love you, Mrs King.' He dropped a kiss on the tip of my nose.

'I love you too,' I said, dredging up a smile.

'Then that's all that matters,' he said, gazing into my eyes. 'Life is short, Mags. Don't stress. It's not good for you.'

'You're right,' I said. I moved towards him. Kissed him full on the mouth.

He reciprocated. I found myself responding. Kissed him harder.

'Is my wife getting playful?' he teased.

'Maybe,' I murmured.

In one swift move, I plonked myself down on his lap. Cupped his face between my hands. Began to kiss him with alacrity. But suddenly Greg was unwrapping my arms from his neck. Pulling away.

'What?' I said in confusion.

He touched his head. Rubbed around his temples.

'I might have to pass on the fun and games,' he grimaced. 'I suddenly have a headache.'

'Isn't that my line?' I quipped, as Greg continued to massage his forehead.

'Sorry, darling.' He gently tipped me off his lap and stood up. 'Ouch, *ouch*. I've never had one like this before. If you don't mind, Mags, I'll head upstairs.'

'Okay,' I frowned. Suddenly Greg didn't look too great. 'Maybe you're coming down with something,' I suggested. 'I ran a bath twenty minutes ago. It's untouched. Do you want first dip? I don't mind having your dirty water.' I smiled at him fondly.

'No.' Greg shook his head. Rubbed his forehead again.

'I'll shower in the morning instead.'

But Greg never took that shower. And I never oversaw a plumber for that blocked loo. Neither did I telephone my accountant to cancel our appointment, nor do a recce of my client's wedding venue. Everything went out the window. Because, when I awoke the following morning, Greg wasn't by my side.

Concerned, I'd hastened downstairs. He was slumped on the sofa. Unresponsive. Upon the occasional table was a glass of water. Next to it, a packet of paracetamol. The blister-pack showed that he'd taken two tablets.

'Greg?' I'd quavered.

But I'd already known from the pallor of his skin that my husband was dead.

To this day, the morning-after-the-night-before remains a blur. As did everything that followed. There had been an ambulance. A postmortem. A verdict – aneurysm. And then a funeral. Everything had seemed to happen at warp speed.

The Golden Oldies had been shocked. The kids, devasted. And me? Well… I'd been numb. Totally numb. However, I do remember the wake. It had been held at our local pub. The Angel. Someone – Tim? – had hired the smaller of its two function rooms. Freya had buttonholed me in the Ladies.

'A good send off, Maggie,' she'd declared as we'd stood at the washbasins. 'But tell me. Why an oak coffin? Cardboard ones are so much more eco-friendly and far better for the environment.'

Chapter Twelve

After an hour or so, Dylan and I returned to the rehoming centre with Bess and Charlie.

During this time we'd struck up conversation with some ramblers. They'd been enjoying an ice-cream while sitting at the table next to us. They'd patted Bess and Charlie and then told us about the dogs they'd once had. Consequently, there had been no personal conversation between Dylan and me – other than his earlier tale about Mabel, the puppy Rottweiler. We'd companionably enjoyed our coffee and cake, but he'd imparted no personal details while we'd sat in the pretty woodland clearing.

'How did you both get on?' Rachel asked upon our return.

'Well' – Dylan put his head on one side as he considered – 'Maggie is a very nice lady, but it's Charlie I want to take home. No hard feelings, eh, Maggie!' he dimpled.

'Ha!' Rachel laughed.

'Funny,' I said, rolling my eyes. Nonetheless I grinned at Dylan's humour.

'And what about you, Maggie?' Rachel gave me an enquiring look.

'Bess is lovely,' I said. 'I'd very much like to rehome

her.'

'Fantastic,' she said, taking both dogs' leads from us.

'Oh,' I said. Suddenly I felt overcome with emotion. I didn't want to be separated from Bess. Rachel caught my expression.

'Would you like to walk her back to her kennel?' she asked kindly.

'I think we'd both like to do that,' said Dylan.

'No problem.' Rachel passed back the leads. 'And then we'll do the paperwork?'

'Absolutely,' I said. 'Can I take her home today?'

'We'll chat about that in a minute,' said Rachel tactfully.

Bess returned to her kennel with her tail between her legs.

'Don't be sad,' I said, squatting down beside her. I gave her a rub behind one ear. Wow, look at me! Up close and personal with a German Shepherd no less. 'I'll be back. And the next time, it will be to take you home.'

Behind me, Rachel tactfully cleared her throat. I stood up, moved out the way, and she secured Bess's kennel door.

'We like our prospective adoptees to take their dog for a second walk. Just to make sure they feel the same way and haven't had a change of heart.'

'I won't change my mind,' I assured.

'That's good to know, but nonetheless it's this centre's policy.'

'Ah.' I nodded. 'Okay. When can I walk her again?'

'Count me in,' said Dylan, returning from Charlie's kennel. 'We could walk together again,' he said. I opened my mouth to speak, but nothing came out. 'Sorry,' he apologised. 'I shouldn't have presumed. If you want to take Bess out alone or' – his eyes flicked to the gold ring on my left hand – 'with your husband, then I'll understand.'

'Oh, no, it's not that,' I said hastily. 'My husband wouldn't want to come. I mean' – I cast about wildly, unused to admitting the truth out loud – 'it's not his bag. Anyway, he can't come.'

'Busy chap, eh?' Dylan smiled.

'N-No,' I stuttered. I could feel my neck prickling and becoming stained with red blotches. 'He, er, he's not around. I mean…' It was no good. I just couldn't say it. I couldn't get my mouth to spit out the words. No way was I going to stand in this rehoming centre and tell two virtual strangers that my husband was dead. Because he wasn't. Not to me. In my mind, Greg was there. He'd *always* be there. 'I'm a widow,' I blurted instead.

Rachel looked momentarily shocked. I'd blanked her earlier question. The one about whether there was anyone else at home. I'd simply told her that I had an empty nest. A quick look at Dylan told me he hadn't expected to hear this either. But there was something else in his expression. In his eyes too. Understanding. He smiled sadly.

'Snap,' he murmured.

'O-Oh,' I stuttered. Suddenly I seemed to have too much air in my lungs. 'Sorry,' I gasped. My hand shot out and clutched one of the bars on Bess's kennel. I steadied myself. Forced myself to exhale, then inhale again.

That's it, Maggie. Breathe. In. Out. And repeat.

Now isn't the time to have a panic attack.

'Sorry,' I repeated. 'Just' – I struggled to compose myself – 'still adjusting.' I forced a smile.

'It's okay,' Rachel assured. 'Do you want a glass of water?'

'I'm fine,' I said, nodding frantically.

Don't be nice. Don't say kind words. Just let me be. I don't know if Rachel had taken a course in telepathy, or whether she was simply good at reading body language, but suddenly she was her usual brisk self.

'Right then,' she said, straightening up. 'Let's go to my office and fill in the reservation forms. Once they are completed, we'll get that second walk in the diary.'

Chapter Thirteen

'Honestly, Greg' – I beamed at the photograph of my husband – 'Bess is wonderful.'

I'd spent an uneasy night, tossing, and turning, debating how to tell him my doggy news.

Earlier, in the shower, I'd rehearsed what I was going to say – that, this afternoon, I would be revisiting Bess for that second walk.

And Dylan, reminded my inner voice.

Yes – I silently acknowledged – but that's because Dylan is planning on rehoming Charlie. It's not a date. My date is with Bess. Not Dylan.

Hmm. That's a nice lipstick. Not your usual colour. Very bright. It enhances the blue of your eyes. Are you sure you're not trying to impress someone?

Don't be ridiculous – I mentally scoffed. I'm simply taking a bit of pride in my appearance. For a change. Is that all right with you?

Oooh, touchy. You don't have to justify yourself to me, dearie.

Good.

The fact that I'd taken care with my hair, threaded some rather dressy hoops through my ears, and then teamed a decent top with a casual-smart pair of jeans – as opposed to scruffy joggers – was merely a coincidence.

I'd blurted out my plans to Greg on this sunny Thursday morning while waiting for the kettle to boil. My husband had stared back at me. The image was that from a past moment. Caught on camera. Mounted in a photo frame. Now residing on the windowsill.

'Bess has been bereaved, just like me,' I prattled.

The kettle came to the boil, sending a jet of steam over the worktop. I poured boiling water over coffee granules.

'As German Shepherds go, Bess isn't huge. Maybe that's because she's female. Perhaps it's the boy dogs that are bigger,' I mused. 'Anyway, I know you're funny about the lawn. That you like every blade of grass standing to attention, but I promise you Bess won't wreck it. She's not a digger.'

Well, I didn't think she was. Time would tell. It might be best to gloss over that for now.

'And, um, I got chatting to a man yesterday.' My eyes slithered away from Greg. I busied myself with the milk. Stirred my coffee. 'His name is Dylan. I'm not sure about his surname. He didn't tell me. Not that it's important. I mean *he's* not important,' I gabbled. 'Dylan is just some randomer who happened to be there while I was dithering about Bess. Anyway, moving on.' I cleared my throat. 'The proprietor of the shelter – Rachel – says that adoptees must have a second walk. It's part of the matching process. And when I say *matching*, I'm talking about the dogs. Obviously. There's no other match going on. I don't even know why I mentioned that word.' I could feel my face burning, even though I had nothing to hide. 'Dylan wants to rehome a cute little rascal by the name of Charlie. So… er… we're going to walk the dogs together. Like we did yesterday. Isn't that nice,' I said brightly.

I dared to look at Greg again. He held my gaze.

'You can come along too, if you like,' I invited.

No, I wasn't going to pick up the photograph and pop it in my handbag. Of course not. But Greg's essence… soul… whatever you wanted to call it… was more than welcome to join me. And anyway, I felt sure he was around most of the time. Either that, or I had a fanciful imagination. Although if Freya found out, she might be more succinct. Simply tell me I was going round the bend.

'Anyway,' I chirped. 'I'll let you decide what you want to do.'

I took a sip of coffee just as the landline rang.

Saved by the bell, said an amused inner voice. It sounded very much like Greg's.

I snatched up the handset.

'Hello?'

'Who's that?' said a confused female voice.

I let out a sigh of exasperation.

'Mum, it's me. Maggie.'

'Oh, hello, dear. How nice of you to call.'

'Mum,' I said gently. '*You* rung *me*.'

'Nonsense,' my mother declared. 'I was turning the television on, and you began speaking out of the remote control. Technology is very strange these days.'

I shook my head and suppressed a smile.

'I think you'll find that you're holding the telephone, not the remote control.'

'Really?' There was a pause while my mother evidently studied the handset she was holding. When she next spoke, there was a shift in her tone. 'I suppose you're after your father,' she said frostily. 'Well, he's not here. He's out with his floozie again.'

If my mother was to be believed, my father had several women on the go. At the last count it was three. This trio comprised of the cleaning lady, the immediate next-door neighbour, and their lady GP. When I'd pointed out that Dad was ninety-two and struggled to get his legs to work, never mind anything else, Mum had been derisive.

'You're clearly in cahoots with him because my husband is *not* ninety-two. I'm only forty-one myself. Do you really think I'd marry an old man?' she'd snorted.

'Is Dad there?' I now asked.

'I just told you,' said Mum indignantly. 'He's out with *her.*'

'Are you sure he's not upstairs in the loo?'

'I never considered that,' said Mum thoughtfully. I sensed her getting to her feet. 'TREVOR!' she bellowed. I held the phone away from my ear. 'ARE YOU AND THAT WOMAN IN THE BATHROOM?'

I raised my eyes to the heavens. Just another crazy conversation. Of feeling like a part of me had teleported to a mad house.

'Mum?' I prompted. No answer. 'MUM!' Oh God,

what was she doing? At that moment there was the sound of a door opening.

'Ah, there you are,' I heard my mother say. 'Thanks for telling me you'd cleared off.' Sarcasm dripped from her voice.

'I did tell you I was going upstairs, Deirdre,' I heard my father reply. There came the sound of some vigorous toilet flushing. Now the washbasin's tap was running. Evidently, handwashing was going on. 'You simply forgot what I told you earlier,' Dad explained.

'There's nothing wrong with my memory,' Mum snapped. 'You're the one who needs some sense knocked into you.'

There was a pause, but when my father next spoke, he sounded alarmed.

'Deirdre?' he quavered. 'Deirdre, what are you–?'

'TAKE THIS!' my mother roared.

From the other end of the line came the sound of a scuffle. It was punctuated with thuds and bangs. What the hell was going on?

'Mum?' I said, gripping the handset.

'Stop it,' I heard my father implore. 'Deirdre, I said–'

My father emitted a bloodcurdling scream followed by another thud. And then the line went dead.

Chapter Fourteen

Frantically, I redialled my parents' telephone number. It rang unanswered. Shit. What the hell was going on in their house? There was only one way to find out.

I grabbed my handbag and keys. Within minutes I was roaring along the rural lanes of Little Waterlow, keeping my fingers crossed that a tractor wouldn't appear around the next bend.

Minutes later I was on the M20. Eyes scanning all three lanes for gaps in the traffic. Daring to break the speed limit in order to knock time off the journey.

My brain kept replaying my father's chilling scream. What had Mum done? Her behaviour was getting increasingly erratic. More and more disruptive. This situation couldn't go on. It just couldn't.

I roared into my parents' quiet residential road and performed an emergency stop on their driveway. Flinging the driver's door wide, I leapt from the vehicle, not even bothering to shut the door. Arm extended, spare key in hand, I fairly flew into their hallway.

'MUM!' I bellowed.

'Is that you, Freya?' came my mother's voice. Ha! Hell would freeze over before my sister dealt with any parental emergency. 'I'm in the bathroom,' Mum trilled. 'I'm keeping your dad company.'

I belted up the stairs.

'Maggie?' my father called out. His voice was reedy.

I edged my way into the bathroom, taking care not to push the door into my father. He was sprawled across the tiles. My mother had put the loo seat down. She was sitting upon it, as if it were a chair. She greeted my wild-eyed expression with a smile.

'Hello, darling,' she chirped. 'Your father has been enjoying a little lay down, although it beats me why he can't use the sofa. Are you comfortable down there, Trevor?'

'God's sake,' I breathed.

I hunkered down by my father. He had cuts and grazes over his forehead and cheeks. There was a huge bruise on the bridge of his nose, which looked swollen. I wondered if it was broken.

'Dad, what happened?' I asked anxiously.

'I fell over,' he said.

'Before that,' I grimaced.

The television's remote control lay abandoned on the floor. I grabbed it. There was blood all over the buttons. The plastic panel that usually housed two batteries was broken. 'I could make a bad joke about assault and battery' – I waggled the handset at my father – 'except this situation isn't funny.'

'Oh, I don't know.' My father gave a weak grin. 'If I'd been murdered, a certain person might have been charged and put in a Duracell.'

'Who's been murdered?' interrupted Mum.

'No one,' I said. 'Thankfully,' I added, under my breath. 'I don't need to be Einstein to work out what's happened here.'

'I had a fall,' Dad insisted. His eyes flashed me a warning. He wasn't going to betray Mum. Not in a million years. 'A *fall*. Do you understand?'

'How on earth did you manage that, Trevor?' tutted my mother. 'You should take more care.'

'Can you get up?' I asked. 'Or do you feel like something could be broken?'

'I'm not in any pain.' Dad shook his head. 'I just need a hand. My legs aren't strong enough to push my body upright. That's all.'

That's all. Nothing major. Laying on one's back like a stranded beetle was simply a minor inconvenience. Inside my head, I was screaming with frustration.

'Right, let's try and get you up.'

My mother immediately shifted off the loo seat.

'I don't need any help,' she said indignantly. 'How DARE you treat me like a child.'

'Sorry, Mum,' I apologised. 'I was actually talking to Dad.'

Her chin jutted for a moment as she hovered on the edge of confrontation. And then her eyes clouded over. She'd forgotten what she'd been about to say.

'Could you possibly go outside' – I suggested – 'and wait on the landing. There isn't enough room in here for the three of us.'

'Of course, darling,' she said sweetly. She shuffled carefully around my father's splayed legs and took herself off. Moments later, the door to the bedroom opened and then closed. I knew she would already have forgotten that I was here. She would now spend ages in her room. Sometimes she was there for hours, happily emptying out her wardrobe, or unravelling toilet rolls.

I took my father's hands in mine.

'Okay, ready? After three,' I said.

'Oof,' he gasped, as I hauled him upright. One of his hands slipped out of mine. He quickly grabbed the edge of the washbasin to steady himself. 'All fine and dandy,' he declared, although he was trembling slightly.

'How do you feel?' I asked, reluctant to let go of his hand.

'I'm right as rain,' he assured.

Of *course* he was! My father was never anything but. Get assaulted by a motorist? Right as rain. Fall over a kerb? Right as rain. Can't get up off the floor? Right as rain.

'Let's get you downstairs,' I said. 'I'll make you a cup of tea.'

'You don't need to fuss, Maggie.' Dad shook me off. 'It was simply an accident.'

'I think a doctor should look at your nose,' I suggested. 'It's swollen.'

'It's fine,' he insisted. His tone had an edge, which spoke volumes.

No doctors. No explanations. No busybodies muscling in. Especially where your mother is concerned.

Minutes later, my father was seated at the kitchen table, sipping his tea.

'Look, Dad,' I said gently. I placed the remote control on the table, next to his cup. 'We both know that Mum assaulted you.'

He pursed his lips.

'I fell,' he said obstinately. He picked up his cup. For a moment, it wobbled alarmingly. Tea slopped on to the table. He took a sip before speaking. 'Don't interfere in our lives, Maggie.'

'Pardon?' I said. My mouth dropped open. 'I've just belted up the motorway to help you. Hardly interfering.'

'You know what I mean,' he said gruffly.

My father's eyes held mine as he once again put the cup to his lips. The air began to vibrate with tension. Carefully, he set down his cup. 'I've had Social Services on the phone.'

I let out an involuntary gasp, then instantly checked myself. Wow. That was quick. Hurrah. Relief flooded through me.

'I did tell you that I'd been in touch with them.'

My tone was defensive. Dad picked up his tea again. For one tense moment, I thought he was going to throw it at me.

'You did tell me,' he acknowledged.

'So when are they visiting?' I asked.

'They're not. I told the woman at the other end of the phone – a nice enough lady I'm sure – to spend her funding on someone else. And then I invited her to fuck off.'

'Dad,' I snapped. 'This has got to stop. I've had enough

of this stress. I'm done with the worry. What if Mum hadn't accidentally called me? What if I hadn't driven over? You'd still be lying on the bathroom floor.'

'There's always Freya to fall back upon,' Dad shrugged.

'And how would you have raised Freya?' I countered. 'By pointing your remote control at the bathroom wall and zapping my sister from her office?'

'Now you're being ridiculous,' my father tutted.

'No, Dad. *You're* the one being ridiculous. I shall phone Social Services and reinstate the assessment they were no doubt trying to arrange.'

'There will be no assessment,' my father exhorted.

'I'm not arguing with you,' I said, getting to my feet. 'And now, as you deem yourself perfectly okay, you must excuse me. I have things to do.'

'What things?' my father scoffed. 'We both know you don't work. Occasionally, you do a bit of point-and-click. Hardly proper employment.'

'Well, thanks for that, Dad,' I said. 'It's good to be reminded that my job isn't worthwhile, even though my *point-and-click* sees me paying tax and national insurance like any other worker.'

'Whatever,' Dad sniffed. 'It's not like Freya's job.'

'I'm going now,' I said carefully. 'Before I say something I might regret.'

'You'd better not be off to visit Social Services, Maggie. If you do, I'll never talk to you again.'

'I'm not off to Social Services,' I said through gritted teeth.

'So where *are* you going?' my father demanded.

I paused in the kitchen doorway. Gave him a defiant look.

'To see a man about a dog.'

Chapter Fifteen

Once again, I got in my car and, once again, I dissolved into tears. The makeup – so carefully applied earlier that morning – was washed away in seconds. The lipstick remained. Pink. At least my lips now matched my eyes.

As the car ate up the miles between my parents' house and the animal shelter, I reflected over this latest event. I should have been more assertive. I should have stayed longer. I should have been more patient.

Yet again I felt like a failure. Oh God, oh God, oh God. Was I an awful human being?

As I drove through the sanctuary's entrance and into the carpark, I spotted Dylan getting out of his car. He looked up. Waved. I flashed him a smile and headed over to an empty bay.

My face felt stiff from the earlier tears. Hopefully I didn't have any salty tramlines across my cheeks. At least my mascara had been waterproof so there were no giveaway black trails. My heartrate inexplicably picked up. Taking a deep breath, I stepped out from the car.

'Hey,' Dylan smiled, as I approached him.

'Hello,' I chirped. My jaunty tone belied the sudden butterflies in my stomach.

'How are you feeling about seeing Bess again?'

'A bit jittery,' I confessed. *Although the jitters might be more to do with seeing you.* 'What about you?'

We fell into step, crossing the carpark and heading towards Reception.

'The same,' he chuckled. 'Although I've been anxious too. Probably because I want Charlie so much. Between you and me, I've fretted about another visitor falling in love with him. Even worse, that he would prefer them over me.'

'I'm sure that won't be the case,' I said warmly.

I briefly touched Dylan's forearm by way of reassurance. The gesture had been automatic on my part. Something I'd have done to anyone. But the unplanned physical contact left me inadvertently gasping. It was as if I'd received a static shock. Zingers rippled through my fingers and whizzed around my palm.

I hastily stuffed my hands in my pockets. It was another warm day. Possibly I looked faintly ridiculous, walking along, hands buried deep in my jacket's lining. I took them out again. Suddenly I didn't know what to do with my arms. It was as if they'd multiplied, and I had too many of them. I walked alongside Dylan feeling like Kartikeya, the six-armed God, but minus a spear.

We arrived at Reception. Dylan held open the door for me.

'After you,' he said.

I ducked under his arm.

'Thanks,' I said gratefully.

I turned just in time to see Rachel approaching. At her

heels was a black Labrador. It strained on its lead.

'A new arrival,' she explained. 'Let me hand over this chap, then I'll take you to Bess and Charlie. I'll be right back.'

'Sure,' said Dylan.

Rachel strode off, the Lab trotting at her side.

'He seemed like a nice dog,' I said, suddenly feeling sad. 'I wonder what his story is.'

'Who knows?' Dylan sighed. 'If my garden was umpteen acres, I'd likely take every dog home with me.'

'Mm,' I agreed. 'And what about the cats? There are loads of them, too.'

Dylan pulled a face.

'I know. However, let's not get melancholy. Let's remind ourselves that two residents will soon be happily rehomed.'

'Yes,' I agreed, perking up.

Rachel reappeared, slightly out of breath.

'Sorry to keep you waiting,' she said. 'Righty-ho. Let's head over to Bess and Charlie.'

Chapter Sixteen

As previously, Rachel took us into the area where dogs had been thoroughly vetted and deemed ready for rehoming.

As I approached Bess's kennel, I was heartened to see her get out of her basket. She regarded me for a moment, eyes alight, and gently wagged her tail. My heart instantly swelled. Then, just like a switch being flicked, she jammed her tail between her legs and made to turn away.

'It's okay, girl,' I crooned. Bess looked back at me. I gave her a reassuring smile. 'I told you I'd be back, and I've kept my promise.'

'Here you are,' said Rachel, handing me a Halti and lead. 'I'll let you get Bess ready while I give Dylan a hand with Charlie.'

'Thank you,' I said.

As I took hold of the headcollar and leash, a cacophony of barking broke out. Charlie had spotted Dylan. The little mongrel had recognised him and was ecstatic that this particular visitor had returned.

From my viewpoint, I surreptitiously watched Dylan. He bent down and scratched Charlie's muzzle, rubbed his ears, stroked his fingers along the brown-and-white spine, then gave the plumy tail a playful tweak. Lucky, lucky

Charlie.

Would you like Dylan to do that to you, Maggie? asked my inner voice, slyly.

Don't be absurd, I silently retorted.

I hunkered down, slipped the noseband over Bess's muzzle, then fiddled with the headcollar's strap.

You need to control your thoughts.

You're the one that whispered in my ear, I replied indignantly.

Hmm. Fair comment. That reminds me. What's the difference between a restriction and a line of dogs waiting for Dylan to stroke them?

What? God, I don't know.

One's a curfew. The other's a fur queue. Ha ha!

Why are you burbling on about ridicul–?

Rachel was coming over. I pressed the pause button on my inner chatter.

'How are you doing, Maggie?' she asked.

'Ready,' I trilled, checking the Halti's clip.

I stood up, knees creaking slightly, and gave Bess's ears a gentle tweak. My goodness but they were big. Still, all the better to hear with. Hopefully. I wondered what Bess's recall was like if ever off the lead.

I pushed open the kennel door and joined Rachel and Dylan.

'Take as long as you like, guys,' she said chummily. 'I know you've both told me that you want to rehome these dogs, but this second walk is critical. I need to be convinced that you both want Bess and Charlie to spend the rest of their days with you. It's a serious commitment.'

'I know,' I said.

Listen to what she's saying, urged my inner voice. *No more jetting off abroad at the drop of a hat.*

I've never made a habit of jetting off anywhere, I responded irritably. And anyway – I added – haven't you heard of kennels?

Do you really think Bess would enjoy being caged again while you sun yourself in the Med?

Then I'll get a dog sitter – I silently answered – or, better still, holiday in England. That way I can take Bess with me.

'Nothing is going to make me change my mind,' said Dylan to Rachel. 'Me and this boy will be buddies for ever.'

Rachel smiled.

'Good to hear. Well, off you both go. Enjoy.'

'Um' – Dylan looked awkward for a moment – 'is it okay with you, Rachel, if Maggie and I let the dogs off the lead for a stretch? We're going to the woods again, so they won't be near any roads.'

Rachel blew out her cheeks.

'Ordinarily, I'd say no. However, between you and me, now and again I take some of our hyper inmates out across the fields so they can let off steam. Charlie is one of them. However, his recall isn't great unless you have treats. Then he's like an arrow. Let me grab a packet from our shop. Take them with you. Wave them about and Charlie will be as good as gold.'

Five minutes later, armed with the treats and filched poo

bags, we set off for Trosley Country Park with our prospective dogs.

Charlie bounced along at Dylan's heels. He reminded me of a tennis ball all set for a high-speed serve. Bess simply kept pace with me. She neither pulled on the lead nor appeared overly excited. However, I noticed those big ears were very erect. Every now and again they quivered slightly, responding to the sound of traffic, birdsong, and – once we were in the woods – twigs snapping underfoot.

There were lots of dogwalkers on the trail today. A Poodle, off lead, rushed over to Charlie who immediately barked his displeasure.

'Sorry,' said a female jogger, as she pounded past. 'He's with me. Bertie!' she urged. 'Leave that dog alone and come with me. I said COME!'

The Poodle dithered, then scooted after its owner.

'It's okay,' said Dylan, giving Charlie a reassuring pat. 'I get it. You're not a fan of other dogs saying hello when you're still restrained. Not a problem. I'll let you off.'

Dylan unclipped the lead and Charlie instantly took off.

'Crikey,' I said, as the mongrel belted off. He then disappeared down a fork in the path. 'Do you think he'll come back?'

'I hope so,' said Dylan, looking bemused. 'Let's put Charlie's recall to the test.'

Dylan stuck two fingers between his teeth and let out a piercing whistle. A second later and Charlie shot out of some trees to our right.

'Good boy,' said Dylan, producing a treat.

Charlie skidded to a halt and gobbled up the biscuit. He was instantly distracted by a squirrel on an overhead branch. Letting out a joyful bark, he took off again.

'Right,' Dylan grinned. 'That's Charlie safely entertained for the next hour or so. What about you, lovely lady?'

The question caught me off-guard. My mouth fell open and my vocal cords shrivelled.

'Come here,' he said softly.

I stared at him, transfixed. Omigod. He wanted me to go to him. Quivering with anticipation, I stepped forward.

'Let's remove that headcollar,' he said.

He's talking to Bess, you berk, hooted my inner voice.

Oh, I mentally gasped.

'Yes, let's have it off,' I twittered.

'Give me the lead,' said Dylan. His hand brushed against mine. Instantly an explosion of zingers went through my palm. I could literally *feel* all the flexion creases burning by way of reaction. I wondered what a palmist might make of it.

Fortune teller: Uh-oh…

Me: What? WHAT?

Fortune teller: Sorry, I'm just being a palmist alarmist…

Ahem, my inner voice interrupted. *Dylan is speaking to you. Pay attention.*

'Sorry,' I gasped. 'What did you say?'

'She's loose. Look.' Dylan nodded at Bess. 'She's off the lead but not leaving your side.'

'O-Oh,' I stuttered. The zingers were still fizzing and

popping. 'That's amazing,' I added.

What's amazing? The dog or the zingers?

I ignored the little voice and glanced at Bess. She was making no attempt to chase after Charlie. That said, I could see her scanning the nearby trees and bushes. She was looking for her hyperactive mate.

Charlie catapulted out of some undergrowth, straight in front of a couple who were walking a Border Collie. Bess let out a yip, as if to say, "Watch what you're doing!" But she made no attempt to join in with Charlie's fun.

'What a good girl,' I said, delighted that Bess was behaving so impeccably.

'The joy of an older dog,' Dylan chuckled. 'A well-behaved lady.'

'She is,' I happily agreed.

'Come on,' said Dylan. 'Let's see where that rascal has gone.'

We set off again, and took a trail that meandered for a mile. Charlie made periodic reappearances, as if to say, "I'm here, don't fret," before whooshing off again.

Bess never left my side. She was unfazed by other dogs coming over. She showed no desire to chase after the occasional jogger or squirrel. She remained calm when a horse rider trotted past, despite me jumping with fright when the pony let out an ear-piercing whinny. Just like a human being, Bess liked to snack, and she cadged a few treats off Dylan every time Charlie responded to rewarded recalls. In short, Bess was wonderful.

The path eventually looped back on itself and led into a

clearing. It was here that the Bluebell Café was located.

'Coffee?' asked Dylan, as we paused outside.

'Yes, please,' I said gratefully. My stomach chose that moment to imitate a washing machine on its final spin.

'Hungry?' Dylan laughed.

'A bit,' I confessed. The air was heavy with the scent of frying bacon, and I sniffed appreciatively. 'Mm, smells divine. Also, it's been a while since breakfast.'

'Go and bag a table,' said Dylan. 'I'll get us a couple of bacon butties.'

'Here,' I said, slipping my handbag off my shoulder. 'Let me give you some money.'

'My treat,' Dylan insisted.

'Okay,' I smiled. 'That's very kind of you.'

'A pleasure,' he said. 'You take Charlie's lead, and I'll get the grub.'

Once again his hand brushed against mine. And once again zingers scorched my fingers before hotly zigzagging up my arm. Lovely.

Lovely, lovely, lovely.

Possibly my eyes glazed over.

'Are you okay?' said Dylan, giving me a curious look.

'I'm lovely,' I sighed.

Chapter Seventeen

Dylan and I sat in the woodland clearing, munching our bacon butties and chatting companionably. However, I couldn't tell you specifically what we talked about. Everything and nothing. We didn't discuss our deceased spouses, although our children cropped up in the conversation.

Dylan mentioned his daughter, Terry. Apparently, she was the same age as Tim and engaged to be married. The wedding was imminent and the bride-to-be very excited.

I shared that Tim was married, also that I hoped to be a grandma in the not-too-distant future. Dylan looked faintly horrified at the grandparent reference.

'The idea of being a grandfather seems preposterous,' he mock-grimaced. 'I'm not old enough. This heart' – he touched his chest – 'still feels twenty-one, even though the body is fifty-three.'

Ah, so he was quite a bit younger than me. Eight years to be precise.

After a toyboy, Maggie?

No – I silently retorted – and could you please stay out of my thoughts.

I am your thoughts.

'I know what you mean,' I said to Dylan. 'My heart still feels eighteen.'

'Ha!' he laughed. 'That makes you three years younger than me.'

'Actually, I'm significantly older than you,' I said wryly. 'Which might explain why I *am* ready to be a grandma,' I added.

Dylan gave me a searching look.

'I know it's rude to ask a lady her age, but–'

'Sixty-one,' I said, answering his unfinished question.

'You don't look it,' he said gallantly. 'I thought you were younger than me.'

'Thanks,' I said, not really believing him. Likely he was being polite – making me feel better, because I was more of a wrinkly than him.

Eventually, we finished our butties. The dogs licked up the crumbs from the plates. Draining our mugs, we headed back to the sanctuary.

Rachel was pleased that all had gone well and that we'd ticked off another condition of the centre's criteria.

'All that now remains' – she beamed – 'is to visit your respective homes and inspect the gardens. I need to make sure they're a safe space for Bess and Charlie.'

'Right,' I blanched. There was a hole under one of the fence panels. A local fox had dug a sizeable entry point. I'd have to go to the garden centre on the way home. Buy a socking great plant to plug the hole.

'Tomorrow morning suit?' asked Rachel.

'Sure,' I nodded. 'I'm not going anywhere.' I'd give

Mum and Dad a miss tomorrow. After the earlier stress and tears, I felt I deserved a break.

'Tomorrow is fine for me too,' said Dylan.

'Fabulous.' Rachel nodded her approval. 'Well then, guys, until then. Afterwards, you'll be able to collect your new family members and live happily ever after.'

'Wow,' I said, grinning from ear to ear.

'See you tomorrow,' said Dylan to Rachel, as we both made to leave.

Outside in the carpark, Dylan stalled.

'I hope you don't mind my saying, Maggie, but…'

'Yes?'

'You looked a little apprehensive when Rachel mentioned the garden inspection. Is there anything that needs doing? Something you need a hand with? A new fence panel, perhaps?'

'No,' I assured. 'It's nothing like that. Rather, it's a hole under a fence panel. Courtesy of Mr Fox. However, I'm going to drive straight over to the garden centre and buy a plant to hide it.'

'Good old Mr Fox,' Dylan chuckled. 'Once Bess is in residence, he'll likely avoid your place.'

'I hope so,' I nodded. 'Mr Fox can be quite a nuisance. He loves to raid the wheelie bin. He's quite accomplished at lifting the lid. Last week he ripped open a sack of rubbish and left mouldering pizza crusts all over the driveway.'

'Didn't he eat them up?'

'Regrettably not. You see, I'd burnt the pizza. The crusts were like concrete.'

'Ah, so Mr Fox didn't want to break a tooth. Wise fella.'

We both laughed. And then, when the sound petered out, we simply stood there. For a moment it was suddenly awkward. What more was there to say?

Me: I hope your home inspection goes well.

Dylan: Likewise.

Me: All the best.

Dylan: And you.

It suddenly dawned on me that this moment was pivotal. It marked the end of our brief friendship. And as that thought registered in my head, my heart felt an inexplicable sense of loss.

Chapter Eighteen

'So…' I said, feeling more uncomfortable by the second.

'So,' Dylan repeated. 'I've really enjoyed our walks, Maggie. And our chats.'

'Me too,' I said, fidgeting slightly and feeling horribly self-conscious.

'I hope everything goes well with Bess.'

'And I hope Charlie settles in quickly with you.'

Small talk. That was suddenly dying on our lips. Dylan opened his mouth to say something, then hesitated.

'Look, I, um…'

'Yes?' I prompted.

Dylan fished in one pocket. Removed his wallet. Seconds later he was pressing a business card in my hand.

'If you ever fancy going for a walk again, when Bess has settled in, and if you want some company' – I realised he was gabbling – 'then, er, give me a call.'

'Oh,' I said, surprised and delighted.

No need to look like you've won the lottery, Maggie. The guy is simply being friendly. He's not exactly suggesting you swap phone numbers and follow up with a candlelit dinner.

I know, I know – I mentally replied – but, even so, this

has cheered me up no end. It means our fledgling friendship isn't over.

I glanced at the business card. It was plain, not remotely flashy. The print was an understated black over a white background.

Dylan Alexander, Manager followed by a mobile number.

Manager of what, I wondered. A shop? A garage? The local McDonald's?

I had a sudden vision of Charlie sauntering in, putting two paws on the counter and saying, "Make mine a Big Mac." I wondered how being a manager of anything meshed with owning a rescued dog.

Questions, questions. Maybe they would be answered another time. Maybe on our next dog walk. Yes, why not!

'Thank you,' I said, pocketing the card. 'Well then…'

What now? Keep fidgeting from one foot to the other? Bravely lean in and peck him on the cheek? Or scamper off across the carpark, pink-faced with joy?

'Take care, Maggie,' said Dylan.

He briefly touched my forearm. Instantly one side of my body was engulfed in a tidal wave of zingers. And then he was off. Striding towards his car. A man on a mission. A man with a sense of purpose. A *man*ager of something-or-other.

For a moment, I stared after him, then turned and walked towards my own vehicle.

Chapter Nineteen

When I drew the curtains on Friday morning, I was greeted by golden sunshine and the promise of another warm day. I stretched, trying to remember last night's dream. Greg had been in it. He'd had a message. Something to do with Dylan.

However, the more I concentrated on trying to recall what he'd said, the more the dream eluded me. By the time I'd put the kettle on, I couldn't remember any of it.

I hummed to myself as I made a coffee. Rachel would be along shortly to inspect the garden.

I took my drink into the conservatory. The room was already warm. Lovely. Later it would be stifling. Such was its nature. Stinking hot in the summer and freezing cold in the winter.

A bird flew past, and something stirred in the corners of my mind. A sense of déjà vu. What was it?

I flopped down on one of the cushioned sofas. Gazed at the view on the other side of the French doors. Admired the Rowan sapling I'd picked up at the garden centre. Mr Fox's entry point had gone.

Another bird swooped low. The sense of déjà vu prevailed. It was definitely something to do with Greg. But what? I tutted and shook my head.

'Do you like my Rowan?' I said aloud. There was no photograph of my late husband in the conservatory. However, my fanciful imagination now conjured him up. He was sitting next to me, on the sofa. 'I'm so proud of myself for planting that tree,' I told him. 'I did it without any help. It was hard work making Mr Fox's hole even deeper. My shoulders still ache after hauling those sacks of compost across the lawn. However, it was worth it. I reckon my little Rowan tree will look amazing in another year or two.'

I sipped my coffee thoughtfully, happily imagining Greg next to me. One arm casually slung along the back of the sofa. His hand brushing my shoulder.

A blackbird landed on the fence. The déjà vu persisted as the bird peered at me. And then, like a cloth removing a stubborn bit of dirt, I remembered last night's dream with absolute clarity.

My husband and I had been sitting right here, in the conservatory, looking at the garden beyond. A blackbird had landed on the fence – just like the one now looking at me – and Greg had asked a very pertinent question.

'I gather you've met someone, Mags?' he'd said. It hadn't been an accusation. Not at all. In fact, he'd seemed slightly amused. 'I'm pleased for you, darling.'

I could feel myself blushing as I now recalled the dream while still imagining Greg sitting alongside me.

'It's not like that,' I'd answered. I found myself repeating it now. Saying it out loud, in this conservatory. Talking to thin air.

In the dream, I'd told Greg about Bess. In fact, we'd gone to the sanctuary together. We'd crept inside the building, then stood outside Bess's kennel. She'd been fast asleep, nose on paws, muzzle twitching as she'd dreamt. Greg had smiled and said that she seemed like a nice dog, and that he knew all about her deceased owner.

'Have you met Bess's owner?' I'd asked in surprise. At the time, it had seemed perfectly normal to ask that question.

'No,' he'd replied. 'But I've checked out your man.'

'My man?' I'd gasped.

'Don't get yourself in a tizzy, Mags,' he'd chuckled. 'You're allowed to befriend other guys. It's called *moving on*.'

'I'm not moving on,' I'd protested. 'I'm simply rehoming a dog. Bess will give me the companionship I crave.'

'Hey, I'm teasing you,' Greg had laughed. 'No need to rise. That said, I think we should have a chat about your future, sweetheart. I think it's time. Dylan seems like a nice guy. I want you to know that I approve.'

My face had heated up with indignation.

'There's nothing going on between me and Dylan.'

'I *know* nothing is going on. Stop being defensive. I'm simply saying that *if* you want something to be going on, then it's fine with me.'

For a moment, my face had worked, as I'd wrestled with conflicting emotions. Happiness at Greg giving me the thumbs up. Irritation at being sussed. Delight at the possibility of something developing with Dylan. Guilt for even thinking about it. Ultimately, embarrassment at Greg knowing I had a secret crush. Consequently, I'd been prickly.

'Are you spying on me?' I'd demanded.

'Of course not,' Greg had snorted.

The dream was now unrolling in full technicolour, as clear as that blackbird on the fence.

'However' – Greg had pointed out – 'you talk to me a lot. So, it's only natural that I'm around when you chat. And anyway, don't deny your attraction to Dylan. It's so obvious. You're all hot and bothered. You've also gone a bit googly eyed. It's how you used to look when we were first dating, do you remember?'

In the dream, Greg had slung an arm around my shoulders. Given them a reassuring squeeze. Was it my imagination, or could I now feel the lightest touch upon my shoulder?

'Dylan is simply someone I met at the rehoming centre,' I now said aloud. 'He gave me his business card. He suggested we might occasionally walk our dogs together. That's all. But I won't be following up. No way am I ringing him. I'd feel too shy. And I didn't give him my phone number, so he can't ring me.'

Hmm, I now heard Greg say in my head. *I'll have to see what I can do about that. Everyone deserves a second chance of happiness.*

'What do you mean?' I said, just as the doorbell rang. That would be Rachel. 'Saved by the bell,' I said to the empty space beside me.

Chapter Twenty

Rachel stood on my doorstep positively bristling with energy and efficiency.

'Good morning!' she trilled.

'Hello,' I beamed. I stepped aside to let her in. 'I was just having a coffee.' I waved my mug at her. 'Can I make you one too?'

'No, thanks,' she said. 'I've not long since had one.'

Her eyes swivelled. She was already assessing the house. Hopefully she approved of the hallway's larger-than-average dimensions. Had noted that there was plenty of room for a dog basket or three in this area alone.

'I have several homes to vet this morning' – she continued – 'so time is of the essence. It's fabulous that so many people are rehoming, but we're flat out. It seems that for every resident that leaves, another two come in.'

'That's sad,' I acknowledged. 'Anyway, come on through.' I shut the door after her.

'You have a lovely house,' she said. 'Are you sure you want a dog shedding hair all over the place? And, oh! Look at your gorgeous cream carpets. They won't stay that colour if Bess has a muddy walk!'

'It's fine,' I said. 'To be honest, I was thinking of

making some changes to the place. Removing those carpets might be the first thing.' The air seemed to quiver beside me. Greg had always resisted change. 'I'd much rather have flooring that can be mopped. Plus, it looks trendier,' I added, as we walked through the kitchen and into the utility room.

'Although less cosy,' Rachel pointed out.

I shrugged.

'That's why rugs were invented,' I grinned. 'Anyway' – I opened the rear door – 'here's the garden.'

The area behind the house was revealed in all its gorgeous May glory.

'This is lovely,' said Rachel, stepping outside.

And she was off. Powering around the lawn. Examining the fence. Parting plants. Looking for potential escape routes. I was glad my little Rowan was safely in situ.

'What a terrific space,' she said, striding back to me. 'Your garden is big enough for a dog to run around *and* play ball. This makes me very happy. If you don't get a chance to walk Bess some days, she's not going to be deprived of exercise.'

'Does that mean I pass?' I asked, fingers crossed behind my back.

'Most definitely,' she nodded. 'It's wonderful that one of our seniors has a second chance for happiness. Everyone deserves that.'

The hairs on the back of my neck prickled. Those were almost the words I'd imagined Greg to say when I'd been sitting in the conservatory earlier.

'Are you off to see D-Dylan next?' I stuttered.

I'd meant for the question to sound casual. However, stumbling over his name rather made it sound like I was being nosy – which I was.

'No. I have other people to see before Dylan. He lives the furthest away, so is last on my list.'

'Oh,' I said, trying to hide my disappointment at this news.

So, what time might Dylan pick up Charlie? I'd rather hoped our paths would cross. That we might even walk our dogs together again.

'Right,' said Rachel. She rubbed her hands together. A gesture of being done. 'I won't hold you up.' We retraced our steps to the front door. She hesitated for a moment. 'Could I ask a favour?'

'Of course.'

'If you could head over to the sanctuary now, it would be helpful for the staff. Free up a kennel sooner, so to speak.'

'Okay,' I nodded.

Oh well. That was that. Absolutely no chance of bumping into Dylan now. Mind you, it was probably for the best. Was it appropriate for a sixty-one-year-old to be mooning around and – as Greg had phrased it – looking all *googly eyed*?

Rachel stuck out a hand.

'It's been lovely meeting you, Maggie.' Her firm handshake rivalled that of a man's. 'I wish you all the best with your rescued companion. And remember, any teething problems, any questions, we're at the end of the phone.'

'That's very kind of you,' I said, releasing the latch on the front door. 'And thank you for all the help to date. I'm very grateful to you and your husband.' Along with another man I suddenly couldn't stop thinking about.

Oh, stop it, Maggie, and start acting your age.

'A pleasure,' said Rachel. She stepped outside. 'Bye-*eee*.'

'Bye,' I called after her.

I watched as Rachel slid behind the wheel of her car. She put up one hand and I waved back. Then, in a cloud of exhaust, she was gone. I shut the front door. For a moment I leant back on it. Exhaled gustily.

Come on, Maggie. Shake a leg. The staff need Bess's kennel.

Repressing another sigh, I grabbed my keys and handbag.

Chapter Twenty-One

'Well, darling,' I warbled. 'We're on our way. Back to my place. Yours too, now. Your fur-ever home.'

I glanced at the car's rearview mirror. Bess was sitting on the back seat, her body ramrod straight and blocking all view of the traffic behind us.

Bess had refused to jump into my hatchback's boot. One of the kennel maids had pointed out that my German Shepherd's hips weren't up for leaping. I'd had the foresight to bring an old towel along with me. It had then been laid across the rear seat's upholstery.

'Let her clamber in through the side door,' the kennel maid had said. The advice had worked a treat.

I glanced again at the rearview mirror. A pair of brown eyes met mine. There was now a light in those eyes – a light that had been missing when I'd first met Bess. The tips of her enormous ears were firmly pointing north, and a long pink tongue flopped south.

Upon leaving the sanctuary, I'd buzzed down the rear windows – not so far that Bess could jump out, but enough for her to stick her head out should she so wish. After all, I didn't want her overheating. Summer was just around the corner, and although the temperature had yet to truly rise, I knew dogs in hot cars was a no-no.

'Is that a nice breeze?' I asked her.

Bess's nose continuously twitched, catching different scents wafting through the open window.

'Mummy can't wait to show you the house,' I prattled.

Was it okay to refer to oneself in such a way? Did other dog owners speak to their charges as if they were children? I tried to remember if Dylan had done the same with Charlie.

Dylan.

Dylan with his dark hair, a touch of grey making him dashing and distinguished.

Dylan with eyes that matched the seas portrayed in holiday brochures.

Dylan with the build of an athlete and the height of a male model.

Gorgeous Dylan.

I sighed. Bess emulated me and eased down on her belly. Oh good. I could see in the rearview mirror again. I now did so – and gulped at what I saw.

A lorry was fast approaching. The driver was showing no inclination to reduce speed, despite us both heading towards traffic lights on a major junction. I felt a frisson of alarm as the lights began to change to red.

Gently, I deployed the brake, and my vehicle began to slow. My eyes flicked back to the rearview mirror. Bloody hell, was that lorry going to hit me? I tensed, relieved that Bess wasn't in the boot.

My car rolled to a stop just as the lorry driver belatedly applied his brakes. There was a horrendous squealing sound accompanied by the blare of a horn. I jumped, heart pumping unpleasantly. Why had he beeped me? I'd done nothing wrong.

My eyes once again darted to the rearview mirror. There was movement behind the windscreen. A second later, the cab door swung open. Uh-oh.

A pair of trousered legs were briefly revealed, then a pot-bellied balding man jumped down to the tarmac. He strode over to my car and rapped on the window. I buzzed it down an inch.

'Yes?' I quavered.

'You silly cow,' he snarled.

'I beg your pardon?' I spluttered.

'Why didn't you drive through those lights?'

'Because they were on the change,' I retorted.

'But they weren't red, were they?'

'No, but–'

'Do you know how long it takes for this junction's lights to change?'

'I don't, but–'

'Four minutes and thirty-nine seconds,' he interrupted. 'I timed it the last time a driver prematurely stopped – another bimbo.'

Bimbo?

'Well, really–'

'That's four minutes and thirty-nine seconds of my life that I won't get back.'

'There's only another three minutes and thirty-nine seconds to wait,' I said sarcastically.

'Is that meant to make me feel better? Because it doesn't. Women like you shouldn't be on the road. You meander from lane to lane, checking your lipstick, taking a selfie, posting to Instaprat, Facesplat, and Twatter–'

'How dare you!' I protested. 'I do no such thing.'

I could feel my sap rising. This guy was bang out of order. I'd been driving safely. Sensibly. I certainly didn't need this fruit loop shouting at me.

'Fluffy women like you' – he ranted, now in his stride – 'should stay at home baking fluffy cakes and refolding your fluffy towels.'

'And men like you' – I snarled – 'should stick to sitting on the loo reading your comic newspaper before shoving it right up–'

'Women like you...' he interrupted, his face puce with rage.

Except he got not further. Ominous growling rent the air. Suddenly the man was up close and personal with Bess. She'd stuck her head through the open back window. Her chest strained against the door.

The lorry driver visibly paled and took a step backwards. He'd failed to notice a huge German Shepherd languishing on the back seat.

'I think what you meant to say' – I said sweetly – 'is that women like me need to be respected, or else we get girls like her' – I jerked my head at Bess – 'to sort out PLEBS LIKE YOU!'

And with that, Bess let rip with a volley of ferocious barks. The lorry driver turned on his heel and scuttled back to his cab. I buzzed the window fully down.

'ONLY ANOTHER THIRTY-NINE SECONDS TO WAIT,' I yelled after him – just as a cop car cruised to a standstill in the next lane.

Ploddy slowed. Gave me a stern look. Bess deigned to give Ploddy a warning woof too, then retracted her head. I hastily shut all the windows. That was the last thing I needed. Ploddy demanding to know why a furious woman and her equally furious dog were causing a burly lorry driver to flee.

Apart from anything else, if the incident made the local papers, Little Waterlow's gossips would have a field day. I could imagine the headlines now:

LORRY DRIVER GOES MUTTS

Or

ALSATION PROVOCATION

Or even

LIGHT BITES AT THE TRAFFIC LIGHTS

Sixty-one-year-old Maggie King's pooch went bark-serk when lorry driver Fatso Dickhead angrily questioned Mrs King's driving skills. Mr Dickhead told re-paw-ters that he'd regrettably lost his temper due to having a ruff day, but assured local paw-lice that his bark was worse than his bite.

I let out a shaky breath.

Bloody hell. I mean, *bloody* hell.

'Okay, darling,' I quavered. 'Good girl. Settle down.'

Bess, lowered her bottom, all the while grumbling to herself. My goodness, she'd been quite fearsome. But at no point had she tried to bite the lorry driver. She'd just warned him off. And protected me too.

'Thank you,' I said, glancing at her in the rearview mirror. 'Us girls have to stick together, eh?' She stared back at me benignly, although I could've sworn she winked.

The lights changed. I shoved the gear into first and accelerated away. Behind me, the lorry crossed the junction and took a right turn. Thank heavens. I didn't fancy another second of him travelling behind me. Stupid man.

My mobile suddenly rang, making me jump for the second time in as many minutes. Freya. I pressed the handset icon on the car's steering wheel.

'Hello?' I said, my voice a little shaky.

'What's up?' she said. 'You sound as if you've been electrocuted.'

'I've just had an unpleasant altercation with a lorry driver eager to demonstrate his road rage skills.'

'Hope you gave him the middle finger,' said my sister.

'I did better than that,' I chuckled. 'My dog terrified the living daylights out of him.'

There was a pause.

'Your dog?' said Freya eventually. Her tone was incredulous.

'Yes, my dog,' I said happily. 'I'm on my way home with her. Her name is Bess. She's an eight-year-old German Shepherd rescue and–'

'No pun intended,' interrupted Freya. 'But have you gone barking mad?'

'What do you mean?' I said, instantly defensive.

'How is a huge dog going to fit in with Mum and Dad?'

I frowned.

'Bess will be living with me, not our parents.'

'I'm talking about when you go over to their place. Or are you leaving this dog alone in your house for hours on end?'

'No, of course not. Bess will come with me.'

'Maggie, what world do you occupy?' Freya's voice had gone up an octave. 'Large dogs do not mix well with Zimmer frames, walking sticks and pensioners with doddery legs. Anyway, I need you to spend tomorrow with Mum and Dad. I promised I'd take them out for coffee and cake, but unfortunately Vernon's aunt has summoned us for tea. We can't turn her down. She might be a cantankerous old bat, but Vernon is her sole beneficiary. We need to keep her sweet.'

'Sorry, Freya,' I said. 'Tomorrow I'm working.'

'Tomorrow is Saturday,' Freya pointed out.

'That's right,' I said evenly. 'And I have a client who is getting married.'

Freya huffed with annoyance.

'So get another photographer to cover it. Use one of your contacts.'

My mouth dropped open. Oooh, the audacity.

'No,' I said firmly. 'No, I won't do that. My client has booked *me*. She's seen *my* portfolio, not the work of another photographer. So, sorry. No can do. If Vernon's aunty disinherits him over not turning up for a cuppa, then she's a control freak.'

'Yes, she is, so I really need you–'

114

'No,' I repeated. 'You'll have to take Mum and Dad with you. Now please excuse me, Freya. Ella is trying to get hold of me,' I lied. 'Talk soon. Toodle-oo.'

I didn't have another call waiting. However, it was best to cut off my sister before I impersonated Bess and delivered a few growler howlers of my own. I glanced at the rearview mirror again. Gave Bess a wicked grin.

'That was Freya,' I said. 'My bossy sister. You have permission to put her in her place whenever you like.'

Chapter Twenty-Two

Once home, I gave Bess a guided tour.

The inside of the house made no obvious impression upon her. However, once outside, she broke into a trot. Nose down, tail up. She sniffed and snuffled in various places before finally dropping a *curtsey* alongside the Rowan tree. I could almost hear Greg protesting in dismay.

There goes my lawn.

'Never mind,' I said aloud. 'It's only a bit of wee.'

Leaving Bess to it, I went back inside, and put the kettle on. While waiting for the water to boil, I texted the children. We had a family group chat, and I was keen to tell the kids my exciting news:

Bess is home!

One by one they replied with messages of congratulation. Tim said he couldn't wait to meet my new *daughter*. Ruby suggested we all get together on Sunday for dinner at mine, so that Bess got to know everyone in one hit. Ella seconded that idea.

I dithered. Might it be overwhelming for Bess? But then I decided it would be fine.

Don't invite Auntie Freya and Uncle Vernon. This from Tim. *She'll only pour a bucket of cold water on your joy.*

She's already done that, I replied. *We spoke on the phone earlier. She basically told me I was off my rocker. That Bess would be a disaster with the grandparents.*

Negativity is Aunty Freya's middle name. This from Ruby. *Will the grandparents be joining us on Sunday too?*

No. I didn't hesitate with my answer. *I want to relax on Sunday. I've seen both of them a few times this week, so refuse to feel guilty. Another time!*

Ella then independently messaged asking if she could meet Bess sooner.

Can I come over tomorrow, Mum? Archie has been given a free pass to see Arsenal play at home. You know what my boyfriend is like when it comes to his team. Totally obsessed!

I texted back immediately.

Football, huh! Of course, darling. That would be lovely. However, I'm only around in the morning. I'll be covering a wedding in the afternoon.

Ella sent me an emoji eye roll, but then added:

That's fine. I'll dog-sit while you're out. Let's walk Bess in the morning. I fancy coffee and cake at the Bluebell Café. That said, it will have to be your treat. I'm skint!

It was then my turn to send an emoji eye roll.

Happy to treat you! See you tomorrow xxx

A scrape on the back door let me know that Bess was done in the garden.

Together, we went through the things I'd bought earlier at the rescue centre's shop; a large cosy basket – hmm, that might go unused for a while due to the warm weather – a squeaky squirrel toy, a tennis ball with plastic launcher, a grooming brush, and two large ceramic bowls – one for water and one for food.

'Which reminds me' – I said, as Bess trailed me – 'I'd better fill this up.'

I went through to the kitchen, dog at my heel. She watched as I stuck one of the bowls under the tap. Sure enough, as soon as the dish was set down, she lapped at the water. Quite a lot splashed over the floor tiles at the same time.

I decided not to walk her today. She'd had quite a bit of upheaval already, one way or another. From kennel to car. From irate lorry driver to unfamiliar house. For now, I'd just let her be. Give her a chance to settle in. Instead, we'd have a play in the garden.

I made myself another cuppa, then picked up the tennis ball and launcher.

'Come, Bess,' I trilled.

The two of us went outside again. I set my drink down on the little wrought iron table. Greg had bought it two summers ago for the patio area. I pulled out a chair and was about to sit down when I caught Bess looking at me. She had her head comically on one side.

'Want to play?' I asked.

She wagged her plumy tail by way of reply.

Picking up the tennis ball, I launched it across the lawn. Bess immediately gave chase. However, after returning the ball twice, she lost interest. Instead, she opted to wander off to a shaded area.

Tongue hanging out, gently panting, Bess sank down on the grass. For a minute or two, she watched a butterfly doing a fluttery dance over some nearby flowers. After another moment or so, she lowered her head. Nose to paws. Her eyes closed. Her sides rose and then fell as she heaved a sigh. Contentment.

Chapter Twenty-Three

'Oh Mum, she's lovely,' Ella smiled.

My youngest dipped her shortbread in her tea, then regarded Bess fondly. The three of us were at the Bluebell Café, having completed a mile-long loop around the woods. We were now enjoying a cuppa.

Bess was working her way through a bone-shaped biscuit. The café baked a batch every day for visiting dogs. I was reminded of the last two times I'd been here. With Dylan, of course. Momentarily distracted, I scanned the outside seating area, half-hoping to see him here with Charlie. However, there was no sign of him, and I felt a frisson of disappointment.

'Who are you looking for?' asked Ella.

'No one,' I said quickly. 'Anyway, I'm glad you approve of Bess.'

'She's utterly gorgeous,' Ella nodded. 'How on earth did you manage to choose one dog from so many?'

'It was tough,' I admitted. Dylan once again popped into my head. I could see him now, touching his heart. *You feel it here,* he'd said. He'd been right. 'I noticed Bess because she looked so depressed. Her owner had died.'

'Bereavement,' Ella acknowledged. 'Yes, you both have

that in common.'

'Indeed,' I said. 'She looked like she'd given up all hope.'

'But not anymore,' Ella observed. 'In fact, she looks pretty perky to me.' My daughter's eyes swivelled to me. 'Like you. Is it the dog that's put a spring in your step? Or is it something else – that you're not sharing?' she added.

I flushed, and hoped Ella didn't spot it.

'Just Bess,' I muttered.

Fortunately, Ella didn't further question my *perkiness.* In fact, what she said next, rather took the wind out of my billowing sails.

'I don't mind admitting, Mum, that after Dad died, you gave us all a bit of a scare.'

'What do you mean?' I frowned.

'Well, obviously, Dad's sudden departure was a terrible shock. It hit us all hard. Dad was here one minute – larger than life – then gone the next. It was awful. I think we were all a bit traumatised, one way or another. After all, it's a harsh reminder that there's a thin line between this world and the next.'

'Agreed,' I nodded.

'But… don't take this the wrong way…'

'Go on,' I huffed. I steeled myself for a lecture of some sort.

'It's just that… well, me, Ruby and Tim… although we found the bereavement hard… we didn't sink.'

My frown deepened.

'I didn't sink,' I protested. 'I got on with life. I had no

choice. My goodness, there was a diary full of photographic appointments for starters. I could hardly let my brides down. And, work aside, I've had two elderly parents keeping me on my toes. I haven't had the luxury of being able to retreat from the world.'

'Message received, loud and clear.' Ella flapped a hand in a conciliatory manner. 'Maybe I didn't phrase my words properly. Perhaps I should have instead said *you seemed to lose the plot.* Just a bit,' she added, as if those last three words softened the blow of the previous ones.

My frown was replaced with astonishment. I gaped at my daughter.

'Lose the plot?' I repeated. 'In what way?'

Ella paused for a moment. Dunked her biscuit again. Looked thoughtful as she sucked up soggy shortbread. When she next spoke, her voice was soft.

'All those framed photographs, Mum. They were everywhere. All over the sideboard. In the lounge. On the coffee table. More in the kitchen. From worktop to windowsill. Then there was the collection in your study. I counted six on your desk alone. Not forgetting your bedroom. Tim made a bet that you'd get a life-sized cardboard effigy of Dad. And the way you spoke to Dad. As if he were still there. Asking his opinion about this, that and the other. And then the way you'd pause, as if hearing him answer. It was unnerving. We were worried about, you know, your mental health.'

'I see,' I nodded. I wasn't going to confess that I still spoke to Greg, albeit in my head rather than out loud. 'So, you thought your old mum had gone bonkers.'

She popped the last of the shortbread in her mouth.

'You're offended,' she said.

I shrugged.

'Okay, maybe I was a bit… odd.'

'Mum, you were downright weird.'

'So are you inferring that I'm no longer weird, or just a *little* weird?'

'Let's just say that we're happy to see you've decluttered the photographic display. What are you down to? One in each room?'

'Yes,' I lied.

I wasn't going to mention the pics still on my dressing table. There had been a time when I'd taken one of them to bed. Hugged it for months. It was Greg and me on our wedding day. Happy. Carefree. I'd thought we'd have decades together. Celebrate our one-hundredth birthday together.

I'd only recently stopped hugging the photograph – mainly on account of rolling on it while sleeping. My torso had cracked the glass. It was a wonder I'd not cut myself.

'We all miss Dad,' said Ella gently.

I lowered my eyes, so she didn't spot their sudden watery sheen.

'Of course,' I agreed.

'But life goes on,' she added. 'And we must all move on with it.'

I blinked. Looked up sharply. Gazed at this daughter of mine. Such wise words for one still so young. Also, those words had very recently been imparted by someone else. Greg.

He'd teased me about meeting Dylan. Told me I was allowed to befriend other guys. That it was called *moving on.* Not that I'd tell Ella about that conversation. After all, I didn't want my daughter thinking I was having a *weird* relapse.

Chapter Twenty-Four

'So, you'll definitely be okay?' I asked Ella, chewing my lip.

We were home, but I needed to head off again. There was a wedding to photograph. However, my stomach was flipping with anxiety.

'Yes!' my daughter sighed. 'Why would I not be?'

'Because you've never looked after a dog before,' I fretted.

'Neither have you,' she pointed out.

'Fair,' I acknowledged. 'However, I've had a day's head start over you.' Sometimes point scoring was appropriate.

'Listen,' said Ella. She adopted her *I'm a very patient person* expression. The one that equally conveyed *I'm also talking to an imbecile.* 'I will let Bess out every couple of hours. We'll play with Mr Squeaky Squirrel. I won't let her climb on the furniture, and I won't share my crisps with her. How does that sound?'

'It sounds okay,' I said reluctantly. 'And don't forget she has her dinner at five o'clock.'

'I won't,' Ella promised. 'And I'll make sure she has a nice cup of Horlicks if you're not back in time to read her bedtime story.'

'You're so funny,' I said, giving her an eyeroll.

'Go, Mother.' Ella made shooing gestures with her hands.

'Right,' I said, picking up my bag of camera equipment. 'Any problems, any problems at all–'

'Rest assured that I will ring 999 and request an ambulance.'

I rolled my eyes again.

'I'm going.'

'I think that's a very good idea,' said my daughter firmly.

Minutes later, I'd left Little Waterlow and was on the motorway, heading towards the wedding venue.

Goldhill Grange was a beautiful country hotel set in fifteen acres of manicured grounds. I'd covered bridal events at this location before, but they'd always been winter affairs. I was looking forward to overseeing this wedding without concerns over fading light or, even worse, frightful weather.

My client, a young woman by the name of Theresa, had booked me almost a year ago. It was impossible to recall every one of my brides' personal details, so I always made notes to later refer to.

Today, my info sheet reminded me that Theresa's wedding was a small affair. There had been a family bereavement not long after Theresa's engagement. The young woman had confided that she couldn't face a wedding with pomp and ceremony. It wouldn't have been the same without her mum being there. Consequently, Theresa had swapped the church for a hotel and scaled down the invitations. There would only be immediate family at the ceremony followed by a small and intimate wedding breakfast. Afterwards, the bride and groom would depart to Heathrow, and a Bali honeymoon. No frills and fuss-free.

I arrived in plenty of time and busied myself taking shots of the hotel, the grounds, and then the empty ceremony room. The latter was decked out with beautiful blooms. Order of Service sheets had been placed upon beribboned chairs. Petals covered the short, carpeted walkway that led up to a small platform. It was here that the couple would stand and say their vows.

I then went into the hotel's orangery. This was where the wedding breakfast would take place. A large table was covered in crisp white linen, ornate candelabra, polished silver cutlery and crystal glassware. Centrepiece was an elaborate flower arrangement. I moved in, snapping pics of the blooms, zooming in on the named place settings, also the individual menus which were beautifully handwritten in italic script.

Nipping about, I captured an air of expectancy, then hastened outside again.

The groom arrived minutes later. Tobias Green was tall and fair. He was also incredibly nervous and steadily turning the same colour as his surname.

'Try and relax,' I encouraged. 'The day will flash by. I promise that you'll later look back at this moment and wish you could do it all over again without nerves getting the better of you.'

'R-Really?' he stuttered. 'I keep worrying that I might forget my lines. Or get a frog in my throat and have a coughing fit.'

'So what if you do?' I shrugged. 'It won't stop you marrying the girl of your dreams.'

'I guess not,' he said, brightening a tad.

'That's better,' I smiled. 'Now then, let's have a few shots of you over here by the fountain. That's it. Relax. Wonderful. And again, this time with your best man. Shake hands. And hold that pose. Perfect.'

I scampered about, clicking away, adding the proud parents into the small group. Mum then asked if she could have one of *just me and my boy*. I could almost see the umbilical cord joining her and Tobias. I wondered how Theresa would get along with her future mother-in-law. Whether there would ever be a power struggle between them. I'd heard of that happening many a time when the bridegroom was *Mummy's boy*.

Due to the family's circumstances, there were no bridesmaids to photograph. Not even a Maid of Honour.

Tobias stuttered that Theresa had given him strict instructions; when the wedding car arrived, he was not to greet her. Instead, he was to be in the ceremony room. He was also to watch his future wife walk down the aisle – preferably looking ecstatic, and not like someone about to upchuck.

'Excellent,' I murmured. 'So, make sure you do that.'

'Do what?' he asked, his Adam's apple bobbing nervously.

'The former, not the latter,' I bantered.

'O-Oh, right. Y–Yes,' he stuttered. 'I'd better go in. Stand on the spot marked X,' he joked weakly.

Dear Lord, this boy's nerves were at breaking point. I hoped the bride wasn't in a similar state.

'C'mon, Tobes,' said the best man gently. 'If you're feeling faint, lean on me.'

'Give him a drink of water,' I said sharply. I was deadly serious too.

I'd once covered a wedding where the bride, overcome by nerves, had swooned prettily at the altar. Not so attractive was her broken nose after faceplanting down on the altar step.

Other guests were now arriving in quick succession. I stood to one side. Watching. Observing. Taking discreet photographs. Catching the moment two women air-kissed on account of their huge hats colliding. Snapping a rotund gentleman's delight at a relative not previously seen for years. Capturing a blonde's concern as she checked her handbag for confetti. It was all there.

Eventually, everybody went inside. I paused. Took a few breaths. A bee buzzed over some nearby marigolds. I was reminded of yesterday when Bess had watched the butterfly in the garden.

For a moment I dithered about giving Ella a quick ring. Just to make sure all was well. But the brief window of opportunity disappeared. A beribboned car had come into view. The vehicle, complete with chauffeur, was purring towards me. It slowly made its way along the single-track gravel road. The bride had arrived.

I began clicking away. The vehicle rolled to a standstill and the chauffeur got out. As he went to open the rear door, I moved in ready to capture Theresa exiting. But as the door opened, the breath whooshed out of me.

For sitting next to the blushing bride, was Dylan.

Chapter Twenty-Five

'Whatever are you doing here,' I said foolishly.

'Getting married,' said Theresa, giving me a peculiar look.

'I'm so sorry,' I said, quickly recovering. 'I meant Dylan. I mean… I didn't realise…'

'Maggie,' said Dylan, equally astonished.

'I take it you two know each other,' said Theresa, gathering up her skirts.

'Er, yes. Sorry, Theresa' – I quickly shifted to professional mode – 'don't get out of the car. Hold it there. Bring the bouquet forward a bit. That's it. Now turn towards me. Smile. Beautiful.' I snapped away. 'And just to say, you look absolutely gorgeous.'

'Thank you,' she said.

Theresa was looking at me curiously. Likely trying to figure out how I knew her father.

Dylan was now out of the car and moving over to Theresa's side.

'Lovely to see you, Maggie,' he murmured.

'You too,' I muttered.

'Who's looking after Bess?'

'My youngest. What about Charlie?'

'He's with my neighbour.'

The snatched conversation ended as Dylan moved in to assist Theresa. Once again, I reverted to photographer mode.

'Let me stop you there,' I said to Dylan. 'Take Theresa's hand – as if you're helping her out of the car. Perfect.' I stood back, framed father and daughter in the viewfinder, clicked, then moved smartly out of the way. After all, the bride wouldn't thank me for treading on her trailing hemline when she exited the vehicle.

'Give me your flowers, Terry,' said Dylan. 'You need to gather up your dress.'

Terry. Ah ha! When Dylan and I had taken the dogs on that second walk, he'd mentioned a daughter – Terry – and that she was getting married. Blimey, he'd never said it was *this* weekend!

I'd failed to join the dots. Not only regarding my client, one Theresa Alexander, sharing Dylan's surname, but also her mother being Dylan's deceased wife. Flipping heck, sometimes it was such a small world. Emotions were always elevated at weddings, and I suspected this one would be running at full throttle.

I had yet to deal with Ruby or Ella getting married without Greg by my side. No doubt, when that day came, it would be tricky for all.

My eyes momentarily brimmed. What must this father and daughter be feeling right now? I blinked rapidly. Gave myself a swift pep talk.

Concentrate, Maggie. You're on a professional

assignment.

The bride was now out of the car. She smoothed her dress, then retrieved her bouquet from Dylan.

'Theresa… Terry,' I said. 'Link Dad's arm, please.' I pointed the camera at them both. 'Perfect. Okay, I'm now going to run ahead and will shortly take a series of candid shots as you make your way into the building. Before you walk down the aisle, give me a moment to get in position. I need to be behind the officiant.'

I didn't wait for either of them to reply. Time was of the essence. I scampered ahead, pausing only to photograph father and daughter strolling towards me… Terry turning to look at her father… a moment of anxiety on her pretty face… Dylan reassuring her… Terry nodding… her features tensing as she became emotional… Dylan mirroring Terry… his eyes suddenly very bright… continuing forward… heads held high… two people so obviously thinking about someone else. A missing mother. An absent wife. It was all there. Captured on film. Or, rather, digital memory. It had been a long time since I'd used a Hasselblad.

I disappeared inside the hotel leaving father and daughter to take a moment. Hastening to the rear of the ceremony room, I moved past Tobias and the best man.

'You're okay, mate,' the best man said. 'Another twenty minutes and it will all be over.'

He sounded like a dentist reassuring a patient who was about to have a tooth extraction.

Once in position, I took an informal shot of Tobias looking like he was about to have that extraction without local anaesthetic, then hid a smile in the palm of my hand. Poor chap.

The wedding officiant stepped forward. She greeted everyone and suddenly Vivaldi's Four Seasons filled the air. The bride appeared, pausing for effect as everyone's heads swivelled.

I snapped away, capturing guests' reactions. Delight at the bride's beauty. Pleasure at her gorgeous dress. And then Dylan and Terry were off; walking sedately down the aisle.

Tobias was now staring at his future wife. He looked awestruck. And surprised. As if that hypothetical tooth extraction had been better than he'd dared to hope.

Dylan passed Terry's right hand to the groom's left, then melted into an aisle. For a moment his eyes snagged on mine. Held my gaze. And then he winked.

Daringly, I did the same.

Chapter Twenty-Six

The wedding flowed seamlessly and without a single hitch.

Tobias shed a tear. I managed to zoom in and capture the moment before he flicked it away with his cuff.

Throughout the ceremony, Terry gazed at her man as if he were the newly crowned Mr Universe.

Dylan looked on. His face was an open book to read – both choked and proud.

Halfway through the ceremony, a blonde woman appeared from nowhere and sat next to Dylan. She was very elegant. Attractive. She reminded me of Jemima Khan – albeit an older version.

She hadn't been beside Dylan earlier, and I was puzzled as to why she'd moved seats. Previously, the chair had been empty. As if reserved for a guest. An *absent* guest. I'd deduced this to be deliberate. A nod to the bride's mother. So, who was this woman? And why was she now sitting there?

I cast my mind back. I vaguely remembered her arriving. She'd blended seamlessly in with the small gathering. Had she been with anyone? Did she have a partner? If so, where was he?

The best man was now reading a poem. I'd already

taken a picture of him on the podium, so took the opportunity of scanning the guests.

My eyes travelled along each row. *Hat Lady* was with *Bow Tie Man. Bespectacled Man* was with *Bespectacled Woman. Stuffed Shirt* was with *Lady Aloof. Mr Uptight* was with *Mrs Uptight. Mrs Too Short* was with *Mr Too Tall. Mr Glam* was with *Mr Good-Looking. Miss Apologetic* was with *Mr Grumpy.* My eyes kept travelling across the rows. He was with her. She was with him. De-da-de-da-de-da. Right, so except for the bride's father, everyone was coupled up. Everyone, that was, apart from the blonde lady who was now firmly stationed next to Dylan.

As my eyes once again rested upon the blonde, I was unnerved to find her staring at me. She held my gaze. Without breaking eye contact, she linked her arm through Dylan's.

It was a proprietorial gesture. I suspected it to be deliberate on her part. Her eyes remained firmly on mine. She'd wanted to make sure I'd noticed her claiming him. I reddened, and she smirked. Her expression said it all.

This man is mine. You can look, but you don't touch. So, hands off.

With a sinking heart, I realised she must have spotted me winking at Dylan. Oh, how embarrassing. She wouldn't have known that he'd been the first to wink.

And then I found myself doubting. Had Dylan *meant* to wink at me? Perhaps he'd had something in his eye. A stray lash. Or a bit of fluff from his suit. Or maybe he'd been having an emotional moment, and it had been his way of halting a tear. Perhaps he'd been trying to squeeze it back into its duct. *Squeeze… squeeze… wink.*

Oh, flipping cosmic. In which case I'd stood before everyone and delivered the bride's father a come-hither look.

I wondered if anyone else had noticed. If so, what might they have thought?

Stuffed Shirt: Good heavens, did you see that?

Lady Aloof: Ay say, what-what?

Stuffed Shirt: That photographer winked at Terry's father.

Lady Aloof: Crikey!

Stuffed Shirt: Let's hope Jemima didn't see.

Lady Aloof: Jemima is a possessive woman.

Stuffed Shirt: Uh-oh. Jemima is glaring at the photographer.

Lady Aloof: By Jove, golly gosh.

Stuffed Shirt: I predict handbags at dawn.

Lady Aloof: How thrilling!

I looked away. Fiddled with my camera. Made a show of being enraptured by the best man who was droning to a finish.

Finally, the bride and groom were pronounced man and wife.

I discreetly moved past the witnesses while Terry and Tobias signed their Marriage Certificate. I then snapped away as Tobias shook the officiant's hand. Eventually, as guests surged forward to take their own pictures, I made sure that I'd blended into the wall.

The new husband and wife exited the ceremony room. The guests followed, showering the newlyweds with confetti. I quickly finished off with some official group photographs.

I wasn't booked to stay to the end of the wedding, or to cover the speeches. That was usually the job of a videographer. However, this wedding was so lowkey no cameraman had been booked.

That said, I knew some of the guests had been discreetly filming with their mobiles. No doubt someone would capture Tobias as he stammered his way through a speech, thanking everyone for coming, and declaring he was so lucky to have Mrs Theresa Green as his wife.

I wondered what Dylan's speech would be like. Polished for sure. He would mention Terry's mother. How she'd watched the ceremony from Heaven. How angels would have tooted their trumpets by way of celebration. Then he would ask everyone to raise a glass to both the newlyweds and absent loved ones.

Or maybe he wouldn't say that at all – because of Jemima. Perhaps it would make her feel awkward. Yes, of course. Dylan would be alive to Jemima's feelings. Maybe he'd omit mentioning his dead wife all together. Perhaps he'd instead mention Jemima.

'Jemima and I are both proud and delighted to see Terry now married to the man of her dreams. Can we all please toast Jemima who has been a second mother to Terry and a tower of strength to me.'

And everyone would raise their glasses and chorus, "To

Jemima."

My lip involuntarily curled. I pushed such thoughts away and swiftly collapsed my tripod, then zipped my camera into its protective case.

The best man, who I now knew to be called Simon, interrupted me. He handed me an envelope.

'The balance,' he said. 'Cash. Is that okay?'

'Absolutely,' I nodded, slipping the packet inside my camera bag. 'Thank you.'

'Don't you want to count it?' Simon frowned.

I smiled and shook my head.

'That won't be necessary. Um, Simon? Listen, I can see that Terry and Tobias are busy with their guests, so I'm going to slip away. Can you give them my best wishes. Tell them to have a fabulous honeymoon, and to give me a tinkle when they're back. Terry has my number.'

'Of course,' Simon nodded.

'Thanks.'

I briefly scanned the crowd for Dylan. There he was. Oh, he had his back to me. Jemima was still clinging to him like a limpet.

I turned on my heel and quickly walked away.

Chapter Twenty-Seven

On the drive home, I rang Ella. She answered on the first ring.

'Hey, Mum.'

'Hi, darling,' I warbled.

'What's up?' she asked. My youngest had an inbuilt antenna when it came to other people's emotions. 'You sound upset.'

'Nonsense,' I said, deliberately lightening my tone. 'I simply wondered how Bess was. I've been worried about her.'

'No need,' Ella assured. 'We've been out in the garden. Played with all her toys, and now we're watching the *101 Dalmatians*. That said, I keep covering Bess's eyes when Cruella Deville appears. I don't want Bess having nightmares later.'

'Quite,' I said.

'Are you sure you're okay?' Ella persisted.

'Yes!' I mock-huffed. 'Why would I not be?'

Because you made a fool of yourself winking at Dylan and was later put in your place by his glamorous girlfriend, said my inner voice.

'I know my mother,' said Ella simply. 'I suspect you're

not telling me something.'

'There's nothing to tell,' I assured.

'Okay, be like that,' she sniffed. 'I'll get to the bottom of it eventually.'

I loved my youngest daughter to bits, but sometimes she was too astute.

'Put the kettle on,' I said, intent on distraction. 'I'm only ten minutes away. We'll have a nice cuppa together.'

'Stuff the cuppa,' Ella snorted. 'Let's take Bess to the pub and have a glass of wine.'

'I don't think wine is good for dogs,' I quipped.

'Ha, funny.' I could visualise Ella rolling her eyes. 'Now that we're in the merry month of May, it doesn't get dark until eight o'clock. We'll be fine walking along Little Waterlow's country lanes that are so wonderfully devoid of street lighting.' Her voice dripped sarcasm. 'Anyway, there's no point in me going home yet. Archie won't be back for ages. He'll probably have eaten too. I'm starving. Are you?'

Ella was currently dropping more hints than a litter lout on a rubbish-throwing spree. She wanted to go out. That was obvious. Usually, I'd be thrilled to have one of my children all to myself for a few hours. But perversely, all I really wanted to do, was get out of my work clothes and kick back in front of the telly. I didn't want a million questions on why I wasn't being jolly-jolly or wanting to rah-rah down.

'The glass of wine sounds good,' I admitted.

Yes, maybe I'd have a glass of Prosecco. Or, to hell with it, go mad and drink an entire bottle. Stagger about,

141

with my trusty German Shepherd by my side. Spot Mabel Plaistow, the local gossip. Hear her tutting as I stumbled past her. Her hubby looking on curiously, as he supped his Guiness.

Mabel: Oooh, look at that Maggie woman. She's a bit worse for wear. I 'eard she rescued that dog, but it looks to me like it needs rescuing again.'

Fred: At 'er age she should know better than to get sloshed.

Mabel: Yer right, Fred. Let's tell the RSBA.

Fred: Doncha mean the RSPCA?

Mabel: Nah. I mean the Right Sodding Blotto Association.

'Let's go to The Angel,' Ella chirped. 'It's within walking distance. Also, they don't mind dogs in the bar area. We can have chicken in a basket with a side of chips and salad. Oooh, and they always have a fab selection of ice-creams.'

'All right,' I agreed. 'You've talked me into it.'

'Lovely,' said Ella happily. 'And then you can tell me what's *really* bugging you.'

'Nothing is bugging me, child,' I said in exasperation.

'Less of the *child*, Mother,' Ella said dryly. 'I sense a bit of role reversal coming on.'

'Oh, please,' I shuddered. 'Don't say that.'

It was bad enough that I felt that way with my own parents. The last thing I wanted was Ella feeling that way about me.

'Chill, Mother,' she tutted. 'I'm winding you up. That

said, while you were out, Grandad telephoned.'

My heart immediately quickened.

'Was he okay?'

Ella considered.

'No. He was grumpy. He wanted to know why you hadn't turned up earlier. He was expecting you to take him and Granny out. Something about coffee and cake. Apparently, Aunty Freya told him you'd be along.'

'Oh for…'

I exited the motorway, gnashing my teeth. A passenger might have described my expression as one of chewing on a lemon.

'I told Freya to take the parents with her to North London.'

'North London?' said Ella sounding perplexed. 'Why would she go there? No, don't tell me.' I sensed Ella holding up one hand, like a traffic cop. 'A peace rally. Or an environmental protest. Yes, that will be it. Right now, she's probably waving a banner that says *Climate Change is a Hoax*.'

'No, it's nothing like that. It's–'

'Don't tell me, don't tell me,' Ella gabbled. 'Got it! She's in the local shopping mall asking shoppers if they'd like a pamphlet on saving the planet. You know what I'd say?' Ella tittered naughtily. 'Bro, sure.'

'What?' I frowned.

'Bro*chure*. Geddit?' Ella dissolved into giggles. 'Oh, Mum, you're not laughing. Lighten up!'

But I was disgruntled. Fuming with my sister. I'd *told*

her I was working. I'd *told* her I wouldn't be allocating a substitute photographer. And yet she'd ignored me. Disregarded everything I'd said. Dismissed my work as unimportant – again. Not to mention setting our parents up for disappointment.

For a moment my heart squeezed as I imagined the scenario. Two Golden Oldies. Buttoned into their coats. Shoes on. Waiting expectantly. Waiting and waiting.

Oooh, Freya. We'd be having a few words when you'd finished sucking up to Vernon's rich ancient aunt.

'I'm nearly home,' I said to Ella. 'Do you think I should divert and pick up the grandparents? We could all go to The Angel.'

'Ah, I detect a guilty conscience.'

'Yes,' I said honestly.

'I don't know why,' Ella tutted. 'It's Aunty Freya who should feel guilty, not you. Personally, I think you should put yourself first today. You've been working. You also have a new dog settling in. Apart from anything else, we have a rare opportunity of some uninterrupted mother-and-daughter time.'

'True,' I nodded, as I signalled left and turned into my road.

'Plus, I suspect you really need that glass of wine,' Ella pointed out. 'And if you fetch Granny and Grandad, you won't be able to drink and drive.'

'You're right,' I nodded. 'I'll see them tomorrow.'

'Good call, Mother,' said Ella happily.

'I'm here,' I said, pulling up outside the house.

'See you in a sec,' said Ella happily, before ending the call.

Chapter Twenty-Eight

Ella and I set off to The Angel with Bess padding alongside us.

The country lanes were beautiful at this time of year. Spring had well and truly sprung. The leafy hedgerows that bordered the single-track road bordered of grazing sheep and cows. Wildflowers were in abundance. Trees were smothered in blossom. Birds were in song as they swooped and dived against a late afternoon blue sky.

'How did the wedding go?' asked Ella.

'Fine,' I said flatly.

'Really?'

'Ah, it's nothing,' I sighed.

'Oh, come on, Mum.' Ella pulled a face. 'Spill the beans.'

I chewed my lip. To tell my daughter, or not? That was the question. And really, was there anything to tell? It seemed faintly ridiculous to confide about a crush on a man I'd known for all of five minutes. And anyway, if I *did* tell Ella, she'd then tell Ruby. And then Ruby would tell Tim. And then Tim would be agog and call me up wanting to know if I'd lost the plot.

'Aw, look at the tiny lambs,' I cooed. I stopped and

peered through a gap in the hedge.

'Never mind the flipping sheep,' Ella tutted, as we approached The Angel. 'This conversation is to be continued.' She waggled a finger. 'Meanwhile, you take Bess and find a table. I'll put in our orders.'

'Sure,' I agreed, as we walked into the main bar area.

'Don't forget that it's your tab,' said Ella, flashing an impudent grin.

'I said I'd pay,' I retorted mildly. 'Unlike my sister, I keep my promises.'

At the mention of her aunt, Ella rolled her eyes. She then turned and headed over to Cathy, the landlady, who was serving behind the bar.

I found a table in a corner and sat down.

'Nice dog,' said a gruff voice.

I glanced to my right and experienced a moment of déjà vu. Fred Plaistow and his wife, Mabel, were sitting at the next table. The pair of them were nursing a Guiness apiece.

'Thank you,' I said politely.

Mabel was scrutinising me.

'I know you,' she said. She picked up her pint glass with gnarled fingers. Sipped thoughtfully. Regarded me over the rim. She set the glass down again. 'Yer name is Maggie King.'

'That's right,' I nodded.

She wiped some froth from her upper lip.

'An' yer a widow.'

'That's right,' I said again.

'So yer single.'

Nothing like stating the obvious.

Mabel shifted in her seat. She reminded me of a *Mastermind* contestant. Special subject Maggie King.

I was relieved to see Ella heading towards me, a glass of Prosecco in each hand. Mabel then scrutinised my daughter.

'And this is yer youngest,' she said triumphantly.

'Hello,' said Ella warily.

She placed the drinks upon the table. Pulling out a chair, she sat down. My daughter flashed me a look accompanied by a pair of raised eyebrows. I wasn't sure what she was trying to convey. Was it:

Shall we sit elsewhere?

Or

Uh-oh. If we engage in chit-chat with Mabel Plaistow, it will become village gossip more nonsensical than Chinese Whispers.

I returned Ella's look with one of my own.

I don't know what to do, so you decide.

But Mabel was holding forth again. This time she was addressing Ella.

'I was just sayin' that now yer dad's passed yer mum is single.'

'Thanks for pointing out the obvious' – my daughter wasn't afraid of offending – 'but my mother's change of marital status is both personal and painful. So, if you don't mind–'

'Painful?' Mabel scoffed. 'Don't be daft, lass. Yer mum is well over yer dad.'

'I beg your pardon?' Ella blinked. 'With the greatest

respect, Mrs Plaistow, you don't know my mother, and therefore have no idea about–'

'You can drop the hoity-toity speech, love,' Mabel sniffed. 'I 'ave it on good authority that yer mum might be single, but she don't wanna be.'

Now it was my turn to blink.

'What did you say?' I gasped.

'You 'eard.' Mabel tapped the side of her nose. 'I know yer secret. You've met a man. And 'e don't belong to yer.'

My face instantly reddened. It didn't go unnoticed by my daughter.

'Wh*aaat*?' Ella spluttered.

'They met at the animal shelter,' Mabel informed Ella. 'Yer mum 'as bin enjoyin' walks with 'im.'

Ella gave me a questioning look.

'An' this afternoon' – Mabel continued – 'yer mum met 'im again.'

'This afternoon, my mother was at work,' said Ella haughtily. 'She's a photographer.'

'I know. An' she woz caught givin' the bride's father the come on.'

Ella was starting to look a little wild about the eyes.

'Now you listen to me–'

'Ella,' I warned. 'Take no–'

Mabel cackled with delight.

'Take no notice, eh? But everyone *was* takin' notice! One of me mates was there. She saw it all.'

'One of yer… your mates?' I gasped. Good Lord. Was Mabel acquainted with Mr Stuffed Shirt and Lady Aloof?

'Agnes,' said Mabel helpfully. 'That's the name of me mate. She cleans at the 'otel, includin' the weddin' ceremony room. She likes slippin' in unnoticed an' quietly watchin' on the sidelines. An' that was when she saw yer.' Mabel jerked her head at me. 'Bold as brass. In front of everyone. Makin' a play for the bride's dad.'

'Mum!' Ella gasped. 'Is this true?'

Chapter Twenty-Nine

'Of *course* it's not true,' I protested. My cheeks were so hot, eggs might have fried upon them. 'I'm a professional photographer. Not a… a…'

'Hussy?' interrupted Mabel. 'The man in question has a lady acquaintance. Some friendly advice, dearie. Love triangles are bad news. Remember Sophie Fairfax?'

I did. She'd lived at Catkin Cottage before upping and moving to Italy. Before her departure, there had been a public rumpus. However, unlike this pair of octogenarians, I wasn't invested in village gossip. Therefore, the details about Sophie evaded me.

'And let's not forget Annie Rosewood either,' Mabel continued. 'A right old hoo-ha with that 'usband of 'ers. Never liked Keith. It was his eyes. Too close together.'

'If you'll excuse us,' I said, standing up. Ella did likewise and picked up our Proseccos. I took hold of Bess's lead.

'Off already?' asked Mabel.

'Yes,' said Ella bluntly. 'As far away from you as possible.'

Cathy the landlady, suddenly appeared with our meals.

'Ladies?' She frowned, alive to the tense atmosphere. 'Where are you both going?'

'To another table,' said Ella, casting a dark look at Mabel.

Cathy gave me a knowing look, then turned to my tormentor.

'Now then, Mabel. I hope you've not been upsetting my customers.'

'I'll tell yer later, love,' said Mabel cosily.

I inwardly groaned. Cathy wasn't exempt from gossiping. Later, she'd likely pump Mabel for the juicy details. Meanwhile, we were guided to the far side of the bar and the last empty table.

'Here we are, lovelies,' said Cathy, setting the plates down. 'Enjoy, and don't let the likes of Mabel upset you.'

'We won't,' Ella scowled.

'Nice dog,' said Cathy. She paused to give Bess a pat on the head. 'Did you get her from the rehoming centre?'

'I did,' I said, cranking up a smile.

'A little bird told me that's not all you picked up.' Cathy gave me a conspiratorial wink. 'In case you're wondering, it was Rachel. The sanctuary's owner,' she added. 'She and her husband come in here now and again. She was chatting. Said that two dogs had been rescued on the same day, and that the man and woman in question had seemingly rescued each other too. She said that sparks had been flying. She also mentioned you both by name. Maggie and Dylan. So, I knew it was you the moment you walked in with your German Shepherd. Anyways, can't linger to chat. I have customers to serve.'

Cathy bustled off leaving me staring after her open-mouthed.

'Well, really,' I spluttered.

'Yes, *well really* indeed,' said Ella dryly. 'It seems to me, Mum, that everyone knows what's going on in your life apart from your family. Perhaps it's about time you gave me an update. Who is Dylan? And why are you making passes at a man who isn't available?'

Chapter Thirty

Updating Ella had been somewhat embarrassing.

As I'd refused to elaborate in the pub, we'd eaten our food in a rather tense silence.

On the walk home, I'd told my youngest how I'd met a man at the rehoming centre. His name was Dylan, and he was a widower. Yes, I'd thought him attractive – but only in the sense of observation.

'I mean, sometimes you can look at a person and think *whoa, mega monobrow.* Or *oops, bad hair day.*' I was aware that I was choosing my words carefully. 'Equally you might admire someone and think *yeah, she's pretty* or *he's attractive.*'

'So you're basically saying that you met Dylan and thought *whoa, hot guy alert.*'

'Don't be silly,' I ridiculed, hoping she didn't spot the flush creeping up my neck. 'I simply thought he was a nice man. That's all.'

I wasn't comfortable with this conversation. Not with Ella. If I'd been with one of my girlfriends or my bestie, Lyn, then it would've been different. I'd have cackled along with them. Glugged my wine. Tipsily regaled how those zingers had hit one or two erogenous zones. But no way could a mother share such info with her daughter. It simply wasn't right. Apart from anything else, Ella would be repulsed that her ancient mother even had a fully functioning set of erogenous zones. As far as she was concerned, anyone over forty was a wrinkly.

'So you didn't hang out together?' Ella pushed.

'We went for some walks together. With the dogs, I hasten to add. It was a stipulation of the rehoming centre – to take potential adoptees for two walks. Dylan happened to be there at the same time as me.'

'Hmm.' Ella narrowed her eyes. 'Rather coincidental.'

I shrugged.

'It could have been anyone. Even a woman.' I spread my palms wide. 'Anyway, we went for those walks and, yes, we had a coffee too. As I said, it could've easily been a woman. She might have become a new mate.'

'Is that what happened next? Dylan became a mate?'

I made a see-saw motion with one hand.

'We made idle chit-chat. He mentioned he was a widower. Also, that he had a daughter who was getting married.'

Ella looked at me suspiciously.

'He never asked for your number?'

'No,' I said truthfully. 'That said…' I trailed off awkwardly.

'Yes?' she prompted.

'He gave me his business card. He said if I ever fancied a walk with our respective dogs, then to give him a call.'

Ella's head jerked up.

'And did you?' she asked shrilly.

'No!' I shook my head vehemently. 'Nor did I ever intend to.'

'Why?' she demanded.

'Because I'm old-fashioned!' I exclaimed. 'You young things' – God, now I sounded like my parents – 'you don't think anything of ringing up a member of the opposite sex. However, my generation rarely did that. We waited for the boy to ring.'

'But regarding this man, it would have been a phone call about going for a walk. Not a candlelit dinner for two,' Ella pointed out. 'Or are you hinting at wishing it to become something else?'

I opened my mouth to speak but struggled to find the right words.

'I guess it's complicated… for someone of my age,' I added. 'I wouldn't have minded calling Dylan up at some point. Asking if he and Charlie would like to take some air' – jeez, now I sounded like a maiden aunt – 'but, equally, I didn't want to send out the wrong signals… like I was keen on him. O-Or something,' I finished lamely.

For I *had* been keen on him. There was no denying it. Until Jemima had appeared from nowhere – with her blonde hair and dagger eyes.

'Dylan didn't mention that his daughter's wedding was so imminent,' I continued. 'It never crossed my mind that she might be a client. No one was more surprised than me when he turned up with the bride.'

'So what's all this about you making a public play for

him?'

I rolled my eyes and tutted.

'Do you really believe that?'

'You tell me,' said Ella primly. 'I won't deny that Mabel's gossip had me imagining all sorts. My mother flinging her camera to one side… propositioning the bride's father… the livid girlfriend shoving the wedding cake in your face...'

'What a rampant imagination.'

'So, what *really* happened?'

'What *really* happened' – I parodied Ella's tone – 'was that Dylan walked his daughter down the aisle, took his seat, and smiled at me.' No way was I going to mention that wink. 'And… and…'

'Yes?' Ella prompted.

'And I smiled back.'

I hoped my nose wasn't impersonating a certain wooden puppet's breathing apparatus.

'And that's it?' said Ella. She didn't sound convinced.

'That's it,' I assured.

For a moment or two we walked on in silence. The light was now fading.

'Something doesn't stack up,' said Ella. 'Why was Mabel prattling on about love triangles? Did this guy's girlfriend give you a hard time over this exchange of *smiles*?'

My daughter was rapidly morphing into an interrogating police officer. Any minute now, she'd be asking me to provide an alibi. I sighed.

'To be honest, I have no idea who this woman was.

Dylan told me he was a widower. So, this lady can't be his wife. He never mentioned a partner or a girlfriend. No one was more surprised than me when this woman glared at me.'

Ella pounced.

'What, like *feck off, Bitch Face*?'

'Er, yes, I suppose,' I said reluctantly. 'She then linked her arm through Dylan's. That immediately told me they were an item.'

'I see.' Ella pursed her lips.

'So that's that,' I shrugged. 'Even if I wanted to go for an innocent dog walk, it won't be happening. No way will I ever phone Dylan. Satisfied?'

'I guess,' Ella conceded. 'But you know, Mum…' she trailed off for a moment.

'What?'

'It seems strange to imagine you dating again but… well, if you want to… what I'm trying to say is… if someone came along… someone suitable–'

'Someone suitable?' I repeated with a hoot of laughter. 'You make it sound like you'll be conducting an interview.'

Ella gave me a serious look.

'Me and my sibs can't have you dating any old Tom, Dick, or Harry. He'll need our approval.'

'Oh,' I said, eyes wide. 'You mean, like I gave you, Ruby and Tim?' I questioned.

'Okay.' Ella had the grace to look abashed. 'I know you and Dad never gave any of us a hard time when we rocked up with someone… who could've been better.'

'That's putting it mildly,' I muttered.

'I know what you're thinking. That Troy was a bit of a prat.'

'A *bit* of a prat?' I regarded my daughter incredulously. 'The guy was completely workshy. He endlessly sponged off you. He was one of those people who thought the world owed him not just a living, but a big fat inheritance too.'

'All right, all right.' Ella made a placatory gesture with one hand. 'All I'm trying to say is, so long as you don't date a Troy–'

'Or a Jayden, or a McKenzie, or a Shane, or a Daz, or a–

'Point taken,' said Ella peevishly. 'As long as the guy isn't a dickhead, then I don't mind you having a male friend.'

'Right,' I nodded. 'A male friend. Good to know.'

I wondered if Ella would approve of a male friend that zinged all my erogenous zones.

Chapter Thirty-One

By the time I'd got home, settled Bess, and had a hot soak in the bath, I'd mentally consigned Dylan Alexander to a wheelie bin. As an afterthought, I'd revisited the bin, and tossed in a piece of paper. Upon it had been the words *Lucky Escape.*

In fact, as I now dried myself off, I started to feel mildly outraged. How dare Dylan give me his business card with contact number when there was another woman in his life. Or was I getting way ahead of myself? Where men were concerned, I was so badly out of touch I couldn't read any subtext.

Even so, I suspected Jemima wouldn't let her man walk his dog with another woman.

I revisited the moment when I'd spotted Jemima standing next to Dylan. Observed her stylish outfit. The slim figure. The immaculate hair and makeup. She was a glam ma'am. Common sense told me that Jemima *must* be special. Why else would she have been standing by Dylan's side?

Men. I'd been so lucky with Greg. He'd never been two-faced. Years ago, a neighbour had had a soft spot for my husband. She'd made it known to him, too. And me, for that matter. She'd reminded me of Dorian, from *Birds of a Feather*. All tight leather trousers and leopard-print tops. Greg had admired her figure but never flirted back.

'As Paul Newman once so famously said' – Greg had declared – 'why have a burger when you can have steak at home.'

But not all men were like my departed husband. Some guys were nightmares. Drinkers. Gamblers. Adulterers. Going on dating apps behind their partner's back.

When I'd been growing up as a child, I'd overheard my mother chatting with my father about the couple two doors down. She'd told Dad that Margo Darcy had popped over and cried on her shoulder. Margo had confided that husband Philip had a mistress. That it had been going on for twenty years.

'What's a mistress?' my eight-year-old self had piped up.

'Never you mind,' my mother had said, aghast that I'd overheard.

'Why can't I know,' I'd persisted.

In order to appease me, my father had given a diplomatic answer.

'It's a person who works with someone that is rubbish at their job.'

This false explanation had backfired when I'd gone to a friend's house for tea. I'd overheard my friend's father moaning about his secretary. I'd then informed my friend's mother that her husband's secretary was a mistress. And no. I hadn't been invited to tea again.

'Are you there, Greg?' I said aloud.

Silence.

'So much for your little homily about *moving on.* It seems that Dylan Alexander has already done that. Is there anyone out there for me? Not that it really matters,' I sighed. I folded up the bath towel and hung it over the hot rail. 'But I do miss company. And yes, I miss romantic company too.'

Ha! So, you're after someone to light up your erogenous zones, Greg chuckled inside my head.

'Ah, there you are.' I squirted deodorant under my arms. 'Well, my darling, I seem to recall that you liked that too.'

I smiled as a misty memory came to mind. A Saturday night. *Date Night* we used to call it. Greg dressed up in smart jeans and a shirt. Me dolled up. Taking care not to cross the line of mutton impersonating lamb. Going out in a cloud of perfume. Driving to a restaurant.

Sometimes we'd go miles out of our way just to have a different experience. Like going to the coast. Brighton. A wild walk along the pier. Then we'd sip wine in a candlelit bistro. Get mildly tight. Then I'd rest my palm on Greg's thigh as we drove home. He'd put his hand over mine. Tell me I looked beautiful. Once home, Greg would shut the door on the world. Pull me into his arms. Impersonate a Mafia Don speaking to his moll.

'Get naked, babe.'

I'd giggle along with the role play. Afterwards he'd always tell me that he never got tired of making love to me.

I slipped into my pyjamas. I knew it wasn't good to

have these imaginary conversations with my departed husband. But I couldn't help it. A psychiatrist would have a field day.

Therapist: So, you like talking to dead people?

Me: Yeah. It happens every time I go to McDonald's and order 'medium' fries, ha!

Therapist: Death isn't a laughing matter, Mrs King.

Me: Would you prefer me to be grave?

Therapist: I suspect you're full of suppressed anger. You should write letters to all the people you dislike, then burn them.

Me: Okay – but should I keep the letters?

I brushed my hair, then spoke to Greg again.

'I had an altercation with someone today. It was that blasted old biddy, Mabel Plaistow. It all was rather embarrassing. And afterwards I had twenty questions from Ella about Dylan Alexander.'

Ella is young. She's also protective of her mum.

'I guess so. Mabel Plaistow aside, it was nice going out earlier.'

You should go out more often.

I will, now I have Bess.

I meant romantically. I want you to be happy, Mags.

'Thank you, darling. And Greg' – I added – 'I want you to know I still love you.' Suddenly I was choking up. 'I love you *so* much. Can you hear me, Greg. Can you *really* hear me? Can you send me a sign or something? Because, between you and me, I *am* a bit concerned about my mental health. Do you remember that conversation we once had?

163

We made a pact. That whoever died first, the other person would send a sign. A red balloon. I've yet to see that red balloon, darling. Did you forget? In which case, I'm reminding you now. Meanwhile, if you could text me – somehow – I'd be over the moon.'

I jumped as my phone, propped against the washbasin, suddenly dinged. For a moment, my heart raced as my brain whirred with possibilities. Greg? Yes, of *course* it was Greg! But… but… my husband couldn't really text me from Heaven. In which case, was this a further indication that I was going loopy?

I picked up the mobile. A text message from an unknown number. Puzzled, I clicked on it. Then gasped aloud.

Chapter Thirty-Two

I read the message with growing astonishment.

Hi Maggie

I hope you don't mind me messaging you. Terry gave me your number. It was both unexpected and lovely to see you earlier. I was looking forward to talking to you properly, after the ceremony. However, upon seeking you out, you'd vanished. It's due to rain tomorrow, so I won't suggest meeting up for a dog walk. Rather, can I take you out for Sunday lunch?

Dylan x

Oh my goodness. Oh-my-oh-my-oh-my goodness. But what about Jemima? How did she figure in all this? Or would she be coming along too? In which case, no thanks. I wasn't up for an altercation over the roast beef.

'Greg?' I said aloud. 'Did you arrange for Dylan to message me?'

Silence.

Oh, don't be so silly, Maggie. It's just a coincidence. Nothing more, nothing less.

Meanwhile, what to say to Dylan?

Me: Yes, please!

Dylan: Yayyy (or however a 53-year-old man might

respond)

Me: However, a small matter to clear up first.

Dylan: Oh?

Me: Who is Jemima?

Dylan: An old bat who gate-crashed my daughter's wedding.

Me: Excellent news xxxxxxxxxxx

But if I accepted this invitation, where would we go? No way was I stepping into The Angel to have the likes of Mabel Plaistow giving her tuppence worth. No, it would have to be somewhere far away from Little Waterlow.

However, I really did need to know who Jemima was. No way was I up for accepting this invite if Dylan was romantically involved with someone else.

I tapped the screen.

Hi there, Dylan

Yes, I slipped away while you were talking to your psychotic looking girlfriend–

I immediately hit the backspace key. Tried again.

Yes, I slipped away while you were talking to the lady who was clinging to you like poison ivy strangling a rose... backspace, backspace...

Yes, I slipped away due to you being otherwise engaged with a woman who I suspect is a possessive, proprietorial, condescending, self-satisfied, smirking... backspace, backspace, backspace, backspace, backspace...

God, how hard could this be?

Hi there, Dylan

I'd love to go for lunch but who is Jemima Khan–

SHIT!

Instead of some agitated stabbing on the backspace key, I'd inadvertently hit the send button. I stared at the screen in horror. But… wait… Autocorrect had changed my message.

Hi there, Dylan

I'd love to go for lunch but who is Jemima Puddleduck

Oh brilliant. The guy would think me barking. Quick, think, Maggie.

Hurriedly, I typed a second message.

Sorry. Predictive text. Ha! Meant to say:

My finger froze and hovered over the phone's keyboard. Hang on. There was something I'd forgotten all about. I'd invited the kids and their partners over tomorrow for Sunday dinner. They were going to meet Bess. With a sinking heart, I finished the message.

I'd love to go for lunch but have the family coming over for Sunday dinner. They're meeting Bess x

Dylan responded immediately.

What about early brunch and a cheeky Prosecco? x

I didn't hesitate.

Sounds good to me! x

His next text was immediate.

Wonderful – it's a date! x

I momentarily hugged the phone with delight. Stuff Jemima bloody Khan-cum-Puddleduck. I'd ask Dylan who this wretched woman was when I saw him, face to face.

Chapter Thirty-Three

I went to bed alternating between excitement and terror.

When I opened the bedroom's blinds on Sunday morning, those two emotions were still see-sawing through my body; excitement at seeing Dylan without any dogs in the equation, and terror because… well, without our dogs, did this mean it was a date?

Dylan's last text had said it was, but had he meant a *date* date, or had those words been a casual throwaway comment? After all, I frequently used such a phrase with my kids and my parents.

Why are you trying to put a label on it? said Greg, inside my head.

'Morning, darling.' I smiled at one of the photographs on my dressing table. 'I guess I'm over-thinking the matter.' I turned and made the bed while continuing the conversation. 'It's probably nerves.'

I arranged the pillows and then overlayed the duvet with several decorative scatter cushions.

'Anyway, it likely isn't a date. Not in the romantic sense. After all, there was another woman on the scene at the wedding. Jemima. You know who I mean. But Jemima aside, I can't help feeling thrilled about seeing Dylan.

I feel… fizzy. Bubbling with excitement. Ha! How weird that I should, in this moment, understand the literal meaning of that expression.' I finished making the bed, then blew Greg's portrait a kiss. 'I'm going downstairs. See you in the kitchen. I must give Bess her breakfast and let her out.'

Downstairs, I greeted my dog – along with another snap of Greg smiling from the kitchen windowsill.

Bess didn't seem to mind my chatter as I continued to prattle away to my absent husband. Instead, she gently wagged her tail, which sped up when I spooned a rather whiffy tin of tripe into a bowl.

As I opened the back door for Bess to go out and do her doggy business, I noted the sky had changed from yesterday's beautiful blue to an intimidating gunmetal grey. Rain was due.

In that moment, I made up my mind to give Bess a quick walk along the lane. We'd head towards the dairy farm, then about turn and get back before the heavens opened. I had some old towels to dry her off. Although wiping down a huge dog was something I'd prefer to avoid if possible.

Forty minutes later, having neatly avoided a downpour, I set about getting ready to meet Dylan. He'd texted again while I'd been out with Bess, this time to ask that I meet him at The Swan in nearby West Malling. Good choice. Expensive, but no matter. I was at a stage of my life where I was comfortably off. Going Dutch wouldn't be an issue.

Despite the rain, it wasn't cold. However, British weather is notorious for being temperamental. It was prudent to be prepared.

I pulled on a pair of white jeans and teamed it with an electric-blue *body* and co-ordinating dog-tooth box jacket. What I'd have given to instead wear one of my daughters' crop tops. How lucky were the girls to show off taut bejewelled navels. Sadly, my sixty-one-year-old torso bore testament to not just a loss of collagen, but also the gift of three pregnancies. On the upside, I didn't have a muffin spilling over my waistband. One had to be grateful for small mercies.

Every now and again, my eyes flicked to Greg's photograph on the dressing table. This portrait of him was a little disconcerting. Just like the portrait of the Mona Lisa, no matter where I stood in the bedroom, Greg's eyes followed me.

I spritzed some perfume behind my ears, then checked my handbag. Made sure my reading specs were inside. The menu would be a blur without them. Footwear next. What to wear? Boots or sandals? In the end I chose a pair of raffia wedges. Sod the rain.

'Right, darling,' I said to Greg's portrait. 'I'll be off. I wish it were me and you going out together.' For a moment my mouth drooped. 'But it isn't.' I picked up my bag and slung it over one shoulder. 'Keep an eye on Bess for me. I feel a bit guilty going out and leaving her on her own for a couple of hours. But then again, she seems happy enough snoozing in her basket. Meanwhile, the kids are coming over later. We'll be together again. All of us. That includes you.' I smiled at the photo. 'So, see you later.'

I walked across the landing and, as I did so, a netful of butterflies took off in my stomach. Interesting. Since when had I felt so nervous? And then I remembered. It had been on my first date with Greg.

Chapter Thirty-Four

I drove along the busy West Malling High Street, eyes scanning left and right in the hope of securing a parking space. Unfortunately, not a single bay was to be had streetside.

Taking a sudden left turn, I dipped into the carpark at the rear of Tesco. Cheeky, but needs must.

After feeding the pay and display machine, I pinged up my brolly and dove into the hustle and bustle of the main thoroughfare. A minute later, I took a right turn into Swan Street. This was where the restaurant was located.

Once a fifteenth century coaching inn, the pub was now a hugely popular contemporary brasserie. Save for a few beams, the place had been totally refurbished to blend old with new. Fashionably distressed tables – a combination of wood and steel – were strategically placed amongst a backdrop of neutral tones and soft fabrics.

I shook out my umbrella, then went inside. Dylan was already standing at the bar. His eyes lit up upon seeing me.

'Maggie,' he said. It seemed like the most natural thing in the world for him to drop a kiss on my cheek. I was momentarily privy to the scent of his aftershave as his lips touched my skin. *Zinggg*! 'Mm,' he said, sniffing appreciatively. 'You smell lovely.'

'I was just thinking the same thing,' I grinned. 'About you. Not me. Obviously.' I gave a shrill laugh.

Settle down, Maggie. Greg's voice.

Oh no. What was my husband doing here? And then I told myself to stop being ridiculous. It was just my mind. The inner voice. Playing tricks again. Some called it one's conscience. Others, the ego. At times I appreciated the inner voice sounding like Greg. Like earlier. It was comforting. But at other times it was a nuisance. And then there were the *other* other times when I simply worried that I was halfway round the bend.

Don't mind me. Greg's voice again, this time faintly amused. *I'm going to eavesdrop on those two young lads over there. One of them is bragging about becoming a famous motorcycle stuntman. I might have a bit of fun – knock the upstart's beer down his front.*

'Good idea,' I said, without thinking.

'What's a good idea?' said Dylan.

'O-Oh, sorry, I thought I heard you say… cider,' I finished lamely. 'Although, on second thoughts, I'd prefer that Prosecco you mentioned last night. I'm not really a fan of cider. It's a bit… gassy.' Oh, terrific, Maggie. First, talking to thin air. Second, casually telling Dylan that cider makes you fart. 'Anyway' – I said, keen to get off the subject of my gurgling intestines – 'how *are* you?'

'I'm good, Maggie.' His mesmerising blue eyes held mine for a moment. 'All the better for seeing you.'

A barman interrupted, asking what he could get us. As Dylan set about ordering our drinks and asking for a table for two, I fiddled nervously with the strap on my handbag. I wondered when it might be a good moment to ask about Jemima.

There was a roar of laughter on the other side of the bar. One of the young lads had somehow managed to tip half his lager down himself while his mate convulsed with laughter.

'You want to be the next Evel Knievel?' the lad hooted. 'You can't even hold your glass, never mind the handlebars of a motorbike.'

My eyes widened, and my mouth formed a perfect O.

Greg? I said silently. *Did you just do that*?

Silence.

'Are you okay, Maggie?' said Dylan. 'You look like you've seen a ghost.'

Bloody hell. I mean, bloody *bloody* hell.

'Fine,' I chirped as the barman set my drink before me. 'And I'll be even better when I have this inside me.'

Terrific. Now I was coming across as not being able to function without alcohol coursing through my veins. Even so, that spilt beer was too coincidental. Or was it? Could it be that I *wasn't* going potty and that, in fact, Greg was haunting me? Or, even worse, that a ghost *pretending* to be Greg was making mischief?

Omigod, did I have a poltergeist trailing me? Maybe I'd hit Google later – when I was home and on my own. Type in *Ghost Busters in the Little Waterlow Area*.

'Cheers,' said Dylan, raising his glass. He lightly clinked it against mine.

'Bottoms up,' I said.

174

Did one say *bottoms up* when having bubbles at eleven o'clock on a Sunday morning? It wasn't a phrase I'd ever used, and I had no idea why I'd uttered it now.

I took a few swift glugs in the hope that it would calm me down. Right now, I felt like a nervy racehorse about to embark on the Grand National. An *older* nervy racehorse, obviously. I was more than aware that it had been a long time since I'd been a filly.

An aproned girl tapped Dylan on the shoulder. She apologised for interrupting our conversation and asked if we'd follow her through to the restaurant.

'After you,' said Dylan, inviting me to go first.

A moment later and I was parking my derriere on a sumptuously upholstered chair. The two of us were handed menus.

'I know what I'm having,' said Dylan. 'Full English. I'm starving.'

'Me too,' I said. Well, I *had* been ravenous up until the moment that lad's beer had gone everywhere.

'Another Prosecco?' asked Dylan.

Steady, Maggie, my inner voice cautioned. I was pleased to note that it sounded just like mine and nothing like Greg's.

'Yes, please,' I said, mentally sticking two fingers up to my conscience.

I'd have a Full English too. Blotting paper would be required. That and a strong coffee afterwards.

The waitress returned, took our orders, and then disappeared again.

'How's Bess settling in?' asked Dylan.

'Fantastically,' I beamed. 'It's so strange, but I feel like I've had her for years. And how's Charlie?'

Dylan laughed.

'He's… adjusting.'

'What does that mean?'

'It means, he gets on the sofa, and I tell him to get off. Then he climbs into an armchair, and I tell him to get off. And then he jumps on the bed, and I tell him to get off. He's also learnt that the refrigerator is where his opened tin of dog food resides during the day. His current strategies have failed to bust open the fridge. However, he did manage to upend the kitchen bin. He scoffed a load of vegetable peelings and a teabag. He is totally food obsessed. That aside, he's very loving. Whenever I step over the threshold it's like dealing with both a welcoming committee and a press conference – with me as the star.'

'Aw, that's nice,' I smiled, as the waitress delivered my second Prosecco. I was now starting to relax. 'And did Charlie behave himself while you were at Terry's wedding yesterday?'

Dylan gave a wry chuckle.

'It wasn't the smartest move rescuing a dog the day before my daughter's wedding. However, sometimes you just have to go with the flow. No, I didn't leave him alone.' Dylan shook his head. 'I wouldn't have dared. I discovered almost immediately that Charlie has a low boredom threshold. My neighbour kindly agreed to look after him. In fact, Charlie is with Denise now. She has a very energetic cockapoo who has become Charlie's BFFL. Together they loll around on her sofas, eat endless treats, and generally do all the things Charlie isn't allowed to do at home,' Dylan laughed. 'What about Bess?'

'Yesterday, my youngest came over and dog-sat.' I took a sip of Prosecco. 'That said, Bess seems very laid back. I've left her on her own while I'm here with you. I suspect she'd have been fine on her own yesterday too, but I didn't want to stress her. Just in case. Thankfully, she's not interested in monopolising the sofa or raiding the biscuit tin.'

'An older dog,' Dylan acknowledged. 'Calmer and very refined.'

'And talking of refined' – I twinkled – 'you looked very debonair yesterday.'

'Why thank you.' Dylan inclined his head graciously. 'I like to think I scrub up well.'

'You did,' I assured, emboldened by alcohol on an empty stomach.

'I got the surprise of my life when I saw you standing there, pointing a camera at Terry and me,' Dylan smiled. 'And then I remembered you saying – when we walked the dogs – that you were a photographer. But, somehow, I hadn't connected you with wedding photography. For some reason I imagined your subject matter to be wildlife or landscapes.'

'Oh, I've done plenty of those,' I said with a light shrug. 'Sold them online too. Blown them up. Framed them. But mostly it's portraiture. Like a new mum wanting to capture three, sometimes four, generations in one shot. That said, my bread and butter is weddings. Terry made a beautiful bride. How did your speech go?'

'I kept it short and sweet,' said Dylan. His tone had changed. A shift. 'Terry requested, prior to the wedding, that I refrain from giving a lengthy speech. She didn't want to hear anything that would tug heartstrings. She said she knew her mum would be watching from Heaven, and that was good enough for her. She didn't need any reminders. So, I honoured that.'

'That's good,' I nodded. 'And surely a relief for the lady by your side.' Dylan looked baffled. 'The blonde,' I pointed out. 'In the ceremony room.' He continued to look confused. Come on, Dylan. Don't try and pretend she wasn't there. 'Clinging to you as if her life depended upon it,' I tinkled, then immediately regretted the comment. It sounded catty.

'Oh, you mean Jill,' said Dylan eventually.

Jill. Not Jemima.

'I didn't catch her name,' I said lightly.

'Yes, you're quite right,' Dylan agreed. 'Jill was grateful that I didn't wax lyrical about my late wife. It would have been hard for her too.'

A part of me instantly deflated. Ah. So, Jill *was* a significant other. And my presence with Dylan today at The Swan was merely a friendly rendezvous. And all because I'd turned up at his daughter's wedding. This wasn't a date. There was no chance of this leading to romance. It was simply a catchup. And afterwards? Well, who knew when I might bump into Dylan again?

Chapter Thirty-Five

'So, um' – I twirled the stem of my glass – 'if you don't mind me asking, Dylan–'

The waitress reappeared, instantly blocking our view of each other as she set down our plates.

'Any sauces? Drinks?' she asked.

'I wouldn't mind an Americano, but there's no rush. I still have my Prosecco,' I added.

'A cappuccino for me,' said Dylan.

'I'll give you both ten minutes,' said the waitress. 'Is that okay?'

'Perfect,' I agreed.

She turned and, as she did so, Dylan came back into view.

'You were saying, Maggie?' he prompted.

'Er, yes. Jill.'

'What about her?' Dylan picked up his knife and fork. 'This looks delicious by the way.'

'Yes, it does.' Stuff the bacon and eggs. I was a little disappointed that Dylan hadn't taken the initiative in explaining who Jill was. I'd have preferred not to ask. But ask I must. I took a deep breath.

'Where is she this morning?' I ventured.

He frowned.

'She said something about outstanding chores yesterday. The weekly shop, I think. Yes' – he nodded – 'she's likely at the supermarket.'

Right.

'And, she didn't mind you coming out with me instead of going with her and, er, lending a hand?'

'No,' he said, then popped some sausage in his mouth.

'That's very generous of her,' I said.

I stabbed a sunshine-yellow yolk with my fork. What was this? Some sort of open relationship?

Jill: I'm off now, darling. Shopping to do.

Dylan: Okay, sweetie-pie. I'll be out with Maggie.

Jill: (chuckling naughtily) Don't forget to tell her about me.

Dylan: I will. Meanwhile, have fun flirting with Steve the shelf stacker.

Jill: Ha! He's usually in the fruit aisle and stares at my melons.

Dylan forked up some baked beans.

'I much prefer to do my shopping online,' he said. 'Don't you?'

I frowned.

'Sometimes. But – forgive me, I'm confused – why didn't you do the shopping online and spare Jill a trip to the supermarket?'

Dylan stopped cutting up a tomato. He looked at me.

'Wait… are you thinking that Jill is…'

He trailed off. Regarded me. I had my head on one

side. In that moment I felt a bit like Bess when she was trying to work something out. I met Dylan's eyes. No, I wasn't going to look away. Nor was I going to finish his sentence. I continued to wait patiently. Now I knew how Bess felt when anticipating a juicy treat. In this case I was waiting for the juicy revelation of who this woman was.

Dylan shook his head imperceptibly.

'Jill is Jennifer's sister,' he said.

I carried on looking at him, none the wiser.

'Jennifer?' I repeated. Who the heck was Jennifer?

'Jennifer is… was… my wife.'

Chapter Thirty-Six

'Oh,' I said, completely flabbergasted. 'So, Jill is your sister-in-law.'

'Yes,' said Dylan, looking slightly bemused. 'Did you think' – he looked awkward for a moment – 'that she was…?'

He trailed off. His unfinished question was left hanging in the air.

'Well' – I shifted in my seat – 'she did seem rather proprietorial. So, er, yes, a part of me wondered… wanted to ask…'

And now it was my turn to feel uncomfortable.

'Jill is…'

Oh, good heavens. What was going on here?

Dylan fiddled with the stem of his glass. Stared at the liquid within, as if the bubbles might somehow hold the answer. I waited for him to reply. Jill was what? A devoted family member who just happened to be united with Dylan in mutual grief? Or Terry's loving aunty who'd elected herself as a mummy substitute? Or simply a menopausal lunatic who devoured men like Dylan for breakfast?

Oooh, catty, Maggie. Stop it.

'Jill is tricky,' said Dylan carefully. 'She's…'

For God's sake, man. Spit it out!

'Yes?' I prompted. At this rate it would be Christmas before I learnt anything further about Jill.

Dylan took a deep breath, as if he were about to make a confession.

'Look, Maggie, I'll come clean,' he said frankly.

Deep joy. Here it was. Revelation of the century. Jill and Dylan were lovers. Or maybe ex-lovers. In which case, if they *had* been lovers, that meant Dylan had cheated on Jennifer, and Jill had betrayed her own sister. And if *that* had happened, maybe Jill wanted to rekindle things now Jennifer was out of the way. But maybe it was awkward – because of Terry. Perhaps Terry hadn't been aware of the relationship between her aunt and father. Or maybe–

Maggie, why don't you stop the runaway thoughts and listen to the guy, eh?

Greg's voice.

I stiffened. No, I was not up for having a silent conversation with my dead husband. Not here. And certainly not right now.

'Are the two of you dating?' I blurted.

Dylan looked startled.

'No!' he said. The word came out like a pistol shot. 'But... but...'

Arghhh. Gahhh! TALK TO ME, I mentally shouted.

'I can't deny' – Dylan stumbled over his words – 'that she'd like for us to be an item.'

I blinked.

'She'd like to be with you?' I whispered, my eyes wide.

183

'That's about the gist of it,' Dylan nodded.

'Isn't that a bit close to home?' I ventured. 'I mean, she's your sister-in-law, wouldn't that be–'

'Incestuous?' He looked up sharply. 'Jill is my sister-*in-law*, Maggie. Not my sister.'

I put up my hands. Made a backing off gesture.

'Yes, of course,' I muttered. 'Anyway, it's nothing to do with me,' I added.

'Just to be crystal clear' – Dylan gave me a level look – 'nothing has ever happened between me and Jill. Nor will it. I'm not interested. However, Jill made it plain, years ago, that if I was up for a fling, then she was too.'

'Omigod,' I gasped. 'What sort of a woman does that to her own sister?'

'One that is devious in order to get what she wants,' said Dylan frankly. 'At the time, I categorically told her it would never happen. That I loved Jennifer. I pointed out to Jill that if she'd fallen out of love with her own husband, then to get divorced and find someone who *did* make her happy.'

'And did she?' I asked, agog.

'No.' Dylan shook his head. 'Jill stayed with Frank. My brother-in-law was a thoroughly nice guy. He had no inkling of his wife's feelings towards me.'

'Did Jennifer know?'

Dylan looked thoughtful for a moment.

'She did once make a comment dressed up as banter. She said she'd never leave Jill alone with me in case her sister made a pass. I told her not to be daft. Said that Jill flirted with anything in trousers.' Dylan cleared his throat. A regrouping gesture. 'All that aside, one day Jill's husband had a freak accident at work. Frank passed away weeks after cancer claimed my wife. Since then, Jill has let it be known that she's… available.'

'Have you ever told your daughter any of this?' I asked. 'I don't mean the bit beforehand when Jennifer and Frank were still alive. I mean the bit afterwards. The *now*, so to speak.'

'Absolutely not.' Dylan's words were emphatic. 'Terry isn't that close to her aunt. Jill might be her mother's sister, but in Terry's eyes the woman is a biological connection rather than an emotional one. Jill and Jennifer are… were… chalk and cheese. My wife was a sweet lady. You'd have liked her, Maggie. There wasn't a bad bone in Jennifer's body. Whereas Jill is something else.'

'I see.' I blew out my cheeks. 'So why was Jill clinging possessively to you at Terry's wedding?'

'I did try to shake her off, but she was having none of it. Apart from anything else, I wouldn't have put it past her to create a scene. That was the last thing I wanted on my daughter's big day.'

'Quite,' I agreed. 'So, how have things been left with Jill?'

'After the wedding, she buttonholed me. Came straight out with it. Said Jennifer would approve of us being a couple. That it might be a little strange for Terry to start off with but that it would be in her best interests. That families should stick together. I told Jill – as kindly as I could – that she was deluded. That there was more chance of electric

185

cars being banned than her and I ever becoming a couple.'

'Blimey.'

'I also said' – Dylan suddenly looked self-conscious – 'that I'd met someone.'

'Oh,' I said, both startled and rattled by this admission.

'Jill took it badly,' he added.

'Oh dear. And is it serious with the woman you recently met, or was that a smokescreen?'

Dylan's head shot up. He gave me a strange look.

'A smokescreen?' he frowned. Suddenly his hands were reaching for mine across the table. *Zing, zing, zinggg.* 'Maggie, you must surely realise that the person I'm talking about… is you.'

Chapter Thirty-Seven

Dylan and I finished brunch, then had a second coffee together – but this time it was accompanied with some handholding across the table. We also did rather a lot of staring into each other's eyes, complete with silly smiles.

We were under no delusions about anything. Both of us were widowed. Both of us were the wrong side of fifty. I'd reminded Dylan that I was eight years older than him.

'And your point is?' he now asked.

'My point is' – I took a deep breath – 'you can take your pick of younger women. Wouldn't you prefer a female who is forty-something rather than–'

'Maggie.' Dylan's voice was grave, but his eyes held a soft light. Tenderness? 'I don't let my brain make romantic decisions. I let my heart do that. And my heart swells every time I see you. With joy. Happiness.' He gave my hand a gentle squeeze. 'Sorry, I don't want to frighten you off by coming on too keen too soon.'

'You're not,' I grinned. Right now, I felt like a teenager in the first flush of crush.

'And anyway' – he added – 'I have another confession for you. Recently I secretly read one of Terry's girly magazines. It said that sixty was the new thirty.'

'Thirty?' I scoffed. 'That seems like a lifetime ago.'

Well, it did, and it didn't. Some things seemed like donkey's years ago. Others, only moments ago. Time was a weird thing. It could mess with your head if you let it.

'When I first met you' – Dylan continued – I thought you were in your late forties. Fifty at an absolute push.'

'You're too kind,' I giggled.

'I'm being honest,' he insisted. 'And I'm also being open about my feelings for you. I like you.'

'I like you too,' I said shyly.

'I like you a lot,' he murmured.

I gave him a smile gooier than a cream cake.

'Ditto,' I whispered.

'What I'm trying to say is…' For a moment he looked bashful. 'I feel like an awkward teenager right now. I want to ask you something.'

'Go on,' I urged.

'Will you be my girlfriend?'

I snorted with laughter.

'Can a sixty-one-year-old legitimately be called a *girl*friend?' I teased.

'Can a fifty-three-year-old male be called a *boy*friend?' he countered.

'I think so,' I said, my eyes dancing with merriment. 'After all, we're not ancient.'

'Of *course* we're not ancient,' he cried, pretending to shudder at the very idea. 'However, you've not answered my question.'

'I've forgotten what it was,' I laughed. 'Uh-oh,

memory blank. You see! That's an age thing.'

He rolled his eyes, feigning exasperation.

'I think you're pretending to have forgotten, and that you're secretly thrilled to see me squirming like a gauche adolescent. But it's fine. I'll ask again.' He tutted theatrically. 'Maggie King. Will you be my girlfriend?'

My smile was now so wide, it was a wonder I didn't have wraparound lips.

'Dylan Alexander,' I bantered back. 'I'd be delighted to be your girlfriend.'

And with that, Dylan leant across the table and planted a kiss on my mouth.

The subsequent zingers scorched my lips, shot through the back of my head, exploded through my brain, and possibly made my eyeballs rotate like a fruit machine.

'You're beautiful, Maggie,' Dylan murmured.

'Give over,' I muttered, blushing like mad.

'It's true,' he insisted. 'You have the most amazing eyes and your hair is the colour of autumn leaves. I'd love to run my hands through it. And one day I will,' he twinkled. 'But for now, how about we see where we go? No pressure.'

'Sounds good to me,' I murmured. He could run his hands through my hair – and anywhere else for that matter – whenever he liked.

'I know we only met a few days ago,' he said. 'But I feel as if I've known you for so much longer.'

Never a truer word. It was that timeline thing again. It could make things go out of whack. I felt like I'd known Dylan for yonks.

It was with great reluctance that we ended brunch. However, I needed to get back to Bess, and Dylan had Charlie waiting. Also, I had a load of veg to prep. Sunday dinner wasn't going to cook itself. The kids – and their partners – were always starving when they came over.

'Can I call you tomorrow?' Dylan asked, as he signalled to the waitress for the bill. 'And put your handbag down, Maggie,' he said firmly. 'This is my treat.'

'Thank you. And yes, of course you can call me tomorrow.'

'I don't want to come on too strong.' He gave an imperceptible shake of his head. 'I'm so badly out of touch with dating a woman. If you prefer, you can call me. Do you still have my business card?''

'I do,' I nodded. 'That reminds me,' I frowned. 'The card says *manager*, but not what you're a manager of.'

And then Dylan said something that completely took me by surprise.

'I manage a care home. For old folks, obviously. Actually, I own it.'

I blinked in astonishment. Of all the potential professions *out there,* running an old peoples' home was the last thing I imagined this man doing. Somehow, Dylan seemed more like… maybe a football coach. Or a personal trainer. Even the manager of a gym. His athletic build was at odds with someone who dealt with the nuts and bolts of people approaching the end of life's journey.

'When my parents needed care' – he explained – 'I couldn't find professionals prepared to do the job long-term.

And the person that I did temporarily find, wasn't honest.'

The waitress brought the card terminal, momentarily interrupting the conversation. After an exchange of pleasantries, Dylan tucked his wallet into his back pocket before continuing.

'My late father was obsessed with money. He'd draw out cash, then hide it in bizarre places. He'd then forget what he'd done with it and accuse me of stealing. It was a defining moment when a large sum of money couldn't be accounted for, and the carer wouldn't look me in the eye. I had Power of Attorney, so sold Dad's home. Then, with Jennifer's agreement, remortgaged the family home. We bought a large Victorian house in West Malling and turned it into a care home. The venture gave me peace of mind. I could now spend quality time with my parents *and* keep an eye on them at the same time. My parents have since departed this world, but Primrose House goes on. I have kind staff, and immense job satisfaction. I'm helping not just old folks, but their families too – people who are usually at their wits' end.'

'I know that feeling,' I muttered.

Dylan regarded me kindly.

'In which case, I know what you're going through,' he said with sympathy. 'They call people like us the *sandwich generation*. People who have raised their kids only to find themselves caring for ageing parents. Except the parents behave like small kids. Their tantrums can be epic.'

'You can say that again,' I nodded. 'And how does young Charlie fit into your work schedule?'

Dylan chuckled.

'As from tomorrow, Charlie will be coming to Primrose House with me. He's going to be the home's *pat dog*. All my Golden Oldies will love it.' Dylan stood up. 'Come on.' He jerked his head. 'The waitress is looking our way. I think our table is required for the lunchtime sitting.'

Outside, the sky remained a leaden grey although the rain had stopped. Dylan walked me back to my car. He also took me in his arms and gently lowered his mouth to mine.

'I'd like to kiss you properly,' he murmured. 'But Tesco's carpark isn't particularly romantic.'

Dylan was wrong. Right now, the cars, the shoppers, the sounds of harassed mothers trailing grizzling children, all seemed to fade into a haze dreamier than a Santorini sunset.

'I'll call you tomorrow, darling,' he promised.

Darling! I mentally squealed with delight. How wonderful to be referred to so endearingly.

As I watched Dylan walk away, it would be fair to say my smile was slushier than one of those neon-coloured ice drinks.

'Ex*cuse* me,' said a pained voice. I turned to see a motorist, a dead ringer for Victor Meldrew, impatiently waiting for my space. He leant out of his window. 'Are you going to keep me waiting all day, or what?'

There was nothing like a grumpy old pensioner to pop your rosy bubble.

Chapter Thirty-Eight

I arrived home to my beautiful Bess. She greeted me with her waggiest tail yet.

'Hello, sweetheart,' I said, gently pulling her ears and then giving her a muzzle rub. 'Did you have a nice snoozy while I was out?' I went through to the kitchen and dumped my handbag on the worktop. 'I've had *such* a lovely morning,' I confided. 'But before I tell you all about it, I'd first better let you out.'

'Woof,' said Bess, her tail going from side to side. I was reminded of a conductor's baton doing two beats to the bar.

I unlocked the back door and watched as Bess did an impression of a curtsy. She bounded back, tongue hanging out one side of her mouth, then stopped in front of me.

'What?' I asked.

She put her head on one side.

'Do you want to play ball?'

But upon producing the ball launcher, she showed no inclination to play *fetch*.

'Would you prefer Mr Squirrel?' I asked.

I lobbed Mr Squirrel through the air. He landed on the grass with a squeak and zero reaction from Bess.

'I'm totally out of ideas,' I told her. 'Sometimes I wish

you could speak and tell me what you want.'

'Woof,' said Bess, and licked her lips several times.

'Ah!' I laughed. 'Message received and understood.'

I returned to the kitchen, dog at my heels, and produced a large rawhide bone.

'Is this more like it?'

The tail wagging sped up. Now the conductor's baton was overseeing a run of quavers. Bess gently took the treat, then went outside again to chomp peacefully on the lawn in the company of Mr Squirrel.

Feeling like a new mother, I smiled indulgently. Leaving the back door open for Bess, I went inside again. Time to put the chicken in the oven and start prepping veg.

'Oh well,' I said, addressing Greg's portrait on the windowsill. 'As my pooch currently prefers Mr Squirrel's company to mine, I'll instead tell *you* all about my morning with Dylan. I gather you were there at the beginning – if that stunt with the spilt lager was anything to go by,' I tutted. 'But I didn't sense you around afterwards. And even though I know the thing with the lager was likely a coincidence, I really *really* would like a proper sign that you're around. I mentioned it last night, remember? The red balloon. So, keep it in mind, eh?'

I smiled at Greg. He beamed back. For a moment I could've sworn he blew me a kiss. And then I told myself it was simply sunlight glinting off the frame and distorting the image.

I went to the fridge and removed the chicken – already pre-basted and in its roasting pot – then gathered up fresh carrots, courgettes, green beans, and a large bag of potatoes. Moments later the pot was in the oven, and I got to work with the vegetable peeler. I briefly glanced up at Greg.

'Dylan said he likes me,' I confided, as the peeler whipped back and forth. '*Really* likes me.' In no time at all, I had a pile of peeled carrots. I picked one up. Held it aloft. 'And later' – I whispered to Greg – 'he kissed me. I gave the carrot a goofy look. 'It was such a lovely kiss.' I put the carrot to my lips. Closed my eyes. Puckered up. Hmm. Not quite the same. I tossed the carrot to one side and filled a saucepan with water. 'And then Dylan asked me to be his girlfriend.' I turned a dial on the stove. Watched the heat ring turn red. Placed the saucepan upon it. 'And I said yes!' I squeaked. 'What do you think about that then?'

'I think' – said a voice that had me shrieking out loud – 'that it's time you and me had a proper chat.'

I spun round, eyes wide, to find Ruby standing in the kitchen.

'G-Good grief, darling,' I stuttered, clutching my heart and getting carrot stain over my top. 'What are you doing here so early? You gave me the fright of my life.'

'I used my spare key,' she shrugged.

'I didn't see your car on the drive.'

'I walked. I've been here a while. I was upstairs in my old bedroom. Hope you don't mind.'

'Of course not,' I said, turning back to my prepping.

'I've met Bess.' She leant against the worktop. Peered at my pile of peeled carrots. She picked one up and took a bite. 'Nice pooch,' she commented. 'But not a great guard

195

dog. She didn't even bark at me.'

'She's not much of a barker,' I confessed. 'Where's Josh?'

'Dunno,' she said flatly. 'And I don't care. We've had a row.'

Oh no.

'What about?' I said carefully.

'His family.'

'Oh?'

'More specifically, his mother.'

I started dicing the courgettes. When Ruby was in one of these moods, it was best to just listen.

Archie's mother was often a bone of contention with Ruby. She swore that Margaret didn't approve of her, although Josh denied this. However, I suspected the umbilical cord wasn't completely severed between mother and son. Ruby was mostly tolerant but objected to playing second fiddle. Their last major row had been on Valentine's Day – which had happened to be Margaret's birthday. Rather than presenting my daughter with a dozen red roses, Josh had instead sent a bouquet to his mother.

'Look,' I cajoled. 'We both know that Josh is a bit of a mummy's boy. However, he's a nice enough lad. He doesn't give you the runaround.'

'I guess not.' She popped the last bit of carrot in her mouth. For a moment, she crunched noisily, then fixed me with a look. 'However, now it's my own mother causing me concern.'

I abruptly stopped dicing.

'Pardon?'

'Mum, it's bad enough that you talk to Dad's photographs. But how do you think I feel catching you snogging a carrot?'

I reddened.

'Look, Rubes. I'm sure there are things you do in the privacy of your own home–'

'Oh, yes, of course, absolutely.' Her voice dripped with sarcasm. 'I'm having a passionate affair with a cauliflower, and this Saturday I have a date with an aubergine. Meanwhile my mangetout are so jealous they've turned into green beans, and Josh is at his wits' end about my veggie fetish.'

'I was mucking about,' I muttered. The dicing went into overdrive as I let a curtain of hair hide my hot face.

'Mum, it's got to stop.'

Oh for…

I flung down the paring knife and plonked my hands on my hips.

'I have never kissed a carrot before,' I said defiantly.

'Stuff the carrot,' Ruby retorted. 'I'm talking about Dad. This… this…' – she jerked her head at Greg's portrait – 'this ridiculous one-sided conversation.'

'Oh, please, Ruby,' I sighed. I picked up the knife again. 'Just give me a break, eh?'

For a moment the two of us didn't speak. The only sound was that of the knife against the chopping board. Ruby was the first to break the silence.

'Are we having wine with dinner?'

'Yes,' I said, glad at the change of subject. Truce time. 'Shall we have a drink together, before the others arrive?'

'Okay,' she said, giving me a small smile.

Was I forgiven? I appreciated it must be unnerving seeing your mother chatting to your dead father, then having a lip-lock with a carrot.

The saucepan of water had since come to the boil. I found a steamer pan, chucked all the veg in, then sealed it with a lid. Behind me, a cork popped. Seconds later came the glug-glug of wine being poured into glasses.

'Cheers,' said Ruby, handing me a flute.

'Happy Sunday,' I said, clinking my glass against hers. 'Why don't you give Josh a ring and tell him to come over.'

'I'll text him instead,' she said grumpily. She reached for her phone, did the necessary, then sat down at the table. She crossed one long leg over the other, then regarded me beadily. 'And now' – she took a sip of her own wine – 'instead of chatting to Dad, you can talk to me.' She took another sip, then set the glass down. 'I'm all ears, Mum. Tell me about this stranger who has asked you to be his *girl*friend.'

Chapter Thirty-Nine

The doorbell rang, and Ruby's question went unanswered.

'Saved by the bell,' she tutted.

'Look, Rubes.' I gave my daughter a frank look. 'If you don't mind, my private life is exactly that. Private. However, when we are all together, I'm happy to share my news about Dylan. After all, he's not a tawdry secret. But when I tell the others, I'll be keeping it low-key, okay? The guy is a friend. Not a fiancé.'

'A friend, eh?' She raised one eyebrow. 'Since when did *friends* kiss?'

Ruby gave an involuntary shudder. Her body language wasn't lost on me.

Bleurgh. My ancient mother has kissed a guy.

The doorbell rang again.

'Instead of sitting there and judging me' – I huffed – 'could you instead do something useful?'

'Good idea,' Ruby grunted. 'What's this guy's second name? I'll look him up on social media. See if he makes it a habit of getting women – and their carrots – in a tizzy.'

The doorbell was now giving a series of short and sharp staccato bursts.

'Lay the table,' I snapped.

Bess, alerted to the constant doorbell ringing, came in from the garden. Like a bodyguard, she accompanied me to the front door. Ella and Archie were standing on the doorstep. Bess gave a joyful yip. *People,* she seemed to say. *How nice.*

'Hey, Mum,' said Ella, plonking a kiss on my cheek.

'Hello, darling.' I hugged my youngest briefly, before her attention diverted to Bess.

'Hello, baby girl,' she cooed, rubbing behind Bess's ears. 'Aren't you beautiful!'

Archie stepped inside. His arms were full of flowers and a bottle of wine.

'For you, Maggie,' he said, pecking me on the cheek. 'Oooh, what a lovely dog.'

'She is,' I beamed. 'Gosh, these are beautiful,' I said, sniffing the fragrant blooms. 'Guys, go on through. Ruby is already here. We've both made a start on the wine.'

'Aye aye,' said my youngest. 'My female intuition tells me something's going down.'

'Only the wine,' I assured.

Ella gave me one of her looks.

'Rubbish,' she scoffed. 'Not to worry. I'll get to the bottom of it. Come on, Archie. And you, Bess. Let's go and find Ruby and suss out the goss.'

'There's no gossip,' I called after her.

'Oh yes there is,' Ruby trilled, just as the doorbell rang again.

This time it was Tim and Steph.

'Hell*ooo*,' said Steph. She gave me a hug and squashed

my flowers in the process. 'Oops. Sorry. Let me take them from you. I'll find a vase.'

'Thanks, lovey.'

She headed off to the kitchen, and I opened my arms to my son.

'How's my boy?' I grinned.

'Good,' said Tim, giving me a bear hug. He then stepped back. Gave me an appraising look. 'Hmm.'

'What's that supposed to mean?' I frowned, just as Josh stepped through the open doorway.

'Hey, Maggie,' said Josh, looking a little awkward. 'Me and Ruby…' he trailed off.

'Don't worry about it,' I said. 'Go on through.'

'Make it snappy, Josh,' Tim teased. 'I need to have a quick word with my mother.' He peered at my face. 'You're looking very pink. And rather flustered. Like you're hugging a secret. Are you?'

'Don't be ridiculous,' I spluttered.

'Official announcement,' Ella yodelled from the kitchen. 'Mum has got herself a boyfriend.'

'What?' said Tim incredulously. 'I thought you'd got a dog.'

'The dog is in here with us,' Ruby called. 'Come and get a drink, Tim. I think you're going to need one.'

God, my kids. A woman couldn't kiss a bloody carrot without it becoming a newsflash.

Chapter Forty

Needless to say, Sunday dinner was a lively affair.

My children teased me mercilessly about having a *boyfriend* at the age of sixty-one. I shook my head in exasperation.

'I'm not an octogenarian with a blue rinse and a penchant for Parma Violets,' I tutted.

'We're pleased for you, Mum,' said Tim. He gave me a cheeky wink.

'Are we?' said Ruby archly. 'I'd like to check this guy out first.'

'So, when are we going to meet him?' asked Tim.

'Not yet,' I said firmly.

'Yeah, we don't want Ruby frightening him off,' said Ella loyally. 'I'm sure Dylan is a respectable guy.'

'He is,' I said.

'What does he do for a living?' asked Ruby, eyes narrowing.

'Um, he's in healthcare,' I said vaguely.

No way was I telling my kids that Dylan owned and managed an old folks' home. They'd make jokes about the pair of us living there together. Wearing his 'n' hers bobble slippers.

'How old is this guy?' asked Tim.

'Er, a year or two younger than me,' I said, picking up my wine glass.

'Omigod,' Ella crowed. 'Mum has got herself a toy boy.'

I made a show of sipping my wine and being unable to answer. If Ella discovered that Dylan was *eight* years younger, she'd be aghast. Ruby would wonder why a fifty-three-year-old wanted to hang out with a wrinkly like me. And if she saw how muscled-up Dylan was, she'd be doubly perplexed. I could almost hear her now. Hypothesising about Dylan being up to no good. Targeting old biddies who had a few quid in the bank.

'Is he divorced?' asked Tim.

'No. Like me, Dylan is widowed. He also has a daughter. Terry. She's just got married.'

'What's his surname?' said Tim, pulling his mobile from his back pocket.

I knew it. It wasn't just Ruby who wanted to check out Dylan on social media. Knowing my son, Tim would go one step further. He'd be feeding Dylan's name into bankruptcy searches or anything else that gave information about a person via the internet.

'I can't remember,' I said lamely.

'Bollocks,' Tim scoffed.

'She wouldn't tell me either,' said Ruby. 'Why so secretive, Mum? Does this man have a criminal record?'

'Not that I'm aware of,' I spluttered. 'Now can we please talk about something else? I invited you all here to meet Bess.'

'And she's lovely,' said Archie gallantly. 'Just like you.'

'No need to suck up to my mother,' said Ella. 'I think one toyboy in her life is enough.'

'Oh, but I didn't mean–' said Archie, turning bright red.

'Take no notice of my daughter,' I said, shooting Ella a look.

'Sorr-*eee*,' she laughed. Her eyes danced with mischief. 'Just teasing.'

She picked up her glass and giggle-snorted into her wine. The sound made Archie laugh too.

I'd moved Bess's basket from the hallway to the kitchen so she could be with us while we ate. She continued to behave like the lady she was. There was no begging at the table. That said, she was looking hopeful at the possibility of leftovers. Overall, she was content to be in everyone's company and was unfazed by the laughter and shrill chatter.

'So, you met this guy at the rehoming centre,' said Tim.

I mentally sighed. There was no getting off this subject.

'Yes,' I nodded. 'Dylan has rescued a brown–and–white mongrel called Charlie. We've already enjoyed some lovely walks together. Hopefully, we'll have many more.'

'Ah!' my son exclaimed. 'I *see*.'

He flashed his oldest sister a look. One that conveyed that Ruby should take a chill pill. All was well. Their old mum wasn't testing the bedsprings with a stranger. Perish the thought! Instead, she and this Dylan dude were pottering around the village with their pooches. And later, when they'd chastely pecked each other's floury cheeks, Mum would return home in time for cocoa and Coronation

Street.

I didn't know whether to laugh or be offended. What would the children say if they knew their father and I had enjoyed an active sex life? Did young people truly believe only they had the right to be sexy?

Okay, I was no *Love Island* contestant. I wasn't a twenty-something female with hair extensions, fake eyelashes and a chest bursting out of my swimsuit. But I could be sensual too, dammit. Albeit in a maxi dress and with some ambient lighting thrown in for good measure.

'Who wants apple crumble?' I asked, standing up. A clamour of affirmative cries rent the air as I gathered up the dinner plates. 'So, that's everyone.'

I tottered over to the dishwasher. Dumping everything down on the worktop, I risked a quick peek at Greg's photo on the windowsill.

They've been taking the rise out of me, I silently informed him. I pulled on the dishwasher's handle. *Over having a boyfriend*, I added. *Dylan rather sweetly told me that sixty is the new thirty.*

That's great, darling, Greg answered in my head. *But don't get banned from driving eh!*

It took me a moment to get the joke, but as I bent to stack the plates, I laughed out loud.

Chapter Forty-One

And so, my foray into the dating world began. However, it wasn't quite as anticipated.

In all honesty I hadn't been entirely sure what to expect. I was old-fashioned enough to let Dylan set the pace. Although I was now starting to wonder if he was waiting for me to take the lead.

My mind went back to Tim and Ruby over dinner. Tim had given his sister a look that had summed up his take on this so-called relationship. That this stranger and their ancient mother would partake in dog walks, trips to cafés and maybe do some handholding – but only if Dylan had consumed a lager and I'd indulged in a sherry.

The thing was, so far, my son had been spot on – apart from the sherry indulgence. To say I was baffled was an understatement. Every time Dylan held my hand I would happily zing away. But on Dylan's part there had been little reaction. In all truth, it was starting to make me somewhat paranoid.

Six weeks on, and now in the middle of a hot July, I wondered if Dylan was having second thoughts about me. Was it because of my age? Had he spotted the way my neck wrinkled attractively? That I was more *tortoise* than *gorgeous*? Was he too embarrassed to say, "Look, Maggie. I'm sorry. I've made a mistake. I've since met a younger woman… yes, quite a bit younger… okay, a lot younger… she's thirty-five."

That said, *life* was not allowing me much time to ponder over this puzzle. The Golden Oldies had been keeping me on their toes. There'd also been several photography bookings to oversee – a kiddie's party (*photoshoot* according to Birthday Girl's mother); a couple of pet portrait bookings; and a bride that had wanted *The Works.*

Despite keeping busy, I often found myself mentally rewinding to that first date – brunch in West Malling. Dylan had called me *darling.* Later, he'd taken me in his arms and gently lowered his mouth to mine. "I'd like to kiss you properly," he'd murmured. "But Tesco's carpark isn't terribly romantic."

Well, he was still referring to me as *darling.* And that was lovely. But he hadn't yet kissed me properly. Okay, he could hardly go for it at Trosley's country park café. But he could have snogged me in the woods. Or in his car when he'd dropped me home after having dinner. If he'd really wanted to, he could've puckered up *in* the car, then flipped back the seat and suggested we steam up the windows. Or hoarsely told me to lead him by the lapels into my house, up the stairs, and inside my bedroom to finish what, so far, hadn't even started.

Nor had it been lost on me that, so far, he'd completely bypassed us going back to his place. Not even a hint of inviting me in for a nightcap with a bit of eyebrow waggling and a meaningful look.

As every couple in lust knows, one kiss leads to another. And that leads to a fumble… then a grope… to getting naked… concluding with the bedsprings being put through their paces.

Or perhaps there was a much deeper issue here, and it was nothing to do with my age. Rather, more to do with Dylan's age. Maybe Dylan – despite looking in peak condition – *wasn't*. If you get my drift. Perhaps things *down there* were a little… soft.

The thought had sent me off to Google. Here I'd been reliably informed of some statistics. Apparently one in four men between the age of fifty to fifty-nine experienced Mr Stiffy doing a runner at an inopportune moment. In other cases, Mr Stiffy had gone completely AWOL and been replaced by Mr Floppy.

I'd clicked off the internet and puffed out my cheeks. Greg hadn't experienced any of those issues. I'd rather naively thought that impotence was a rarity. I mean, look at Hugh Heffner and all those bunny girls. Stamina or what? Another recent example was ninety-one-year-old Rupert Murdoch. Only last year he'd been set to marry for a fifth time. I mean, presumably one wouldn't be up for marriage if one's willy wasn't up for it too?

I decided to broach the subject with Dylan and ask him outright. By that, I don't mean, "Tell me, Dylan. Are you impotent?" Of course not. I wasn't insensitive. Rather… well, I wasn't too sure about how to approach the subject. Maybe Google could provide me with some clues.

'Er, Dylan, sweetheart, have you heard about, um, Erectile Dysfunction? No? What is it? W-e-ll, it's, um, it's, um, it's…'

Or perhaps I should, on the quiet, start up an Erectile Dysfunction Support Group. Then I could invite Dylan to it. But then I might have some explaining to do if nobody else turned up. A case of a big flop and nobody coming.

I'd have to give it some serious thought.

Meanwhile, my parents were stressing me big time. It didn't help that my mother had telephoned only last night – actually, it had been three in the morning – demanding to know if I'd stolen her handbag. However, after being on Social Services' waiting list these last several weeks, a house visit was finally being made.

And so it was, on this beautiful July morning, that I set off to see the parents. Bess was on the back seat. Together, we cruised along the M20. Irene, the lady from the Old People's Team, would conduct the assessment.

As I overtook a lorry, I found myself earnestly talking to Him. *Please God, let there be help.*

Chapter Forty-Two

With Bess at my heel, I let myself into Mum and Dad's house using my own key.

'Yoohoo,' I called.

No reply.

I shut the front door and walked through to the kitchen. Removing a large bowl from the china cupboard, I filled it with water for Bess.

'Here you are, sweetheart,' I said, setting it down on the floor. She took several noisy laps, then stood by the back door. 'Do you want to go out?'

I unlocked the door and Bess stepped out into my parents' small garden. The lawn was unkempt. The grass was long and raggedy with an explosion of dandelions. There were also some spectacular weeds in the flower borders. Freya had recently volunteered her husband to do some gardening. Evidently Vernon hadn't been up for it. After Social Services had concluded their visit, I'd wheel out the mower from the garage and tidy things up.

Overhead, a floorboard creaked. I moved back to the hallway.

'Dad?' I shouted up the stairs.

'Who's that?' came a befuddled reply.

'It's Maggie,' I answered.

My father's head appeared over the upper landing's safety rail.

'What are you doing here?'

For a moment I didn't speak. Surely, he hadn't forgotten?

'I telephoned yesterday, remember? We talked about a lady called Irene. She's coming to visit you today.'

'Who?' he said crossly.

I inhaled sharply, and mentally counted to ten.

'Irene from Social Services is visiting to have a chat with you and Mum.'

There was a pause while he digested this.

'Oh, yes. It had slipped my mind.'

His head bobbed back. Seconds later he appeared at the top of the staircase. A vision in boxer shorts and a string vest.

'Dad, you're not even dressed,' I said, unable to hide my exasperation.

'So?' he said belligerently. 'Can't a man do what he likes in his own home?'

'Yes, of course,' I said, trying not to get irritated. 'But it's getting on for noon. At this time of day I'm usually thinking about having a sandwich, but clearly you haven't even had breakfast.'

'So?' he repeated, his bottom lip now protruding. I was reminded of a pouting toddler testing parental boundaries – but in geriatric form.

'Where's Mum?' I said, changing the subject.

'Probably in the bathroom. Let me fetch my dressing gown. I'll use the downstairs loo.'

'Can't you get some clothes on first?'

'What for?' he growled.

I opened my mouth to tell him about Irene again, then smartly shut it. This. *This* was what frustrated me. One cantankerous old man refusing to co-operate. No doubt my mother was holed up in the bathroom shredding loo paper faster than a Labrador puppy in a TV ad.

'Tell you what, Dad,' I said. 'You sort yourself out, and I'll make you and Mum some scrambled eggs.'

My father visibly perked up at the thought of eating without the effort of cooking. This. This *again*. The feeling of guilt that I wasn't here every day, doing everything for them. Realistically I knew it wasn't possible to do that. Not unless I gave up work and put my life on hold.

Some sons and daughters would do that. In some cultures, it was expected – and the adult children complied too. Indeed, the little voice in my head was often very opinionated on the matter.

What sort of a daughter are you not to move in with your parents?

What sort of a daughter are you not to let them move in with you?

What sort of a daughter are you not to sacrifice your life for them?

Usually I would silently scream my reply.

A SELFISH ONE, OKAY? HAPPY? YES, I'M A SELFISH DAUGHTER!

Pushing aside the inevitable feelings of guilt, resentment, and frustration, I returned to the kitchen to crack eggs into a pan.

Chapter Forty-Three

I left the scrambled eggs, along with some toast, on a low heat in the oven. I was just putting the kettle on when the doorbell rang.

Bess bustled in from the garden, eager to see who was visiting. Together, we walked to the front door. A kindly-looking lady was standing on the doorstep.

'Morning,' she beamed.

The woman was about ten years younger than me. She had a lovely vibe. Warm. Comforting. Like crumble and custard on a winter's day.

'Hello.' I returned her smile. 'You must be Irene.'

'Indeed,' she nodded. 'And you must be Maggie.'

'I am.' I opened the door wider and grabbed Bess's collar. 'Do come in. Are you okay with dogs?' I held on to Bess in case Irene had the heebie-jeebies at a German Shepherd checking her out.

'I adore dogs,' she assured. 'I have a Labrador. A rescue. In fact, I got her from the local rehoming centre.'

'Snap!' I beamed. I was liking Irene more and more by the second.

'Rachel and Luke were so helpful. Hello, darling,' she cooed, rubbing Bess's ears.

'Go through to the kitchen,' I said, letting go of Bess's collar. 'Second door on the left.' I paused at the foot of the stairs. 'Dad?' I called. 'Our visitor is here.'

I caught up with Irene. Bess had disappeared into the garden again. A quick glance through the window revealed her settling down in the shade of a tree. The back door could stay open. The weather was warm, plus tension in my body was making me feel hotter than usual.

'Would you like a cuppa?' I asked Irene. 'Or would you prefer a cold drink?'

'Tea would be lovely,' she said, sitting down at the kitchen table. She set down her bag, then placed an A4 notepad on the table's surface. 'One sugar and a dash of milk, please.'

'Coming right up,' I said, just as Dad wandered in. Thankfully he was now dressed.

'Hello, Trevor,' said Irene warmly.

'Hmm,' Dad replied. He pulled out the chair opposite Irene and sat down heavily. 'You seem to know me, but I don't know you. What do you want?' he demanded rudely.

Oh Lord. His bottom lip was protruding again. Belligerence was emanating from every cell of his body.

'I've come to see how you're coping and–'

'Perfectly well,' Dad interrupted.

'And if we – by that I mean Social Services – can help in any way,' Irene added.

Dad narrowed his eyes.

'My daughter is the culprit behind this meeting.'

'Yes, Maggie did reach out to us,' Irene confirmed. 'She

told us that you're managing splendidly' – I silently thanked Irene for her diplomacy – 'but that your wife could do with a little extra help.'

'Not true,' said Dad. 'Deirdre is perfectly fine.' His tone dared her to contradict him. As far as he was concerned, this matter was now closed.

I set the teas down on the table.

'Dad,' I said gently. 'While Mum isn't in the room, we can talk freely. So, let's have an open and honest discussion, eh?' I moved to the oven and withdrew his scrambled egg and toast. 'As Irene said' – I set the plate before him – 'you've been amazing.' Yes, I was shamelessly borrowing the social worker's tactics. 'You've done a wonderful job looking after Mum.'

'And I still am,' he said, picking up his knife and fork.

'But you deserve a break now and again. Mum doesn't give you any opportunity for respite. You can't even leave her alone for a minute. You can't even go to the corner shop to buy a newspaper.'

'Yes, I can. And do,' he added.

'But she shouldn't be left alone,' I said quickly. 'She wanders off. Goes looking for you. And stops strangers in the street, asking for help. Not everyone is scrupulous, Dad. Mum could get mugged.'

'Don't be dramatic, Maggie,' Dad tutted. He loaded his fork, then paused for a moment. 'And anyway, after that last episode, I now lock your mother in. She can't wander off.' He popped the food into his mouth. He gave me a crafty look as he chewed. One that conveyed, *you won't catch me out – I've covered all bases.*

'But Dad, it's dangerous to leave Mum alone,' I pointed out. 'What if she tried to make herself a hot drink?'

'She's perfectly capable.'

'But she really isn't,' I said gently. 'Have you forgotten the time she put the kettle on the stove?'

Dad put some more food in his mouth. He didn't want to answer. Instead, he glared at me while he chewed. Nobody spoke until he'd swallowed.

'And your point is?' he finally asked.

'My point is that one doesn't put electric kettles on gas hobs.'

Dad waved his fork in the air. The gesture implied such an action was a blip.

'At our age, one is allowed to make the odd mistake.'

'Where is Deirdre?' asked Irene. 'I'd love to meet her.'

'Upstairs,' said Dad. 'Getting dressed. I don't know why Maggie has dragged you here. I'm sure there are more pressing things for you to do. You don't need to waste your time on us. Spend the taxpayers' money on something worthwhile. For once,' he added nastily.

'Dad,' I hissed. 'There's no need to–'

But my words died on my lips. My mother was standing in the kitchen doorway. And she was completely starkers.

Chapter Forty-Four

'Mum!' I exclaimed.

I was aghast that my mother couldn't recognise if she was in a state of undress, and shocked at her skinniness. No way could Mum be eating three meals a day. Or, was it that she no longer recognised when she was hungry, so didn't eat?

When I'd first contacted Social Services with the dramatic claim that I believed my mother was dying, maybe I hadn't been far off the mark.

'Hello,' said my mother vaguely. 'Er, are you Freya or Maggie?'

'I'm Maggie,' I said, swooping over to her. 'Um' – I whispered – 'are you aware that you're naked?'

'Am I?' said Mum. She glanced at herself in confusion.

'Deirdre,' my father spluttered, having frantically swallowed a mouthful of food. 'What the devil do you think you're playing at, woman?'

'I'll see to her,' I said, guiding Mum out of the kitchen.

'Let go of my arm, Maggie,' she said testily. My mother shook me off. 'I'm not a child.'

'Okay,' I soothed, steering her towards the staircase. 'But we have a visitor, and you need to get dressed.'

'And now you're *speaking* to me like I'm a child,' Mum retorted. 'I don't know what all the fuss is about. God gave us skin to wear. Why do we need to put clothes on? And anyway, I'm hot. I don't want to wear a sweater and trousers.'

'Of course you don't,' I agreed, leading her into the bedroom. 'That's why I'm going to find you a nice summer dress and some sandals.'

'Go away, Maggie.' My mother gave me a little shove. 'I'll find myself a dress. I don't need you standing over me.'

'Mum, let me help you. Please. It won't take a second and–'

'GO AWAY!' my mother shrieked.

I put my hands in the air. Backed off.

'Right,' I nodded. 'You sort yourself out. I'll see you shortly.'

I knew better than to argue with my mother when she was in one of these moods. And anyway, it was better for Irene to see firsthand what was going on in this house.

I scampered back downstairs but paused three steps from the bottom. Irene was calmly talking to my father. Words floated my way. I held my breath. Listened. Tried to piece the conversation together.

'… must see, Trevor, that Deirdre is… mentally… dementia… struggling a little… assistance… no one taking over… an hour… morning… dressed… bathtime… cooking…'

Oooh. These words were music to my ears. I willed my father to take on board what Irene was advising.

When I walked into the kitchen, Dad was sitting at the table with his head bowed. Irene looked up and gave me a sympathetic smile.

'Is Deirdre not with you?'

'No, er…' – I gestured vaguely – 'she said she could see to herself. I've suggested she put on a summer dress.'

'Your father and I have been having a chat,' said Irene. 'I'd like him to consider a carer visiting every day. Just for an hour, to begin with. Deirdre can then get used to another person being around. Maybe even make a friend of her.' Irene gave Dad an encouraging smile. 'Another woman can provide companionship for your wife, Trevor. Then you can go out. Stretch those legs. Take a breather. Recalibrate.'

My father looked up and rolled his eyes.

'You're seriously suggesting that my wife would befriend another woman?' he jeered. 'My life wouldn't be worth living. Deirdre would have a field day accusing me of shenanigans. I'm surprised she didn't accuse *you* of being my mistress.' He gave a mirthless laugh, then looked Irene in the eye. 'I know you mean well, but we don't want any carer. Not for one hour. Not for one minute. Just leave us be.'

'Dad,' I warned. 'I'm not taking no for an answer. Years ago, you and Mum made a Power of Attorney. You did so in case one or both of you lost capacity. That time has come. I've had enough. I can't cope–'

'And you don't need to cope,' my father interrupted. 'It's not your job to look after your mother. It's mine.'

'Yes, but the thing is, Dad' – I licked my lips nervously – 'recently *your* memory hasn't been great either.'

'How DARE you!' he roared, his face flushing with anger.

'Now then, Trevor,' said Irene. 'Let's discuss this—'

'And you can sod off,' said Dad, turning on her. 'Go on. Get out of here.'

My mother reappeared in the kitchen doorway. She was now decent but wearing a nightdress.

'Who can sod off?' Mum demanded.

'Her,' said Dad, pointing at Irene.

I had no doubt that my father was anticipating my mother to round on Irene, call her a hussy, and to back up his request for her to go away.

Instead Mum looked at Irene blankly.

'Who are you?'

'I'm from Social Services, Deirdre. I've been having a lovely chat with Trevor and Maggie. Did you know that you're entitled to all sorts of help but haven't been taking advantage?'

'Really?' said Mum, her eyes lighting up.

'Yes,' Irene confirmed. 'You and Trevor have both worked hard all your life.'

'Quite right,' Mum agreed. 'I was a nurse, you know.'

'And I'll bet you were a very good one too,' said Irene.

Mum's chest swelled.

'I was,' she agreed.

'For years you have paid your taxes and National Insurance contributions. Now it's time to have something in return.'

'How wonderful,' Mum cooed. 'What are you going to

give us?'

'Well, for starters, how about a safety rail on your staircase?'

'Sounds good,' said Mum excitedly.

'And also a battery-operated chair to help you in and out of the bath.'

Mum clapped her hands together in childlike delight.

'What else?' she asked.

'Someone to come in every day and help you,' said Irene.

Mum clapped her hands again, while Dad looked on. His face was thunderous.

'And how much is that going to cost?' he demanded.

'Not much,' Irene assured. 'After all, we're only talking about an hour a day.'

'To start with,' I quickly added. 'Isn't that nice, Mum?' I cajoled. 'A kind lady is going to visit every day and help you.'

'Help me with what?' said Mum, looking puzzled.

'Housework,' suggested Irene. 'After all, no woman loves doing that, do they!'

Mum frowned.

'I don't need any help. I do everything around here.'

My father snorted but didn't contradict her.

'What do you do, Deirdre?' asked Irene gently. 'Are you able to tell me?'

'Of course I can,' said Mum indignantly. 'I just said. I do everything. The cooking. Laundry. Ironing. Housework. The food shopping. A woman's work is never done and I, for one, never stop. Do I, Trevor?'

Dad didn't answer. But, even if he'd wanted to, my mother would have spoken over him. Right now, there was a light blazing in her eyes. She was remembering the past. The days when she really had done everything. Juggled a job while raising her children. Balanced working days with school holidays. Put a meal on the table within minutes of getting off duty. Helped us with homework as she'd washed up. All while waiting on her husband hand, foot, and finger. Oh yes, she'd been the rock. The foundation of the family. A warrior. And in her head, she still was! A warrior in a nightdress.

'That's marvellous, Deirdre,' said Irene. 'And what sort of meals do you cook?'

'Everything you can think of,' said Mum airily.

'And how do you cook?'

'What do you mean?' Mum frowned.

'On the stove? In the oven? Or do you prefer using a microwave?'

Mum frowned again.

'Er, the last one.'

'The microwave?'

'Yes,' she nodded. 'I use that.'

My mother then pointed to the small television screen on the kitchen wall. Dad opened his mouth to say something, but Irene held up one hand.

'Let Deirdre speak for herself, Trevor.'

'Thank you,' said Mum importantly. 'He's always interrupting me. I tell him over and over. Shut up, Trevor, for fuck's sake.'

There was a stunned pause. My frail mother's robust words hovered in the air. Irene was the first to break the silence.

'That's a lovely microwave, Deirdre,' she said diplomatically. 'Do you use anything else for cooking?'

Mum went over to the grill. She pulled down its door and peered within.

'Remind me what I'm looking for,' she said.

'That's perfect, Deirdre,' said Irene. She added a few more words to her copious notes, then turned to my father. 'What sort of foods do the two of you eat, Trevor?'

'Well,' Dad blustered. 'We eat plenty – that I can tell you.'

'What foods?' Irene persisted.

'We're very partial to salmon and sweetcorn. In fact, we love it so much, we eat it all the time.' Dad nodded his head vigorously.

'Do you not get bored eating the same thing every day?' she asked.

'Nope.' Dad gave Irene a stubborn look. One that said *stop trying to catch me out because it won't work.*

'Oh for heaven's sake, Dad,' I huffed. 'Mum needs *brain* foods. Avocados. Walnuts. Coconut. You should both be having fresh vegetables. Eating the rainbow. And what about a bit of fillet steak now and again? Heavens, it's not as if you can't afford it. You have a decent pension.'

Irene was evidently used to dealing with people like my father.

'I think you're an amazing man, Trevor,' she said. 'Indeed, I wish my husband was as hands-on as you. However, I think you're tired. You're now in your nineties. That's awesome. But there's nothing wrong in having some assistance.'

'I don't want it,' said Dad stubbornly. 'Everything is fine as it is.'

'I'm going to ask you a question, Trevor. Think carefully before you answer. You've reached an amazing age. But none of us can go on forever. If anything happened to you, who would look after your wife?'

I flinched, waiting for Mum to kick off. However, she was currently distracted by something under the table. There was a horrible silence. The clock on the wall tick-ticked as the second hand passed its painted numerals. Dad glared at Irene. He'd been cornered. Like a rat in a trap. And he didn't like it.

'Trevor,' said Irene gently. 'None of us like to feel as if we're losing control. However, I strongly suggest you put a back-up plan in place.

Dad rolled his eyes.

'If anything should happen to me, I have two daughters. They can step in.'

'Your daughters are not yet retired,' Irene pointed out. 'Both are working. Neither of them can give your wife the fulltime care she needs.'

Irene shut her notebook and put the pen away. She delved into her bag and removed a clutch of leaflets. When she next spoke, it was to me.

'These are for you and your sister. There is a lot of advice within these pages. There's also a list of telephone numbers. These offer support for people in this situation. Unfortunately, we can't force anyone to have care assistance. We can only advise.'

I took the leaflets.

'But what about my mother?' I bleated. 'She's skin and bone. This situation is tantamount to supervised neglect.'

'As I said, Maggie. We can't force your father to do anything against his will.'

I stared at her helplessly.

'I thought Social Services had the power to… well…'

My voice trailed off. What had I been expecting? That Irene would lecture my father? Turn to him and say, "Now you listen here! If things don't change, we will seize your wife and put her up for adoption." That was never going to happen. Of course not.

I put my head in my hands.

'I don't know what to do,' I whispered.

'Read the information I've given you,' said Irene. She stood up. I followed her out to the hallway. 'If anything changes – if something happens to your father – there's a list of care homes that would look after your mother. It's an expensive path,' she warned. 'When you were upstairs, your father told me he's a homeowner. Unfortunately, you'd probably have to sell this house to pay for long-term care.'

'Right,' I nodded.

C'est la vie. People worked hard all their lives. Some, if they could, bought a house. Made it their home. Thought it would be something to pass on. To their children. Grandchildren. Maybe even great-grandchildren. Instead, when they were old and decrepit, they had to sell up to fund their last days on Earth.

As Irene released the catch on the door, a wave of depression threatened to engulf me.

'The thing is' – I blurted – 'I don't believe my father is the full ticket either. There are two old people in this house muddling along. Both are frail. Both are registered disabled. One has lost their marbles. The other is in the process of doing so. This situation is an accident waiting to happen.'

'You said your father made a Power of Attorney.'

'Yes,' I nodded. 'Years ago.'

'Then I suggest you get it registered – before he loses capacity.'

'Right,' I nodded. 'That's a good idea.' I chewed my lip thoughtfully. 'In fact, recently my father spoke of renewing his Will. I could make an appointment with his solicitor. Kill two birds with one stone, so to speak.'

'Do that,' Irene urged. 'Don't prevaricate.'

'Yes,' I nodded. 'I'll talk to Dad about it right now.'

'Good. Meanwhile, it was lovely to meet you, Maggie.' Irene shook my hand. 'There's only one thing left for me to say.'

'Oh?' I raised my eyebrows.

She gave me a frank look before stepping through the open doorway.

'Good luck.'

Chapter Forty-Five

Having said goodbye to Irene, I returned to the kitchen and sat back down at the table. Mum had nodded off in her chair. Chin on chest. I turned to Dad.

'A little while ago, you said you wanted to revise your Will. Shall we make an appointment with the solicitor?'

'Oh, that,' said Dad vaguely. 'I think I've already done that.'

'What do you mean?' I frowned. 'You've revised your Will, or made an appointment with the solicitor?'

'The latter.' Dad waved a hand at the kitchen wall where, on a nail, hung a calendar. 'Have a look for me.'

I stood up and read the entries for July. My eyes widened with surprise.

'Dad, the appointment is for *tomorrow*.'

'That's right.'

Oh, terrific. I tried to remember what, if anything, was happening tomorrow in my own diary. At home, on my desk, was a large A4 affair. I didn't carry it with me on account of it always being full of work-related inserts. Apart from anything else, it was too big to fit into my handbag. Nor could I check the calendar on my Smart phone because I never used it. However, I was fairly sure I was available.

'When were you going to tell me?' I grumbled.

'Now,' said Dad defensively. 'I had to wait for that woman to leave first.' *That woman.* Letting me know he was still cross. 'I need you to taxi me, Maggie, because…'

He trailed off, suddenly shifty.

'Because what?' I prompted.

'Because I've had a letter from the DVLA. It says I mustn't drive until a doctor has passed me fit to do so.'

My mouth dropped open.

'Oh,' I said. What else was there to say? No doctor in their right mind would pass my father to drive a car. They'd take one look at his cataracts, swollen feet and stiff legs and suggest he use a local taxi. Or me, in this case.

'Why are you looking so surprised?' said my father. His expression had changed. 'After all, you're probably the person who reported me.'

'What?' I spluttered. 'Of course I didn't report you,' I protested. Not that it hadn't crossed my mind. Ultimately, I'd held off because I'd dreaded my father's wrath. Although it looked like I was about to take some verbal blows anyway.

'Sometimes, Maggie, you are a total cow.'

Ouch. I took a deep breath.

'Dad, please don't speak to me like that. You know perfectly well that, a few weeks ago, you had a row with a motorist.'

My father's eyes narrowed.

'What are you talking about?'

I looked at my father in disbelief.

'Sanjit told me.' I waited for my father's expression to

change. For his memory to kick in. For him to say *oh yes, I remember now.* Instead, he continued to look at me blankly. 'You almost had a collision with another vehicle,' I reminded.

'This is preposterous,' Dad spat.

'Sanjit told me that the other driver was furious. The motorist leapt out of his car, banged on your window and then, when you opened it, he leant in and snatched your keys. He shouted that he was going to report you to the DVLA. Well, it looks like he did.'

Dad closed his eyes. For a moment he didn't say anything.

'Ah, yes. It's coming back to me now. There was a bit of a kerfuffle.'

'Apology accepted,' I said sarcastically.

Oh, stop it, Maggie. Get off your high horse. You're talking to a man whose memory is fading like the sky at dusk.

'Look, Dad, I hate to say this but… well, I can't help noticing that, of late, your memory isn't what it used to be.'

'I'm tired, Maggie. That's all.'

'If you say so,' I muttered. 'Right.' I stood up. 'I'd best be heading home. Things to do. I'll pick you up in the morning. We'll have to take Mum along. I'm not leaving her at home alone. How about I take you both out to lunch afterwards?'

Dad perked up.

'That would be lovely, sweetheart.'

Sweetheart. I sighed. Better than *cow.*

Chapter Forty-Six

That evening, Dylan phoned.

'Hey,' I said, lowering the volume on the television.

'How's you?' he asked.

'Oh, you know.' I found myself doing a see-saw motion with one hand, even though Dylan couldn't see. 'Muddling along.'

'The Golden Oldies?'

'Yes, although I'm thinking about changing that name to the BOBs.'

'Meaning?'

'Bad-tempered Old Buggers.' I chuckled into the handset.

'Ah, yes. I remember when my parents behaved in an unpleasant way. I privately called them the GOGs – Grumpy Old Gits.'

I laughed.

'I mustn't complain. Better to have them here than not.'

'Exactly,' Dylan agreed. He paused. A regrouping gesture. 'I've booked tomorrow off work. I thought I'd tag Friday onto Saturday and Sunday and enjoy a long weekend. Are you available tomorrow for lunch? I know a lovely pub that is dog-friendly. We can take Bess and Charlie along.'

'Oh,' I said, my disappointment evident. 'That would have been wonderful. However, I've promised to take my parents out for lunch tomorrow.'

'Ah, okay. That's a shame. It will keep.'

There was something about Dylan's tone that caught my attention.

'What will keep?'

There was a pause at the other end of the line. Suddenly I had a bad vibe.

'I wanted to have… a chat,' he said carefully.

My heart skipped a beat.

'That sounds rather ominous,' I said, trying to ignore the chill that had settled around my heart. 'Why don't you chat to me now, instead?' I said lightly.

'No, I'd rather do it face-to-face.'

Do what?

Well, isn't it obvious, Maggie? said my inner voice. *This sounds like the bullet to me.*

Oh God. Was it? Or… wait. Maybe it was more to do with the intimacy thing. Or rather, the lack of it. Perhaps Dylan wanted to have a face-to-face about why our 'relationship' had yet to get off the ground.

I cleared my throat.

'Er, I think I know what you want to talk about, Dylan,' I said carefully.

There was pause before he spoke.

'You do?' He sounded nervous.

'Yeah…' I trailed off. How to word this? 'Have you

thought about…'

Should I mention the *medication* word?

Hey, Dylan, there's a new opium-based medicine on the market. It's called Poppycock.

Should I offer to buy it for him? I felt sure it could be bought over the counter.

'Do you think I should see someone?' Dylan asked.

'Only if you're worried.'

'To be honest, I *am* worried. It's been going on for too long. It started not long after I met you.'

Wow. Well, they said honesty was the best policy. Although I felt a bit rocked to hear *not long after I met you.* Hopefully that was an unfortunate coincidence, and that my sagging jawline hadn't been a major turn off.

'Well, as I said, if you're worried, it's best to talk to a professional.'

'It's not that I'm worried,' he said carefully. 'It's more a case of not knowing where to start. I mean, I've gone down the reasoning path. Addressed the situation. Had a conversation, as they say.'

I had a sudden mental picture of Dylan, in his bed, trying to reason with his penis.

C'mon, old fella. Don't do this to me. Maggie is a nice lady. I'm sure you'll like her when you meet her.

I shook away the mental image.

'Do you think a counsellor would help?' asked Dylan.

Another unexpected vision popped into my head. Dylan on a therapist's couch. Trousers down. Therapist addressing said penis.

'Now then, Mr Willy. I appreciate this is difficult for you. After all, the subject isn't one that can be raised easily.'

Oh God, stop it, Maggie.

'I'm sure a counsellor is a good starting point,' I assured.

'Perhaps the counsellor could then potentially speak to a doctor on my behalf.'

'Can't you see the doctor yourself? I mean, it's nothing to be ashamed of. No biggie.' *Oops. An unfortunate choice of words there, Maggie.* 'I mean, why don't you tell the doctor yourself,' I said hastily. I adopted a silly voice to lighten the mood. 'Hey, doc! I need some medication to put a twinkle in my wrinkle.' Best to joke about it. Keep the topic light.

From the other end of the line came a stunned silence.

'Er, I think we may be at cross purposes, Maggie.'

Eh? Now it was my turn to go silent. Had I got the wrong end of the stick?

More puns, Maggie?

Oh dear. This was nothing to do with impotency and everything to do with my first worry. Dylan didn't want to see me anymore. Unlike a coward, he didn't want to send a dump text, preferring to do it face-to-face.

'The problem I have, Maggie' – Dylan continued – 'is to do with my sister-in-law.'

Ah, Jill. The woman who'd given me dark looks at Terry's wedding.

'What about her?' I asked in a small voice.

Dylan didn't miss a beat.

'She's living with me.'

Chapter Forty-Seven

'W–What?' I stammered.

My world tipped on its axis. Jill was living with Dylan? *My* Dylan. Except… except he wasn't my Dylan. And, let's face it, he never had been. Not in the proper sense.

A part of me couldn't accept what he was saying, and yet I instinctively knew it was the truth. This explained so much. Why Dylan had never properly kissed me. Why he'd never invited me back to his place.

His words echoed in my brain. *It started not long after I met you.* I inhaled sharply. Wow, bummer or what.

Still, better to find out now than months later. I was annoyed for believing the tosh about Jill having the hots for Dylan and him putting her straight. Lies!

'I see,' I said coolly. 'Well, better to find out now, than later.'

'You sound miffed,' said Dylan.

I shut my eyes. After the day I'd had so far, I wasn't in the mood for keeping my feelings to myself any longer.

'Yes, Dylan. I am a taddy miffed,' I said in my best schoolmarm voice.

'You see,' he sighed. 'This was why I wanted to talk to you face-to-face.'

'It wouldn't have made a scrap of difference,' I said crisply. 'I'm not up for seeing a man who is co-habiting with another woman.'

'I'm being open and honest with you,' Dylan protested. 'I told you how Jill felt about me.'

'There's one small detail you left out.'

'Oh?'

'You omitted to tell me how you felt about her.'

'I did not,' Dylan protested. 'I want nothing to do with the woman.'

'So why is she sharing your house?'

I'd been about to add *and your bed*, but my emotions were starting to get the better of me and my voice had cracked. Dylan must have heard.

'I told you before, Maggie, and I'll say it again. There is nothing going on between Jill and me.'

'Then why…'

I clamped my mouth shut.

'Why haven't I taken our relationship further?' Dylan finished the sentence for me. 'That's what you were about to say, wasn't it?

'Yes,' I admitted, after a small silence.

'Because I felt awkward. I wanted to be transparent with you about Jill being in my house. After all, if I gave you a thorough kissing only to wave you off on my doorstep, wouldn't you be rather perplexed?'

'Obviously,' I said irritably, still not understanding where this conversation was going.

'After all' – Dylan pointed out – 'I could hardly ask you

to come in with Madam in situ. You'd have wondered what the hell was going on, especially if Jill had kicked off. Likewise, if I'd stayed over at yours, I'd have felt guilty about you not knowing about the situation under my roof. I'm at my wits' end. Jill asked to stay over for Terry's wedding, and I said yes. However, she found my spare house key and took it. After our brunch date, I came home to find her unpacking a suitcase of clothes. As I said, she's been here ever since.'

'You mean… she's refusing to leave?'

'Yes!' Dylan exclaimed.

'Oh,' I said. This put a different complexion on things.

'I honestly thought Jill would have tired of this charade by now and left. It's because she hasn't, that I'm now forced to have this conversation with you. I'm so sorry I didn't tell you earlier. But I never thought I'd be in this ridiculous situation all these weeks later.'

'It's fine,' I sighed, hugely relieved. 'Thank you for telling me. I had been a bit puzzled. I thought you'd had a change of heart and were…'

I trailed off. Suddenly it seemed a bit silly to say *going off me.*

'Maggie, my feelings for you haven't cooled in the slightest. Rather, they've intensified. You're a wonderful woman. I never thought I'd feel this way again. I'm not going to start making declarations because I don't want to frighten you off. But trust me, Maggie, you make my heart sing.'

'Oh,' I said, grinning foolishly.

I sat there with a goofy expression on my face. Me, a woman in her sixties, made this gorgeous man's heart sing! I felt something stir in my heart. Like a fanfare of trumpets, or a choir singing *Hallelujah* at top volume.

A thought occurred to me. Could Jill overhear this conversation?

'Where are you?' I asked.

'At work. I didn't want Jill eavesdropping,' he said, echoing my thoughts.

'I don't know what to suggest,' I said, shaking my head.

'And I don't know what to do,' Dylan countered. 'She's Jennifer's sister. I can hardly chuck Jill out on the streets.'

'I have an idea!' I sat up straight, a forefinger shooting up in the air. 'Wait for her to go out, then change your locks.'

'That thought had crossed my mind. However, until I go to work, she's there, by my side. Like glue. She greets me like a wife when I get home. "Hello, honey. I've cooked a nice roast dinner and there's a bottle of wine chilling in the fridge." The whole situation is absurd. Nor does Terry know about this. I don't want her getting stressed. She told me today that she's expecting a honeymoon baby–'

'Oh, Dylan! That's wonderful news,' I said, unable to stop myself from gushing. 'Your first grandchild. Yes, I can understand why you don't want to burden Terry.'

'Exactly,' Dylan sighed. 'So that's why I thought of a counsellor. To see what advice they might give. Maybe that person could pop round. Talk to Jill. Persuade her to go home.'

I chewed my lip thoughtfully.

'You know, a few years ago I read an article about a houseguest who refused to leave. From what I can remember, and from what you've told me, Jill is trespassing. Call the police. Tell them.'

'Oh, but, Maggie, I've already done that. They weren't as helpful as you would think. They asked if Jill had her own key. I said yes, and that it had been acquired dishonestly. That was when they said that a keyholder can claim to be a tenant. It would be my word against hers that she was staying unlawfully.'

'Oh, Dylan,' I breathed. This situation sounded intolerable.

'Apparently' – he was starting to sound exasperated – 'a tenant can't be removed from a property without a court order for eviction. However, the police were helpful in other areas. They told me to make her stay as uncomfortable as possible. Jill can't bear Charlie. She calls him a smelly mongrel. But other than my beloved dog, I can't think how else to provoke her into leaving.'

'I can,' I said. 'Although you might not like it.'

'I'm open to all suggestions.'

'Move into your nursing home. Is there a spare room?'

'Not currently, although one of our lovely residents looks like she's on her way out. But how long is a piece of string?'

'I have another idea.' My brain was racing, and my heart was starting to flutter with nerves. 'It sounds a bit mad… incredibly crazy… a quick-fix solution…'

'What?' said Dylan, sounding perplexed. As well he might.

I took a deep breath. Closed my eyes.

'Move in with me.'

Chapter Forty-Eight

There was a long silence as Dylan digested my words.

My hand immediately fluttered to my mouth. Oh Lord. What had I said? But it was done now. I couldn't unsay it.

Moving in with me might resolve Dylan's immediate problem with Jill, but it could potentially create two issues for me.

First, the kids.

I mentally flushed to my roots at the thought of my children's faces when they next came over for Sunday dinner. Dylan sitting at the head of the table – once Greg's place. Ella, trying not to look irked, while Ruby threw Tim a questioning look.

I thought you said Mum and this Dylan dude were just companions?

Tim volleying back a shrug.

How was I to know this man would move in? Anyway, don't worry, Rubes. If they ARE having sex, it's likely to be infrequently.

Ruby raising her eyebrows.

Infrequently – is that one word or two?

Second, my parents.

Both were old-fashioned enough not to approve of a

live-in lover, especially if they found out I'd only known Dylan not quite three months.

'Shame on you, Maggie.' I could already hear my father's voice in my head. 'I can't believe my daughter has shacked up with another man.'

'Isn't *shacking up* what teenagers do?' This from my mother. 'Oooh, Maggie! Does this mean you're a teenager again? In which case, I can't be ninety-one years old. Shame on YOU, Trevor King, for having me believe otherwise.'

Cue my mother walloping Dad with her handbag. My father, bristling with hostility, then getting to the crux of his fury. For what he'd really want to know was how this new situation would affect him and Mum.

'What about *us*, Maggie?' he'd rant. '*We* are the ones who should have moved in with you.'

Maybe I shouldn't tell the family. Perhaps I could get away with it if I banished Dylan every time the family came over. I had a mental picture of shooing Dylan out the back door.

'Sorry, darling. I know it's pouring with rain and – oh dear, yes that was a clap of thunder – but never mind! Look what I've got for you. A Captain Birdseye sou'wester and matching hat! That's it, pop them both on. Oh, perfect. Yes, you do look a bit like Paddington Bear, but never mind. Off you go. Bye-*eee*.'

And then I'd slam the door on Dylan only to find Charlie sitting at my feet wondering why Daddy had gone for walkies without him. How would I explain the presence of a second dog?

Tim: *Another* dog, Mum?

Ruby: There's a medical name for people who rescue lots of dogs.

Ella: Yeah, it's called a *Rover*dose.'

My thoughts fragmented as Dylan finally spoke.

'Maggie,' he said tenderly. 'I truly appreciate your offer. But I'm not going to take you up on it. This is my problem. Not yours.'

'Okay,' I said, feeling a mixture of both regret and relief.

'However, your suggestion has given me a lightbulb moment. I don't know why I didn't think of it before. I'm going to rent something. A place that's dog friendly. After all, it might take a few months to resolve this matter. Also, there's a local firm, Gardener and Stewart Solicitors, who have a good reputation. I'll give them a ring and make an appointment.'

'I know the firm,' I said. 'My father is one of their clients. I also know of Gabe Stewart, one of the partners. He married Wendy Walker who lived in the village with her first husband. Derek Walker was rather–'

'Peculiar.' Dylan finished my sentence. 'Yes, thanks to the gossips, I did hear about Wendy's bit of bother. I think Gabe is the divorce lawyer. It's the other chappie I'll see. He can sort out Jill's eviction order.'

'Just remember, Dylan, that if you get stuck, my offer remains.'

'I truly appreciate your kindness, darling,' said Dylan softly. 'And maybe one day…'

He trailed off, leaving the words unspoken. Even so, they hovered in the air.

Maybe one day, we will move in together.

'However, before that ever happens' – Dylan's voice took on a playful tone – 'I need to get around to the matter of holding you tight and giving you ten thousand kisses.'

I squirmed deliciously on the sofa.

'It certainly is a little overdue,' I said teasingly.

'In which case' – Dylan's voice had taken on a suggestive tone – 'now that you know the situation, and a cunning plan has been devised, how about I take you out for a romantic dinner on Saturday evening?'

'Only dinner?' I said mischievously.

'Did you have something else in mind?' said Dylan, feigning innocence.

'I most certainly did,' I said huskily.

God, this was thrilling. I was zinging all over the place and Dylan wasn't even here. Heaven help me when we did finally go to bed together. The duvet might go up in flames.

'Are you suggesting I bring my toothbrush?' said Dylan, sotto voce.

'Go mad,' I whispered. 'Bring your pyjamas too.'

'I have two more confessions,' said Dylan. Oh God. What now? But I needn't have worried. 'First, I will have to bring Charlie with me.'

'That's fine. He can sleep downstairs with Bess. What's the other thing?'

'I don't wear pyjamas,' Dylan whispered.

Zinggg.

Chapter Forty-Nine

The following morning, I was up with the sparrows. Bess needed walking before the temperature soared.

We enjoyed an hour's stroll along the village's meandering lanes. Together we took footpaths across fields of grazing sheep, then picked up a trail that led to the woods. I'd now walked here many times with Dylan and Charlie. The café had yet to open and the woodland trail at this hour was somewhat lonely.

Retracing my steps, I skirted the tree-lined paths and instead walked through the neighbouring village of Vigo, before heading back to Little Waterlow.

Once home, Bess flopped into her basket and snoozed while I caught up with paperwork and admin. I then had a quick shower and slipped into a cotton dress. I was taking the parents out shortly.

'Be a good girl for Mummy,' I said to Bess. 'I'll be back after lunch.'

Blowing her a kiss, and feeling faintly ridiculous for doing so, I let myself out of the house. Since becoming a dog owner, I now understood that a hound was much more than a hairy beast. Bess was a family member. Another daughter – albeit in black-and-tan form.

Humming to myself, I hopped in the car. Within minutes Little Waterlow was behind me, and I'd joined the M20.

I wondered – if Greg were still alive – how he'd feel about Bess. Would he love her, like I did? But then again, if Greg hadn't died, I wouldn't have adopted a dog. I knew he would have been unimpressed with the lawn. Thanks to the garden being my girl's loo, the grass sported several brown rings. I had no idea why a dog's wee caused such damage. A part of me was glad Bess couldn't cock a leg. I'd take a shrivelled lawn over dead shrubs.

Morning, Mags, said Greg in my head.

'I was just thinking about you,' I said aloud.

I know. And, yes, I have noticed the marks on the lawn.

'Ah, sorry.' I pulled a face. 'In the beginning, I used to rush about with a watering can, sprinkling where Bess had been. However, I can't police every wee my girl has.'

Don't worry about it. I think she's a lovely dog.

'She is, isn't she!' I beamed.

A driver overtook me. As he passed, he glanced my way, then gave me a strange look. One that said I was possibly a bit bonkers.

'What?' I said, as the driver accelerated past. 'Haven't you ever seen a woman talking to herself before?'

It's okay to talk to yourself, said Greg. He then chuckled. *It's when you ask yourself to repeat something that you have a problem.*

'Ha!' I laughed. 'Very good.'

246

For a moment neither of us spoke. Ahead, a lorry pulled into the middle lane. The vehicle was struggling to overtake a car-transporter. I signalled and manoeuvred into the fast lane, swiftly overtaking both vehicles, before returning to a clear inside lane.

'You still there?' I said aloud.

I'm here, said Greg.

'When are you going to send me that sign? I've now asked you several times. Have you forgotten our pact? Whoever died first was meant to send the other a red balloon.'

I know, I know. I'm sorry. I've been busy.

I rolled my eyes.

'Doing what exactly? Chatting up a few angels?'

Funny! I haven't yet seen anyone here wearing halos.

'Hmm,' I mused. 'Do people – or souls – hook up over there?'

Are you worried that I'm going to go off with someone else, Greg teased.

'Well, now that you've mentioned it…'

I frowned. That was a point. What happened in the afterlife – assuming there was one and I wasn't a candidate for a straitjacket? Did husbands and wives still hang out with each other?

I'd taken it for granted that Greg and I would one day be together again. But what if my fledging relationship with Dylan turned into the real deal? What happened when *our* time was up? Would I arrive at the Pearly Gates to find two men slugging it out on who would spend Eternity with me?

And what about Jennifer? Would Dylan's deceased wife roll up too?

My thoughts turned to Dylan. I was keen on the guy. In the middle of a full-blown crush. But love? Did I love Dylan? I had a sneaking feeling I was *falling* in love. I'd tried not to think too much about it. After all those years of being married to Greg … of raising a family with him… to think of a future with another man was *huge*.

As yet, Dylan and I had skirted around the *love* word. I knew he was keen on me. Last night's phone conversation had confirmed that. And there was a huge anticipation about Saturday night. Not because we would be sleeping together for the first time, but also – in my book – the act was a physical demonstration of having deep feelings for someone.

Or was I, perhaps, terribly naïve? Maybe most women of my age were happy to simply bed hop and have one-night stands. I sighed. The truth was, I didn't know. Why were relationships so complicated?

Wow, that's an awful lot of thoughts going through your mind, said Greg.

'Stop eavesdropping,' I said mildly.

I wasn't. To answer one of those thoughts, yes, one day we will see each other again. And that is because of love. To keep things simple, you always see whoever you love. So, if you fall in love with Dylan, you will see him too. As regards to relationships… well, it's different here, Mags. When you get here, you'll understand. For now, get on with living your life.

'Okay,' I nodded. 'And what about my red balloon?'

I'm working on it.

'Really?' My heart gladdened and for a moment I felt giddy with happiness. 'I shall keep my eyes peeled.'

Stop looking, said Greg. *It's only then that you will see it.*

And telling myself that, for now, I'd have to be satisfied with that answer, I toggled the left indicator. The car shot up the slip road and left the motorway.

Chapter Fifty

'Where are we going?' said Mum.

'To see a solicitor,' I said, for the umpteenth time in five minutes.

We were in the bedroom. My mother was still in her nightdress and refusing to take it off. Meanwhile, my father's temper was rapidly fraying.

'DEIRDRE,' he bellowed. 'Stop prevaricating and GET SOME RUDDY CLOTHES ON.'

'Don't you shout at me, Trevor King,' Mum glowered. 'Nobody ever tells me what's going on around here. If I'd have known we were going out, I'd have been ready. Instead, you didn't tell me, and so I'm not.' She shot him a defiant look. 'Where are we going?' she repeated.

'To see a solicitor,' I said through gritted teeth. 'Seriously, Mum, can you just do as I ask and get some clothes on, otherwise Dad will miss his appointment.'

'What appointment?'

'The solicitor's appointment,' I intoned, moving over to Mum's wardrobe. 'We are going to see a solicitor.' I rummaged within the cupboard. 'You need to get dressed.' I flipped through garments and extracted a dress. 'We are seeing a solicitor.' I walked towards Mum with determination. 'You need to get dressed. And you need to get dressed because we are seeing a solicitor.' I handed Mum the dress. 'We have a solicitor's appointment. You need to get dressed. And you need to get dressed because we're seeing a solicitor. Get dressed. We have an appointment. To see a solicitor. You need to get–'

Mum snatched the dress from me.

'Shut up, Maggie. You sound like a blithering idiot.'

Hurrah. My repetitive diatribe had penetrated her fuzzy brainbox and fired a neurological pathway. The lights were momentarily on. The action of getting dressed was about to take place.

We arrived at Gardener and Stewart's offices with literally a minute to spare.

A kind receptionist greeted us. Dad was using two canes and Mum was hanging on to her walker. Together, we moved at a snail's pace along a carpeted corridor. The receptionist tapped on a door and indicated we go in. Moments later we were greeted by one of the firm's legal executives.

'Good morning, everyone.' A little apple dumpling of a lady twinkled at us all. She was sitting behind a huge desk. 'I'm Judy Tiller. Do take a seat.'

Dad sat down heavily on one of the three available chairs. However, instead of sitting alongside him, Mum unexpectedly sank down on her walker's seat. As the handbrakes weren't on, it shot backwards, and sent Dad's canes crashing to the floor.

'Oooh,' screeched Mum. 'My chair has wheels. Help!'

I grabbed the handlebars, steered my mother so that she was facing Judy, and deployed the brakes.

'Sorry,' I muttered. 'Wasn't expecting her to do that.'

'No worries,' said Judy. She looked at Mum. 'Would you like to sit on a chair?'

'Whatever for?' Mum frowned. 'I already have one.'

The solicitor looked perplexed. As well she might. I caught her eye.

'Dementia,' I mouthed.

'Ah,' said Judy.

'What are you two whispering about?' said Mum, her eyes narrowing.

Oh, how I hated this. How I abhorred this condition. The endless repetition. The moments of paranoia. The whole damned awkwardness and frustration of this ongoing situation.

'Nothing, Mum,' I reassured.

'Nothing what?' she said, looking surprised. Already her question had been forgotten.

'Right,' said Judy. She steepled her fingers together. 'It's lovely to meet you all.' She turned to Dad. 'Mr King, some years ago you and your wife each made a Power of Attorney. I have the copies here. However, the documents were never registered. This is vital if you want to act for someone in certain legal, financial, personal, or medical spheres of life and' – she smiled at Mum before conveying a look at Dad – 'I suggest that time is now.'

My mother was so confused at the pace of the meeting, thankfully, she fell silent. She spoke up again when the receptionist returned with a tray bearing four cups of black coffee, a jug of milk and a bowl of sugar cubes. The meeting ground to a halt while my mother added increasing amounts of sugar to her coffee. After stirring in the seventh lump, she proclaimed the drink still wasn't sweet enough. I had an overwhelming urge to tip the whole lot into her cup.

The meeting eventually continued. Judy went through the relevant paperwork. She explained that, post-Covid, for some reason registration of the documents would take months rather than weeks. She said we'd have to be patient.

She then turned to the matter of the parents' Wills.

'Now then, Mr King. You wanted to renew your Will. That's fine, but regrettably your wife won't be able to renew hers due to losing capacity.'

Mum's head shot up.

'Who's lost capacity?' she demanded.

'No one,' I said placatingly.

I then stared at my mother in dismay. She'd been quietly occupying herself by putting the remaining sugar cubes in Judy's cup. The drink was now a semi-mush of caramel and gold.

'Let me take that from you,' I said, removing the cup and its sugar mountain. I set it to one side. 'Sorry,' I mumbled to Judy.

'It couldn't matter less,' she said, before turning back to my father. 'Meanwhile, I took the liberty of reviewing the Wills you both made in 2018. Frankly, I can't see why you would want to change them. Is there a specific reason?'

'Well, I thought it prudent. You see, my other

daughter, Freya, got married for the fourth time. Her name has changed again.'

'That won't affect anything,' Judy assured. 'A change of surname doesn't invalidate the document.'

'Oh,' said Dad in surprise. 'That's good to know. In which case, we'll leave things as they are.'

'I think that's wise,' Judy smiled. 'Before we wrap up our meeting, is there anything else I can help with?'

'Can I trouble you to take two photocopies of the Wills?' asked Dad. 'I'd like my daughters to each have a copy.'

'Certainly,' said Judy. 'Would you like me to post a copy to your other daughter, Mr King?'

'If it's no trouble,' said Dad.

'Of course we can do that for you.' Judy stood up. 'I'll do the copies right now. Won't be a mo.'

I'd never seen a copy of my parents' Wills. Dad had always opined that such a document was private. That it shouldn't be revealed until the person had demised. I looked at him curiously.

'Why have you decided to give Freya and me copies of your Will, Dad?'

He shrugged.

'I'm ninety-two, Maggie. I could leave this planet at any moment. It seems a bit daft to continue being secretive. However, I'll keep the originals here, with Judy, for safekeeping.'

'Of course.' I gave Dad's hand a squeeze. 'I appreciate that. And thank you for reviewing your affairs today. It's a depressing task that none of us particularly like to face.'

Dad grunted.

'I've had my head buried in the sand,' he admitted. 'I'm aware of that now. We all think we're immortal. But, after that business with your Greg, well…' He trailed off. No further words were required. 'Anyway.' He cleared his throat. 'Our Wills are straightforward. Mum and I have left everything to each other. When we're both gone, whatever is left is to be divided up between our children and grandchildren.'

'Thanks, Dad,' I said softly.

His eyes briefly watered as he smiled at me.

'Enough of this talk of death,' he said gruffly. 'I'm looking forward to our lunch.'

'Me too,' I agreed, giving his hand another squeeze.

'And as the Grim Reaper isn't calling by today, I'll have a double gin and tonic to go with it.'

Chapter Fifty-One

Taking my parents out to dinner was always hard work.

Trying to make sure my father didn't lose his balance while directing my mother's walker, was tricky.

Frankly, it should have been my father using the walker and my mother sitting in a wheelchair. However, due Dad's stubbornness, it was best to give in and let him use his sticks rather than nothing at all.

Part of my father's refusal to use a walker was due to his crush on one of the waitresses. He wanted to appear as a man who might be a little stooped but who was otherwise a virile silver fox. Indeed, Dad was a man with a twinkle in his cataracts and a fine line in flirtatious patter.

If my children believed having a relationship at my age was rather *ewww,* heaven knows what they'd have thought if they'd seen their grandfather in action.

Heads always turned when we clattered into the restaurant. This was mainly due to my father's sticks hitting people's legs as his eyes sought the object of his desire.

My mother was a different matter. She staggered inside, breathless from exertion, all the while shrieking, "Where am I going?" before crashing her walker into chairs and diners alike.

By the time we were seated at a table – walking paraphernalia stowed to one side – I felt as if I'd run a marathon.

A beaming blonde woman approached our table. A badge pinned to her ample bosom informed everyone that her name was Gemma. Dad's eyes lit up.

'How are my favourite customers?' said Gemma, handing out three menus.

'We're all very well, thank you,' I said with a smile.

'And all the better for seeing you, my darling,' said Dad, patting Gemma on the bottom.

She looked momentarily startled, then took a discreet step to one side.

'What are we all having to drink?' she asked.

Dad batted his eyelashes coquettishly.

'Double gin and tonic. Tell me, dear girl. Would you be allowed to join us?'

'Er, Dad, Gemma is working,' I pointed out.

'Oh, you're so sweet,' said Gemma, playing along. 'But I don't think my boss would approve.'

'Nonsense,' said Dad. 'Tell your boss to sod off. How dare he refuse my favourite girl a break.'

'Ha, ha,' tinkled Gemma, unsure how to respond.

Whenever around her, Dad always behaved like a lovestruck schoolboy. Recently, however, it had started to get embarrassing.

'I'll have a Prosecco, please,' I said quickly. 'And Mum will have a tonic water.'

'Coming right up,' said Gemma.

'That's my girl,' Dad cackled. He lunged sideways and caught hold of Gemma's hand. 'At my age, those words are magic to my ears. A woman who comes quickly. Ah ha ha ha!'

There was a stunned pause. Omigod. *What* had my father just said? He'd well and truly crossed the line between flirting and smutty innuendo. Gemma and I exchanged a frozen smile before she turned and hastened off.

I rounded furiously on my father.

'What the bloody hell are you playing at?' I spluttered.

'What?' said my mother, snapping out of her stupor. 'What's going on?'

'Nothing,' I muttered, while glaring at my father. 'Behave, please.'

'I don't know what you mean,' said my father nonchalantly. 'I was simply making conversation with our waitress.'

'Was he flirting?' said Mum, her eyes narrowing.

'No,' I lied.

The last thing I needed was my mother kicking off in public. It was bad enough that she thought my father was having affairs with their doctor, the postmistress, and all the checkout girls at the supermarket, never mind our waitress.

My mother reeled her neck back in and disappeared behind her menu.

'And stop being so touchy-feely with Gemma,' I hissed.

'Oh leave me alone, Maggie,' Dad retorted. 'Take one of your chill pills. I'm simply having a bit of fun.'

I pursed my lips and studied my own menu. However,

I noticed when Gemma returned to take our orders, she stood next to me, rather than my father.

Likewise, when Gemma brought our meals to the table and, later, cleared the plates, she was stationed at arm's length from my father. He, in turn, was put out at having his *fun* halted.

When I eventually drove the parents back to theirs, it set me wondering what my father had been like as a young man. In his youth, he'd been a good-looking guy. I could still remember, as a child, how my mother had accused him of having affairs. To this day I had no idea if he'd ever messed Mum about. I was momentarily tempted to ask him, but then dismissed the notion.

Sometimes secrets were best left alone.

Chapter Fifty-Two

When Saturday morning rolled around, I awoke with a huge sense of anticipation. I had no wedding work to oversee. The day had yet to get underway. Right now it was warm, golden, and full of possibilities.

This was the day that Dylan and I were – finally – taking our relationship to the next level. Or whatever one called it when you were a sixty-one-year-old having a second chance at romance.

Once again, I walked Bess early, before the temperature rose. A thorough vacuuming of the house then took place. Finally, I stripped my bed.

Fresh sheets, Maggie, I chortled to myself.

As I bundled up the old linen, I caught sight of Greg's photographs on the dressing table. I froze.

'Sorry, darling,' I apologised. 'But I'm going to have to put you away.' My late husband remained silent as I gathered up the various frames. 'You see, I can't have you staring at me and Dylan later on.'

The silence prevailed.

I carefully stashed the photographs in a drawer, then instantly felt disloyal.

Don't be daft, Maggie, said my inner voice. *You're a*

widow. You've already established that you're allowed to move on.

Absolutely.

Nonetheless, something felt off.

I paused; my arms still full of the bundled-up linen. I looked at the bed. The *marital* bed. No man, other than Greg, had ever slept on that bed alongside me. I wasn't entirely sure I could let Dylan sleep in this room. It felt … wrong. No, not wrong. More… weird. Perhaps, later, I'd lead Dylan into one of the kids' bedrooms instead.

Back in the day, when the children were growing up, they'd all had their own bedrooms. Each room had been big enough to take a small double bed.

I now opened the door to Tim's old bedroom. It had long been emptied of childhood things, but his old duvet remained the same. A no-nonsense navy-and-white affair.

I stared at Tim's bed. In the corner of my mind, I could picture my son. Standing over there. Wagging a finger with disapproval. Nope. I couldn't bring Dylan in here.

It was the same when I went into the girls' old bedrooms. There was Ruby. Hovering like Moaning Myrtle, the Muggle-born witch at Hogwarts.

Oooooh, Motherrrr! Put your clothes on NOWWWWW!

Ella too.

Mum! Why can't you take up crocheting like other wrinklies?

I reversed out onto the landing. Took stock. Returned to the marital bedroom. Dumping the dirty linen, on impulse I rearranged everything within.

That was better! Now the bed was on *this* wall instead of *that* wall. The dressing table was *here* instead of *there*. And the wardrobes... well, the wardrobes had to stay put due to them being fitted. But at least the room looked different. Less like the room I'd shared with my late husband.

I then removed all the prints on the wall and, on a whim, nipped off to Bluewater shopping mall. I returned home with brand new linen and complimentary artwork for the walls.

By the time I'd finished, hours and hours had passed. However, the bedroom was transformed. Perhaps I should, at some point, repaint it too? But at least, psychologically, I could now handle bringing Dylan in here.

I glanced at the new clock over the dressing table. It was time to get ready for my dinner date.

I disappeared into the shower, washed my hair, and soaped myself from head to toe. Afterwards, I covered myself in a hideously expensive body lotion used only for special occasions. Mm. Lovely. I rubbed some of it into my cheeks too, taking care to avoid my eyes. In which case, would that be *moist-your-eyes*?

I gave my pits a double dose of body spray and then, sneezing violently, got to work with the hairdryer. Twenty minutes later, my red mop had been transformed into a waterfall of titian waves. They curled over my shoulders and down my back.

Finally, I put on new lacy lingerie that I'd also grabbed

while at Bluewater. After three pregnancies, my knickers had more elastic than my belly. Distraction strategies were therefore required.

Oh yes, I was pulling out all the stops. New bedroom. New bedding. New undies. New dress. And all for the new man in my life. I made some overexcited squeaking noises, then told myself to calm down.

With a slightly trembling hand, I applied my makeup, then zipped myself into a new dress – yes, something else I'd impulsively bought. The garment was easy to get off. A case of it slithering to the floor, rather than hopping about with a foot caught up in clothing. Tonight was all about seduction.

The fact that I was horribly out of practice was neither here nor there.

Chapter Fifty-Three

'You look stunning,' said Dylan, as I opened the door to him and Charlie.

'Thank you.' I grinned foolishly, trying not to salivate at the sight of my man. 'You don't look too bad yourself,' I bantered.

He was dressed in chinos and a shirt that was undone 'just so'. Very… Man at C & A.

You're showing your age, Maggie, Greg snorted. *He's more David Gandy at M & S.*

I stiffened. Oh no. Tonight was not a night to imagine Greg talking to me.

I was passing through, he assured. *Just wanted to wish you a lovely evening. And by the way, you look gorgeous. Dylan is a lucky man.*

Thanks, darling, I mentally replied, but I was talking to myself. Greg had gone.

Meanwhile, Charlie was noisily greeting Bess. She was wagging her tail but also giving the mongrel's ears soft nips, as if to rein in his overexcitement at being in new surroundings.

'I'll let the dogs out for a quick wee,' I said. 'And then we'll be off. Come on you two,' I instructed. 'Heel!'

'That's it,' said Dylan, bringing up the rear. 'You tell Charlie who's boss. Your house. Your rules.'

I opened the back door and the dogs bounded out. For a moment they frolicked playfully together, then Bess watered her favourite patch of lawn. This particular area now resembled burnt toast. Charlie cocked a leg over a rosebush. I wondered if the flowers would wilt, and the petals fall to the floor. Time would tell.

'You have a gorgeous garden,' said Dylan, as we waited for the dogs to return. 'And a lovely home, too.'

'Thanks,' I said. 'Although the house is too big now. I suppose I should think about moving. Downsize. Declutter. I've yet to find the right moment.'

Dylan nodded his understanding.

'There has to be a period of adjustment.'

'You're right,' I agreed. 'I went from empty nest to widowhood in swift succession. A big upheaval.'

'How's the heart?' he asked.

'Surprisingly good,' I smiled. 'What about yours?'

'In these last few months' – his eyes snagged on mine – 'it's been coming along nicely.'

'Pleased to hear it,' I said softly.

The moment was broken by Charlie discovering Mr Squirrel on the lawn. He grabbed the toy, then belted in through the open doorway with Bess in hot pursuit. They shot into the lounge with lots of playful growling.

'Right you Herbert,' said Dylan, taking the toy off Charlie. 'Settle down. You too, Bess. Your parents are going out for the evening and we don't want any nonsense.'

I suppressed a giggle-snort.

'Quite right,' I added. 'Don't raid the biscuit tin. No lolling about on the sofas. And don't squabble over the remote control.'

Charlie looked at me quizzically, while Bess yawned. She ambled over to her basket, then collapsed into it with a contented groan. A second later and Charlie had flopped down beside her. He put his nose on his paws and regarded us mournfully.

'Be good,' said Dylan sternly. He turned to me, eyes twinkling. 'Meanwhile, Maggie, your conveyance awaits.'

'Conveyance, eh?' I laughed. 'I do hope it's a brand-new Bentley with sumptuous leather interior.'

'Regrettably not,' he chuckled. 'It's a BMW that's been through the carwash and also had the dog hair removed.'

'That sounds most acceptable,' I said, affecting a posh accent. 'Do lead the way, my good man.'

Chapter Fifty-Four

Dylan was old-fashioned enough to open the passenger door for me.

I sank into the depths of the BMW and tucked my legs in. As he walked around to the driver's side, my mobile began to ring.

'Is that you or me?' asked Dylan, as he started up the engine.

'Definitely me,' I said, rummaging within my bag.

A glance at the screen told me the caller was Freya. Uh–oh. That could mean only one thing. She was after me going over to Mum and Dad's.

I felt a flash of irritation. No, I wasn't complying. Not tonight. I'd spoken to Dad earlier when I'd been at Bluewater. He'd insisted all was well.

I sent my sister's call to voicemail, then switched the phone to silent. There were going to be no interruptions by Freya or anyone else this evening. The only person claiming my attention tonight was the man sitting by my side.

I suppressed a shiver of excitement. Dylan noticed.

'Cold?' he asked.

'Hardly,' I shook my head. 'Not in the middle of July.' I wasn't going to confess the real reason behind that quiver.

Delicious anticipation. 'It was one of those moments where you could say someone had walked over your grave. That's a very strange expression when you stop to think about it. I wonder where it came from.'

'Folklore probably,' said Dylan.

My phone began to vibrate within my handbag.

'You're popular this evening,' said Dylan.

'Indeed,' I frowned. 'Excuse me for a sec.'

I peered at the screen. Freya again.

'It's my sister,' I said, unable to hide my irritation.

Once again I sent her call to voicemail.

'Problem?' he asked.

'Unlikely.' I shook my head. 'After all, she hasn't left a message.'

With that, the phone lit up with a WhatsApp notification. I briefly caught sight of Freya's message before the screen went dark.

Where the bloody hell are you, Maggie? I have a bone to pick with you.

I didn't click on the message. I didn't want Freya knowing I'd read it. Otherwise she'd give me a hard time for not picking up. If she wanted a rant about something, it could wait.

Nonetheless, I was perplexed. My sister's choice of words indicated she was aggrieved. I wondered what about. Had I failed to do something for our parents? I mentally checked the parents' calendar entries against my own.

Both parents had recently had dental check-ups. Tick. One had visited the podiatrist. Tick. The other had seen the nurse for a blood test regarding iron levels. Tick. I'd renewed Dad's car insurance. Tick. Organised the car's MOT and service. Tick. Taken Mum to the hairdresser, and Dad to the barber. Tick, tick. I'd also recently driven them both to the next county to visit my uncle – Dad's brother – who was now in a care home. Tick. Finally, there had been that visit to the solicitor to tie up loose ends. Tick.

My conscience was clear. For now, I'd done my bit. Over to you, Freya! Take your *bone of contention* and deal with it!

When my phone began to vibrate for a third time, I switched it off.

'Are you sure you don't want to speak to your sister?' said Dylan. 'After all, it might be important.'

'It really isn't,' I said emphatically. 'Now, never mind Freya,' I smiled. 'Tell me where we're going.'

I let my hand move across the space between us and placed my palm on Dylan's thigh. I resisted the urge to stroke it. But later, I would. Along with other body parts. I mentally hugged myself. Oooh, the anticipation. Of everything. It was so lovely!

'We're heading back to my part of the world,' said Dylan. 'West Malling.'

'What?' I squeaked. 'We won't bump into Jill, will we?'

'No chance,' he laughed. 'I left her in front of the telly. She was prattling on about finding a nice film for us to watch while I went out to get a takeaway. I slipped out with Charlie. Together we made our getaway.'

'Is your overnight bag in the boot?' I asked.

Dylan pointed to the inside pocket of his jacket.

'Toothbrush.' He then patted his jacket's side pocket. 'Clean pants.'

'Is that all you've taken?' I said, eyes wide. 'You're joking, right?'

'Nope.' He shook his head. 'Sadly, I wasn't able to bring a tin of Chum for Charlie.' He gave a deprecating smile. 'Hopefully Bess won't mind sharing her breakfast with him.'

'Yes, that's fine,' I said faintly. Wow. He really had snuck off.

'Sooner or later, Jill will realise Charlie isn't about, but likely presume I've taken him for a walk. It will probably be a couple of hours before she susses that I've done a bunk.'

'It all sounds horribly…' I trailed off.

'Horribly horrible.' Dylan finished my sentence.

'No, I was going to say horribly *domestic.*'

'It really isn't.' Dylan shook his head. 'I'm a free agent with an unwanted houseguest. And, actually, I have some good news. I was going to tell you in the restaurant – we're going to The Swan again by the way – but as the subject has come up, I shall reveal all now.'

And with that Dylan told me all about the two-up-two-down he'd found in the heart of Little Waterlow. Catkin Cottage had been offered to the market for a six-month letting. It was the perfect stopgap for him to rent while Gardener and Stewart Solicitors dealt with Jill's eviction order.

'Catkin Cottage,' I said thoughtfully. 'I know the property. It's chocolate-box pretty and not without a history of drama.'

'Oh?'

'One of the village's biggest rumourmongers lives further along the lane.'

Dylan groaned.

'Don't tell me. Will Mabel Plaistow be a neighbour?'

'Yup,' I said, trying to not giggle. 'She and husband Fred make gossip a national pastime. The owner of Catkin Cottage is a woman called Sophie Fairfax. She now lives in Italy. Mabel told anyone and everyone that Sophie divorced her new husband after he got drunk and his false leg fell off.'

Dylan raised his eyebrows.

'A whole new meaning to getting legless,' he said dryly.

I snorted.

'Sophie was apparently so traumatised, she spent her honeymoon alone.'

'And where was that?'

'The Amalfi Coast.'

'I've been to that part of Italy,' said Dylan. 'It's beautiful. Absolutely stuffed with lemon groves, the likes of which you've never seen.'

'Maybe Sophie felt like a bit of a lemon, because she never returned to England. According to Mabel Plaistow–'

'You do realise that your info is likely highly inaccurate,' Dylan pointed out.

'I'm sure,' I chuckled. 'Nonetheless, according to Mabel Plaistow, Sophie rented the cottage out to someone called

Lottie Lucas.'

'I know that name,' Dylan frowned. 'But I don't know why I know.'

'I can tell you,' I said helpfully. 'Lottie shot to fame as a crime-writer. She wrote one of her bestselling novels at Catkin Cottage. Her books always dominate the Amazon charts. One of them has even been made into a movie.'

'You're right!' Dylan clicked his fingers. 'I've seen the trailer. Looks brilliant too. We'll have to watch it.'

I wriggled with happiness in my seat. It was so good to be making plans with a man again. Just the simple idea of watching a movie together was giving such a thrill.

'Lottie now lives in Cornwall' – I continued – 'but before she left Little Waterlow, Mabel Plaistow did her usual thing and spread rumours. Mabel told anyone who'd care to listen that the reason Lottie could write a good thriller was because she'd killed her ex-husband.'

'Blimey,' Dylan gasped. 'And did she? Please don't tell me I'll be living in a house with a body under the patio.'

'No, silly!' I giggled. 'For a long time, Lottie had no idea where her ex was. I believe he came out of the woodwork when he heard his former wife was suddenly in the money.'

'Ah, a gold digger,' said Dylan. We were now heading along West Malling's High Street. 'Oh look. A spare parking bay. Result!'

The car dipped into the space. Dylan then hastened around the BMW to open the passenger door for me.

'I could get used to this,' I joked, as he helped me out.

He squeezed my hand.

'I hope you do,' he said gruffly. 'Because I'm loving every moment of being with you.'

Chapter Fifty-Five

When it came to eating out, The Swan was West Malling's jewel in the crown. The last time Dylan and I had been here, we'd enjoyed brunch. Tonight, we would be sampling the fine dining.

Our table was covered in crisp linen and polished silver. A jug of roses was centrepiece along with champagne cooling in an ice bucket. The whole thing was romantically set off with flickering candlelight.

'Oh my word,' I said to Dylan. 'This is fabulous. And *bubbly*!' I clapped my hands in delight. 'You've been so extravagant. A bottle of house plonk would have been just as appreciated.'

'Nonsense,' said Dylan. 'Every time I see you, Maggie, it's a celebration. But, tonight – as we both know – is extra special.'

Eeeep! Absolutely. Let the romance begin!

Best to eat first, eh, Maggie! said my inner voice in amusement. *Got to keep up your strength for later.*

That's enough of the smut, I silently retorted.

Although I had to confess, I couldn't wait to unbutton Dylan's shirt. Check out those muscles. I knew he worked out. That he was a bit of a gym bunny. Which was another reason why I'd recently started doing the same – albeit at home, or when out with Bess.

At Trosley Country Park, while Bess exchanged doggy chit-chat with other hounds, I'd been working out on the *Trim Trail*. Here, I'd climbed and dangled off various bits of apparatus that the Council had installed for children and adults alike.

I'd also been on Instagram and checked out some inspirational females. I was now following several women who sported grey hair and pleated cheeks. However, they all had washboard stomachs and the silhouettes of a twenty-year-old. Motivating, or what! Each woman – clad in vibrant *active wear* – had insisted it was never too late to build muscle or rediscover your abs.

At home, Bess had watched, head on one side, as her human mummy had performed tummy crunches, squats, and lunges, before swinging her arms about, all the while clutching tins of baked beans. I couldn't do much about crepey skin, but I could stop my bingo wings from getting bingo wings.

I knew the work was paying off because Ella had made a comment about my arms looking more defined.

'Go you,' she'd said, when I'd told her what I'd been doing. She'd reached for her phone and tapped the Insta app. 'Who are you following?' she'd asked.

I'd looked faintly embarrassed.

'Mainly a ninety-one-year-old woman,' I'd confessed.

'*How* old?' she'd said in disbelief.

I'd then shown Ella the lady in question. An Australian

female who, it had to be said, looked three decades younger than her age – and acted it too. The woman had incredible vitality, an amazing physique, and not a hint of a dowager's hump. I'd deduced that if a great grandma could do press-ups, then I could too.

Also, the lady in question had been mentally sharper than a butcher's block of knives. Given that she was the same age as my mother – who was mentally away with the fairies – I figured that exercise was also good for the brain.

Meanwhile, a camp waiter was hovering. He poured the champers, then took our orders. He gave Dylan a few smoulders accompanied by lots of head tossing and hip wiggling.

'You look beautiful, Maggie,' said Dylan, after the waiter had minced off.

'Thank you,' I beamed. 'I did make a particular effort this evening. Note the lack of muddy walking boots and no sign of a bobbly cardigan.'

'That dress is amazing,' said Dylan. His eyes briefly roved over my body. 'And being a bloke, I haven't the faintest idea what you've done to your hair, but it looks amazing.'

'I employed a heavy-duty dryer and vast barrel-shaped hairbrush. There were a few expletives when the latter got entangled in my hair,' I confessed.

I decided that if the waiter could flirt, then so could I.

'And might I add' – I said huskily – 'that you're looking rather delectable too, my darling.'

'Why thank you.' He inclined his head graciously.

'Sadly, I don't have enough hair to use a barrel-shaped brush.'

'But at least you still have hair,' I pointed out.

'True,' he acknowledged. 'And my own teeth,' he added, with a wink.

'Excellent,' I dimpled. No way was I telling him about my two implants. It had either been that or a *piece* – as my dentist had called the alternative. Yes, a denture. *Quelle horreur!*

'Anyway,' said Dylan. 'To us.'

'To us,' I echoed, grinning from ear to ear.

It felt both right, and yet strange, to make such a toast with another man. I half expected to hear Greg make a comment – if he'd ever truly been there, of course – and was relieved at the inner silence.

I cleared my throat. Fingered the stem of my champagne flute thoughtfully.

'Do you ever…' I trailed off awkwardly.

'Do I ever what?' said Dylan.

There was a long pause while I tried – and failed – to continue.

'Come on, Maggie,' he encouraged. 'Spill the beans.'

I pulled a face.

'I wondered if you ever, in a quiet moment, talk to… if you ever chat to…'

'God?' he asked.

'Er, no. Not God.' I paused. Then gave him a frank look. 'Jennifer.'

For a moment, Dylan looked startled. Then he shifted

awkwardly in his seat.

'As it happens' – he was looking uncomfortable now – 'yes, sometimes I do. Why? Do you talk to Greg?'

I nodded slowly.

'Yeah,' I admitted. 'Now and again. In the beginning I spoke to him all the time. Asked him where he was. What it was like *there*. What he was doing. If he'd seen my grandparents. His parents. Jesus.' I attempted a deprecating laugh, but it came out shrilly. Like that of a bonkers person. 'Do I sound like a nutcase?'

Dylan's mouth quirked, but he shook his head.

'Not at all,' he said quietly. 'I think it's perfectly normal to talk to someone you loved – still love – and tell them about your day. How much you miss them. How you wish they were still here. I guess it's part of the grieving process. On Terry's wedding day, I spoke to Jennifer throughout the entire day. I said, "Wow, that's our daughter getting married. We *made* her. Hasn't she grown into an amazing human being! And stunning with it. We did a great job!" Obviously, I said all that silently. In my head,' he added. 'I didn't want strange looks from the guests.'

'Of course,' I acknowledged. 'And… and…' I faltered.

'Go on. Spit it out.'

'Okay, this sounds daft, but… do you, sometimes… now and again…'

Dylan sighed. Gave me a knowing look.

'You're going to ask if I ever hear Jennifer answering me. Am I right or am I right?'

'You're right,' I said.

278

Now it was Dylan's turn to toy with the stem of his glass. For a moment he didn't say anything. Just stared at his fingers as they twirled the champagne flute this way and that. The pale golden liquid sparkled as the candlelight bounced off the crystal.

'To answer your question, yes. Sometimes I heard her voice in my head.'

I sighed with relief.

'Me too,' I confessed. 'Not Jennifer's voice, obviously,' I added.

He laughed. Then the smile faded, and for a moment he looked serious.

'Are you worried you're a bit… potty?' he asked gently.

'Sometimes. In the beginning, my kids thought I was losing my grip on reality.'

'I suspect it's a coping mechanism. After all, we're not *truly* hearing Jennifer or Greg. It's our brains filling in what we'd like them to say if they were still here.'

I wanted to tell Dylan about the last time we were at The Swan together. How I'd heard Greg tell me that he was going to have some fun with a bragging lad. Take him down a peg or two. How the youngster had ended up with beer slopped down his front. And to suggest that this incident was proof that Greg had been present. But I didn't. Dylan would say it was a fluke. Coincidence. And anyway, it didn't put Greg in a very good light, now I came to think about it. I didn't want Dylan thinking my late husband had been a delinquent.

The subject changed. Dylan spoke of his shock and

delight upon Terry's baby news. That he was astonished that he would soon be a grandfather. Also, that he was looking forward to a fresh start at Catkin Cottage. How Charlie was his best buddy, albeit a bestie with four legs. Small talk. *Wonderful* talk.

The waiter reappeared with our starters. He set it down with a flourish of limp wrists and flared nostrils.

'Enjoy your din-dins,' he said to Dylan, all the while batting his eyelashes.

I reached for the champagne. Dylan had told me to make free. After all, he was driving. And I wasn't one who liked to waste. Especially the bubbly stuff.

The mains were sublime and the dessert delicious. By the time we'd got to the coffee stage, I was feeling extremely mellow. I had one elbow resting on the table, propping up my chin. I gazed dreamily at Dylan. My other hand was enfolded in his. Our fingers were interlocked. He stared deeply into my eyes, while I impersonated the candle – melting all over the place.

We were so preoccupied with each other, neither of us heard the pub door crash back on its hinges or see a woman – eyes scanning diners like a hawk looking for prey – head our way.

Dylan was now playing with my fingers and stroking my palm. Endless zingers were shooting up the underside of my arm causing mini explosions down my spine.

'I am so glad I found you,' Dylan murmured.

'And I'm so glad I've found you too,' shrieked a female voice. 'YOU TOTAL SHIT!'

Chapter Fifty-Six

There was a stunned silence. Diners turned to stare at the blonde woman screeching at the dark-haired man sitting opposite the flabbergasted redhead.

'I wondered where you'd got to,' Jill ranted. She dumped her handbag on the table, then stuck her hands on her hips. 'I had a feeling you were up to no good, so I put a tracker on your car. I thought you'd gone to get a takeaway. When I realised the dog had vanished too, I checked the tracker's notifications. And what did I find? You' – she stabbed a finger at Dylan – 'visiting a property in Little Waterlow and then' – the finger jabbed the air again – 'returning to West Malling. But instead of coming home, you drove here' – the jabbing finger went into overtime – 'with this FLOOZIE!'

'*Excuse* me,' I interrupted. 'But I'm not–'

'Shut up, you partner-pinching TROLLOP!'

My mouth dropped open just as Dylan came to his senses. He sprang to his feet.

'Jill,' he said, voice placating. 'Now is neither the time nor the place–'

'Ay say,' said a plummy-voiced female at the table to my left. 'Ay couldn't help overhearing this lady and ay think' –

she gave Dylan a furious look – 'that you should be thoroughly ay-*shamed* of yourself. You might be a handsome man, but you're also a cad.'

'You tell him,' snarled Jill.

And with that she shoved Dylan hard. He fell backwards into his seat. Without missing a beat, Jill emptied the centrepiece of roses over his lap.

'What the…' Dylan spluttered, as the camp waiter zoomed over.

'Excuse me, madam,' said the waiter, barging past Jill.

Plucking petals from Dylan's crotch, for a moment he looked like he'd died and gone to Heaven.

'Er, thanks,' said Dylan, swatting away both the waiter's hands and wrecked flowers.

'The pleasure was all mine,' gushed the waiter. He turned to Jill. 'Madam, I'm going to have to ask you to leave.'

'I'm going to have to ask you to leave,' Jill mimicked in a silly voice. 'And I'm going to have to refuse,' she growled. 'I want everyone in this restaurant' – her voice rose an octave – 'to know that Dylan Alexander is a lying, cheating, two-faced, devious TWAT.' She took a huge juddering breath, and glared at me. 'As for you' – she jabbed a finger in the air – 'you are a tarty farty witchy bitchy ginger MINGER.' And with that she grabbed the ice bucket and emptied the slush over my head.

The shock had me springing to my feet. I'd had enough of this unjustified public humiliation.

'How dare you,' I gasped, as freezing water dripped

inside my dress. 'This woman' – I told anyone who cared to listen, which was everyone judging by the rapt faces – 'is totally deluded.'

'Bollocks,' shrieked Jill.

Dylan once again attempted to pacify his apoplectic sister-in-law.

'Jill,' he said quietly. 'Please–'

'Ay think it's a bit late to plead for forgiveness,' interrupted Plummy Woman.

'I AM SO UNHAPPY,' bawled Jill, and promptly burst into tears.

All around us came the sound of chuntering. From the overheard snatches of conversation, it was clear that the diners were on Jill's side.

'That poor woman…'

'She's distraught…'

'Just awful…'

'A cheating husband…'

'A shameless mistress…'

And then Jill overplayed her hand. Leaning across Plummy Woman, she grabbed a steak knife.

'Ay say,' Plummy gasped. 'Ay was about to use that.'

'My need is greater than yours,' hissed Jill. She waved the knife in the air. Instinctively, I shrank away. Jill focussed on Dylan. 'I've a good mind to stick this in your throat,' she spat.

The entire restaurant did a collective intake of breath. Someone screamed.

'Don't be silly,' said Dylan calmly.

'Silly?' Jill gave a manic laugh. 'SILLY?' she yelled.

'Madam,' quavered the hovering waiter. He looked like he was about to faint. 'Please, put down–'

'And you can fuck off,' Jill warned. She spun round and pointed the knife at him.

What happened next seemed to take place in slow motion.

Jill turned back to Dylan. Knife raised, she lunged towards him. At the same time, Plummy's dining partner reared up from his seat. He came at Jill from behind. Seizing the deranged woman's raised arm with one hand, he then grabbed her free wrist. Using both momentum and body weight, the two of them crashed down on the floor. The steak knife flew out of Jill's hand. Quick as lightning, the man whipped Jill's wrists behind her back. Holding them in a vice-like grip, he then sat on her.

'Someone call the police,' squealed the waiter.

'I *am* the police,' growled Plummy's partner. 'Albeit off duty. However, I'm perfectly entitled to intervene and uphold the law. Now hurry up and phone for assistance.'

'I'll do it,' I squeaked. I scrabbled in my bag for my mobile, then blanched as I caught sight of a torrent of messages from Freya. Oh God. I'd deal with her later. But as I went to call 999, my hands – still wet from the ice bucket's impromptu delivery – dropped the phone. It skittered off under the table.

'I'll ring them,' said Dylan hastily. He patted his pocket and promptly pulled out a balled-up pair of underpants.

'*Ay* will ring the police,' said Plummy imperiously. She

then proceeded to do so with her pink iPhone.

'Geddoff me,' screeched Jill. She wriggled desperately trying to shake off the hefty off-duty copper. 'Dylan,' she wheedled. 'Tell him I meant no harm.'

'That's not what me and a load of witnesses saw,' barked the copper. 'Sorry, sir' – he looked up at Dylan – 'but I regret to inform you, your wife is going to the police station.'

'She's not my wife,' said Dylan grimly.

Jill's handbag was still on the table, where she'd left it. Dylan reached inside and pulled out a set of keys. Seconds later, he'd reclaimed his spare housekey. He squatted down and spoke to Jill.

'I'm truly sorry it's come to this,' he said, rocking back on his heels. 'But now is as good a time as any to tell you that you are no longer a guest in my home.'

Chapter Fifty-Seven

'Freaking hell,' muttered Dylan, as Jill was handcuffed and led from the restaurant.

I pushed back my wet hair – now an attractive frizz – and glanced about.

Diners were agog. The chuntering was back in full force. Dylan and I were being flashed dark looks. People were discussing us behind their hands.

Despite Jill's threatening behaviour, patrons were still of the opinion that the nutty blonde had been pushed over the edge by a philandering husband and meddlesome mistress.

If looks could kill, then I'd have been a goner several times over. Numerous scowls were winging my way – mainly from the women within this establishment.

'Would you both like a brandy?' simpered the waiter.

'I think we could do with one,' Dylan agreed. 'However, I'm driving. Just give me the bill, please.'

'Ay could do with a brandy,' said Plummy. 'Ay'm feeling a little queer.'

'You and me both,' muttered the waiter, before turning on his heel.

Dylan turned to the off-duty policeman.

'I really must thank you,' he said. 'You quite possibly

saved my life.'

'All part of the job,' said the cop modestly.

Wow. What a night. Dylan had wanted it to be memorable, but attempted murder hadn't been on the agenda.

'But who *was* she?' said Plummy, confused.

'My sister-in-law,' said Dylan.

'You were having an affair with your sister-in-law?' spluttered Plummy.

'I wasn't having an affair with anyone,' said Dylan in exasperation. 'She was a guest at my daughter's wedding who wrongly believed we had a future together.'

Plummy shook her head, then looked at me.

'So who are you?'

'I'm Dylan's… girlfriend.'

Plummy pursed her lips, then looked back at Dylan.

'And what does your wife have to say about all this?' she persisted.

Dylan took a deep breath.

'My wife is deceased.'

'Oh,' said Plummy, the cogs visibly whirring. 'Ay say. Did your sister-in-law kill your wife?'

Dylan ignored the question. Instead, he turned to the copper.

'What will happen to Jill?' he asked. 'Will she get cautioned?'

The policeman shook his head.

'A person who has threatened someone with a knife faces a minimum sentence of six months in prison.'

'What?' I gasped, as Dylan's eyes widened.

Omigod. A split second of madness. One pivotal moment. From freedom to incarceration. But then again, perhaps it hadn't been a split second of madness. After all, Jill had demanded Dylan love her. Refused to accept they didn't have a future together. Stolen his housekey. Declined to go home. Not exactly the behaviour of your average woman when dealing with unrequited love.

If I'd been her, I'd have bought a box of chocolates, a bottle of plonk, and watched *Love Actually* on repeat with a packet of tissues to hand.

The waiter returned with the bill. Dylan tapped his pin number into the terminal. We thanked the copper again. Then, ignoring the many eyes upon us, and holding our heads high, we left the restaurant.

Chapter Fifty-Eight

As we walked back to the car, Dylan caught hold of my hand. His fingers interlocked with mine.

The night air was cool and soothing after the events of the last thirty minutes. As we strode along, our heels clicked loudly on the pavement. We were a couple eager to be elsewhere. Keen to put something behind us.

It dawned on me that Dylan might have had a lucky escape. Yet again I was reminded of the thin line between this world and the next. Maybe Dylan was thinking likewise. Certainly, the pair of us were quiet, each with our own thoughts.

As we eventually headed out of West Malling, Dylan was the first to speak.

'I guess I can cancel my appointment with Gardener and Stewart Solicitors,' he said wryly. 'After all, an eviction order is no longer required.'

I blew out my cheeks.

'Indeed. Likewise, your rental of Catkin Cottage. Thanks to Jill overseeing her own eviction, you can remain in your own home.'

Dylan cleared his throat.

'You'd be right to think that. But you're wrong.'

I glanced at him.

'Oh?'

'You know, it's amazing how some high drama can put your life in perspective,' he declared softly. 'I'm going ahead with the rental. I shall move into Catkin Cottage and put my property on the market. That way, there will be no chain. My house will be easier to sell.'

'Wow,' I said in astonishment. 'Is this decision because you have bad memories of Jill being there?'

'Yes, and no,' he said. 'The fact is, Maggie, I've been rattling around the place for ages.'

The car slowed for a pedestrian crossing. A gaggle of rowdy youths, high on alcohol and camaraderie, staggered across the road. We set off again.

'Jennifer is gone' – Dylan continued – 'and Terry left home yonks ago. Now it's just me and Charlie. What am I doing living in a family-sized home? Of course there are good memories. More recently, some unpleasant ones. But the latter isn't the real reason for coming to this decision. I think tonight simply flagged up that it's time to move on. Let someone else live there. A young couple. Preferably with little ones or wanting to start a family. They can put their own stamp on the place. Make their own memories. But for me, I'm ready to write new chapters. As I said, tonight's episode simply put it all into perspective.'

For a moment I didn't say anything. I knew what Dylan was talking about. What he was touching upon. Recently, I'd had similar thoughts myself. Now and again. The kids too. Only recently Ruby had buttonholed me.

'For heaven's sake, Mum! Why are you changing the linen in bedrooms that nobody sleeps in?'

Ella had seconded Ruby's sentiments but also gone one step further. She'd dared to suggest I was bored and needed something to do.

'Why else would you keep vacuuming rooms that are empty?' she'd persisted. 'I can't understand why you don't sell up.'

Tim had flashed his sisters a sharp look.

Girls, pipe down. Mum feels that Dad is still here. And she's not leaving Dad any time soon.

Ruby and Ella had both made fair points. Indeed, why was I making work for myself with those empty rooms? Not forgetting the garden. Huge. And vast flowerbeds that required hours of backbreaking weeding.

But I'd felt that I was doing the latter for Greg. And the former… well, again for Greg. Because, despite all the photographs dotted about, it was my way of keeping him close to me.

Nonetheless, Dylan's words resonated with me. If I moved too, I'd not really be leaving Greg. After all, he was in my heart. And always would be.

'Food for thought?' said Dylan, glancing at me.

I opened my mouth to say something. For a moment nothing came out.

'I think…'

'Yes?' Dylan prompted.

'I think you've spoken wise words,' I said thoughtfully.

He flashed me a smile.

'I was hoping you'd say that.'

The BMW took a left and came to a halt on my driveway.

Home. The *marital* home. The house I'd shared with Greg. I suddenly realised that I wanted — as Dylan had so succinctly put it — to write some new chapters of my own. It was time. But a fresh start couldn't be made here. And it was in that split-second moment that I made my decision. I'd do the same as Dylan. Put my house on the market. In fact, I'd do it first thing on Monday morning.

I had no idea where I'd go. Or what area to look at. Maybe I'd leave Little Waterlow. After all, it was only a matter of time before Mabel Plaistow got wind of tonight's episode in The Swan. Heaven only knew how she'd rehash the drama. By the time Mabel had finished, Jill might have swapped that steak knife for Chef's carving blade, with Dylan's heart on the menu. I could almost hear the camp waiter: "Would you like that with chunky chips or mash?"

I mentally shook the gruesome thought away. Unbuckled my seatbelt. Turned to Dylan.

'Come on in,' I said with a smile.

Chapter Fifty-Nine

Bess and Charlie greeted us, yawning and stretching.

'Shall we now have that brandy?' suggested Dylan.

'Good idea,' I agreed. 'You do the necessary. In the lounge – door straight ahead – there's a bottle in the cabinet. You'll find some glasses in there too. I'll let the dogs out. And then we'll, er…' I trailed off.

'Take our brandies upstairs?' Dylan raised an eyebrow.

'Yes,' I nodded.

Brandy was most definitely required. Not just as a pick-me-up after the earlier hoo-ha, but also for courage – because suddenly I felt horribly nervous.

My hands fluttered over the key to the back door. As I levered down the handle, I was all fingers and thumbs.

The dogs bounced out. A beam of moonlight revealed next door's cat perched on the fence. Bess gave a territorial woof.

This is my space, not yours.

Charlie scampered over to the fence, all set to give chase. The cat gave him a condescending look. Then, with a flick of its tail – a sort of feline one-fingered salute – it dropped into the adjacent garden.

There then followed a bit of foot tapping on my part,

while Bess decided where to have a wee – the usual spot possibly unacceptable now that the grass had died a death. Charlie, possibly by dint of being able to cock a leg rather than curtsy, watered several rosebushes and Greg's prized hydrangeas.

'Come!' I said sternly.

Both dogs scooted back and shot through the open door at the same time. Bess gave Charlie a soft growl, as if to say *ladies first, thank you very much*.

I locked the door after them. As I turned, I was surprised to see Dylan standing there. He was holding a tumbler in each hand.

'I didn't like to presume,' he said, looking a little awkward. 'You know… to go upstairs without you.'

I realised he was feeling as nervous as me. I took one of the glasses from him.

'Cheers,' I said softly.

Gently, I clinked my tumbler against his, then tossed the drink down my neck. As it travelled down my gullet, it burnt a fiery path. I tried not to cough.

'All gone,' I wheezed gamely.

Dylan looked at me in amazement, then did likewise.

I took the glass from him. Put them both in the sink. Emboldened, I gave him a suggestive look. Quite a feat considering I was a woman with a wrecked hairdo, smudged makeup, and a damp dress.

'You're very desirable, Maggie,' whispered Dylan.

'So are you,' I quavered.

Awesome, Maggie, said my inner voice. *No need for*

Dylan to shed his clothes because your dull repartee will bore the pants off him. What next? A cup of Horlicks? Or perhaps a game of Scrabble could be part of your foreplay?

I'm feeling panicky, I retorted silently.

Dylan stepped closer.

'And I also want to tell you' – he added softly – 'that I love you.'

My jaw fell open.

'Do you?' I gasped, as my heart leapt with joy.

'Yes,' he nodded. 'I do. I've wanted to tell you for ages. But I was scared of frightening you off. And I'm *in* love with you. Desperately so.' He put his arms around me. Held me tight. 'Do you… feel the same way?'

And in that moment, I knew I did. That I had done for ages. I'd simply been too afraid of the implications to properly acknowledge it.

'Yes,' I whispered. 'I feel the same way too.' I looked up at him under my eyelashes. 'Although' – I murmured bravely – 'I'd much rather show you.'

Dylan's eyes lit up.

'Is that so?' he whispered, as my arms coiled around his neck.

I leant into him. Tilted my head back. Let his lips meet mine. And at last, kiss, after glorious kiss, enfolded. At first, gently. Then, hungrily. And suddenly our hands were going everywhere. Mine feeling the way down his shirt. Undoing buttons. Slipping one hand under the fabric. Thrilling at the touch of soft chest hair. Him, feeling his way around the back of my dress. Me undoing the belt on his trousers. Him, locating the dress's zipper and peeling me like a banana. All in my kitchen.

Oh God, Maggie. Not here, implored my inner voice. *The days of you straddling the table or laying on a cold floor are over. Think of your arthritis.*

I unglued my mouth from Dylan's.

'Upstairs,' I said hoarsely.

Down to our undies, we left our clothes in a heap on the tiles. I then took Dylan by the hand and, giggling like teenagers taking advantage of an empty house, we scampered up the staircase.

Chapter Sixty

I was amazed at how easy it was to lead Dylan into the bedroom that I'd once shared with Greg.

Maybe it was because I'd moved the furniture around. Or perhaps it was because I'd put away my husband's photographs – especially the one where Greg's eyes always seemed to follow me around the room.

Either way, Dylan and I crossed the floor to the bed with the sort of choreography that affirmed this was meant to be. I wrapped my legs around his hips and welcomed him inside me relieved that, after a lengthy break, everything was popping and fizzing nicely.

Lyn, my mate, had insisted that a woman of a certain age should regularly use a vibrator. She swore that it kept things *down there* ticketty-boo.

'That and lots of lube, Mags,' she'd shrieked, as we'd giggled tipsily over our Proseccos. 'Did I tell you about the time I made the thing so slippery, it shot right out of my hands. Catapulted across the carpet. And Sooty' – Lyn's Cockapoo – 'thought it was her new toy. She grabbed it and wouldn't give it back. It was most embarrassing when the doorbell rang. I greeted a courier in my kimono only to have Sooty dash past with a rubber penis hanging out of her mouth.'

I smiled at the memory then, as Dylan flipped me on top, batted the thought away. Right now, I didn't want to think of Lyn, Sooty, or chewed-up vibrators.

Instead, long hair trailing over Dylan's chest, I leant in for a full-blown snog.

Careful, Maggie. Your mouth isn't a vacuum nozzle.

Coming up for air, I leant back and cupped my breasts suggestively. Gave Dylan an eyeful of cleavage that was… uh-oh…

Warning! Crepe alert!

I instantly dropped my boobs. They yo-yoed attractively down to my navel.

Diversion tactics urgently required!

I stuck a finger in my mouth. Ran my tongue suggestively over the tip. Licked it lasciviously up and down, up and down, while making the sort of sounds heard in a porn movie. Oh yes, baby. Right now, was I hot, or was I *hot*? I suppressed a burp.

Caution! You're still full of champagne. Stop the voracious bouncing or you'll burp again, and next time you'll sound like Fred Plaistow after he's drunk a pint of Guinness.

I instantly switched to a woman on horseback sedately rising to the trot. But Dylan was having none of it. He flipped me over again and was suddenly doing the sort of thrusts that might challenge anyone who'd had a hip replacement.

As he sped up, his breath hurricaned in my left ear while

I cosied up to his right earlobe and loudly affirmed my pleasure.

Perforated eardrum alert!

Oh for…

I shifted my neck, thus directing all sound over Dylan's shoulder. At least if I was unable to stop screeching – and right now I really couldn't – my lover's hearing apparatus wouldn't be damaged.

Hearts pounding, gasping for breath, things came to an energetic and noisy crescendo. Spent, we finally flopped back against the pillows.

'Wow,' panted Dylan.

'Wow, indeed,' I said, my ribcage going up and down rather alarmingly. That had been quite a work-out. A calorie burner for sure. I wriggled closer to Dylan. Looked up at him seductively.

'What?' he asked in bemusement.

'Fancy some chocolate?' I grinned.

Chapter Sixty-One

Dylan regarded me in amusement.

'I think most couples light a post–coital cigarette,' he said.

Oh. Was Dylan a secret smoker? Or did he prefer, on the quiet, to vape?

'I don't smoke,' I said. 'Do you?'

He laughed.

'No, definitely not. In my teens I tried it. I stopped when the girl I fancied told me I smelt like an ashtray.' He gave me a loving look. 'But if you're up for some après-sex chocolate, then so am I. What have you got?'

I cogitated. At the start of the week, there had been some fruit and nut in the fridge. However, I'd crammed the whole lot in my mouth after the Golden Oldies had frustrated me. Mainlining on sugar had been comfort food after Mum and Dad had both refused to have a bath – for the third week running.

But wait. I was sure I'd seen something sweet and sugary lurking at the back of the fridge. As yet untouched.

'I think there may be something green and black,' I said tentatively.

'Sounds great,' said Dylan happily. 'I love their

chocolate. Shall we have a cuppa with it?'

Oooh, a man after my own heart.

'Definitely. You stay right here. I'll get it.'

'I have no intention of moving,' Dylan assured. 'You've worn me out.'

'Ah ha!' I gave him a saucy look. 'I guess that means you're *shagged*?'

'Funny,' said Dylan, rolling his eyes.

I grinned.

'Won't be a mo.'

I grabbed my robe from the back of the door. Wrapping it around me, I bounced down the stairs, humming as I went. Once the kettle was on, I let the dogs out for a final wee before lights out. I then busied myself putting cups on a tray. I added a plate of biscuits – suddenly I was ravenous again – and located a small box of chocolates.

Tea made, and tray loaded, I let the dogs back in, then returned to the bedroom. Charlie was all set to barge in and steal the biscuits.

'No,' I said to him sternly. Lifting my foot, I gently shooed him out. 'Stay with Bess.'

I shut the door, then padded over to Dylan. He was now sitting up in bed. Carefully, I placed the tray on the bedcovers – mindful not to slop the teas – then perched alongside.

'Lovely,' said Dylan. He rubbed his hands together. 'First, I'm seduced by the most beautiful woman in Little Waterlow. Second, she plies me with cookies and a builder's brew. And what's this?' He reached for the box of chocolates. 'Oh.' He wrinkled his nose. 'Not Green and Black's.'

I frowned.

'No, but the *box* is green and black.' I picked it up. Waggled the After Eights at him.

'You can have those,' he said with a shudder. 'I'm not a fan of the fondant goo. However' – he reached for a chocolate Hobnob – 'these are my favourite. I might scoff the lot because, suddenly, I'm starving.'

'I know,' I agreed, cramming an After Eight in my mouth. 'I feel the same, despite enjoying a three-course meal earlier. Weird.'

'It's the sex,' said Dylan matter-of-factly. 'Our bodies are seeking to replenish their energy stores.'

'Oh!' I nodded, as the dawn came up. 'So *that's* why Lyn is always so trim when she has a new man in her life. Sexercise.'

Dylan raised his eyebrows.

'Who's Lyn?'

'My bestie. I love her to bits. However, she's a bit of a maneater and a terrible flirt.'

'In which case I hope you'll protect me if I ever meet her.'

I giggled.

'I'll do my best,' I teased.

I drained my tea, then hopped back under the covers with Dylan. He put his cup on the bedside table, then put an arm around my shoulders. I snuggled into him, loving this moment. Loving him. Loving all of it.

'Can I ask you something?' he said tentatively.

'Fire away,' I said happily.

'Have you recently moved the furniture around in this room?'

I blinked.

'Er, yes. Why?'

Dylan pointed at the opposite side of the bedroom.

'Your carpet. It has huge indentations. I'm guessing that your double bed spent years over there.'

'You're very observant, Mr Alexander,' I said lightly. 'And also, absolutely correct. I have moved the bed. I mean, I did it ages ago.' My tone was suddenly defensive. 'I simply fancied a change.'

Dylan squeezed my shoulder.

'You don't have to explain, sweetheart,' he said gently.

Ah. He'd sussed. He knew that I'd moved everything about in order to feel comfortable about him coming into this room.

'It was time,' I said, attempting nonchalance. 'In fact, your earlier conversation – about going ahead with the rental of Catkin Cottage – got me thinking too. On Monday, I'm putting this house on the market.'

'What?' said Dylan in surprise. 'Are you sure you're doing the right thing?'

I shrugged.

'As sure as I'll ever be. This place is full of memories. Me and Greg. The kids. Wet paintings from schooldays. Fridge magnets. Then, later, the teen years. Rows about wanting boyfriends staying over. Girlfriends too,' I added.

I could still remember an adolescent Tim declaring that if I didn't permit Poppy – a fellow Sixth Former – to stay over, they'd only go and do it elsewhere.

'Elsewhere is fine by me,' I'd snarled, adamant that no doe-eyed siren would be eating cornflakes with us the following morning.

It had been Greg who'd made me see reason.

'Better to have them all safely here,' he'd said. 'Under our wing. We don't want them getting charged by the police for having sex in a field.'

And then, later, the kids going off into the big wide world. Greg and me living in our empty nest. When he'd suddenly died, it wasn't just my husband's voice I'd heard. I'd listened to many echoes in my head. Tim. Ruby. Ella. The girls arguing.

'I *told* you not to borrow my new top without asking.' This from a shrill Ruby. 'And look at it now. *Covered* in your wanky makeup.'

'RUBY!' I'd roared. 'Don't use that word.'

'I said MANKY,' she'd bellowed back.

Sometimes I'd had to pause, in the hallway, convinced I'd heard Tim. Upstairs. Playing music. Oh yes, the mind had delivered some fantastic tricks.

I now looked up at Dylan.

'All your talk about writing new chapters…' I trailed off. Paused. Chose my next words carefully. 'It resonated with me. However, I won't move far. I want to be near my children. Especially if any grandkids come along.'

'I won't be going far either,' said Dylan. 'The care

home – my work – is in West Malling. And next year there will be Terry's baby. A grandchild. I'll probably draw a ring on a map – a twenty-mile radius – and eventually look for a property somewhere within that circle.'

I nodded thoughtfully.

'That sounds very sensible.'

For a moment we were both quiet, each with our own thoughts.

'Maggie…' said Dylan cautiously.

'Yes?'

His body shifted. A regrouping gesture.

'Writing those new chapters…'

'What about them?'

He hesitated for a second. Then his words came out in a rush.

'How do you feel about writing those new chapters with me, at Catkin Cottage?'

Chapter Sixty-Two

I stared at Dylan, both surprised and stunned. My jaw seemed to be overcome by gravity. A gormless expression prevailed.

For heaven's sake, Maggie, change the face. Village idiot comes to mind.

'Sorry,' Dylan apologised. 'I can see you're horrified by the idea. My fault. I'm going along at a hundred miles an hour, planning my new life, and expecting you to fall into it. Please disregard—'

'N-No,' I stuttered. Touched his arm. 'It's fine, honest,' I assured. 'You just caught me unawares. And I'm *not* horrified,' I promised. 'More… flabbergasted. But also' – my mouth curved into a vast banana grin – 'delighted. And… well… if you're sure…'

'Never been surer,' he murmured.

'Then… omigod... yes! Yes, I'll move into Catkin Cottage with you.'

Bloody hell. We were going to live together. What would my parents say?

Never mind your parents, said my inner voice. *What about your kids?*

I paled. Yes, indeed. What *would* the children say?

Ruby: (morphing into Victor Meldrew) I do not believe it!

Ella: (turning into Lance-Corporal Jones) Don't panic!

Tim: (looking eerily like Geoffrey Adams) Good God!

And never mind my children. What about Dylan's daughter? What might she think? Would Terry be aghast that another woman was potentially stepping into the shoes of her mother? I gave Dylan an anxious look.

'Will Terry mind?' I asked.

'What has my life got to do with Terry?' he asked with bemusement.

Fair comment. And actually, a flipping good one. Yes, if any of my children protested, I'd point that out – my life, my decision. But *would* they protest? Might they not – now I came to think of it – be rather pleased for their old mum.

Less of the old, Maggie.

In fact, might they be relieved? Happy that someone else could shoulder the concerns they'd had about me?

'Gosh, all those mad conversations she kept having with Dad.' This from Ruby. 'At least she won't be able to do that any longer.'

Ella nodding her head in agreement.

'Yeah, and all the photographs of Dad everywhere. Mum can't do that if she's shacked up with another man.'

Then Tim adding his thoughts.

'Unless this guy has pics of his dead wife everywhere. Then the two of them can turn Catkin Cottage into a shrine.'

But, deep down, I suspected my children would approve of Dylan. Once they'd properly met him. After all, he was a decent guy. A *catch* as my mother would have said, before dementia claimed her. And would my parents really be against their daughter finding happiness again? If anyone was going to be surly, it would be Dad. And purely for his own selfish reasons. I could imagine him now. Mouth pursed.

'I suppose you won't have time for us anymore, Maggie.'

I'd have to reassure him. Guide him to be a little more flexible, and less vehement about employing a carer. But I knew in my heart that it would take something monumental before Dad sought alternative help. Hmm. I'd have to pick the right moment before breaking the news to my father.

And then there was Dylan's daughter to consider. Despite him stating that his decisions were nothing to do with Terry, they *were* to a degree. After all, having someone in a stepmother role was massive. Hopefully Terry would give me the thumbs up.

But, all that aside, right now I felt deliriously happy. Over the moon.

'You've gone very quiet,' said Dylan. 'A penny for your thoughts.'

I leant my head on his shoulder. Took his hand in mine.

'Sorry, I was miles away. Just trying to gauge everyone's reactions. Wondering if they will tell me I'm being ridiculous for finding love again in my sixties. Or whether they will be happy for me.'

Dylan squeezed my hand.

'If someone loves you then they will have your best interests at heart,' he assured.

'Yes,' I agreed. 'You're right.'

'And listen' – he squeezed my hand again – 'if it turns out that you think you've made a mistake… or that my little ways annoy you…'

'Little ways?' I bantered. 'Tell me about them.'

He looked bashful.

'You know. A typical man who forgets to pick up his socks. Or leaves the cap off the toothpaste. Or forgets to spritz the smallest room after being in there with the Sunday papers. I won't blame you if you say, "Sorry, Dylan, but I'm off." Remember, I was going to rent Catkin Cottage anyway. So, if at some point you have a change of heart, it won't be hugely different for me. If that makes sense. However, it's monumental on your part. I simply want you to be sure.'

'I am,' I said, looking up at him. 'And anyway, your reasoning works both ways. After all, you might be exasperated by my makeup littering the dressing table. And I, too, leave the cap off the toothpaste. Also, you might find yourself competing for the smallest room with the Sunday papers. That said, I never forget to spritz.'

Dylan roared with laughter.

'In that case' – he twinkled – 'I'd venture to say we might just be the perfect match.' He cleared his throat. Suddenly looked a little shy. 'Maybe one day we will buy a place together.'

I gave him another huge grin and hugged him tightly.

'Omigod,' I squeaked. 'I'm so excited. I don't think I'll sleep a wink tonight.'

'Me neither.' His expression shifted. Became furtive. 'Er, there's something else I want to tell you.'

'Go on,' I prompted.

'Well…' He took a deep breath. 'I've had this ambition…'

'Y-e-s,' I said.

'It's something I've always wanted to do. I'm hoping you might be up for doing it too.'

I looked at him curiously. What was it? Dancing naked in the moonlight? Joining a cult? Becoming a vegan?

'What is it?' I prompted.

'I'd like to buy a campervan. At some point, I'd like to take a month off work. Tour around the UK. I've travelled abroad extensively but never properly explored the island upon which I live. I'd like to visit' – he raised his hand and began ticking off on his fingers – 'Devon, Dorset, Hampshire, Cornwall, the Lake District–'

'Oooh, yes,' I interrupted, squeaking again in excitement. 'Loch Lomond, the Isle of Skye–'

'And don't forget Wales,' Dylan added. 'I've heard Shell Island has stunning views of the Welsh countryside.'

'We'll need more than a month,' I pointed out.

'That's to begin with,' said Dylan. 'We can spend the rest of our lives hopping in the campervan and exploring.'

'Oh, Dylan,' I said, my eyes shining. 'It sounds wonderful. We can take Charlie and Bess with us and not have a care in the world.'

'Indeed,' Dylan agreed.   He grabbed hold of me. Hugged me fiercely. 'I love you, Maggie. You're my dream woman.'

'And I love you, Dylan.'   I kissed him hard on the mouth.

'How much?' he asked.

'More than words can say,' I assured. 'What about you?'

'To the moon and back,' he said without hesitation.

I gave him an enquiring look.

'What about to the kitchen and back?'

He frowned.

'I'm not following.'

I gave him a playful punch on the arm.

'I fancy another cuppa.   And it's your turn to put the kettle on.'

Chapter Sixty-Three

On Sunday morning, after Dylan and Charlie had left, I picked up the phone. I wanted to share my news with the kids. However, I was brought up short by my sister's last text.

Hell, after all the excitement, I'd completely forgotten about Freya trying to contact me. I paled slightly at the memory of her first message. My phone had dinged while I'd been out with Dylan.

I have a bone to pick with you.

Since then, she'd sent several more WhatApps, so wordy they were more like essays.

I began to skim read and, as I did so, my eyebrows almost shot off my forehead.

I have a bone to pick with you... solicitor mailed me copies of our parents' Wills...

why are your children mentioned?

What did she mean, why were my children mentioned? Obviously because our parents wanted to remember their grandchildren. That was why!

I had yet to properly read the copy Wills myself, but now recalled Dad telling me he'd included his grandchildren. Well, if Mum and Dad had gifted something to Tim, Ruby, and Ella, then how very generous of them. And how lovely that, one day, the kids would have a bit of money to bolster their bank accounts. Maybe to pay off a chunk of their mortgages. Or perhaps replace their clapped-out cars. Youngsters struggled to balance the money books. I, for one, was grateful my parents wanted to take away some of that struggle for their grandchildren. After all, they could have opted to give everything to charity. It was their money. Their wishes.

Absolutely not fair…

Outrageous that my inheritance is being shared with Tim, Ruby, and Ella…

I've never had kids…

Don't see why my future bank balance should be compromised…

Frigging flaming flipping Nora!

Quite obvious to me that you knew about this all along…

You've never liked me…

Oh, stupid woman. What was she on about?

Certainly I've never liked you…

What? Wow, thanks for that, Freya. Thanks a bunch.

You have coerced our parents…

I will contest this in a Court of Law…

She had to be kidding, right?

YOU give your kids money from YOUR share…

I WANT MY FIFTY PER CENT!

Bloody hell. Our parents weren't yet dead. How disgustingly distasteful.

I immediately tried calling Freya only to discover my number had been blocked. Oh, this was ridiculous. What on earth was going through my sister's head? I knew we'd had our squabbles over the years. Some disagreements. But surely no more than any other family? To accuse me of never liking her was nonsense. And to cap it all off by saying she'd never liked me, was hurtful to say the least. Who was it that had said *money is the root of all evil*? Someone wise, for sure. I'd have to find an alternative way to contact her.

I logged on to Facebook. I'd send Freya a direct message. Less than a minute later, I had discovered that she'd blocked me on all platforms where we were mutual friends.

'Pathetic,' I said aloud. 'And actually, how dare you, Freya. How *dare* you make such horrible and untrue accusations.'

At the sound of my voice, Bess wandered into the kitchen. I was currently perched on a chair with my phone. My girl looked at me quizzically, as if to enquire who I was talking to.

'Hello, darling,' I said, stroking her silky head. 'You're not going to believe what my daft sister has said.'

I stood up. Made for the kettle. Whenever drama struck, I made a brew. Either that or stuffed my face with chocolate. I reached for the biscuit tin. Damn. Empty. Dylan had polished off all the Hobnobs.

What about the freezer? The top drawer contained some ice-lollies. Hmm. Did an orange popsicle go well with a cuppa? Not really. I shut the door.

'I'll have to go shopping,' I said to Bess. 'We need biscuits.'

At the mention of that last word, her tail–wagging went into overdrive.

'Message received and understood,' I smiled. I reached into the cupboard where her treats were kept. 'Here you are,' I said, giving her a chew.

She took the treat from me, and trotted off to the lounge. I knew she would spend the next few minutes in a sun puddle happily munching away.

'What the heck am I going to do about Freya?' I said to myself.

Email her, said my inner voice. *Tell her you're outraged, disgusted and that she's a total bitch.*

No, I silently replied.

Much as my ego wanted to respond in an enraged way, I refused to give Freya ammunition for her gripe. And never mind *her* objections. What about our parents? If anything happened to Mum and Dad, then I'd need my sister's help. How the hell could I contact her if she had blocked me? Even emailing was a gamble. For all I knew, my plea for a face-to-face might go straight to her Junk folder. It could be unseen for weeks. Lost amongst the usual spam that offered penis extensions or *pay up* scams. Well, that was the sort of thing you'd find in my Junk folder.

Taking a deep breath, I instead found my brother-in-law's contact details. If Freya wouldn't speak to me, perhaps Vernon would.

Chapter Sixty-Three

'Vernon?' I said. No answer. 'Hello? Are you there?'

There was a pregnant pause.

'Oh, er, yes. I'm here,' he said. 'Unfortunately,' he muttered. 'Hello, Maggie. How are you?'

His wary tone conveyed that he knew of his wife's displeasure with me. Fully up to speed, thank you very much. Also, that he wanted no part of it. He was a *yes* man. A guy who trotted after Freya like a loyal hound.

After three shitty husbands, Vernon suited Freya. I wasn't so sure Freya always suited Vernon. However, my sister was a decade younger than him. She was also an excellent cook. Perhaps he was happy to indulge her moods in exchange for a youthful wife and decent grub.

'I'm not so good, Vernon,' I said honestly. 'I've had a number of unpleasant texts from Freya. Can I speak to her, please?'

In the background I heard Freya reply.

'Tell Maggie I've gone out.'

'Um, er, she's says she's gone out,' said Vernon nervously. 'I-I mean–'

Evidently Vernon was getting himself in a pickle. Breaking out in a muck sweat at being caught between his furious wife and irked sister-in-law. I could imagine him now. Glasses steamed up and sliding down his nose. One damp hand raking his hair so that it stood up on end, like Ken Dodd.

'Tell Freya I can hear her,' I said calmly.

'Er, right. Y–Yes. Um, Freya, dear. Maggie says she can hear you.'

'Improvise, Vernon,' Freya ordered. 'Tell her she's mistaken. It's the radio. Or the television. Or I'm otherwise engaged with the bible bashers.'

In the background, a doorbell rang.

'Um, one moment, Maggie,' said Vernon nervously.

Suddenly it sounded as if all hell was breaking out.

'I frigging knew it!' I heard Freya crow. 'Don't you lot have anything better to do on a Sunday? Oh, you're saving me, are you? From what? Ah, myself! And why would I need saving from myself? No, I'm not mad. Well, I wasn't before you rang my doorbell. But now I'm steaming. So, take your haloes and saintly smiles and–'

Chuntering was now filtering down the line. That and a few expletives. Oooh, I say. *That* word wasn't in the bible.

'Do I look like a woman possessed?' I heard Freya roar. I had a feeling she was doing an excellent impression of one. 'Well at least I don't wear socks with my sandals. Now clear off!'

There was the sound of a door slamming.

'Um, darling,' Vernon quavered. 'I think Maggie now knows you're at home.'

'Tell her…' – snarled Freya – 'oh, bollocks. I'll tell her

myself.'

There was the sound of the phone being snatched from Vernon. Suddenly my sister was addressing me.

'Maggie.'

'Freya,' I said coolly.

'I was out. But now I'm in.'

'Right.' I pursed my mouth. 'I've read your texts.'

Silence.

'Freya, can we talk about this civilly, please?

More silence.

And then the sound of sobbing.

'Freya,' I said gently. 'Please, tell me what's wrong.'

When my sister next spoke, she sounded broken.

'I'm s-sorry,' she hiccupped.

'It's okay,' I placated.

'No, no, it's not okay,' she gulped, attempting to recover herself. 'I've behaved badly. For that I'm sorry.'

'But…' I didn't understand what was going on here. *Why* had my sister reacted so badly after reading a photocopy of our parents' Wills? 'Listen, if you're not happy about my children being remembered, can we at least discuss it calmly? There's no need to make threats about contesting Mum and Dad's wishes. Good grief, our parents haven't even departed this planet yet!'

'I won't be contesting,' she said in a small voice. 'I was just… surprised to see that Tim, Ruby and Ella had been given a mention.'

'Why?' I said gently. 'They're Mum and Dad's *grandchildren*, Freya. If I have grandkids one day, I'll do the same thing.'

There was more gulping at the other end of the line.

'It's not that,' she said. I sensed her shaking her head. 'I don't begrudge my nephew and nieces. Of course I don't.'

'Then why–?'

'Don't you see, Maggie? I was triggered.'

'Triggered?' I repeated in bewilderment. I stared at the kitchen wall, lost for words. My sister had been triggered. By what?

'I don't expect you to understand,' she said.

My sister's voice was suddenly brisk. I could imagine her standing in her hallway as she spoke to me. Straightening her spine. Squaring her shoulders. She was revving up to tell me something. Something I'd never been privy to.

'When I saw your children mentioned in our parents' Wills, it triggered me over' – she inhaled sharply – 'the children I never had. The children that I *should* have had. Who, had they been born, would also have been included in our parents' wishes.'

I turned away from the kitchen wall. Stared at the oven instead. What the hell was my sister talking about? Children she'd never had. Should have had. Freya had always been adamant that she couldn't stand kids. Snot one end. Poo the other. Sleepless nights. Tantrums. A disruption to one's life. A burden to the planet.

'Hang on,' I said. One of the oven's knobs had some grease upon it. I picked up the tea towel. Wiped it off. 'You once told me you didn't want children. Ever. Are you telling me–?'

I broke off. My brain was whirring. I was trying to make sense of what Freya was saying. I didn't have long to find out.

'It was a coping mechanism, Maggie,' she said quietly. 'A way of dealing with my miscarriages.'

'Miscarriages?' I gasped. 'You never told me–'

'No,' she interrupted. Gave a mirthless laugh. 'I never told you. Never told anyone. Not even our parents.'

'But… why? *Why* didn't you tell me?' I ran a hand through my hair. I'd soon be looking like Ken Dodd too.

'How could I?' she retorted. 'There you were. Carrying Tim. Six months pregnant. Glowing with good health. Excitedly talking about the crib you'd bought. I couldn't rain on your parade. Couldn't tell you that I'd just come out of hospital.'

My mind flipped back in time. There had been moments in my sister's life where she'd stayed in hospital. Albeit briefly. Memory flooded back.

'W-Wait,' I stuttered. 'You told everyone that you'd had a cyst removed from your ovary.'

'No,' she said softly. 'The foetus had died. Despite bleeding heavily, it didn't come away. I had to have it surgically removed.'

I swung round, appalled.

'Freya,' I breathed. 'You should have told us.'

'Well, I didn't,' she said sadly. 'And it happened on two other occasions. Both times you were pregnant again. With Ruby, then Ella.'

'Oh dear God,' I said softly.

'I had to keep my gob shut. I couldn't share my devastating news. Not when my sister was pregnant for a second and third time. I struggled to deal with my losses. I couldn't understand why I lost my pregnancies when you cruised through yours. Why they ended at ten weeks, eleven, twelve, when my sister had textbook deliveries.' Her tone changed. Became bitter. 'I told myself that being a mother wasn't for me. That children were brats,' she added defiantly.

I swallowed. Gripped the phone. Right. So that explained why Freya had been so vocal about how I'd raised my kids. Criticised my parenting. Endlessly told me where I'd been going wrong with breast feeding. Bottle feeding. Colic. Teething. Why she'd put me down. Made me feel like a failure when my kids had picked up nits at school. Scraped their knees in the playground. Why she'd poured scorn on what they were fed. How they were clothed. Even the way they were disciplined. Oh yes. My sister had always been there. In my ear. At times, I'd hated her for it.

'At times, I'd hated you for it,' she said, startling me. 'You see, I was jealous. And that's why I never sought to have a close relationship with your children, Maggie. Don't get me wrong, I loved them. Still do, obviously. But I couldn't be a pro-active aunty. Couldn't say, "Hey, Mags! Greg! Let me take the kids off your hands today. I want to take them to the zoo." I couldn't do it. You see, it should have been *my* kids going to the zoo with *me*. Do you understand?' she implored.

321

I closed my eyes. Gripped the phone harder.

'Yes,' I said quietly. 'Yes, I understand. Everything makes sense now. I just wish you'd shared this years ago, Freya.'

'I couldn't,' she said sadly. 'But, hey.' She tried to lighten the mood. 'Better late than never, eh.'

'So,' I said hesitantly. 'Your texts. Can we draw a line under them?'

'Yes. I'd like that,' she said meekly.

'And Freya' – I sat back down, suddenly emotionally drained – 'you're my sister. I love you.'

There was a pause at the other end of the line. When Freya next spoke, she sounded choked.

'I love you, too, Maggie.'

Chapter Sixty-Four

I didn't tell Freya about my plans to move into Catkin Cottage with Dylan. It hadn't been the right time. But I did pick my moment with the children and, a whole week later, gave them my big news.

They were surprised but unfazed. Strangely, it was a bit of an anti-climax on my part.

'What were you expecting us to say, Mum?' said Tim.

We were gathered around the kitchen table enjoying a family Sunday dinner. I'd held off inviting Dylan. I'd wanted to talk to my children first – just in case any of them wanted to throw a hissy fit about the family home being sold, and their mother going off to live with a man they hadn't yet met.

'I'm not sure,' I shrugged, answering Tim's question. 'I thought you might be annoyed. Or upset. Or think it… not right,' I added lamely.

'What's not right about falling in love?' said Ella dreamily.

'Mum meant the sex,' Ruby smirked. 'Which, when you stop and think about it' – she frowned – 'is a bit gross.'

'Then don't think about it,' I said crisply.

God. My daughter.

'Do Granny and Grandad know?' asked Ella.

'What, that Mum is having sex?' said Ruby wryly.

I pursed my lips.

'Rub*eee*,' I chided. 'No.' I shook my head. 'They don't know anything about my decision.'

'What about Aunty Freya and Uncle Vernon?' asked Tim.

'Nope,' I shook my head again. 'Not yet.' I was still biding my time with my sister. Making sure the dust had well and truly settled between us. I made a mental note to tell my parents, sister, and brother-in-law all together. Two birds, one stone – that sort of thing.

'Do you think Aunty Freya and Uncle Vernon still have sex?' mused Ruby aloud.

'Now that really is gross,' said Ella. She helped herself to some tomatoes and salad. 'Uncle Vernon is so ancient.'

'Will you two please stop,' I said in exasperation.

Archie and Joshua gave each other a quick look and tried not to snigger.

'Archie, pass the garlic bread around,' I said briskly. It was time to get off the subject of anyone over thirty-five being too decrepit for sex. 'Josh, if you could do the same with the cold meats, please, I'd be very grateful.'

It had been too hot a day to do any proper cooking. Plans for the usual Sunday roast had gone out the – open – window when the temperature had soared to a sticky thirty degrees.

Bess and I were currently walking at silly o'clock in the morning to beat the heat. I'd also had her clipped – much to

Tim's horror.

'Her beautiful coat!' he'd lamented. 'Gone!'

'It will grow back,' I'd pointed out. 'She's happy because she's cooler. After all, no one wears a thick coat in the height of summer.'

My daughter-in-law now brought me back to the present moment.

'When are you moving into Catkin Cottage?' Steph asked.

'Soon,' I said happily.

The previous Monday I'd telephoned the local estate agent. By Tuesday, the house had been photographed. The property's description and floor plans hadn't even been uploaded online when I had received a telephone call from the senior buyer.

'Mrs King,' he'd purred down the line. 'We have a small waiting list for properties like yours. This agency prides itself on being pro-active. We always tell prospective buyers what's coming to the market.'

'Er, right,' I'd said. 'Does that mean you have a viewing for me?'

'My dear lady,' he'd said importantly. 'I have *three* viewings for you.'

'Wow.'

I'd also said *wow* the following day. All three viewers had wanted to make offers and it had gone to sealed bids. I'd secured the sale at fifty thousand pounds over the asking price.

'Dylan has already moved into Catkin Cottage,' I said to

Steph. 'However, I'm holding off joining him for now. There's a lot of sorting out to do here – like overseeing furniture clearance. I need to prepare for vacant possession. However, first I need to go through every single cupboard, wardrobe, and drawer.'

I'd never considered myself a hoarder until I'd started emptying out the hot cupboard. *How* many towels were folded upon its shelves? And *how* many spare changes of linen did I possess? There had been enough to start a small haberdashery shop.

I was also very aware that Greg's clothes were still hanging in one of the wardrobes. I'd cleared some of his belongings immediately after he'd died. Donated his suits, ties, shirts, and shoes to a local charity shop. But a goodly proportion remained. Jeans. Hoodies. T-shirts. His dressing gown. I wasn't sure I'd ever be able to part with that. And then I thought of Dylan. He'd kept nothing of Jennifer's.

'They're clothes, Maggie,' he'd said, when we'd had such a conversation. 'Bits of material sewn into a blouse or a dress. They're not Jennifer.' He'd taken me in his arms. Hugged me tight. 'I didn't need to keep her stuff, because she's *here*.' He'd tapped his head. 'And *here*.' He'd then touched his heart.

He was right, of course. And yes, I would eventually let that dressing gown go. It would just be the very last thing.

'Anyway,' I said brightly. I glanced at everyone around the table. 'If there's anything anyone wants – furniture, paintings, whatever – now is the time to speak up and claim it.'

There then followed some squabbles about who was having the mirror on the landing, Greg's prized desk in the study, and the grandfather clock in the lounge.

I listened to my children compromising with each other. Loving the noise. The camaraderie. Also wondering how I would fit everyone into Catkin Cottage when they visited. Plates on laps and bums on floors came to mind.

My thoughts were interrupted by the phone ringing.

'Hello?' I said.

'Mrs King?' said a well-spoken male voice.

'Yes,' I frowned.

'Hello. My name is John and I'm a paramedic. Please don't be alarmed, but I'm at your parents' house. A neighbour telephoned Emergency Services. Your father has had a fall. Rather a nasty one, I'm afraid.'

Chapter Sixty-Five

'Is my father all right?' I asked breathlessly.

All chatter around the table came to an abrupt halt. Six pairs of eyes were suddenly trained on me.

'It's very likely that he's broken his hip, Mrs King,' said John. 'We're going to take your father to Darent Valley Hospital for an X-Ray. The likelihood is that he will be admitted and kept in for several days. I did ask your mother if she'd be kind enough to pack him some pyjamas and a washbag but, er–'

'I'm doing it, I'm *doing* it.' My mother could be heard in the background, shrieking and clearly confused. 'Oh, God, what am I doing? What's happened? Who are you? Get out of my house.'

'My mother has dementia,' I explained to John. 'She can't follow instructions, and she can't be left alone.'

Right now I had a dilemma. I needed to be with my father. To go to hospital with him. I also needed to be with my mother. However, I couldn't be in two places at once.

'One of your neighbours is here,' said John. 'She's volunteered to stay with your mum until you can take her home with you.'

Take her home with me? I stared up at the ceiling,

suddenly feeling overwhelmed. I couldn't look after my mother! She'd have me up all night, asking where she was on a repetitive loop. And if I fell asleep, she might wander. Unlock doors. Disappear into the night. Get lost. Step out in front of a car. Get knocked down by a lorry…

My brain instantly pressed the pause button on such images. My thoughts were not only rattling around my skull like a runaway steam train, they were accompanied by high-pitched toots. Panic threatened to derail my mind.

Freya. I needed Freya's help. Perhaps she could take Mum home with her while I dealt with Dad.

Oh dear Lord. This situation was exactly what I'd always feared. My stubborn parents refusing care. No back-up plan in place. *I have two daughters* my father had told Social Services when they'd asked him the same question. Yes, two daughters who were expected to drop everything and come running. Never mind a bride and her wedding day tomorrow afternoon. Never mind Freya and her job in London.

And that was another thing. Would Freya even be prepared to help out this evening? I wasn't sure she would. I couldn't envisage her ringing her boss. Explaining that an unforeseen family emergency meant she wouldn't be in the office tomorrow.

Well, I'd soon find out on that score.

'I need to phone my sister,' I said to John. 'I'll do it now. While I'm driving over. Or should I go straight to the hospital?'

The children were looking at me anxiously.

'What's happened?' Ella mouthed.

I put up a hand. Signalled that I would reveal everything when the person at the other end of the line had finished speaking.

'I suggest you drive to your parents' house first. Pack an overnight bag for your father. Nightwear. Robe. Toothbrush. Toiletries. Change of clothes. That sort of thing. Also, I suggest you reassure your mother before heading off to the hospital. She's very distressed.'

'Yes,' I nodded, heart pounding. 'I'm on my way, John. Thank you for speaking to me and for your help so far.'

I disconnected the call, picked up my wine and took a huge gulp.

Don't drink, Maggie! You need to drive and have your wits about you.

'Mum?' said Tim.

'Grandad has had a fall,' I said. 'He's broken his hip.' I promptly burst into tears. 'Sorry,' I apologised, snatching up a napkin to wipe my eyes.

Unfortunately, the serviette was caught up under my wine glass. It went over with a dull clunk. Red liquid puddled across the table.

'Shit, shit, *shit*,' I shrieked.

'It's okay, Mum,' said Ruby, leaping to her feet. She hugged me tight as Ella and Steph mopped up the mess between them. 'Presumably Grandad is going to hospital?'

'Yes,' I sniffed. 'I need to go. I must sort out an overnight bag. Reassure Grandma. Ring Freya. And… oh! I'd better call Dylan. See if he can have Bess tonight.'

'Me and Archie will look after Bess,' said Ella. 'We'll stay here for the night. You go and see to the grandparents.'

'And I'll clear up the dinner things, and stack the dishwasher,' said Ruby, giving my shoulder a squeeze.'

'Do you want me and Steph to come with you?' said Tim.

'No, it's fine, darling.' I shook my head. 'Thanks, kids. Your support is hugely appreciated. I'd better get a wiggle on. I'll ring Freya while I'm on the road.'

'Good luck with that,' said Ruby dryly.

Chapter Sixty-Six

'He's done *what*?' screeched Freya.

'Broken a hip,' I repeated.

I was now belting along the M20. Outside lane. Speedometer nudging ninety. I mentally kept my fingers crossed that a cop wasn't about. That was the last thing I needed on top of this evening's events.

'So what's happening?' asked Freya.

'I'm on my way over to the parents' house. The paramedic asked me to sort out a bag for Dad and to reassure Mum. One of their neighbours is currently with her.'

A pigeon swooped low across the carriageway. I squeezed the brakes just as the bird shot upwards. As it did so, a volley of crap pebble-dashed the windscreen.

'Ah, well,' said Freya. 'It sounds like you have everything under control.'

I frowned. Toggled the windscreen wipers and water jets.

'But that's just it,' I said breathlessly. 'Things aren't under control. Far from it. I need to get to the hospital, so if you could drive up and see to Mum–'

'Don't be ridiculous,' scoffed Freya.

'What do you mean?' I asked.

'You'll have to take Mum with you.'

'To Darent Valley?' My brow furrowed. 'You want me to take a confused old lady into hospital while I stay with Dad?'

'That's the gist of it,' said Freya. 'What's the problem?'

'The problem' – I said through clenched teeth – 'is that I don't feel able to manage Dad *and* Mum together. You forget that Mum is physically disabled. What am I meant to do? Say, "Come on, Mum. Keep up!" as I race after a porter trolleying Dad along a corridor.'

'Then put Mum in a wheelchair.' There was a shrug to Freya's voice.

For a moment I was so angry I couldn't speak.

'Freya,' I said, forcing myself to speak calmly. 'Realistically, by the time Dad is seen by a doctor, many hours will have passed. It's already gone seven o'clock. It will likely be the early hours of the morning before Dad is admitted to a ward. If not later. How does that work for our mother?'

'Take a pillow with you. She can kip in the wheelchair.'

Enough was enough. I took a deep breath.

'I'm asking you to drive up and stay overnight with Mum while I stay with Dad. His memory issues aren't as bad as Mum's, but nonetheless he's confused himself. He needs one of us there with him.'

'No,' said Freya stubbornly. I could picture her at the other end of the line. Vehemently shaking her head. 'I have work tomorrow, Maggie.'

'Me too,' I pointed out. 'I have a bride to oversee tomorrow afternoon.'

'The *afternoon*,' she pointed out. 'That means, when you get home from the hospital, you can sleep in. I wouldn't have that luxury,' she sniffed. 'I will be up with the sparrows and squashed into a train with all the other stressed-out commuters.'

'Freya, *please*,' I implored. 'I need your help.'

When my sister next spoke, her voice was like a pistol shot.

'Maggie. I don't think you understand. I cannot – repeat *cannot* – babysit our mother. Comprendez? Not tonight. Not tomorrow. Not the day after. What I *can* do' – her tone became conciliatory – 'is get on the phone, and ring some care homes. See if I can find one that is prepared to take Mum as an emergency. How's that?'

'Thanks, Freya,' I said. 'But don't put yourself out.'

My sarcasm went straight over her head.

'Are you sure? It's not a problem.' She was now all gushing effusiveness. Delighted to be off the hook. 'After all, I appreciate you're in a bit of a pickle, but I'm more than happy to help.'

Happy to help? Freya's assistance was as much use as a chocolate teapot.

'It's fine,' I said. 'I'll sort things out.'

'Okay, as long as you're sure,' she replied, all concern now. 'And don't forget to keep me updated.'

I gnashed my teeth.

'Of course,' I said sweetly.

I ended the call. Quietly seethed as the car left the motorway. Tried not to chomp my crowns down to my gums as I headed up the slip road. Let out a few expletives as the car stopped at a red light.

My fingers drummed upon the steering wheel as I reflected over Freya's idea of *help* – ringing a few care homes on a Sunday night. It would be like Mary's Joseph calling at all the inns and being turned away. And then I inhaled sharply. Because my sister's words had given me an idea.

Chapter Sixty-Seven

'Dylan?' I said, as the traffic lights changed from red to green.

'Hello, darling.' He sounded delighted to hear from me. 'I was just thinking about you. How did it go earlier with the children? Were they horrified that you're going to *live in sin*, and then tour the country in a campervan with a strange man and two hairy dogs?' He chuckled, no doubt delighted at painting this comical picture.

'I did mention it,' I nodded, as the car leapt forward. 'Although I didn't get as far as the bit about the campervan–'

Dylan caught my anxious tone.

'Are all bets off?' he said nervously. 'Do they hate the idea? Do you want me to talk to them? I'm happy to wait and let things settle–'

'No, no, no.' I shook my head. 'It's nothing like that. They're looking forward to meeting you and–'

'Oh, that's a relief.' Dylan sighed gustily. 'You had me worried for a moment. Meanwhile, Terry and her hubby are excited about meeting your brood. If you want to get a date in the diary, we can crack on and do that. Heavens, we don't want our chicks stressing about their *rents* – I do believe that's the term used for old fogies like us.'

He chuckled again, and I found my shoulders unkinking

slightly. This man was part of life that I liked. *My* life. Where everything was hearts and flowers and big fat buzzy bees and flowers nodding on a warm summer breeze. Not strangers calling me up. Ambulances blue-lighting my father to a hospital. My mother beyond understanding anything.

I made myself take a calming breath.

'Not so much of the *old fogies'* reference,' I said lightly, attempting humour. 'I'm actually calling you about another pair of old fogies.'

'Oh?' said Dylan in surprise. 'Who?'

'My parents. Well, specifically my mother.'

'Go on,' said Dylan.

And with that the whole sorry story tumbled out.

'So, let me get this straight.' I could sense Dylan frowning. 'Your sister has refused to help. You've been left to deal with your father who – as we speak – is on his way to hospital. Meanwhile you have nobody available to look after your mother tonight.'

'Correct,' I nodded. 'Freya offered to ring some care homes. To see if there were any vacancies or a chance of an emergency admission.'

'She will be unsuccessful,' said Dylan quietly. 'There are certain protocols that must be followed before someone can be taken in for respite care. With the best will in the world, that won't be done on a Sunday night with a skeleton staff.'

'I thought as much,' I said flatly.

Despair threatened to engulf me. I'd been all revved up to ask Dylan if there was any possibility – the smallest chance – of Mum checking into Primrose House tonight. It would have helped enormously. I could then have devoted my time and energy to Dad, without being torn in two.

I'd have to ask one of the kids to help. To have their granny overnight. But as soon as the thought had registered, my mind swatted it away. They all had their own jobs to go to in the morning. It wasn't fair to dump my mother on them.

'I know what' – I said, thinking aloud – 'I'll take Dad's overnight bag to the hospital. Then I'll return to my mother. Thank the neighbour for her help. Then telephone the Emergency Services. I'll say that Mum has had a funny turn and get her ambulanced off to the hospital. She'll likely spend all night in a corridor, but at least she'll be on a trolley. She'll also be safe. And then I can stay at the hospital and alternate between both parents in one location. Mum can stay in the hospital until I sort out her respite care.'

'Maggie, I don't think–'

'No, it's fine,' I interrupted, perking up hugely.

Sorted! Why didn't I think of that before? Okay, so I'd be calling an ambulance for someone who wasn't ill, but what choice did I have in the matter? However, my conscience had plenty to say on the matter.

Are you sure you don't feel a teensy bit guilty about your mother taking up a hospital bed – be it in a corridor or on a ward – just so you can juggle your own life with your parents' needs?

Oh for…

Fuckity-fuckity-*fuck*. Why did the little voice always guilt trip me?

I thumped the steering wheel in exasperation. Right. Back to Freya's suggestion. Stick Mum in a wheelchair. With a pillow. We'd both stay with Dad. And maybe, just maybe, my stubborn father would finally realise that things needed to change.

I'd be firm with Dad. Tell him enough was enough. He *would* have a carer. After all, no way could he look after either himself or my mother when later convalescing at home.

It was time for me to be more *Freya* and less *Maggie*. In other words, to put my foot down. Tread on a few corns and bunions. Get my life back, for heaven's sake. Ha! If things didn't change, then I wouldn't be going anywhere – never mind travelling around the country in a campervan.

'Maggie?' Dylan interrupted my chaotic thoughts.

'Yes, I'm here,' I said tiredly.

'I mentioned that care homes must follow certain protocols before taking someone in, especially with weekend skeleton staff. But that's *other* care homes. I'm now talking about *my* care home. I can put myself on duty right now. Go over to Primrose House. Load all your mother's needs onto the system – her medical history, GP details, medications – and then get her admitted. She will then be settled and comfortable for however long you need. A vacancy became available forty-eight hours ago. Your mum is welcome to have the room while your dad recuperates in hospital. Primrose House is only a small care home, but it's a good one, if I do say so myself.'

'Oh, Dylan,' I gasped. 'I don't know what to say.'

'Say yes,' he said simply. 'After all' – his tone became playful – 'your parents might one day be my in-laws. So, I'd better keep on the right side of them.'

Chapter Sixty-Eight

Despite the gravity of the situation, I felt as if an enormous weight had been lifted from my shoulders. For now, I could concentrate on Mum and Dad with clarity, instead of dread. You see, a plan was in place. A plan that should have been made a long time ago.

When I arrived at my parents' house, the ambulance had gone. Using my key, I let myself in. Mum was sitting in her usual chair. She looked surprisingly chipper. Their immediate neighbour, June, was sitting on the sofa. A couple of empty coffee cups had been placed on the occasional table.

'Hello, darling,' beamed Mum, as I pecked her on the cheek. 'How wonderful to see you. I've been having a lovely chat with' – my mother frowned – 'sorry, what was your name?'

'June,' said my mother's neighbour.

The poor woman looked slightly frazzled. I had a feeling that she'd told Mum at least fifty times what her name was.

June stood up and I gave her a grateful hug.

'Thank you so much for staying until I could get here.'

'It's no bother, love,' she said warmly. 'All's well that

ends well, eh?'

'Yes,' I nodded. 'Er' – I picked up the empty cups – 'could you possibly help me with, er, the washing up?' I said brightly.

She immediately caught my drift.

'Of course, love.' She turned to Mum. 'We won't be a moment, Deirdre. I'm popping into the kitchen with Maggie to give her a hand. You stay right there.'

'Okay,' trilled Mum.

I placed the cups in the sink and turned to June.

'My father has broken his hip,' I began. 'Do you, by any chance, know how it happened? In fact, if you could talk me through how you came to be involved, I'd be most grateful.'

'Of course, love,' said June.

Her bosom swelled with importance. At eighty-one years of age, she was no spring chicken. But she was spright, nimble on her feet and had a razor-sharp mind. Absolutely nothing like my parents.

'I was putting the bins out – my Norman never does it, the lazy whatsit – and your mum was standing at her front door. She was shrieking but making no sense. So I went over. Asked what was wrong. But she couldn't tell me. Deirdre was in a terrible state. Hanging on to the doorframe. Gasping for breath from the exertion of shouting.'

Oh God. My poor mother.

'Anyway' – June continued – 'that was when I heard your father shouting for help too. His voice was ever so weak. Like he'd been calling for ages. Trevor was quite hoarse, bless him.'

My heart squeezed at the thought of Dad as vulnerable as a newborn.

'Did he tell you how long he'd been lying there?' I asked.

'Yes,' said Jean sadly. 'Over an hour.'

'What? I gasped.

So while I'd been eating dinner with my children… drinking wine… listening to jokey innuendo about *sex in the sixties*… happily joshing along with the kids, my father had been spreadeagled on this floor. I closed my eyes. Instantly saw him unable to move. In terrible pain. I quickly opened my eyes again.

The usual guilt threatened to consume me. I should have invited them to dinner. I should have picked them up. I should have been more available. Should, should, should.

June was talking again.

'Your father told me that he'd repeatedly asked your mother to phone you. But every time she left the kitchen, she forgot his instructions. Instead, she kept saying, "Trevor! What on earth are you doing down there. Get up you daft bugger." I must say, Maggie, I had no idea your mother's memory was so impaired. I mean, I knew she had dementia, but it's been a few months since I last saw her.' She looked defensive for a moment. 'I should have been a better neighbour.' That word again. Should. 'But my Norman isn't terribly well himself. I'm always scampering around after him.'

'June, you don't have to explain yourself,' I said sadly. 'Mum and Dad are my responsibility. Not yours.'

She looked at me earnestly.

'Don't take this as a criticism, love. But why didn't you sort out a carer for them?'

I shook my head.

'Oh, I've tried, June. Believe me. On numerous occasions. I even had Social Services involved. To no avail. Dad wouldn't play ball. He told me I was interfering.'

'I see,' she nodded. 'He's a proud man.'

'And look where that got him,' I said crossly. 'They say pride comes before a fall. Quite literally in his case.'

'Yes, you're right, dear.' She patted my hand before continuing her story. 'Anyway, your father told me that, in frustration, he lost his temper with mother. Yelled at her to go into the hallway… open the door… find someone to help him up. He kept yelling at her until, eventually, she managed to do most of what he asked. Unfortunately, your mum didn't have the wherewithal to knock on our door – or anyone else's for that matter. So, she just stood there, shrieking. It's lucky I was outside. Your mother's voice isn't one that carries. Who knows how long she might have stood there. This is a small cul-de-sac. Folks don't pass by every few minutes.'

'Thank goodness you heard her,' I said.

'That I did, love.' June patted my hand again. 'When I realised your father needed some strong arms to get him up, I went over to Charlotte and Ray's place. They have a couple of strapping lads still at home. The boys were brilliant. They got Trevor on a chair while I called an ambulance.'

'I must thank them,' I said. 'But what I don't understand, June, is how my father fell in the first place. Did he say?'

For a moment, June looked awkward.

'Your mum attacked him,' she said quietly.

'What?' The word caught in my throat. Came out as a strangled whisper.

'Apparently, Deirdre sometimes gets aggressive. I've heard that dementia can do that.'

'Yes,' I said shakily. 'It can.' I remembered how my mother had recently struck me across the face. How my father had sat there. Head bowed. Subservient. Accepting such behaviour, because he'd experienced it too.

'Trevor said he'd been making them both a drink when Deirdre took him by surprise. She came up behind him. Shoved him hard. He lost his balance, and down he went.' June regarded the kitchen's stone floor. 'The poor man didn't stand a chance.'

'No,' I agreed.

'Anyway, love' – she made to move towards the hallway – 'I know you need to oversee a bag for your dad. I'll leave you to it. And I hope you can sort things out for your mum while he's in hospital.'

'Thankfully respite care is already in place.'

'Gosh, that was quick,' said June in surprise. She touched my arm. A gesture of reassurance. 'Don't worry about this place, Maggie. I'll keep an eye on it for you. I have your phone number. I'll call if there are any problems.'

'That's so kind of you, June,' I said, giving her another hug.

'It's the least I can do,' she said. 'Keep your pecker up.'

My mother suddenly appeared in the doorway.

'Who's pecker needs keeping up?' she scowled. 'And where's your father gone? He's always disappearing. Sometimes I think he deliberately avoids me.'

Chapter Sixty-Nine

Two months later

'I have a surprise for you,' said Dylan, coming into the kitchen.

Earlier, he'd disappeared without explanation, simply telling me that he wouldn't be long.

I put down my chopping knife, abandoning the vegetables I'd been peeling, and looked at Dylan. Smiled. Basked in the pleasure of his proximity. His presence. And love. These days I felt like a champagne bottle. Permanently fizzy. Feeling like I could explode with joy.

'I love surprises,' I said, trying not to squeak with excitement. 'Tell me what it is!'

'No, silly, otherwise it won't be a surprise. Close your eyes. That's it. Let me take your hand. I'm going to lead you into the front room.'

That wouldn't take long. Catkin Cottage was like a doll's house. Small and exquisite.

'No peeking,' warned Dylan.

'Spoilsport,' I grumbled, shuttering down my eyelids.

I wondered what the surprise was. After all, there had been so many in the last two months. So much had happened.

My house sale had completed in record time. I'd now been living with Dylan at the cottage for just over a week. We were like two snug bugs in a rug. Catkin Cottage was perfect for the two of us. And Bess and Charlie hadn't minded the change of address. Thanks to a postage stamp of a garden, they now had more frequent walks in the fields opposite – something young Charlie needed. He was a high-energy dog.

July and August had been hectic months. September promised to be calmer. My wedding diary was winding down. I'd also decided to take a bit of a sabbatical from work. After recent events, I felt like I needed to… well, just take a breath. Just *be*.

It transpired my father had indeed broken his hip. He'd had a full hip replacement. The hospital had discharged him three weeks later.

Meanwhile, my parents' house had gone on the market. Freya and I had also had a frank talk with our father. We'd not exactly ganged up on him, but we'd been firm. Insisted he employ a carer. However, Mum had unexpectedly settled into Primrose House. Even more surprisingly, she didn't want to leave. She couldn't remember *home*, the house that she'd lived in for so many years. Instead, she referred to Primrose House as *my place*. It was at that point that my father had realised it was game over. He'd subsequently made the decision to move into Primrose House with Mum.

My children and their respective other halves had since

met Dylan, Terry, and her husband Tobias. The newlyweds were blissfully happy. Terry had enjoyed showing off her little baby bump. Ruby and Ella had asked if they could touch Terry's tummy. My girls' faces had promptly turned gooier than a chocolate eclair. Archie and Josh had looked on with nervous smiles, not yet ready to walk that path.

Dylan and I had been delighted at how our kids had bonded. Ruby had particularly cosied up with Terry saying that Terry could be her substitute sister when Ella annoyed her. Ella had playfully punched Ruby's arm and said, "Likewise!"

Tim had been very jovial with Terry too. He'd asked if he could take on the role of uncle when her baby was born. Ruby and Ella had promptly asked if they could be aunties. Terry had agreed, pink-cheeked with pleasure.

I'd desperately wanted to ask her if I could be Baby Bump's grandma but had felt too nervous to ask. It was one thing to be considered an aunty or uncle, but quite another to assume a role that rightly belonged to the deceased Jennifer. However, the darling girl had instead asked *me*. I'd been so touched. So honoured. And so horribly, horribly emotional. I'd given Terry a fierce hug. We'd both shed a tear or two, laughing as our hands swiped our wet eyes.

As for Freya and me, well, it was amazing how much better the two of us were getting along. Now that our parents were in a care home, all stress had been removed.

In fact, I'd been quietly flabbergasted at how much better life was all round now that our parents were in safe hands and having all their needs taken care of.

I'd never resented looking after my parents, but I had often been left frustrated. With the best will in the world, I'd never had the time nor the resources to give them everything they'd needed. But now a rota of staff fulfilled that side of things. So, when I took them on an outing somewhere, it was a far more pleasurable experience. And I could look back on the memories we were making with appreciation rather than exasperation.

This shift also meant I currently had more time on my hands. I was no longer the chaperone at doctors' appointments. Or the chauffeur taxiing the Golden Oldies to the dentist... the dementia clinic... the chiropodist... the supermarket. I no longer had to make time to do my parents' housework, or washing and ironing. I had a huge swathe of my life back. I was no longer *Maggie in the Middle*. I was *Maggie on the Move*.

'Okay,' said Dylan, interrupting my thoughts. 'You can now open your eyes.'

I blinked, allowing the dark dots behind my lids to turn into dancing light. September sunshine was pouring in through the window. It had turned everything gold. The heat of summer was over. Autumn was just around the corner. I blinked again, and my eyes widened.

'Oh my goodness,' I gasped, with both surprise and delight.

My hands flew to my mouth. For there, beyond the garden gate and parked on the lane, was a campervan. And – omigod – behind the windscreen I could see... yes, I could see *balloons*. Dylan had filled the interior with them by way of celebration.

'Surprise!' Dylan sang. 'Do you like it, darling?'

'I do,' I whispered. 'It's amazing.'

'Come on.' He took my hand. 'Let's go and have a proper look.'

Together we stepped outside, walked along the flower-lined garden path, passed through its rickety gate and on to the lane.

'Wow,' I whispered.

I stared at the balloons crammed within the campervan's cabin. How many had Dylan blown up and squashed into that space? One hundred? Two hundred?

They merrily bobbed about, a pastel assortment of prettiness. Orange. Lemon. Lime. Lilac. Baby pink. Light blue. Lots of different colours. But only one red balloon, I noticed. And then I froze. Paled. Stared at that... one... red... balloon. And then I heard his voice. As clear as a bell inside my head. Greg.

Yes, Mags. This is my sign.

'Omigod,' I said aloud.

Dylan put an arm around me. Held me tight as I tuned in to what only I could hear.

You wanted a red balloon, Mags, said Greg. *But why limit yourself to one, when you can have many? And why just red when you can have the whole rainbow?*

My eyes brimmed and the tears began to flow.

Thank you, Greg, I said silently. This means the world to me.

Live your life with Dylan. Be content, darling. Have your happy ever after.

I love you, Greg.

I know. And I love you too. Always have done. Always will.

'Are you ready to begin our next adventure?' asked Dylan, holding me tight.

I nodded, momentarily unable to speak.

'Yes,' I finally managed to whisper.

'I love you, Maggie King,' said Dylan.

So much love. How lucky was I? So blessed.

'I love you too,' I replied.

Dylan opened the passenger door. Punching balloons out the way, I hopped inside. An old atlas book was perched on the dash. I picked it up. Flicked through its pages. Looked at all the routes that led to everywhere. And I knew, just *knew*, that within these pages was the road to my brand-new future.

THE END

A Letter from Debbie

I love to put my pets in my novels.

Charlie – Dylan's brown-and-white mongrel – is a carbon copy of my current rescued dog, Molly Muddles. Anyone who follows me on social media will know that she was found at just three days old, sadly orphaned, on a Cretan beach. She eventually travelled over sixteen hundred miles to be with us in the UK.

Bess, Maggie's rescue dog, is based upon my rescued German Shepherd, Tess – sadly long departed.

Just like Maggie, I was once terrified of the breed. Back then, I lived in a rough neighbourhood. My first husband felt that such a dog would be beneficial in keeping vandals away. After all, our home was in an area where, when you opened the curtains on a new day, you'd wonder if your car still had wheels, or if the garden fence had been stolen in the night.

Tess, like Bess, was a middle-aged dog that kept getting bypassed through no fault of her own. Her previous owner had been a single lady who'd unexpectedly died. When I met Tess, she was deeply depressed. She wasn't interested in us. She wasn't interested in *anything*.

We took her home. I can still remember how she climbed on to the car's back seat, emanating gloom. I'd glanced nervously at her over my shoulder. Regarded the huge black-and-tan shape and thought, 'Dear Lord. What have we done? This isn't a dog. It's a beast!'

She taught me to understand that looks are deceptive. Tess was a gentle soul but very protective. She'd fluff up like a porcupine if anyone came near me when out walking – which was what I wanted when strolling through wasteland where stolen cars were frequently dumped and torched. Part of our walk was directly under the M25 and somewhat lonely.

One day, Tess led me to a large cardboard box, by the flyover. She stopped, then looked at me as if to say, 'Open it.' So, I did. And discovered a black terrier puppy cowering within. I suspect he'd been flung off the bridge from a fast-moving vehicle. And yes, I took him home. Despite being a pup, he looked like an old man. So, I gave him an old man's name – Wilbur. But that's another story!

I'm a writer who only ever writes about what she knows. I never second guess. So, if you've read any of my previous novels, like *Sophie's Summer Kiss*, then you will know that the location and setting is authentic. I don't refer to guidebooks (as one crusty reviewer suggested!) or try and imagine the emotions of my characters. I know how my characters feel because I've *felt* those emotions too, *experienced* that bit of life, *tasted* that joy or disappointment or loss.

This novel came about because… well… I've had a lot of processing to do in the last twelve months.

I'm not someone who is prone to depression or gets in a rut and wallows. I'm usually the one who says, 'Hey, stop playing victim and sort yourself out.' But I've had to use those words on myself many times over in the last year or so. Why? Because like many people of my age, Maggie's story is one of familiarity – that of supporting your adult children *and* your parents who are sadly now behaving like children themselves.

It is far, *far* harder dealing with the latter. Elderly parents, even with a ravaged mind, still consider themselves to be the head of the household. It is a tricky task negotiating a senior's stubborn pride and inability to reason.

Many times, I've had people say, 'But at least you still have your parents. One day you will look back on your mother screaming and shouting and say you'd give anything to have that day again.' Well, I disagree.

What I would like is to have a day with my mother *the way she used to be.* A conversation *the way she used to be.* Take a trip somewhere *the way she used to be.* There is no magic taking my mum to a restaurant. She no longer recognises hunger nor appreciates delicious cooking smells. She is more likely to tell you that a beautifully presented dish looks disgusting. All you take away from such a situation is fulfilling a sense of duty – and gloomily so at that.

Maggie's story is a work of fiction, but it was therapeutic to write. It has helped me process many emotions. I am grieving the loss of my parents. Despite them being here, they're *not* here – if that makes sense. Their minds are wrecked by dementia.

It is a horrible, horrible, *horrible* condition. Let's just say that if dementia had a physical shape, I would kick it, punch it, slap it, hit it, rant at it, and do my very best to squash it flat before stamping all over it.

Oooh, that sentence helped me release a bit of angst!

I had a lot of fun asking Facebook friends to help me name Maggie's love interest. Special thanks to Claire M Robertson for coming up with *Dylan*, and Paul Harris who suggested *Alexander*. I put the two together and suddenly we had Mr Dylan Alexander!

Maggie in the Middle is my twentieth novel. It sees a return to the fictional village of Little Waterlow. This is a small Kent village not dissimilar to my own stomping ground.

I love to write books that provide escapism and make a reader occasionally giggle. You will also find drama – like family fallouts, illness, isolation – and sometimes that can be uncomfortable. I let my characters decide how a story is going to unfold, but its best to buckle up in case there are tense moments.

There are several people involved in getting a book "out there" and I want to thank them from the bottom of my heart.

First, the brilliant Rebecca Emin of *Gingersnap Books*. Rebecca knows exactly what to do with machine code and is a formatting genius.

Second, the fabulous Cathy Helms of *Avalon Graphics* for working her magic in transforming a rough sketch to a gorgeous book cover. Cathy always delivers exactly what I want and is a joy to work with.

Third, the amazing Rachel Gilbey of *Rachel's Random Resources*, blog tour organiser extraordinaire. Immense gratitude also goes to each of the fantastic bloggers who took the time to read and review *Maggie in the Middle*. They are:

Tizi's Book Review; Bookish Rambles; Wendyreadsbooks; loopyloulaura; Ginger Book Geek; Random Things Through My Letterbox; Captured on Film; Becca's Book Reviews; Bookworm86; Splashes Into Books; Carla Loves To Read; C L Tustin – Author; Nicki's Book Blog; mjporterauthor.blog; My Reading Getaway; Jan's Book Buzz; @teaandbooks90; Kirsty_Reviews_Books; LouiseReads_UK; Eatwell2015; and @Leona.Omahony.

Fourth, the lovely Jo Fleming for her sharp eyes spotting typos, missing words, and the like.

Finally, I want to thank you, my reader. Without you, there is no book. If you enjoyed reading *Maggie in the Middle*, I'd be over the moon if you wrote a review – just a quick one liner – on Amazon. It makes such a difference helping new readers to discover one of my books for the first time.

Love Debbie xx

Enjoyed *Maggie in the Middle*?

Then you might also like *Sophie's Summer Kiss.*

Check out the first three chapters on the next page!

Chapter One

I stared in disbelief at the private Instagram message.

Congratulations on your engagement. Clearly you are unaware that your fiancé is a cheater! From a well-wisher.

What on earth?

I sat down heavily on the edge of my bed and, for a moment, stared blankly at the carpet. The sender of that message couldn't possibly be talking about George. Not *my* George. Not George with the waistline that bore testament to his love of steak-and-kidney puddings. Not George who had recently taken to doing a comb-over to hide his ever-expanding bald patch. I mean, well, George was George. George Baker. Not George Clooney.

My fiancé wasn't around to see the message, having left for work five minutes earlier. My immediate instinct was to search George's belongings for clues but, unfortunately, I was sitting on the bed at my house, not his. Nor were there any of George's belongings under my roof. Not even a toothbrush. He always came to my place fully prepared, having previously neatly packed his stuff in an overnight bag. His holdall arrived with him, and it left with him.

Neither of us had ever got around to giving each other a key to our respective homes and, in truth, I was secretly pleased about that. I told myself that it kept things fresh between us. That it was more fun to have the anticipation of

George staying in my bed once or twice a week or, alternatively, me going over to his place to snuggle up in his vast custom-made bed. However, after we were married, the plan was for me to permanently move in with George, and for my place to be rented out.

I tried not to think about making the transition to George's modern detached house in nearby Kings Hill. It had been tastefully decorated throughout in white and dove grey but – if truth be told – I found it a little cold and depressing. I much preferred the rather hectic colour scheme at Catkin Cottage with its multi-jewelled rugs and bright throws. However, right now, our spare key situation meant I was unable to let myself into George's place for a sneaky look around.

I tore my gaze away from the Axminster and gazed once again at the phone in my hand. The mystery messenger was called *Thomas*. A tabby cat featured as the profile picture. Neither meant anything to me.

I clicked on the name. Immediately, a notification flashed up. *This account is private.* A quick look at Thomas's posts revealed nothing had ever been uploaded, and he – or she – had no followers. Also, Thomas was following just one person. Presumably me.

I took a deep breath, then exhaled gustily, aware that my stomach muscles felt tense and knotted. A sane, sensible part of my brain clamoured to be heard.

This message is nonsense. Utter rubbish. Click off it now!

Shakily, I swiped my mobile's screen, then went straight

to my list of contacts. I should've known my best friend's number off by heart considering how often we spoke to each other, but thanks to digital life this wasn't the case. My bestie answered on the third ring.

'Sue!' I gasped.

'Soph,' she chirped. 'You sound tense. Surely half past seven on a Thursday morning is a little early to be so fraught. What's up?'

'Sorry, but' – I stood up and began pacing the bedroom – 'I've received a weird message via social media, and it's unsettled me.'

'Don't tell me' – I sensed Sue at the other end of the connection, blue eyes narrowing as she concentrated, one hand raking her blonde hair – 'a rich overseas prince wants to deposit a billion pounds in your bank account, then pay you a vast sum of cash by way of reward but only if you help with his money laundering.'

'Nothing like that,' I said, pausing by the window.

I yanked the catch and pushed against the wooden frame, savouring the rush of sweet air as I gazed at the fields beyond the garden hedge. The pasture was full of cows. Oh, look! Overnight, another calf had been born. I gazed at the tiny creature in awe. Another miracle of Mother Nature in this new month of June. Despite the early hour, cornflower-blue skies were promising a day of warm sunshine. The heady scent of honeysuckle wafted through the open window, tickling my nostrils.

'How many guesses do I get?' Sue prompted.

I turned my back on the bucolic scene and resumed my

pacing.

'None,' I said, chewing my lip, willing the anxiety to go away.

'Then spill the beans and make it quick, or Charlie will be after me. He'll want to know why I'm still starkers in the bathroom and not downstairs frying his eggs and bacon. Bloody man. All he thinks about is his belly. When it comes to food, he's more insatiable than–'

There was the sound of a door opening. In the background I heard Sue's husband asking if she'd finished with the shower.

'Oh, er, yes, darling. You go ahead. I'm just on the phone to Sophie.'

'Morning, Sophie,' Charlie called.

'Tell him I said hi,' I said to Sue.

'Sophie says hello too,' Sue repeated.

'Tell her I don't know what you girlies find to talk about so early in the morning.'

'Did you hear that?' said Sue, a grin in her voice.

'I did, and give him my love.'

'Sophie sends her love,' Sue told Charlie.

'And tell her I send all love back but now' – there was a shooing sound – 'I'd like the smallest room in the house to myself, without Sophie overhearing any rampant trumpeting. A man likes to oversee his ablutions without being overheard, so out you go, dear wife. Be off with you. Go cook my breakfast.'

'I'm going, I'm going,' Sue assured. A second later came the sound of a door closing and a bolt being drawn. My bestie tutted theatrically. 'Talk to me while I throw on my dressing gown and get myself downstairs. I'll have my shower after Charlie has left for work and the house is quiet. So, come on, Soph. What's this message all about?'

I glanced at the bedside clock. The big hand seemed to be galloping through its upward sweep reminding that I, too, should be getting ready for work, not gassing to my mate.

'The message said that George is playing away.'

There was a pause at the other end of the line, and I could almost visualise Sue doing some rapid blinking.

'*What* did you just say?'

'You heard. Someone called Thomas – with a profile picture of a tabby cat – messaged me to inform I was betrothed to a cheater.'

'That's insane. Find the message and read it to me properly.'

'Just a minute.' I swiped the screen, then tapped the Instagram icon. 'Oh, I don't believe it.'

'What now?'

'It's gone.'

'The message?'

'Yes, it's disappeared.'

'The author must have unsent it. Tell me exactly what it said.'

'I can't remember now. Not precisely. But the gist was' – I screwed up my face trying to recall the words – 'congratulations on my upcoming nuptials, and was I aware that George was an unfaithful bastard?' My voice rose an octave as I said those last two words.

'Calm down, Soph. Look, listen to me. This is George we're talking about, right?'

'Obviously.'

'Exactly, and George wouldn't do that.'

'How do you know?' I wailed.

'Now, don't be offended. I know George is your fiancé and you think the sun shines out of his briefcase, and that he runs a thriving stationery company that recently flogged a trillion paperclips to WH Smith–'

'Are you insinuating that George is boring?' I interrupted.

'I asked you not to be offended.'

Now it was my turn to rake a hand through my hair.

'Okay, no offence taken.'

'I mean, who, in their right mind, wants to have a fling with George?' Sue asked.

My jaw dropped.

'Well *I'm* having a flipping fling with George,' I said indignantly.

'No, you're not,' said Sue quickly. 'You're having a *relationship* with him. That's totally different. A fling is' – she paused to consider, no doubt her thought processes swiftly back-peddling – 'something tacky. And George isn't tacky,' she added loyally.

'No, he's not tacky, just boring,' I said sarcastically.

'I thought you said you weren't offended? Listen to me, Soph. Let's start again. George is reliable. Okay? *Reliable.*'

'Do you think?' I whispered, collapsing down on the bed again. 'Oh God, Sue. What if Thomas Tabby Cat is telling the truth?'

A background clattering momentarily had me holding the phone away from my ear. Sue was banging pans about as she set to work cooking Charlie's breakfast.

'I think you're getting worked up over nothing,' she said staunchly.

'I'm not so sure. Wouldn't you be unnerved by such a message? After all, I'm marrying George this Saturday. That's forty-eight hours away.'

'Don't you see what this is?' said Sue in exasperation. 'It's a troll. Some jealous saddo with nothing better to do than pour a bucket of cold water on a betrothed woman's happiness. Like many people who use social media, you wanted to share your joy with a pic of your beautiful engagement ring, and some nasty little prat has zoomed in on you, hoping to spoil things.'

I fiddled with a hole in my dressing gown. Sue's words held some truth.

Here I was. Fifty-year-old Sophie Fairfax. One failed marriage already behind her. Then finally – *finally* – I'd found a guy who'd asked me to marry him, who'd sealed the deal by whisking me off to Hatton Garden for a ring. I'd been so delighted. So ecstatic.

Once home, I'd snapped away with my mobile's camera. There had been one of me beaming away, long dark hair falling in waves, brown eyes sparkling with excitement as I'd presented my third finger to camera. I'd then zoomed in on the diamond itself and captured a glitzy close-up. The pics had subsequently been uploaded to Instagram, Facebook, and

Twitter with umpteen wedding-appropriate hashtags. I'd burbled on about my impending wedding and imminent name change. You see, I'd wanted the world to know. Everyone else seemed to have shiny perfect lives, and now I had one too. Hooray!

I rubbed my temples. Despite Sue's words of reassurance, I could feel a headache starting.

'Do you understand?' Sue prompted.

'Yes,' I whispered uncertainly.

'I can tell you're not convinced. Okay, let's go over the facts.' There came the sound of sizzling as rashers began to brown. 'When you were a slip of a girl, you walked down the aisle to wed Teddy who, just like a certain band's song, thought he was far too sexy for his shirt, his trousers, *and* his boxers and frequently shed the lot to cavort with other women throughout your twenty-five-year marriage. Teddy would then come back to you with his tail between his legs, promising it would never happen again. But Teddy only kept half his promise, in that it never happened again with the same woman. So, when you found out about his latest conquest in a rather public way, you knew it was time to either put up and shut up, or bail out. You chose the latter and, for a while, enjoyed not having your nerves jangling with dropped phone calls on the home landline. Then you met George in the chiller aisle of Kings Hill's biggest supermarket while shopping for a lonely meal for one, and he asked you out. Initially you weren't interested, but he persisted. Also, George was different to Teddy. He wasn't loud. And, unlike Teddy, he wasn't sexy.'

'Oh, thanks.'

'You know what I mean,' said Sue hastily. 'You felt secure with George–'

'Because of his boring looks and boring ways,' I cut in.

'Look, Soph. Let's be realistic here. I have nothing against George, but everything about him is… *grey.*'

'What do you mean?' I gasped.

'He has grey hair. Grey eyes. Grey suits. Grey jeans. He even drives a grey car.'

'The car is silver,' I objected. 'Just like George's hair. You know, male magazines refer to these guys as *silver foxes.* That sounds rather glamorous to me.'

'If you say so.' I sensed the shrug in her voice. 'George eventually popped the question but, from what you've told me, the proposal was casual and lacked any romance.'

'It was sweet enough,' I protested. 'Just like him.'

'George isn't sweet,' Sue countered. 'He's *safe*. Men who are safe and look like George do not have a harem of women lusting after them.'

'Well, I lusted after him,' I squawked.

'No, you didn't.'

'W–What?' I stuttered. 'Sue, that's absolutely not true.'

'Yes, it is.' There came the sound of a spatula banging against a pan. 'From what I can gather, you've never once ripped his clothes off. In fact, from what you shared about the first time you both did it, I seem to remember you being rather put out because you'd missed the first half of Coronation Street.'

I opened my mouth, then shut it again.

'I'm fifty, Sue. Not fifteen. Women of our age don't go around ripping off their man's clothes.'

'Don't they?' I sensed Sue arching an eyebrow as the sound of a plate rattled down on her worktop. 'Speak for yourself. Charlie and I still go at it like a couple of teenagers.'

'You can't possibly.'

'We do, and you'd better believe it.'

I felt momentarily flummoxed. Was there something wrong with me? Time under the duvet with George wasn't adventurous. It was very perfunctory.

Very boring? enquired my inner voice.

I recoiled in horror. George was *not* boring. He was, as Sue said, safe. Safe was safe. Safe wasn't boring.

Isn't it?

'So stop fretting about a ridiculous message from Tabby Twitface –'

'Thomas Tabby Cat,' I corrected.

'Him too' – Sue exhorted – 'and know that when you marry George this Saturday, all will be well.'

'Yes,' I said slowly. 'It's going to be a lovely day.'

'Of course it is.'

I stared into space thinking about my big day. It wasn't going to be a grand event. Not at our age. After all, we'd both been married before. Sadly, neither of us had children, nor parents or siblings. Consequently, George had been adamant about not wanting a fuss. Instead, we were each inviting a couple of close friends to the local registry office – Sue and Charlie on my side, and Graham Rollinson and his wife Jackie on George's side.

Afterwards, the six of us would have a celebratory *wedding breakfast* at Little Waterlow's pub, The Angel. George had booked one of the pub's two function rooms. It would be a small affair.

And rather boring, said my inner voice.

Nonsense!

'It will be intimate and classy,' I said to Sue.

'Indeed,' she agreed. 'And I know George wanted to be conservative with his pennies and not splash out on a hideously expensive wedding, but at least he didn't hold back for the honeymoon. I'm quite jealous of you jetting off to the Amalfi Coast immediately afterwards.' Sue's voice took on a wistful tone. 'I've heard it's stunning.'

'Yes,' I said, properly smiling for the first time since reading the troll's message. 'I'm really looking forward to that bit.'

'Surely, you're looking forward to your wedding day, too?' asked Sue curiously.

'Of course,' I quickly answered.

But after we'd said good-bye to each other, I wasn't sure who I'd been trying to convince the most. Sue, or myself.

Chapter Two

I'd barely ended the conversation with Sue when my mobile rang. I glanced at the name on the screen and my heart sank. Teddy Fairfax. My ex-husband.

'Hello,' I said cautiously.

'How's my favourite ex-wife?' he said jovially.

'Your only ex-wife,' I pointed out.

'And that's why you're my favourite,' he quipped. 'How are you, darling?'

'Honestly, Teddy? None the better for hearing your voice.'

'Oooh, that's harsh. Very harsh.'

'What do you want?'

'That's my girl. Straight to the point. You were never one to beat about the bush.'

'Unlike you. That's probably because you spent a lot of time *in* the bush, having your wicked way with your latest conquest.'

'That's all in the past.'

'Ah, a sentence that tells me you're currently between girlfriends.'

'You're right. Fancy a quick one?'

'Are we talking about a drink or sex?'

'Sex, of course.'

'No.'

'Bet you don't say that to George.'

I sighed. Teddy always had the ability to exasperate me. I began to quickly dress, trying to ignore my stomach which was starting to growl with hunger.

'Teddy, you've been calling me a lot lately, and I wish you'd stop. What if George had been here?'

'Then I'd have behaved honourably and asked his permission to give you a quick one.'

'You're not funny.' I headed towards the steep staircase inside my two-up-two-down. Like most of the old cottages in the village of Little Waterlow, the ascent and descent in these properties required one's full attention and utmost caution. 'I'll ask you again. What do you want?'

'I want to persuade you not to marry George.'

'Again?' I sighed, walking into the kitchen.

Teddy had been aghast when he'd found out about my engagement. Not that it had been a secret. In a village like Little Waterlow, gossip was a pastime. At one point or another, nearly everyone fell under the spotlight of scrutiny because that's just the way my village was. A resident couldn't change their washing powder without it being discussed. I could still remember Mrs Bates, two doors down saying, "I heard you'd gone off Persil, Sophie. Is that true?" And me replying, "Yes, it seemed a bit pointless buying it after having all my dirty laundry washed in public." This was a reference to when villagers were gossiping about Teddy and me when our marriage – which had always been on a slippery slope – had finally ended and in a most public way.

We'd been having a drink at our local. Teddy had barely

set his lager down at our table when he'd excused himself to go to the Gents. Unbeknownst to me, he'd then attempted buying contraceptives from the machine on the wall. Unfortunately, the machine had swallowed his money without delivering the goods. He'd promptly had a private word with the landlord but, from my seat, I'd managed to catch the gist of the conversation.

Shocked, I'd waited for Teddy to return to our table before shrilly asking why he'd bought contraceptives when I'd gone through the change. Regrettably I'd been overheard by Little Waterlow's biggest gossip, Mabel Plaistow. She'd been having a quiet Guinness with her husband Fred, out of sight at the table behind me. She'd leant across to tap me on the shoulder, intent on getting my full attention. "I'll tell yer what yer man wants 'em for," she'd declared. "To put on 'is willy when 'e's playin' away."

No shit, Sherlock!

I'd subsequently picked up Teddy's pint and, in front of astonished customers, tipped it over his head. Leaving Teddy open-mouthed and dripping, I'd calmly walked out of the pub. That night I'd ignored Teddy's familiar pleas for forgiveness, and slept in the spare room.

The following day I'd made an appointment with Gabe Stewart, a local no-nonsense solicitor who specialised in divorce. And the rest, as they say, is history.

Teddy had always played around. I'd spent years forgiving, but never quite forgetting. The issue with the contraceptive machine at The Angel had simply been the last straw.

My ex-husband and I now lived at opposite ends of the village. It was inevitable that our paths sometimes crossed. Teddy had wanted to remain friends and – after twenty-five years of marriage and no close family members – I'd felt the same way. Also, it was easier to love him as a mate rather than a philandering husband. However, there was a world of difference between occasionally bumping into him and now having him telephone on an almost daily basis.

'This is the fourth time this week,' I said, using my shoulder to wedge the phone against my ear while filling the kettle. 'Why don't you want me to marry George?' I plonked the kettle on its electric base, then flipped the switch.

'You know why.'

'No, I don't.'

'Yes, you do. The man is a berk.'

I reached into a cupboard and extracted a mug.

'You don't *know* George, so how can you possibly hold such an opinion?'

'I've seen him around.'

'Oh, really?' I went to the fridge. Extracting a loaf of bread, I dropped two slices into the toaster. 'And have you ever bothered to say hello to him?'

'Of course not.' Teddy sounded indignant. 'Why on earth would I want to associate with a man who wears a grey suit?'

I rolled my eyes.

'What's wrong with a grey suit?'

'Grey suits are for boring people.'

Oh God. First Sue. Now Teddy.

'I see. Do you think George would be more likeable if he wore a loud pinstripe, like your good self?'

Teddy was a business consultant with a fine line in patter and an eye for expensive cloth that made a statement.

'I simply take pride in the way I look,' he pointed out.

'Is that why you went to Turkey last year for a hair transplant?'

'I need to look my best to succeed in wooing you back.'

'You'll never woo me back and, anyway, Sue says men who have hair transplants are vain.'

'Says the woman who's had more filling than a sandwich shop.'

'I think you mean *filler*,' I corrected, just as the toaster violently ejected my breakfast on to the worktop. I grabbed it and reached for the margarine.

'That too.' Teddy cleared his throat, an indication that the subject was about to be changed. 'Anyway, never mind Sue. I'm talking about George. Call off the wedding. If you go through with it, darling, you'll be making a terrible mistake.'

I paused from my toast buttering.

'What did you say?'

'You heard. The guy simply isn't your type.'

'And what, exactly, is my type? Someone like you who behaves like a dog with six dicks?'

'You'll be bored to tears if you marry George Baker.'

'That's fine,' I said, reaching for the marmalade and lathering it over the toast. 'It will be my pleasure to be bored to tears, because it means I'll never be stressed wondering what George is up to behind my back.'

'Don't count on it,' said Teddy darkly. 'Sometimes it's the quiet ones that need to be watched.'

'Oh, don't be so ridiculous, Teddy,' I snapped. 'I'm now ending this conversation. If I were you, I'd take a good long look at yourself before you start casting aspersions about other people.'

Annoyed, I abruptly ended the call and aggressively bit into the toast.

It was only when I was later walking to work, that a thought occurred to me. Might Teddy be the author of that strange Instagram message?

As I bowled along the leafy lane covering the distance from my cottage to another not so very far away, the possibility that my ex-husband was Thomas Tabby Cat seemed more and more likely.

Chapter Three

'Hi, Sophie,' trilled my boss. Ruby reversed out of a floor-to-ceiling stock cupboard, a grin on her face. 'How are you this morning?'

I shut the door to the tiny hair salon and shrugged off my jacket.

'Not so bad,' I said, forcing a smile.

Ruby paused for a moment, her arms full of tin foils, hair dye and bleach brushes. She gave me an appraising look.

'Hmm. You look like my mum when she's been walking one of her four-legged doggy clients and had a run-in with an off-lead hellraiser.'

'Oh?'

'In other words, you have a face like a slapped bum.'

'Gee, thanks, Rubes.'

Ruby was only nineteen and said things how they were. Her mother, Wendy, was a lovely woman who'd recently remarried. Ironically, Wendy's new husband had turned out to be my divorce lawyer. Wendy's life had fallen under the gossips' spotlight when her first husband had… well, let's just say there had been some eyebrow-raising tittle-tattle.

Wendy had gone on to buy a dear little house called Clover Cottage but, since marrying Gabe, she'd permanently loaned the cottage to her daughter. Ruby had recently qualified as a hairdresser and gone on to turn a small

376

outbuilding into a tiny hair salon. Her business had taken off almost immediately thanks to Little Waterlow's high street salon – my original workplace – going into administration.

Following my redundancy, I hadn't wasted a moment, and hotfooted over to Ruby's place to see if she needed another pair of hands. Happily, she had.

Despite our age gap, we got on well. Occasionally I babysat Mo, Ruby's little girl, if she and her partner Simon wanted a night out. They were a lovely little family and it made me wistful for the children I'd always hoped to have with Teddy but which, despite our many attempts at IVF, had never come along. Perhaps – looking back at our bumpy marriage – that had been a blessing in disguise.

'So come on then,' said Ruby, scrutinising my face. 'What's up?'

I hung my jacket over the coat stand in the corner.

'It's something and nothing.'

Ruby dumped the foils and hairdressing paraphernalia on the tiny reception table, then stuck her hands on her hips.

'Forget the *nothing* and tell me the *something*. In fact, hold fire while I put the kettle on. We've got ten minutes before our respective clients arrive, so sit down for a minute and take some deep breaths. I can tell you're rattled.'

She disappeared into a small backroom that housed a loo, miniature washbasin, a washing-machine-cum-tumble-dryer, and a slither of worktop upon which sat a kettle and a microwave.

I flopped down on the chair by the washbasin and stared through the window. The view was of Ruby's home. Clover

Cottage was chocolate-box pretty, especially with its arc of pink rambling roses framing the back door. The beautiful blooms gave off the sweetest fragrance throughout the summer months.

I gazed at the roses, my mind wandering to some different flowers. Namely, my bouquet. George had suggested I go for something in silk, claiming they'd make a nice keepsake. Together, we'd trawled through a website. He'd paused to consider some artificial lilies.

'These are nice,' he'd enthused. 'I *love* them in this colour.'

They'd been grey.

I'd since visited Daisy Kingston, another resident of Little Waterlow, who had her own florist shop in the heart of the village. She'd promised to give me a bouquet of mixed blooms in a riot of different colours.

It had struck me – briefly – that George could, at times, be somewhat controlling. However, I'd then dismissed the thought. So long as I agreed to whatever George wanted, there wasn't a problem. That said, I wasn't too sure what he'd say about my choice of bouquet.

Ruby interrupted my musings.

'Here we are,' she said, handing me a mug.

'Thanks, sweetheart.'

I took the drink from her, sipping gratefully as she settled down on the cutting stool. Her gaze met mine. She was an extraordinarily pretty girl with a shocking pink crop that set off bright blue eyes and elfin features. She beamed at me over the rim of her cup.

'So, go on. Spill the beans. Think of me as your personal agony aunt.'

'Hmm. Okay.' I set down my cup and pretended to type, my fingers wiggling in the air. 'Dear Aunty Ruby. I have a problem. I'm getting married this Saturday–'

'Indeed, and I'm doing your hair,' she dimpled. 'Oh, sorry. I've interrupted. Carry on.'

I continued air typing and talking.

'My best friend thinks my fiancé is boring, and my ex-husband says I shouldn't marry George-'

'What's it got to do with either of them? Oooh, sorry. I've done it again. Continue.'

'Something happened this morning. Something that *really* rattled me–'

I paused as my eyes suddenly brimmed.

'Yes?' prompted Ruby, alarmed at a possible display of waterworks.

I frantically blinked the tears back into their ducts.

'I had a message from Thomas Tabby Cat.'

Ruby frowned, cupping her hands around her mug.

'You've lost me.'

'On Instagram.'

'You follow a cat?

'He follows me.'

'I'm not following.'

'I don't follow him either.'

'Sophie, what the heck are you talking about?'

'It was an anonymous message from someone calling themselves by that name.'

'Oh, I see. A promoter, right?'

I shook my head.

'No, a troublemaker. They told me that George was a cheater.'

'*Whaaaat?*' she squawked.

'And now I feel deeply anxious. It's triggered me. You know, after all the shenanigans when married to Teddy.'

'Look, I don't know your George. I mean, I've met him a couple of times when he's popped in here to see you after work, but – first impressions and all that – he doesn't strike me as someone who would muck a woman about. After all…' she trailed off.

'Yes?'

'Well, don't take this the wrong way, Sophie, but he's quite an ordinary looking guy. I privately thought he was punching when you introduced him to me.'

'Punching?'

'Yeah, you know. Punching above his belt. After all, you're way better looking than him.'

'What are you talking about? I'm nothing special. In fact, I'm very ordinary.'

'No, you're bloomin' not,' Ruby snorted. 'Look at yourself!' She jabbed a finger at one of the two huge mirrors on the opposite wall. 'Look at that reflection. You're gorgeous.'

'Ruby, I'm fifty. My face looks like it needs ironing.'

'You have a few laughter lines, that's all. It shows you have a sense of humour. But never mind them. Look at the rest of you. You have a cloud of long, dark hair. Flawless skin that glows with good health. Beautiful brown eyes. You remind me of Nigella Lawson, and my Simon has always fancied her. You're still very attractive. Whereas George…' she trailed off again.

I finished the sentence for her.

'Isn't.'

'No, sorry, he definitely isn't. In fact' – she took a deep breath and looked a bit sheepish – 'I privately wondered what on earth you saw in the guy. I can see he drives a big car and heard he has his own company. I put the attraction down to his bank balance.'

'Bloody hell, Rubes. I'm not that shallow,' I protested. 'I fell for George because' – I floundered for a moment – 'well, because he's a nice guy.'

'So is my dustman but I wouldn't want to marry him.'

'George is dependable. And' – I hesitated for a moment before ploughing on – 'yes, if I'm honest, he's a tiny bit boring. But that's fine by me.'

'In which case you must agree that George isn't the swaggering, cheating type.'

'Yeah,' I sighed. 'It was my first husband who was like that.'

'Teddy. Yes, I've seen him about the village. He's still a good-looking guy. Are you sure you're doing the right thing marrying George?'

'Why? Do you think Thomas Tabby Cat is telling the truth and giving me a genuine warning?'

'Er, no.' Ruby shook her head. 'I meant that you don't sound like you're in love with George.'

I opened my mouth in shock.

'Ruby, that's not true. I love George to bits.'

'Not the same thing,' she said, shaking her head.

'What do you mean?'

'I mean, are you *in love* with George?'

I was saved from answering the question thanks to the arrival of our first two clients of the day.

Also by Debbie Viggiano

Lottie's Little Secret
Wendy's Winter Gift
Sadie's Spring Surprise
Annie's Autumn Escape
Daisy's Dilemma
The Watchful Neighbour (debut psychological thriller)
Cappuccino and Chick-Chat (memoir)
Willow's Wedding Vows
Lucy's Last Straw
What Holly's Husband Did
Stockings and Cellulite
Lipstick and Lies
Flings and Arrows
The Perfect Marriage
Secrets
The Corner Shop of Whispers
The Woman Who Knew Everything
Mixed Emotions (short stories)
The Ex Factor (a family drama)
Lily's Pink Cloud ~ a child's fairytale
100 ~ the Author's experience of Chronic Myeloid Leukaemia

Printed in Great Britain
by Amazon

44002793R00219